A GREY MOON OVER CHINA

A GREY MOON OVER CHINA

Thomas A. Day

Black Heron Press

ISBN-13: 978-0-930773-78-6
ISBN-10: 0-9307730-78-0

Black Heron Press
Post Office Box 95676
Seattle, Washington 98145
www.blackheronpress.com

for Stephen and Alexander,
who are on every page.

PROLOGUE

I opened my eyes suddenly, startled out of my half-sleep. For a moment I thought it had finally started to rain, but the clouds still waited outside the window, patient and grey as ever.

I'd been lost in an old man's reverie, I suppose, sitting at the table and thinking about my encounter the day before. I'd written little that morning, in any case. The highland skies were low and the air was cool, and the winds shifted uncertainly out of the east. It was difficult to concentrate. It felt somehow as though the wars were finally just over the horizon, ready to crash through the leaden clouds and into my life again with all their thunder and blood.

But, no, it remained peaceful. Like the meadow outside, the house was still. When I listened closely I could hear the whispered tick of the brass clock beside me, counting out the passing of its own morning. The kettle sputtered on the stove.

Yet it wasn't the kettle that woke me. It was a sudden and unwelcome memory of the drones. A memory of the quiet machines we'd sent long ago to chart these worlds, the faceless, pilotless ships that had drawn us after them into the darkness. The ships that had vanished into space without a trace in the end, without a whisper of their intentions, as though to mock the very dreams that made them.

Now, of course, on that chilly morning on the Bolton Uplands, those dreams seemed far away and inconsequential. Our triumphant leap to the stars had given way long before to despair, had left in its wake a civilization exhausted and broken, ravaged by the wars that would not end.

Until that morning, however, I hadn't thought to question who was to blame. I'd always thought it was Polaski. But now I wasn't sure, and the doubt left me a little afraid.

I took the kettle off the stove, and the room was quiet again. Nearby

I found my cup, filled with cold tea and forgotten. In among the tins and packets the old cat from the barn sat with his back straight and his eyes closed, rocking almost imperceptibly back and forth. His peculiar green eyes opened just enough to watch me fumble with my tea, then closed again, leaving me to my uncertain steps back to my chair.

My bones ached from the years in the fast ships, and I'd come to limp a little. My heart faltered in the thin air sometimes, although I worried more about what would happen to me when the wars came. Still, if I was to have any time at all, the purpose to which I had put myself and which lent urgency to the otherwise desolate passage of my days was to leave a true record of the events that had led up to the wars.

It was to work on that record that I sat back down at the table. The steam from the tea gathered on the window, making my reflection difficult to see. It was the reflection of an ordinary man, a man born by the side of the road in the winter of 1999, carried north on his mother's back in the closing days of a dying century. The face had the dark look of my Aztec ancestors, lined now and grey with stubble. The eyes were black and wary, the hair close-cropped. The hands were coarse and bent, and the fingers trembled a little as they lifted the tea to my lips.

Yet my pen lay unused on the paper. Early that morning I'd taken my cane and walked down to meet the dairyman's cart, stopping only to look at the grave by the side of the path for a short while. At the road I'd waited with the woman who lives across the way. We stood together and stamped our feet in the chill, peering into the gloom for a sign of the horses. She remarked on the blackness of the sky and said it felt to her, too, like an omen of the coming wars. She didn't say that it troubled her, but I saw the flicker in her eyes and the old hands worrying at her buttons, and I knew that she was afraid. She asked why the wars should come to such a quiet place, a place that wanted only to be left in peace.

Walking back up the hill carrying my parcels, I stopped to catch my breath and listen to the silence after the crunching of my feet on the gravel. She's like the rest of us, I thought. We pursue our own solitary passions and seldom look up, seldom sense that it is we

ourselves who form the swelling flood of history, the dark constel-
lation of events we would sooner lay at the feet of others. Until the
storm finally gathers, and then we look up and we grow afraid, and
we say: This is not what I intended.

And yet, even then, I thought, we do not act. Even then we
hesitate, and always for too long.

I turned to look back down the hill and watched the woman
walking away, and it was then when, very much to my own surprise,
I raised my cane and called out to her, beckoning her to wait.

Next to the table was a metal bed where I took what little sleep would
come to me. I spent much of each night sitting on the edge of that bed,
looking into the embers, and I awoke a little earlier in the mornings
than I would have liked.

Some of those mornings, restless in the last moments of sleep,
I dreamt about Polaski. I saw his expressionless eyes watching me,
and I awoke with a start, struggling for the breath to curse him one
more time.

But now, sitting at the table with a fear of the real truth
growing in my chest, Polaski's face became hard to remember. A
man whom I had charged and condemned a thousand times seemed
to shimmer in my memory and fade, then disappear without a sound
like a child's soap bubble. I was left in that quiet room under the
lowering sky, alone with my story.

To begin the story I tried to think where in all those years
there'd been someone whose words might lend it meaning, someone
stronger and wiser than I. But in the end I was sure there was no one.
No one had understood; no one had seen.

Still, as absurd as it seemed at the time, my thoughts in those
few moments returned again and again to Pham. Had I still believed
in my own innocence I would have dismissed the idea with a kind of
disgust, but as I watched my hand begin its labor across the page, as
I listened to my breath rattle in my chest, I knew that this would be
Pham's story.

PART ONE

FIRE

Chapter One: DARKNESS

There were times on the island, late in the summer of 2017, when I thought I could hear the sun hissing off the ground. It was a sound like the insects made in the jungle, and it pressed down on me like the dust that hung in the air and stained it yellow.

But if I closed my eyes, I could imagine it was the sound of water. On some days there was only the sun, hissing down on the islands and the ocean, but on the afternoon Sergeant Polaski was to arrive it was the sound of water, cool and clear in the shadows. I was standing on the rutted ground by the runway, remembering a picture I'd seen of a river in *Las Serranías del Burro*, when the cough of his airplane intruded, rough and dry on the still air.

It backfired again and throttled down over the jungle, then shuddered onto the runway in a cloud of smoke. When it had rumbled by I closed my eyes again, unwilling to give up my thoughts to a man whose arrival would surely end what little peace I'd found here.

The plane turned and taxied back, then waited out in the sun with its engines idling. Minutes passed.

"Torres."

I opened my eyes. The airplane shimmered in the heat while its crew wrestled a crate down a ramp into the dirt.

When I turned in the direction of the voice I found myself looking into the barrel of a revolver, gripped in the hand of a short, blond man with a pale, unremarkable face and expressionless grey eyes.

"Hello, Polaski."

He let down the hammer. "That's not real bright, Torres, standing out in the dirt with your eyes closed." The crew pushed the ramp back up into the plane.

I hated Polaski. Hated him and loved him. I hadn't seen him

since 1st Engineers, where we'd served together until the unit was disbanded. It was broken up after Polaski killed an officer with an anti-tank round—broken up mainly because the MPs couldn't decide who'd done it. Polaski himself fingered a half-breed Samoan named Tulafono for it; it was the day after Tulafono had beaten me with a tire iron for swearing in Spanish.

Polaski was kicked back to sergeant in a demolitions unit, but I'd kept warrant officer and was sent to join the forward units in the Pacific. Now Polaski was here, too, evidently as part of an Army plan involving heavy demolitions. It was a plan I didn't like because I knew nothing about it, which was why I'd picked Polaski up at the airstrip in the first place. That, and the hint of anticipation I'd felt when I first heard he was coming, the sense of a change in the wind that I didn't yet understand.

"What are they planning for these islands, Polaski?"

"Nothing you need to know about." With a shriek from the brakes the plane jerked forward again, a wavering blob of silver in the heat, and left behind a cloud of smoke and the crate, dumped on the runway like the stool of a great bird. "It isn't going to work, anyway," he said.

The engines spun up and the plane bounced around over the ruts, then rose tiredly up over the jungle.

"What isn't?"

Polaski didn't answer.

"I heard we're looking for someone," I said.

Still he didn't answer. I was almost wishing he'd gone, too, leaving me to my thoughts of how to get out of the war, how to get away and find a place of my own. How to get off of the planet altogether.

"Do you have a priest named Katherine Chan?" he said.

"Yes."

"The crate's for her. Let's go, I'm in a hurry."

Polaski and I had been picked up off the streets in Army sweeps at the age of fourteen, then sent to Technical Warfare School. It was a school designed to provide regular Army units with technologically sophisticated soldiers, able to fight in the Pacific with little support.

Polaski called us the "Shorts;" in addition to whatever the Army thought of as intelligence, it had picked us for endurance, and in the end that had meant squat and tough. So we were squat, tough, smart and educated, and something of an embarrassment: greater knowledge of the war hadn't always brought the Army greater loyalty.

"I need to see your captain," said Polaski. He'd taken over my truck by the runway, and now its electric motors hissed and spat as he ran down trees and rocks in the jungle.

"We haven't got a captain," I said

"A lieutenant?"

"You need to see Bolton."

"Choppers?"

"No. We get them from Airmobile on the big island."

The jungle dropped away with a smack of high grass on the hood and a dry scraping sound as it dragged along underneath. We were in the big clearing by the beach, next to the helicopter pad and the mess canopy with its leaning, rusted poles. Scrub grass and rows of bungalows stretched away to the jungle on the far side.

Polaski dropped me off and drove away to find Michael Bolton. But before he'd gone fifty yards, a familiar furry streak raced in from the side toward the truck's front wheels—McGafferty's dog, low to the ground and barking for all he was worth.

Polaski swerved sharply. But he swerved toward the dog, not away from it, as though hoping the dog would overshoot. But it was a miscalculation, and with a sound muted by the distance into a soft thumping, the dog's body tumbled out from underneath the wheels and lay still in the dirt. Polaski kept going.

"At least you could stop and look!"

I shouted at him again and looked for a rock to throw, but it was too late. He was gone across the clearing.

The dog was dead. Its back and neck were broken and it bled from half a dozen wounds. I stroked its muzzle with the back of my hand and pulled out a rock that had lodged in its mouth with the broken teeth. I moved him away from the track, then trudged back to the mess.

The air under the canopy was heavy and still, punctuated

only by the wet sound of sunflower husks spat across the floor by Technical Sergeant Tyrone Elliot. He was leaning back in a chair with his feet up on the table, a tall, powerful Southerner with mild eyes and black stubble on his dark face. His jaw was broad and square with thick muscles bunching in his neck as he chewed. Deep lines ran from the corners of his eyes and down past his mouth, as though he'd been tired for a long time. The hands on his knees were big and still.

He didn't say anything for a while, but sat and chewed and watched the receding back of Polaski's truck.

"So your old buddy Polaski's here," he said finally. He rummaged in his pocket for more seeds. "So maybe we'll forget to tell him about the water, what do you think?"

"Polaski's all right," I said. "He gets things done."

"Uh-huh."

"He should have stopped, though."

"Uh-huh."

Elliot launched himself out of his seat to slam his hands together overhead, then just as suddenly sat back down and wiped them on his fatigues. "Polaski's crazy, Torres. I been with him in the 89th. He ain't all there, you know, and he don't see you when he looks at you. He's mean, boy, and he's crazy. You stay away from him."

"It's the war that's mean, Tyrone."

"Don't stick up for him."

"It's the war, Tyrone. The whole planet. It's gotten so bad I don't even know any more when I'll wake up puking blood from some new wonder we've dumped in the water. You saw what happened to the lieutenant."

"Yeah, I know." He spat another shell. "Anyhow, nothing we can do about it. Or you back to thinking about getting off?"

"Of course I'm thinking about getting off."

Far off, I was thinking. Off-planet with someone like Katherine Chan, someone still in one piece. As far and as fast as an engine could carry us, away from the memories that followed me everywhere I went. Memories of Mexico and hunger, memories of boats filled with children and the stink of death. Broken dogs, broken children. Memories of the frozen pavement in Chicago, memories of my father hanging from the wires in the desert...

"Uh-uh, no sir." Elliot stuck another seed in his mouth. "Ain't no one gotten off this old ball of trouble for a long time, except rich folks in their tin cans up there. U.S. quit on the space tunnel years ago, I keep telling you. And no one ever built drones smart enough to send through it, anyhow. So that's that. Rich folks is stuck in their cans, and you and me is stuck in 42nd Engineers digging out holes to piss in. So you take what you got, Torres, which is a fine afternoon and something to chew on. Here, have some."

I swatted at a fly. "What's the Army planning for these islands, Tyrone? Polaski won't say."

"You tell Polaski to piss off. Word I got is you're the only one he pays any mind to, anyway. What's happening on these islands is that Army and Air Force are going to try something funny on those skinny little atolls east of here, except folks are saying it ain't going to work."

"Bolton says we're looking for someone."

"Yeah, but that's different. Been going on a long time. DoD's looking for one of their smart-boys, went and slipped out on 'em. DARPA fellow with plans for counter-BCs that's going to save all our asses. He took them a year ago, and now Army's saying he's out here somewhere and we got to get him back before all this other big shit comes down."

Before what came down, though? Too much was happening—the Army poking around after leaving us alone for more than a year, heavy equipment showing up for the MI priests, talk about heavy demolitions...and now Polaski back. To do what I told him to? Not likely. I was an Army hardware engineer, no more. I took care of the island's machines, from the cooling rods in the big antennas to the drones we put up at night to listen in on the Japanese. I tuned them and I studied them, and I spent my nights alone with them and the sounds of the jungle, not wanting to sleep.

Polaski's truck skidded to a stop in front of Bolton's bungalow across the clearing. Smoke trailed from the motors. He strode through the grass and jumped onto the porch.

"Tyrone?" I said.

"Yup."

"Why would anyone steal the plans to *counter*-biologicals?"

He was quiet for a minute.

"I been hearing a long time," he said, "how you're one of the real smart ones, Torres. I think maybe you got yourself a good question there. Japanese sure as hell don't need to defend against their own stuff, huh?"

"Why's Polaski here, Tyrone?"

He shrugged. "Blow something up, I expect. It's what he does."

Clouds scudded along the horizon over the ocean. I tried not to think about Polaski, and tried to remember the daydream he'd interrupted, instead.

There'd been a time when missions to the stars had been planned by the western nations, out through America's "space tunnel." It was a moon-sized torus near Venus that was supposed to pass the ships onward, along with their cargos of colonists and seed and livestock embryos. The project had died from poverty and warfare, but it was those same trees and horses I'd been thinking about that morning. Trees and horses and Katherine Chan, and a piece of land far from Earth and the war. All of it impossible.

"Well," said Elliot, "I guess I don't know what demolition's got to do with MI folks, after all, now that I think about it. But you might have noticed the priests had something to do with a bunch of sonic diggers out behind Bolton's bungalow."

"Diggers?"

"Yup. Big suckers."

"Torres."

Elliot's voice, far away. The dog snarled and pushed its face in through the spokes of the wheel, in under the wagon where I'd crawled.

"Jesus Christ, boy, wake up. What the hell's the matter with you, anyway?"

I was four, and the dog's teeth were red and its breath was hot on my face. Its neck was bloody with open sores. Dogs behind it fought each other and tore at the entrails of an infant they'd dragged away from its *carretero*, away from its sleeping parents in their tin and cardboard house. My mother and father were nowhere. The little girl's face jerked in the dust and blood spattered under the wagon. Helpless men across the road shuffled their feet and threw rocks at the dogs.

"Come on, Torres."

There was foam in the dog's mouth, under its lip where it curled back from its teeth...

"Shit, what's the matter with this boy?"

Later that morning I sat with Polaski on the slope of an island to the east of the base, watching the glare of the sun from under my eyelids. It reflected off the straits between the island where we sat and a deserted peak rising from the ocean two miles away. I was trying to keep from slipping down the stony hillside while I pressed my hands over my ears to keep out the roaring behind me. Two days had passed since Polaski's arrival.

The sound changed pitch again, then surged from the roar into a howl, setting my teeth on edge and sending new pain into my temples. It warbled lower for a moment only to seize on a new frequency and lash out again, tearing the air apart with its shriek and bringing a sweat to my forehead.

On the island across the straits, angry jets of smoke tinged with purple shot into the air each time the digger found a frequency that worked, leaving behind a smoldering socket where tons of earth had been disintegrated. Now and then Polaski let the digger dip its massive barrel too far, and its beam swept across the ocean to send a wall of steam curling into the sky. It settled across us later in a cloud of humid air that mingled with our sweat and stung our eyes.

Squatting on its thick legs behind us, like a tank without treads, the digger probed with its beam higher up the far island until it found a new weakness in the rock, then leapt into its screaming again. The clanging of its cooling pump was like the metallic thumping of a cat's tail as it hurled itself into its kill.

"God *damn* it, Polaski, turn that thing off!" Having Polaski take potshots for fun was more than I could stand. The noise was like an alien presence inside me that stole my concentration and dragged me closer to a pit I needed all of my wits to stay out of. A pit I'd slipped into that morning and stayed in until Elliot had finally kicked me awake.

"Jesus *Christ*, boy!" he'd shouted. "Wake *up!*"

Foam in the dog's mouth, and the wagon collapsing with the dog's head still caught in the spokes...

"Torres!"

Polaski hit the switch in his lap. The digger choked in mid-wail and spun down, muttering and spitting and grumbling in its disappointment. The armor on its haunches clattered, then with a hiss and a *crump* as the armature locked up, the machine was quiet and Polaski and I were left alone with the flies and the sun.

On the blackened ruin of the island across the straits, gullies glowed red and ragged pits steamed along the waterline. I struggled to my feet and climbed the hillside to sit next to Polaski.

"So aside from target practice, Polaski, how come you dragged me out here?"

He squinted at the pitted island with one eye closed, judging his work.

"We have to take test shots once the surface warms up." He squinted with the other eye.

"It's warm," I said. Polaski had asked Bolton to have me assigned to him, but I didn't want to be there.

"Another two hours," he said.

"Christ." I lay back and watched the clouds piling up to the north, wondering what possible use the military could have for such a little island. Polaski lay back, too, then began lobbing rocks up over his head. He was trying for the clang when they hit the digger, but most of them thumped into the hillside and came skittering back down past us. I couldn't see them after they left his hand, so after waiting for the clang I had to wait again to see if one would smack into me on the way down. Each time one found its target I thought he was going to stop, and when he didn't I wanted to snatch the rocks up and throw them back at him...

Don't. I sat up and looked at the ocean. There was another scene from Piedras Negras that came back sometimes, more often than I liked. Running from the stinging sand that blew across the desert, into the heat of our tiny house with its iron roof. Running toward my father where he sat at the table with his hand gripped around his glass, staring at the tabletop and not moving. My mother at the basin, her head turning with the warning in her eyes: *Don't.* That's what I remembered—her dark eyes turning toward me and their warning: *Don't.*

I let out my breath and ran a hand through my hair, then turned to look along the flank of the hill. Polaski was watching me.

"Pretty little thing," he said, "isn't she?"

"Who?"

"Miss Chan."

The image of Mexico faded. "You stay away from Chan."

"Really? I was thinking maybe I could diddle her for you, Torres, tell you what it was like."

"I said leave her alone."

"Sweet on Miss Chan, are we?"

When I didn't answer he picked up a rock and pitched it carefully down the hill.

"Man-u-factured Intelligence," he said. "Man, those MI people have got it made. Jobs when they get out..." He reached for a bigger rock. "Don't go crapping out on me again, Torres."

"I didn't crap out on you. You fucked up and the Army busted us."

He toyed with the rock. "So what do you see in her, anyway?"

"Someone who's still all right, Polaski. Someone whose insides haven't been taken out and pissed all over like the rest of us."

"Nice," he said. "Nicely said. So what's she see in you?"

I didn't answer.

"Come on, Torres, I've seen the way she looks at you all the fucking time. What's she see in you?"

"I don't know. Come on, Polaski, what did you drag me out here for?"

"Because I need you, all right? I need your brains. Is that what you want to hear?"

"For what?" I said.

He didn't answer.

"For what?"

He rummaged in his pack. "You tell me."

"Forget it, Polaski. All I want any more is out."

He got his radio into his hand and called Tyrone Elliot; he'd seen Elliot's helicopter beating its way toward us across the ocean, just above the waves.

"Yes, boss," said Elliot.

"Make a detour, Elliot. Get Torres' ass out of here. He needs something to do."

"Yes, sir, *Herr Feld Marschall,* sir. Tell him we'll snap his little wetback ass off the ridge, *sir.*" The radio shut off with a squeal.

"Get out of here," said Polaski. The helicopter changed course and headed toward us. "Go back where you came from, maybe."

I stood up. "So what about you, Polaski? Where did you come from?"

He was sitting a few yards away from me, facing down the hill, and now he put the radio down carefully between his feet. His movements were slow, calm. He looked down at the radio, then stayed that way, his head down, the muscles working in his jaw.

It was what I'd expected. The only other time I'd asked him about himself was at the school, after we met, when I asked him if he had family, and his reaction was the same. His face lost expression and his eyes narrowed, and he didn't look at me or speak. He walked away. When he returned three days later our relationship had changed: there were things that belonged in it, and things that didn't.

I left Polaski stewing on the hillside and slogged up past the digger toward the ridge, while I scratched at my bites and thought back to when I met him.

I'd been in the U.S. two years when the Army picked me up and selected me out for Tech-War School. Until then I'd been working the reforestations in the summer and trying to stay warm in the winter, asking at doors for books and food and huddling under blankets at night to read them. I walked the streets during the day and tried to sound Anglo and think Anglo, trying to get out of the trap. In cities filled with poor I was the poorest, a wetback off the Gulf boats that snuck around the border wire, and I knew my only chance for a job was English and machines.

Then without warning I was in the Army. Polaski appeared

a few days later, as though out of nowhere. Streetwise and confident, quick on familiar ground and sly when out of his depth. He picked me out for my skill with the books, then over the weeks grew prickly and watchful as though mindful of losing a new possession. The pointed guns began, the half-serious threats, always in private.

The pounding of Elliott's helicopter brought me back to the present. It kicked up a trail of fine sand along the ridge, then threw up a biting cloud as it reared above me. A black arm reached down from the after door and heaved me in, and Tyrone Elliot's big face appeared as he snapped a tether onto my belt. I grabbed at it just as the helicopter spun and plunged down the far side of the ridge. Elliot grinned.

"Getting on Polaski's nerves, huh?"

"Nothing gets on Polaski's nerves, Tyrone." The cabin was packed with people from the company, including a tiny woman named Ellen Tanaka who clung to the back of Elliot's belt.

"Who's Bolton kissing up to to get all this air time?" I said. "Airmobile kills quicker than giving up fuel."

"Oh, this ain't Bolton. This here's straight from Battalion, and it's sure enough major business. Mighty peculiar, too."

"Why?"

"Well, what we're doing here, see, is searching for civvies and yanking 'em up off the island, then hauling their asses back so the Army can see if we got the fellow they're looking for. And we gotta jerk 'em out real quick like, so not one whisper of nothing gets off the island."

"Not one whisper of what?"

"You're asking a man who don't know, friend. I just work here, if you know what I mean." He flashed another grin. "But I do hear that in thirty-six hours a whole lot of this here island ain't gonna be here no more."

With that he turned and shouted at the pilot. The helicopter reared up above the beach with its nose toward the trees, kicking up sand. Elliot shouted into the cabin.

"DeLauder! Your sector! Call in for pickups—go!" Tess DeLauder and two others fought their way forward and dropped from the swaying machine, rifles smacking against the deck.

"They need professional grunts to do this kind of work, Tyrone."

"No, sir. No one's supposed to know that don't have to."

"So why do *we* have to?" A wall of hot sand slammed in through the door as the helicopter spun.

"Lord almighty, boy! Because whatever screwed-up thing's happening to this island, it's us that's doing the screwing! Salvatore, you folks are next! Let's go!"

We went on around the island and dropped the rest of the crews, then ended up over the shoreline less than a mile from where I'd left Polaski. Elliot was about to have the pilot go around again when we saw roofs in the jungle and a satellite dish on the sand, tucked in against the tree line. He slapped the pilot and pointed, and the three of us were dropped on the beach—me, Elliot, and Ellen Tanaka. The helicopter left, and the silence closed in with the droning of insects.

Tanaka nodded toward the tree line.

"What if there're people in those houses?"

"Well, now," said Elliot, "I suppose that's the whole point. Torres, move it back along there and cut the leads to that dish, before someone starts telling someone else that there's choppers fooling around out here. Then let's go on back in and see who it is might be doing the telling."

"Tyrone," I said. "You don't move islands in thirty-six hours."

His eyes widened in mock surprise.

"Why son, we ain't going to move *nothing* in thirty-six hours. We're going to move it in five *minutes*. And we're going to do it sitting right on top of it, too!"

"We're going to blow this island while we're on it?"

"Yes, indeed! You're gonna need *faith*, boy, *faith*."

"*Why* are we blowing it, Tyrone?"

He shrugged. "Shoot, Torres, details like that they ain't telling us. Now get going."

I sawed through the cable leading from the dish into the underbrush. It was a small commercial device and nothing military, so we were probably dealing with civilian recluses or sportsmen. We were so close to the equator that the dish was pointed only slightly north, but it was pointing a fair bit east, probably at one of California's big commercial machines. Someone was using it to listen to the radio and order his milk and eggs.

Elliot and Tanaka had headed straight into the trees, and I cut into the jungle to meet them. I was struck by how quiet it was. No birds or crickets, no scurrying among the trees. Only the snapping of twigs and the crackle of dry leaves under my feet. The jungle was thin and brittle, close to burning. And it stank; down at the water-line, rotting fish lay half out of the water.

"Okey-doke," said Elliot beside me, "let's walk real quiet." We pushed in through the underbrush until a bungalow appeared through the trees. Beyond it a rutted track climbed up to the dirt road, after which the hillside continued up toward the island's ridge. The tangle of jungle followed the slope up a way, then petered out into rock and shale. The door to the bungalow was open, and Elliot motioned me in.

I peered into the gloom. It was empty, stripped of furniture, covered with dust.

"I don't think we're going to find anyone," I said when I came back. "This place is too crummy for air-dropped supplies, and there's not much of a town or boat dock anywhere."

"Yeah. Maybe we got us a long-time-gone rich people's retreat or something."

"Tyrone," said Tanaka, "that was a pretty new McAllister dish on the beach."

"Yeah, true. Okay, here's another one." Tanaka and I waited among the trees while Elliot pushed open the door.

"Nope."

I took the third bungalow. Its door was open like the others. I stepped onto the porch to look, but it was too dark to see in. Yet from the doorway came the steady purring of ventilating fans, and a current of warm air with an odd, sweet smell in it. I held up a hand for Elliot and Tanaka to wait, then stepped in.

There was the luster of wooden floors and off to the side, a little up from the floor, tiny equipment lights. The familiar green lights of MI cabinets. On the wall behind them hung charts and drawings, while papers and books lay scattered on the tables. By the door stood a terminal with a cable hanging from it, most likely to the severed antenna on the beach.

At the far end of the room, a man sat on a straight chair turned away from me, at a table with books and a glowing screen. Small and elderly, he had the dusty yellow skin and fine features of the Vietnamese. He wore a rumpled black shirt and a soiled shawl over his shoulders. Limp, grey strands of hair clung to his scalp.

A keyboard was pushed to one side, while instead he used fast-typing gloves bolted to the table. The arms disappearing into them were thin, and the tendons stood out clearly even in the poor light. A worn blanket hung across his legs, pulled up around his waist, while a wooden cane hung from the back of his chair. He looked fragile, barely alive. A smoking pipe lay next to the screen, made from bone and brass.

He leaned forward with a kind of stiff intensity, the gloves shaking so hard that he had to be working very fast, although every few seconds he gave an abrupt sigh and glanced toward the back room.

I knocked.

His head whipped around, and in the same movement he seemed almost to lunge toward the screen. But his hands were caught in the gloves, and after that one, convulsive movement he remained frozen in that odd position, his eyes locked on mine.

It was clear that he was hiding something, and, from the look that came over him now, he knew that I knew. His eyes lost their focus and drifted to the floor. The tension went out of his shoulders and he slumped back into his chair. Was he expecting this? Had it happened before?

Elliot put a hand on my shoulder.

"We gotta go, Torres." He squinted into the room. "What the hell's all this?" He took another step in and looked around, then came back to the door.

"God almighty," he said. "That's him, ain't it? The one we're supposed to be picking up?"

But I'd already seen the titles on the books.

"It's not biologicals, Tyrone."

He hesitated, then toyed with the flap on his holster.

"Listen, Torres. Battalion's screaming for my ass. We're supposed to be back."

"Go away, Tyrone."

He stared at me. "Come on, Torres, get his ass out of here. What do you mean, 'go away?' You know this place is getting trashed tomorrow."

"I'll take care of it, Tyrone. I'll get out with Polaski."

Elliot ran the back of his hand across his mouth.

"Fine, Torres, fine. I don't know what the fuck you're doing, but fine, I ain't never been here. You watch yourself, boy."

Then he was gone, and a minute later the helicopter roared away overhead. Inside the bungalow, the man hadn't moved.

I walked along the tables and glanced again at the books. They were English-language texts in disciplines I scarcely understood, but whose significance I knew very well.

None of the machines along the near side of the room, idling in their racks or cluttered on top of the tables, appeared to be connected to the outside world, or to the machine the man had in front of him.

Next to the charts on the wall he'd pinned a clump of photographs and articles. He was in some of the photographs himself, standing next to Westerners in what looked like academic settings. One photograph of him alone was partway down an article entitled DEPARTMENT OF ENERGY DISMISSES SCIENTIST'S CLAIMS OF CHEAP POWER.

I looked at the title for several minutes. I scarcely wanted to think what it implied. If the man had really found such a thing, it was worth any amount of money—yet according to the article, he hadn't.

Then I read the rest of the articles. And as I read them, a mixture of anticipation and fear began to leave a sour taste in my mouth. Could it be that no one had ever put all the pieces together?

On the other hand, maybe someone had. The military. Maybe their story about the missing researcher wasn't all a fabrication. Maybe the military had indeed put the pieces together, and had gotten to the man first. Then killed the story, courtesy of the Department of Energy.

And if it was true, and he'd then gotten away from them,

even to this strange, scarcely settled island cleverly in the shadow of the equatorial Pacific war zone itself, he wouldn't have been surprised to find the Army at his door.

Me.

Which makes it easier. I walked around behind his chair to the back room. He turned his head to follow. What was I going to do, though? Or did I already know?

The back room was smaller, with its own door to the outside. The door was half open. On the floor were a sleeping mat and some personal items, including a battered radio and some faded girls' clothing.

I walked back to the table and leaned down to look at his screen. His eyes left mine to watch as I pulled the keyboard toward me, and his mouth opened with a hoarse sound of protest. His breath was strong with the half-sweet smell of opium.

On the screen were mathematical series that meant little to me, so I reached for a key to flip through the pages of the document he was working on. I glanced at the corner of the screen to find a page count, then stopped when I saw something else.

Next to the page count was the machine's free memory count. But what should have been a few hundred billion—a few hundred gigabytes, or maybe a terabyte—was instead shown exponentially in a way I'd never seen before. 1.97×10^{15}. Two times ten to the fifteenth.

Not hundreds of billions. Not trillions. Two *quadrillion*—a thousand times the memory of other workstations. The man's eyes met mine.

Without touching the keyboard I walked to the back of the table, around to the computer cabinet itself. To one side of it, a twenty-centimeter section of the power cord had been stripped of its insulation, and the three copper conductors inside it carefully strung between two small pedestals in plain view on the table, as though between tiny telephone poles. Other than that there were only old-fashioned, transparent fibers leading to the gloves and keyboard and screen, also in plain view—no wireless connections here—but nothing else. Nothing. Everything the man had was inside that one machine. He might have been mirroring his data among multiple memory stores inside the box for redundancy, but it wasn't leaving the machine. He had surrounded his computer with an air-gap and shielding, lest anyone hack his way in, intercept its signals, or add a tracer wire when he wasn't there.

I unfastened the clips and drew off the cover. The man said something and pulled himself out of his chair, then slumped back down, immediately out of breath.

In the center of the machine were two oblong, dull silver shapes side by side, about six inches long and two wide. They bore Department of Defense asset tags. I'd heard rumors about such blocks, but I'd never seen any. They were petabyte memory blocks, one quadrillion bytes each, two to the fiftieth power, all of it static, immune to accidental loss. The document the man was writing couldn't have needed even a fraction of that much memory, but whatever he was writing about must have. It was an amount of memory used only to solve the mysterious equations of chaos, or to simulate the interactions of genetics or particle physics. The blocks would have cost millions each.

Blood was pounding in my ears as I walked back to the screen and began scrolling through the pages. Many of them seemed to deal with the rotation of super-symmetrical particles, the eerie fringe of quantum physics that had caught my attention in the book titles.

Somewhat more familiar engineering work followed. One page was titled SUMMARY DATA: OUTPUT IMPEDANCE. It dealt with the production of electrical power, and the numbers were very low. He was dealing with something that put out a tremendous amount of power, like a power plant generator.

Much farther down, a section was titled CRITICAL THER-MAL THRESHOLDS AND WORKABLE MASS, and there, once I understood it, I stopped. It wasn't a generator at all, but something that weighed only a few kilograms. The size of a car battery. It had to be some kind of pulsing device, then, because anything so small could only put out that kind of power for a few thousandths of a second.

The man was staring into his screen now, at the same time tamping down his pipe with a finger.

The last page was titled OBSERVED SUSTAINABILITY, and had only a few sentences. But I stared at the words in those sentences for a long time. Over and over I looked at them, not believing.

Decades. Not thousandths of a second, but *decades.*

The man was looking directly at me now, his face an awful conflict of what I took to be pride and pain.

I walked away, reeling. A device like the one spelled out in those blocks would give the world the kind of power people were literally dying for. Was it possible?

"Observed," it said. Not theoretical. Observed. A virtual observation in the blocks? It would have been enough.

Power—and wealth.

I was next to the computer's cabinet when I looked up again sometime later, facing the man across the table. The evening had left the room gloomy and dim, and his face was lit only by the screen. He'd smoked his pipe after I'd walked away, and his head was wreathed in amber smoke that drifted through the glow between us, obscuring his features.

My hand rested on one of the blocks. I ran my thumb down one side of it and my fingers down the other, feeling for the flange on the bottom. *Don't.* There was a throbbing in my ears, a roaring sound, coming and going. *Don't speak.*

The man sat in his smoky world of half-light and watched my hand. The block slid upward in its socket.

Don't ask. A pair of dark eyes flashing their warning. *Don't want.*

I slipped the first block into my trousers pocket. The cloth lining the pocket began to tear—the block was much heavier than I'd expected.

The second block slid loose from its case. The man became agitated for a moment and pent up frustration seemed to pull at his features, but the opium soon took back its hold on him and left in its place only the moist, unfocused eyes, leaden already with resignation and the torpor of the drug. The block slipped free and the screen blinked out, leaving only a shadow in the gloom where he had sat, a memory fading away already into the night.

I don't remember finding my way back to the camp that night, but I do remember walking along the hillside above the jungle, smelling the hot air and the dust, and thinking I could hear someone playing a flute far off in the distance. The tune was familiar, but difficult to hear.

By the time I reached camp, though, the music was gone. Polaski was gone, too, leaving me just a sleeping bag and a packet of food.

I lay down on the bag and looked up into night, thinking that maybe my future lay out in the darkness, after all. A future bought with a single, quick, mean-spirited theft.

Just before falling asleep I remember thinking it would be good to hear the flute again. It remained quiet, though, and I reached down for the touch of the blocks instead.

I dreamed that night about a wolf. It walked toward me across a black planet at night, the color of ashes, its face smooth. And it had no eyes.

Chapter Two: THE FIRST MESSENGER

When I awoke the next day the ground was shaking. My sleeping bag whipped in the wind and something heavy slid across my waist. A voice called out from above.

"It's time, Torres."

I put my face in the bag and felt for the blocks. If they were gone, I thought, maybe the punishment would stop.

"Let's *go*, Torres!" The blocks were still there. The thing on my waist slid higher and I grabbed for it. It was a rope, a pair of ropes, and it dragged me out of the bag and lifted me into the air.

The island sank away and I coughed and squinted at the jungle, clutching the rope ladder. The old man's bungalow was gone, lost in the trees. The island had already dwindled to nothing but sand and rock in the ocean, a slash of ocher against the grey.

Turbines exploded in my ears and my head lifted over the deck. Polaski sat in the far gunner's seat with a foot up on the helicopter's magnetic cannon, swinging it back and forth past my face. I snapped myself in and put on a headset.

"Good morning," said Polaski.

"Jesus, Polaski, are we in a hurry, or what?"

"Bolton's got orders."

I came awake as I remembered the Army and its plans. And the blocks. What had I planned to do? The day was starting too fast.

"What happened yesterday?" said Polaski.

"I found something."

"You found something."

Polaski was the last one I should be telling. He'd want to sell the blocks themselves the first chance he got.

"Under a rock, maybe?" he said. "You found something under a rock?"

"No. I took it."

"You took it." The cannon stopped. It was aimed at my crotch. "And you want me to do something about it."

I did and I didn't.

The helicopter plunged nose-low and raced along the beach of the main island, then banked through a gap in the jungle and heaved its tail into the air. The skids struck hard and it spun to a stop in front of the mess.

"Find me after the briefing," said Polaski.

The company was sprawled in chairs under the mess canopy, disheveled but mostly good-humored. Leaning against a table in front were two women wearing the white insignia of the MI controllers, looking crisper than the rest. One was A. W. Paulson, a stocky Midwesterner with hard eyes, and the other Katherine Chan, a slender, honey-skinned woman with a quick smile and glossy black hair.

I nodded to Chan, then sat down next to Elliot and tried to get the sand out of my ears. I glanced up now and then at Chan's figure and dark eyes. Elliot blew elaborate kisses to someone in back, then settled into his seat with a sigh.

"I ain't gonna ask," he said.

"Yeah. That's good."

He leaned closer. "On the other hand, maybe I am. Hell, Torres, you look like you swallowed a cat."

"I think I did."

"You think you *did*? You ain't supposed to say 'I think I did,' Torres, you're supposed to say 'Hell no, Tyrone, I ain't swallowed no cat, what you talkin' 'bout?' I swear I gotta watch you short Mexicans." He stretched out his legs. "I knew a short Mexican once. No one could see him coming, so he got stepped on a lot. Got shorter and shorter all the time."

"You're making that up."

"'Course I'm making it up! Ain't nothing around here to be cheerful about if you don't make something up. See—here comes his nibs. He don't look too cheerful, neither. He better make something up, quick."

Bolton walked in, out of place as ever. He was a small but

good-looking man with broad shoulders and sandy hair, wearing immaculate dress whites. He looked like a freshly-scrubbed school-boy stepping up to the front of the class, eyes alert as he surveyed the troops.

"All right, listen up." He was Welsh, and still had the accent.

"Let's see if we can straighten up a bit first, right where we sit, shall we? We've got a major coming along, and I shouldn't want to be caught less than kempt, hm? He's a Senior Manufactured Intelligence Controller—"

"A *what*?" The slurred question came from a woman in back, followed by snickers around the mess.

"Sorry," mumbled the woman, finally. "I guess they teach you to talk like that in OCS." Her eyes were glassy.

The mess quieted at the mention of OCS, and Bolton looked uncomfortable. "Well, Miss—"

Another spasm of laughter and she jammed her knuckles into her mouth. Bolton actually blushed and looked around the front for help.

Finally he took a breath and leveled his gaze at the back.

"I speak that way, Miss, precisely because I am *not* a lieutenant, and am for that reason making my very *finest* effort to seem like one—I am not even a corporal. You are clearly new here, so that is something you could not have known. Our lieutenant had the ill grace to pitch forward and puke his life onto our playing field, and a decision was made that a replacement would not be well received. Thus his bars were handed to me, and our MI controllers here were kind enough to break into BuPers and make it legal. I apologize if I am not what you expected."

There was an awkward silence, then she wheezed out behind her hands, "Jesus, what a weird outfit."

"It is an organization, *Private*, in which you should find yourself most comfortable." He broke his gaze after a minute and gave the assembly a sheepish smile.

"Now, then, however much it may put us out, we have orders, and we should at least make a respectable show of following them. It seems the Army have a plan for embarrassing the enemy closing on Singapore."

Surprised noises—we were a long way from Singapore.

"There are entrenched armor north of Singapore, and we need to tempt them into showing their hand in terms of their positions and in terms of with whom they are currently allied on the peninsula. There have been sightings of frogs in Johor, and it is of interest whether or not the enemy have access to them."

He described the enemy's order of battle, his command of the facts impressive. He was proving to be a good officer, even while in maneuvers he'd shown himself to be especially cunning and nasty in one-on-one combat. It was something that in the end he was always endlessly apologetic about.

"The way we will tempt them," he said, "is by firing a bouncer out of Guayaquil, Ecuador, aimed for the big strip north of Singapore."

Again, surprise. The giant ballistic transports were so expensive it was unheard of to launch one into the war zone. Yet Bolton was talking about firing one on its arc high above the atmosphere, along the equator from South America right into Asia.

"The moment the enemy detect the aircraft's launch from Guayaquil," he said, "and have calculated its trajectory, they will commit everything they have to that strip above Singapore, ready to capture or destroy the aircraft at any cost—knowing it cannot be recalled. They will also know that, even if the bouncer were able to alter its arc in mid-flight, there is nowhere between Guayaquil and Singapore capable of taking it. Thus they will move immediately.

"The U.S. Army will be there to meet them. The bouncer, ladies and gentlemen, will not."

There was a silence, then hoots and whistles; the position of a bouncer's four-hundred-knot landing was inalterable and was calculated to within inches before it launched.

Bolton looked embarrassed again. "Just a minute, people. Please. This particular bouncer will be equipped with braking rockets, and those rockets will arrest its arc and drop it directly down over the Pacific. Tonight. And in the five minutes after the pilots fire those rockets, this company will turn the island Sergeants Polaski and Elliot surveyed yesterday into a twenty-thousand-foot runway.

"I recognize," he said, "that your love of the cause has

diminished of late, but you will have to admit that this does sound like rather a lot of fun."

Something out in the clearing caught my eye, as the mess erupted into shouted questions. It was a boy, wearing nothing but shorts, which at the moment were down around his knees as he urinated into the company vegetable garden. He was slender and agile-looking, with a long neck and smooth black skin. He was holding something at his side and looking straight up.

The voices in the mess stopped. Glasses rattled and a muffled roar came from the sky. The temperature began to rise, higher and higher until the air was sweltering. People were getting out of their chairs when the roaring stopped abruptly and the air cooled back down. A spattering of rain drops hit the roof and then stopped, as well.

"Fucking frogs."

We knew what it had been. Fuel was so scarce that the U.S. had built tremendous vertical-takeoff transports powered by nuclear fission. But without water to keep the piles cool, they needed to blow huge amounts of air down through them, so much that it took further tons of armor just to hold it down against the lift. The air came out so fast and so hot that the frog overhead could have been a mile up, trailing its characteristic little squall line across the ocean in its wake.

"So, Bolton, you going to be running this little exercise?" The distraction was over.

"Um, actually not—I'll be at Battalion. That is why you're getting this fine fellow of a major, Major Cole. It seems that the phasing of the required diggers and heaters, as well as their coordination with the bouncer, will take a great deal of MI—and it was felt that even the lovely Chan and Paulson here were not up to the task. Thus they have sent us a senior controller—a high priest, as it were."

I told Polaski about the blocks after the briefing. We stood in the shade of the helicopter, watching the cirrus gather into a thin, high overcast. The air had taken on an uneasy grey cast since morning.

"Shit, Torres, these are worth more than we make in a lifetime." He hefted one of the blocks in his hand.

"It's the plans inside them, Polaski. The power cell, not the blocks. Two gigawatt-hours—enough to run a house for sixty years or a car for two hundred. Portable."

"Will it work?"

"His MI said it will."

"Jesus."

He handed back the block and paced.

"So what do we get, Torres? What do we want?"

"Out."

"Oh, come on, limp dick, everybody wants out. So why didn't you just sell these things and buy your way out? Come on, Torres, everyone says how smart you are. What do you really want? An army of your own, a piece of Alaska—"

"Off." My throat was dry, and I wasn't sure he heard me. "I want off."

"Off? A tin-can habitat? Jesus, you're going by yourself, buddy—"

"No."

He looked at me uncertainly, then after a minute took out his revolver and peered through the cylinder as he turned it.

"Come on, Torres—the doughnut? The torus? They didn't finish it, it's not—"

"Yes, they did."

He shook his head. "No, they didn't. Come on, what's with you, anyway?"

"We've all forgotten, Polaski. They did finish the torus. It was the solar collectors they couldn't do."

I had to use the latrines. Polaski was walking around the helicopter, squinting at it from all angles. "All right, okay, all right," he was saying, over and over. I wondered what had happened to the boy in the vegetable garden.

Pinned to the door of the latrines was a warning about insect-borne biologicals—theirs or ours was apparently of no interest—and recommending use of the jungle out back. I gave the building a wide berth.

I'd told Polaski what I'd been thinking to myself, and now it sounded foolish. The plans to anything weren't much good to a lone soldier with no resources.

Still, it was the only chance I would ever get. And the bouncer landing? I wasn't sure. A change in the wind? What I did know was that if I did nothing, I'd be back on the streets after the war. They would hand me my food ticket and send me into a world that had no use for a wetback soldier. I'd be sharpening knives on the curbstone again and fighting for a piece of sidewalk, until somebody was quicker that I was, and I was dragged out and rolled into the sewers. Some nights on the island I still heard the manhole covers grinding against the pavement as the bodies were rolled across them, the long wait before the splash.

I walked back to the helicopter.

"What about the mark?" said Polaski.

"What mark?"

"The guy you took them from. Maybe I should do him for you, keep him quiet. We could do it tonight."

"I don't want people hurt, Polaski."

"Oh, bullshit, Torres! The whole fucking world's dying over the piss-for-nothing oil that's left, and you come along with manna from heaven and expect everyone to be nice about it? Grow up. You brought me the things, so what the fuck did you want me to do with them?"

He turned to urinate on the helicopter skids.

"What about the drones?" he said over his shoulder.

"I don't know. Drones are a problem." They were more than a problem—they were the key to using the tunnel.

The tunnel wasn't really a tunnel at all, but a torus, a dough-nut-shaped thing the size of the moon that could generate a field along its axis strong enough to bend a narrow cone of space. A vessel passing through the hole at its center the moment it energized would find the distance to some far-off point shorter. According to the theory.

But super-smart drones were supposed to be sent through before any colonists, and no one had been able to build them. They were supposed to build another torus at the far end to come back through and tell us it was safe.

Major Cole was crazy. He was a powerful West Indian with bulldog features and wary eyes, who snarled orders and browbeat the company until we were all nervous and jumpy.

We were back on the narrow island where I'd taken the blocks. It was dark, less than an hour before we were supposed to blow off the ridge and make the runway. Polaski and I were at the western end of the ridge, looking back along the island's flanks toward the east; the bouncer would be landing toward us.

Miles away and down the slope was the Vietnamese man's bungalow. Other settlements along the island's shoreline, hastily abandoned and dark, were invisible to us as well.

A few stars shone, but no moon. The metal flanks of the digger in front of me creaked as it cooled from the day's heat. The rest of the digger and heater crews were strung out along the left and right slopes of the island in front of us, two strings of them along what would become the left and right sides of the runway after the ridge was removed. We couldn't see the crews themselves, but we saw their work lights flickering in the night, forming two four-mile-long lines stretching away toward the approach end of the runway.

All the machines on the flanks were slaved to Cole's computers. Polaski himself was responsible for the only two that remained freelance, positioned at our end of the island and aimed back along its length: my own digger, and a big two-barreled heater run by Ellen Tanaka. She was about fifty feet to my right, with Polaski crunching back and forth between us. Tanaka, Polaski and I were the only ones at our end of the runway. We couldn't see anyone else except Tyrone Elliot, holding down the right-side digger position closest to our end.

We had dark goggles pushed up on our foreheads, and wore padded, noise-canceling headsets linked together by ground wire. On a rise to the left was an antenna Cole had put up, linking us to him and to a voice named Bella, the name he had given his MI. We didn't know where they actually were. Chan and Paulson, our own MI people, were somewhere down the slope behind us, monitoring the heavy machines.

"Three minutes to braking," came Bella's silky voice through the headset.

"Paulson, Chan!" It was Cole. "Who the hell's not responding?"

"All diggers and heaters are timed and green on both sides,
sir," said Chan.

"Maybe *now* they are. Polaski—Tanaka and Torres at your
end are the only ones off-line, so listen close. Torres is going to
eyeball the finished runway and take off the rough spots. But there's
going to be about a million tons of dust in the air, and the pilots aren't
going to be able to see. So Tanaka's going to sweep the range with her
heaters and draw the crap off. She doesn't look too bright, Polaski.
You watch her close."

"Lay off her, Cole," said Elliot, a dim shape behind his
digger.

"Sir," said Tanaka.

"Hurry it up. What?"

"When do I stop sweeping the runway with the heaters?"

"When I tell you to, damn it! Listen, you people, this is a
billion-dollar bird and it's my ass, and I'm not going to let a bunch
of piss-ant wireheads blow it for me. Now shut up, all of you. The
clock's running."

"Two minutes to braking," said Bella, reading his mind.
I was listening to all this with a kind of numb disinterest, my hands
sweating on the digger's controls.

"Rather be reading a book, Torres?" It was Polaski, off in the
darkness.

"Who the hell said that?"

"Piss off, Cole."

"Chan! Systems."

"Yes, sir. Clock's stable. Handshaking, no faults. All machines polling—one skip on number six, single retry. RPM's in spec
across the board. Ready, sir."

"I don't want another skip—anywhere. Is that understood?
Paulson, are you backing up Chan?"

"Yes, sir."

"Fifty-six seconds to braking."

"Goggles on."

"I want all the digger crews to switch their ranging lasers on manually," said Cole, "so I can see if anyone's paying attention. Now!"

All the way up the island, thin red beams shot out from the diggers to measure the distance to the slope, lighting up in a herringbone pattern pointing away from us. After an instant's pause, one last laser flickered on way up on the left.

"Who the hell was that? Who the hell's the useless piece of crap that can't pay attention for a whole minute? Well?"

"It's on now, sir." The voice was that of the woman who'd heckled Bolton in the briefing.

"Ten seconds to braking," said Bella. "I have timing."

There was a moment of suspense, then in perfect unison all of the ranging lasers winked out. It was dark and quiet for several heartbeats, then the ground shook with a powerful jolt. I felt sick at what was coming.

Still nothing.

Then all at once the noise hit us, a wall of howling and clanging, even through our headsets, as all the diggers surged in unison through their frequencies, looking for a hit. The noise came screaming out of the blackness, swelling even louder as the farthest sounds began to reach us. Parts of the island began to glow and heave upward.

"Heaters—now!" shouted Cole.

The night erupted into searing white light as bolts of lightning shot out from the heaters and stayed lit, burning off the mass dislodged by the diggers. A single, ripping curtain of thunder pounded us for twenty seconds and then stopped, leaving just the snarling of the diggers and a roar as hurricane-force winds rushed into the vacuum behind the blinding white beams of the heaters. Cole was screaming something into his microphone—then a new voice came on.

"Thunder Island, this is Thunderbird on slope, two-niner miles. We have your lights, thank you. They're mighty pretty."

"Chan! God damn it—"

Bella cut him off. "Thunderbird, I have you at three-zero. I have data channel negative—are you automatic or pilot?"

"Colonel Alice Rajani at your service, with a crew of fourteen of the Air Force's finest. Advise your timing on those lights, please, Thunder Island."

"Three seconds, Colonel."

I tripped my ranging laser and got ready. The world went dark. I ripped my goggles off and strained to see. Stretching away in front of me was a glowing runway, socked in under a layer of grey smoke, eerily quiet. On the surface were a few darker irregularities I was to remove, but one of the heaters up on the left was still lit. Cole was screaming about it.

"Chan! Cut that thing off! Override it! What the hell's the problem down there? Paulson! Take over—get that Chink bitch out of there. And where the hell's the Jap? Why isn't she clearing that smoke?"

Elliot's voice: "Because you didn't tell her to, you son of a bitch!"

Up the runway, heater number six finally blinked out.

"Come *on*, Tanaka," said Polaski. "Your heaters!"

"Two minutes," said Bella. Tanaka's two barrels erupted into sun-bright shafts of light straight down the centerline, smoke rushing in to follow them.

"Four degrees up!" Cole screamed at her. "Four degrees! And swing it! Somebody do something about that piece-of-crap imbecile down there—"

Elliot cut him off.

"Chan, get me off-line! Come on, give me this thing. I'm tired of this shit." Elliot's ranging laser flicked on, still aimed up the runway in its locked position.

Chan shouldn't have let him have control of the digger. Its barrel released from its locked position, then swung across the runway, across Tanaka's heater beams and up toward Cole's antenna. The digger itself flashed into life.

Wherever he was, Cole saw it.

"Jesus Christ! Paulson, get control of that thing! Take—"

The antenna burst into flame as Elliot sliced through it with the digger. Paulson must have taken control back at that moment, because the digger's beam jerked to a stop and started swinging back toward its old position up-range.

It was still on.

I was halfway to my feet and screaming when the live beam from Elliot's digger swept through the first crew on our left. More screams, and the digger swept down the left side of the runway dragging a wall of flame behind it, finally merging with the double lance of Tanaka's huge heaters on the centerline. Elliot's digger flashed out, and a horrified silence settled over the island. Whimpering came through the headsets.

"Sir?"

The question took a while to sink in.

"Major Cole?" It was Tanaka.

Chan screamed.

"Oh my god! Tanaka! Ellen! Kill your heater, now!"

Elliot was already racing toward Tanaka's heater, which was blazing down the runway long after it should have been off. No one had told her to stop. She stood by the heater in confusion, staring at the new wall of flame on the left side of the runway.

Elliot leapt onto the machine and groped for the controls, finally tearing out the breakers. The twin shafts flashed out. We spun around to look down the dark island.

Suspended above the runway was a swirling layer of smoke, drifting in quiet eddies. Floating above it was the moon—huge, round and full, the color of lead through the overcast, lifting into view.

And then, slowly and gracefully, into the grey circle of the moon came a giant silhouette—the breathtakingly huge, powerful shape of an aircraft, gliding silently through the top of the smoke layer, its nose rising majestically as it began its flare for the landing. The nose lifted higher, then higher, then gasps came through my headset as the nose rolled even higher, exposing a glowing, jagged edge where Tanaka's heater had melted the plane in two.

The front end of the aircraft rolled slowly onto its back, settling closer and closer to the runway, the glowing maw of its wound approaching as though to swallow us all. Molten fragments floated across the island and flared into pillars of flame where they hit the jungle, making no noise at all.

Then suddenly the trance was broken as the plane plunged through the wall of smoke and smashed into the runway, spinning furiously toward us along the right side, crushing the remaining crews behind their machines.

Polaski jumped. I strained to see through the smoke, then I saw it too.

Barely outlined against the glow of the flames, a black figure walked toward Elliot where he stood by the big heater. I started to run, pulling off my headset as I went. "Elliot! Elliot, look out!"

Elliot spun just as Cole raised his arm and pulled the trigger, hitting Ellen Tanaka squarely in the face from inches away.

We lifted off in a helicopter two hours later. The island was in flames, a pyre whose smoke churned into the night like oil, blotting out the moon.

Chan sat hunched in a corner of the deck as the turbines swept us through the night, her face in her hands and her shoulders shaking as she wept. Elliot slumped against the after bulkhead, head turned with his cheek against the cold metal. Paulson sat to one side, frowning at her hands and counting something on her fingers. Polaski looked out a window with pursed lips. I stood across from him, holding on to a strap. I was staring out through the door, not wanting anyone to know how frightened I'd been when I'd thought the gun was aimed at Elliot.

The five of us were the only ones left, the only ones who'd been at that end of the runway. The rescue crews hadn't found Cole, or any trace of his body.

Chapter Three: PASSOVER

At dawn the next morning a pillar of black smoke still blotted out the
sky over the island. I sat on the stoop of our bungalow and watched,
far to the east.

During the night I'd gone to find Chan, and she'd taken me
into her bed. But the picture of oily flames and charred bodies hadn't
left me, and finally she'd put a hand on my chest and sent me away.
Elliot had come later, and now sat tossing pebbles into the dirt. They
made faint little thumps in the darkness where they hit.

"Cheer up," he said.

"You should talk."

"Hell, it ain't so bad. We still got stuff to look forward to. We
could have breakfast, you know, with that real good egg shit, then—
Well, come on, Torres, think of all the stuff we could do. Your head
gets to hurting, thinking about it… You don't believe me, do you?
That's the trouble with you, Torres, you take everything so serious.
It's depressing being around you sometimes."

"They're dead, Tyrone. A hundred forty-two of them. How
the hell can you let them go so quick?"

"No, sir, you don't ever let them go. You hang onto them real
tight. But you don't let them drag you back, neither. Don't forget
that, you hear?"

What had the old man done when the fires came? Had he
tried to hobble away on his cane? Call out for help?

Music from a flute brought me out of my sleep. It came from the
trees, the same tune I'd heard the other night. Again, as I listened, it
seemed to bring back some other place, some other time, hard to
remember.

A chair scraped in the room behind me. Elliot was gone. The
air was still, with a light mist hiding in the trees.

The chair squeaked again.

"Torres." It was Polaski's voice.

"What."

"How rich is it possible to get?"

"As rich as you want, Polaski."

Silence.

"I mean, can you have a trillion dollars?"

"Christ." I went inside. Boots hung off the end of my bunk where Elliot slept. I sat down across from Polaski and took a drink from his canteen.

"Okay. No, you can't get trillions. At a certain point money doesn't mean anything any more. In the end it's something the other guy only honors if he feels like it, and if you've got almost all of it, he's not going to feel like it. You reach a point where you've got too big a claim on society's resources and they devalue the money or cut you off, because you're bidding against it for labor and goods it has to have."

"How can they cut you off? It's legal money, isn't it?"

"Grow up."

"Fuck you, too. What if we've got some other kind of hold?"

"Listen, Polaski, if you're talking about selling those plans, you're not going to get anywhere near that kind of money. It doesn't work that way."

He looked disgusted. "No one's getting those plans, Torres. *We* build the power cells, and *those* we sell."

"Forget it. And don't even mention patent rights. They'll duplicate it overnight, and by next morning every company and government out there will have nice tidy reasons why we need to be deported and our facilities appropriated."

Polaski reached for the canteen.

"Fuck 'em."

The overcast had lowered even more an hour later.

"So listen, Torres. You made copies yet?"

"Before we moved out yesterday. There was just the document in the blocks, so I copied it out and wiped them. He was done with the modeling."

"So how long to build a power cell and find out if it works?"

"That's not the way it's done, Polaski. You tell an MI to build it internally and simulate it. That's what the old man was using the big blocks for, and his MI said it works. Assuming all the materials exist."

"Yeah, okay. So what do you need to prove it can really be built?"

"Bigger systems, like Canberra. Or China Lake's better, if California let the U.S. keep it open."

"They did." Elliot was sitting up on the bed. "U.S. got to keep it under the treaty. What the hell are you up to?" He was looking at me.

Footsteps came from the porch and Bolton stepped in, still in his dress whites.

"Whatever you're up to, lads, you can forget it." He threw a yellow flimsy onto the table. "They're breaking us up, with unaccustomed dispatch. Possibility of courts-martial relating to the aircraft, with additional rather cryptic questions regarding our search for a missing researcher—about whom we know nothing, hm? The Army are not amused, gentlemen."

I turned away.

"When?" said Polaski.

What the hell did it matter?

"Fifteen-hundred hours. We have six hours, lads, to come to terms with the wretched little scraps of our lives they will leave us."

For a minute no one spoke, then Elliot left abruptly. When he came back it was with Chan, who stopped and leaned in the doorway. She looked tired.

"Listen, Chan," said Elliot. "Bolton says they're busting us up at fifteen-hundred. How come you can't break into someone's communications and put out a message that we've been picked up or we're dead or something?"

She sighed. "One. That's not the way you work a bureaucracy. Instead you create a classified unit somewhere with no known access code, then you transfer us to that unit. Then you reassign that unit to this island. In the military mind, we no longer exist.

"Two. I can't get that deep into their systems. I can file

personnel status changes, but I can't move units around or requisition equipment or classify information. They change those passwords every ten days, and without a much bigger front-side store it would take me months to crack one. They know that.

"Three. What do you think I've been trying to do all night?" She didn't look at me. "Most of the night."

"All *right!*" Polaski's fist slammed into the table. Chan frowned. But I was reaching into my pockets at the same time. I set the silver blocks on the table.

Chan looked at me. Then in a blur she was moving, snatching up the blocks and pushing her way out the door.

It was sometime after three when a CH-77's lethargic thumping approached from above the clouds. It materialized through the layer just offshore, then beat its way in toward the clearing.

We were sitting under the mess canopy, waiting for the Army and the rain. We hadn't seen Chan since morning, and the brief hope sparked by her departure had faded. We'd told Bolton and Elliot about the plans for the power cells. Bolton listened with a polite skepticism, his eyes flicking restlessly across the landing field. Elliot hummed and spat sunflower husks.

Now we sat and watched the ugly machine coming in across the clearing. It was squat and slow, and spent a while finding the right position before it waddled onto its tiny legs and the pilot killed the engines.

We wandered out to watch. As the rotors spun down one of the cargo doors slid open and an MP stepped out and looked around. The pilot and her chief kicked open their own doors and leaned against the fuselage. It got quiet.

Then all at once Chan was racing around a corner and up to the helicopter. She pushed her way past the pilot with a mumbled apology, then pulled herself up to look at the instrument panel. She slipped back down and ran out of sight between the buildings.

The pilot took the performance with good enough humor, but the MP tensed. He watched her go, then walked over and stopped in front of Bolton.

"I understand we're giving you a lift off the island? Kits

ready? Anything heavy?" He was being friendly, but he looked at each of us in turn and didn't seem to miss much.

We couldn't think of anything to say.

The silence was broken when Chan ran up to the helicopter again, back past the pilot and into the seat. She picked up the microphone and set one of the radios, breathing hard from the run.

The pilot put her hands in her pockets and watched. The chief wandered around the nose to see. The MP folded his hands across his chest.

Chan brought the microphone to her lips.

"Paradise Control, Watchdog Three on guard."

"Watchdog Three, Paradise. Go ahead."

"Paradise, be advised I have a signature on a CH-seven-seven in grid four-two oscar, restricted zone." She was clearly reporting a sighting of the very aircraft she was calling from, although our island's position in 42-oscar had never been restricted.

A pause by the controller.

"We show no restrictions in forty-two oscar, Watchdog. Say your point of origin, please."

Chan ignored him. "Check your overlays, Paradise." The morning's airspace notices, not yet on the master grid.

"Stand by."

Chan's hand shot out to the frequency selector and waited. The MP turned to glance at Bolton, then looked back.

"Thank you, Watchdog," said the controller.

Chan spun the selector and the same controller's voice came up on the new frequency.

"—ster one-five, Paradise Control. Acknowledge."

Chan stuck the microphone out the door to the pilot.

"It's for you."

The pilot raised an eyebrow but took the mike.

"Duster one-five."

"One-five, you have entered restricted zone niner-zulu without authorization—"

The controller stopped.

"Stand by, one-five." Apparently something else had popped up in front of him.

Chan ducked under the microphone cord and walked lightly around the MP to stand between me and Bolton. She squeezed my hand. The pilot and her chief looked at each other. The MP stared at the microphone.

"Duster one-five, our apologies. You are cleared into R-niner-zulu to pick up one Warrant Officer A. W. Paulson for routine reassignment, then return Motherlode-direct. All other orders are superseded. Clearance expires on zone departure. Contact me on engine-start."

"Cleared R-niner-zulu, return Motherlode-direct. Roger one-five." The pilot clipped the mike back and put her hands in her pockets. She and her chief leaned back to watch us.

The MP stood halfway between them and our little group, then finally he, too, turned back to face us, looking grim. No one spoke.

Finally Chan said, "Lieutenant?"

It took Bolton a minute, then he straightened and tugged down his tunic. "Quite." He turned briskly and strode off toward the MI hut.

We stood where we were for a long time—Chan, Elliot, Polaski and I on the edge of the clearing, the crew under the stubby wing of their obese helicopter, and the MP out in the middle. It began to rain.

Drops spattered against the canvas behind us and sizzled off the helicopter's engine housings, putting up a fine mist. The air smelled of wet dust.

Finally we heard feet slapping through the rain and Bolton escorted a sleepy-looking Paulson to the open cargo bay. He handed in her kit bag, then walked back to the MP and saluted.

The MP's eyes narrowed. Rain dripped from his brow as he stared at each one of us in turn. Finally he turned back to Bolton and saluted, spun on his heel, and walked to the helicopter. The crew began their engine-start, and the pilot reached for her microphone.

We're free, I thought. For now, at least, we're free.

Chapter Four: THE EYE OF MOUNT NEBO

Sun hissed off the salt pan of Searles Lake, and China Lake to the west, shimmering between the Mojave and the Sierra Nevada. The temperature climbed above 130 degrees.

Inside the lab, ventilators hummed and dripped water down the walls. Computer screens waited for my instructions, if only I could think what more to ask. In the concrete pits under the grating, processors iced in frost sent up wisps of helium into the room.

The China Lake Naval Weapons Center seemed isolated and adrift. There was an air of resignation, with the staff just waiting for the war to end.

Chan had gotten me in with the rank of captain and a classification high enough that I was isolated even from the staff. The escorts who brought my meals were polite but reserved. The systems I was using were set to purge when I was done.

She'd gotten me in, but she hadn't been happy about it.

"Why are you doing this, anyway?" she said. "And why with Polaski? I don't think he knows when to stop, Eddie."

The day after Chan had gotten our unit classified and the MP had gone, a T-98 light aircraft had landed on the island, flown by a quiet-spoken colonel from the Judge Advocate General's office, with the name HOLKOM on his fatigues. He was a slight, mustached man with greying hair, and was accompanied by a petite woman in civilian clothes named Delaney, who blushed frequently and carried a portable communications terminal.

They were there to conduct interviews, he said.

"If I might ask a question, Colonel," said Bolton, meeting them by the airplane while Elliot disposed of classified documents we'd been reading in the bungalow. "How long has it been since you got your orders? This island has been sealed off, you know."

"Oh, I'm sure it has, son, I'm sure it has. Haven't talked to a soul in two days, is the thing—hell of a trip out from Washington. But I sure would hate to go all the way back without even a postcard for the kids, wouldn't I? And I don't much take orders from anyone, Lieutenant. Don't tell anyone where you're going, I say, or what you're up to—just poke around and you never know what you might find. Over this way, shall we?" With a hand on Bolton's shoulder he steered us off toward the bungalow. "Sarah here"—he moved his hand over to her shoulder—"well, her mom thinks she's in Philadelphia, as I recall. Fine woman, her mom."

Chan had gone back to her quarters briefly and had then stolen a look into the plane, but now she gave me a tight-lipped shake of her head: there was nothing she could do.

The bungalow was clean, although Polaski's mattress bulged more than it should have in the middle.

"Well, why don't you just get set up there at the table, Sarah," said Holkom, "and we can all get acquainted."

The young woman, Sarah Delaney, glanced at Polaski and then Elliot and blushed, then sat down at her terminal. A bright pink heart with lace edges had been sewn onto the breast of her blouse. "Hi," she said. A tiny dish antenna purred out and locked on a certain spot on the ceiling.

"So, what have we got?" said Holkom. He glanced around. "Warrant Officer Chan, Warrant Officer Torres—top of your class, weren't you, son? Pretty good for a boy off the streets. You would have been a good officer, anyone ever tell you that? And Sergeant Elliot, okay..."

Elliot saluted and Holkom turned farther in his seat to take in Polaski. His eyes dropped to Polaski's name tag.

"Oh, yes? Well, well, Platoon leader Polaski, 1st Engineers. Didn't expect to find you here. Or maybe I should have, what do you say? Well, we'll deal with you later."

He turned back to Delaney, now prim and upright in her chair, her fingers poised on the keys. Holkom nodded to her, then spoke to Bolton without turning around.

"You will wait outside, Mr. Bolton."

Bolton straightened.

"Permission to speak, sir."

Holkom didn't answer, and went about organizing his papers.

"Sir," said Bolton. "I have the right and the obligation to remain with my troops during the conduct of inquiries, sir."

Holkom still didn't look up.

"Private First Class Bolton," he said, "you will wait outside."

Bolton hesitated, then glanced around at the rest of us, saluted stiffly, and left.

"So," said Holkom. "Sergeant Elliot..."

He questioned Elliot about the events that led up to the crash of the bouncer. Delaney typed. Occasionally Holkom directed a question to Chan, who stood against the wall with Polaski and me, then finally he came around to the issue of Major Cole's fate.

"Was the major on the runway during the approach, Sergeant?" he said to Elliot.

"No sir."

"And at the time of the crash?"

"Uh...no, sir, I don't believe he was. He was still at his command post."

"I see. Then who killed him?"

Elliot hesitated.

"How did he die, Sergeant?"

"Is he dead, sir?" said Elliot.

It was the wrong answer. Holkom frowned as though disappointed in one of his students. He turned to Sarah Delaney, still speaking to Elliot as he did so.

"Tell me, Sergeant Elliot," he said. He gave Delaney a nod. "What do you suppose could destroy a man so completely that nothing would be left of him?"

"I don't know, sir."

"Oh, I think you do."

At that moment Holkom glanced up in surprise.

Polaski had pushed himself away from the wall and walked the few paces to the table. He seemed uninterested in the proceedings, as though he meant only to wander over to glance at Holkom's papers. But then he took his revolver out from behind his back and put the barrel against Holkom's face. Holkom raised his eyes to meet

Polaski's, not concerned, not yet. Mostly curious.

There was no way Polaski could have thought it through, I thought. All we'd needed was to delay the man, to raise some doubt, get him on his airplane and back to Washington before he filed any charges. Then Chan would have had time to block them, or to reverse them. To think of something. Our records would have been clean, then, our hardcopy records, and we could have backed down from the project and stayed in the Army if we'd needed to.

Polaski shot Holkom through his right eye. The crash of the gun and the blood and the stink of sulfur exploded into the room. Polaski held the gun perfectly steady after the shot. The force of the blast sent papers billowing off the table.

Holkom landed on the floor on his back, twisted around in an odd way.

Sarah Delaney didn't move or call out. She sat motionlessly at her keyboard as her fingers felt back and forth for their correct typing positions. She stared at Polaski. A noise came from the back of her throat.

I hesitated at that point only because I didn't think he'd do it. I remembered that fact later that afternoon, as I dragged the bodies out to the jungle. The idea that Sarah Delaney's death would provide a neat solution to our dilemma hadn't occurred to me while I was still standing there next to Polaski, in front of Holkom's body. I hesitated only because I didn't think he'd do it.

Or so I believed.

When I took my eyes off the blood seeping through the lace around the pink heart on her breast, it was to look over at what she'd typed on her terminal.

ELLIOT, TECH SGT TYRONE R, REFERRED FOR DISHONORABLE DISCHARGE. TYPE "RETRIEVE" TO AMEND TRANSACTION, OR MAKE NO RESPONSE TO CONTINUE.

Polaski read the screen at the same time I did. Or at least he was looking in that direction. He was closer to it than I was, so I didn't reach for the keys myself to cancel Elliot's discharge.

Polaski reached leaned around to the back of the back of the terminal and turned it off.

"Jesus *Christ*, Polaski—"

His eyes met mine and I stopped.

"You were thinking," he said, "of turning back?"

He glanced back once at Elliot, then brushed past Bolton and left. The revolver was still in his hand.

"Is that why?" Chan had asked me. "Because he doesn't know when to stop?"

On the second day at China Lake I sent him a message telling him the power cells would work. The systems had found the principle unfamiliar, but they'd understood the quantum interactions it was based on. After modeling the device and running it through enough iterations of cause and effect, they'd agreed it was stable and that any good manufacturing system would be able to build it. That was as I'd expected.

But in the end it wasn't why I'd come. I'd needed to check on the cells and on the tunnel and electric propulsion, but my real reason had to do with something no one was talking about yet—the drones.

A seldom-advertised fact of the tunnel was that once it had sent us out to some other system, there would be no way back. And we couldn't know much ahead of time about the place we'd be stranded, either—if we sent robot probes ahead of us through the tunnel, it would still take decades for their findings to be transmitted back in the usual way.

So we would have to send super-intelligent drones through and have them build another torus in the new system—not just for further stages of the journey, but through which they could return to Earth with news.

And drones meant China Lake. The center had shifted from its expertise in target recognition to the strange business of applied information theory, which was apparently the key to building drones. One of the scientists explained to me that the theory examined the practical value of hard knowledge—a kind of knowledge that by itself tended to be overrated.

"For example," he said, "if a drone flying over a battlefield senses sulfur and a drop in pressure, it might be able to use these data to calculate a course that improves its chances of survival. But what if it only has millionths of a second to calculate? Can it decide on the usefulness of the calculation without actually doing it? And will improving that decision by spending more time on it outweigh the increasing danger of waiting to act? Has the time already spent on all these decisions changed the significance of the original data?

"In other words, Captain, under time pressure the very process of thinking becomes a factor in what the thinking is *about*, and it is on that self-referential knot that conventional MI balks. Finding the best action with few data and little time amounts to the skill of making snap judgments. It is something animals evolved for and are very good at, but which current MI is not. Manufactured intelligence is less fallible—that's its point—but it isn't very *effective*. We had to concede long ago that infallible intelligence and effective intelligence are very different things, and to this day we can't manufacture the effective kind very well."

But the military needed drones, and drones meant effective intelligence. Thus that superlative mystery, the decision-making rules behind what they called "EI," had become China Lake's great project.

Just the same, when I left after three hard weeks, I believed we would never build a single drone. We had neither the equipment nor the skills.

And yet, I thought, if only we could—because in the files I'd found a destination: Holzstein's Star, a small, cool G-type known to have planets, with no fewer than three of them livable—planets where forests could be made to grow, planets with endless amounts of land. And barely, just barely, within our reach.

The pilot ferrying me back to the island said something as we crossed the equator. I shook off tangled thoughts and looked at her, not understanding. She pointed out the window.

High in the atmosphere, tracing the line of the equator, ran a band of grey smoke like a noose around the belly of the world.

She shrugged and looked back at her instruments, but I watched it until it was lost from view.

Our base had been turned into miles of mud and mosquitos. Tents had been set up and torn down, and at the edge of the clearing stood row after row of the cradles sonic diggers were shipped on. A mud-spattered jump-jet stood nearby.

Polaski worked his way across the muddy field toward me, looking very much in command of this stinking piece of ground. He swatted at mosquitos and flicked a new swagger stick against his calf.

He stopped and waited a few paces away, as though I was supposed to say something. When I didn't, he turned to watch another man picking his way toward us—David Rosler, one of our fellow Shorts from the school. He was compact with soft features and limp black hair across his forehead, with a pair of glasses he alternately wore and held out to the side as though for balance on the rough ground. He wore an old military blouse stained down the front and soaked with sweat under his arms.

When he reached us he brushed his hair away from his face and dug a sleeve into each eye, clutching his glasses. He reached out to shake hands.

"So you're the one with the brains," he said. His hand was slack and moist. "Can't say I'm surprised. Your boss here said he had someone pretty smart sniffing around."

I glanced at Polaski. "Hello, Rosler."

He jerked his head at the twelve-seater. "Let's go."

Rosler reminded me of a man in the Chicago yards who, in the winter I turned twelve, took my blankets and burned them to warm his hands over. It was a memory like that of my father on the border wires. It made me angry, and there was nothing I could do about it.

Rosler swung down the plane's steps and glanced over my shoulder. "He with you?"

It was the boy I'd seen near the mess at Bolton's briefing, nearly a month ago. He was dirty and thin, though now he did have a shirt, and he shifted his weight from foot to foot and looked anxiously from us to the plane. There was a wooden flute in his hand.

"Where the fuck did he come from?" said Polaski. "I thought the place was cleared. And what's he doing out here in the first place?"

"I've seen him before," I said. "By the mess. What's your name, kid?"

Either he didn't speak English or didn't speak at all.

"Hey!" Polaski jabbed him in the stomach with the swagger stick. "The man's talking to you."

The boy gripped his stomach and looked at me with eyes wide.

"Jesus fucking *Christ*." Polaski swung the stick at the boy's face, then turned and climbed into the jet. "Keep him away from me, Torres." I'd never seen him so angry, yet I had no idea what it was about.

The boy's cheek had an ugly gash on it and was bleeding down his chin. I searched in my pockets for a cloth, knowing I didn't have one, then finally just motioned him into the plane. He moved to the farthest seat aft, stanching the flow of blood with his shirt. I watched for a minute, then went to sit behind Polaski and Rosler.

The plane was equipped with full gloves, set like boxing gloves onto stubby columns beside the pilot's seat. They were small enough to be Rosler's own, meaning he would unclip them and use them on other equipment. As he maneuvered the plane out of the field it looked like he wasn't moving a muscle. His typed instructions appeared on the screens while the gloves slid and rotated very slightly to control the plane. We climbed northward.

The boy was looking out the window. He had blue-black skin across fine features, with eyes wide and lips parted as he watched something below. Simple-minded and harmless...and familiar?

In the cockpit I watched the position readouts until latitude reached zero and stayed there. We were hovering at the equator.

"What do you think?" said Polaski.

There was an eerie sight in the ocean ahead of us, a peculiar island all by itself. It was about six miles long and two miles wide, running east to west. It was also over a mile high, with sheer, smooth walls curving to a peak like a roof.

The walls were cloaked in a film of smoke, which near the base flickered with fire. It was like the head of a beast rising from the water in flames. Apparently it had been cut from a much bigger island, with work still under way at the base.

There was something else behind the smoke. On the near end of the island, a darker black showed through now and then, and then closed over again, like a veiled eye. It was thousands of feet up the eastern end.

Rosler raised an eyebrow at Polaski. Polaski nodded curtly and Rosler spoke into his headset. Horns blared and the screens turned bright red, showing splayed hands and the words ALL MANUAL. He pulled his hands out of the gloves and took off his headset, then reached forward and snapped the control column out of its recess.

The world dropped out from under me. The plane fell like a rock as the nose pitched forward, filling the windscreen with ocean. Air screamed past the fuselage and the nose started back up, pressing me into the seat. The island was growing larger in front of us as we dove toward its base.

When we were half a mile away the nose came all the way up and we raced for the eastern face at a breathtaking speed. I silently noted the instant when it was too late to turn aside. The curtain of smoke flew at us and we hurtled into the wall at full speed.

It went dark. There was no sensation at all but the roar of engines. Then all at once I was wrenched forward as the jets spun to stop us in midair, then another jolt shook the plane as it struck ground. The engines spun down.

I stepped out into a cold and moonless night, and suddenly had the uneasy sense of having crossed some kind of line at the very edge of reality. I rubbed my arms against the cold and looked back the way we'd come.

Three miles behind the aircraft's tail was the bright rectangle of the opening we'd flown through, the completely open end of a massive cavern. Smoke drifted across the opening, casting shadows against the floor and walls.

The boy slipped past me and disappeared into the dark.

"Over here," said Polaski. He led me to the nose of the plane.

Set into the bottom of the cavern's end wall, the end we'd been flying toward, were three rectangular openings. Dwarfed by the openings, engineering crews were installing hundred-foot-high blast doors and freight elevators into them. The ant-like appearance of the crews suddenly threw the cavern's true size into perspective. More crews, nearly invisible in the distance and the gloom, worked around the remaining walls under harsh white lights and the flicker of arc welders.

"Heaters," said Polaski. "We used heaters to fuse the surfaces. The runway's a quarter-mile wide, eight hundred feet high. It's the only way in—everything else is a half-mile below us. Forty-damn-million square feet of space down there."

"Torres!" Elliot trotted across the runway toward us, ignoring Polaski. "Chan wants to see you. She's all jumpy like, so maybe you ought to come quick."

"All right."

"Hey, Torres," said Polaski as I walked away. "Do something about the boy."

I ignored him. When we were out of earshot I stopped Elliot.

"Jesus, Tyrone. All of this in three *weeks*?"

"Yeah, I know. He's been pushing folks pretty hard."

"Pushing who? Who the hell are all these people?"

"Well—he brought in most of your Shorts like you planned, but he's got some other specialists in on TDY, down on the shelf. I don't know what he's been telling them."

"What's he been telling the Shorts?"

"That we might have a way off-planet. He ain't exactly let on we're freelance, though."

"Jesus. Okay—what shelf?"

"You didn't see it coming in? Down at the waterline, below the runway mouth. Couple of miles of flat rock. The bays for the big ships are under it—Polaski says right under the runway is the only place we can defend a level area like that. Those bays are big suckers, too."

"He said forty million feet. What's that, a couple of square miles?"

"Mile and a half. Big enough, though. Man, we sucked smoke out of those bastards for ten days, and it still ain't right down there."

I stopped.

But Elliot spoke before I could. "Listen, Torres. No one liked having you gone. I know we planned this and all, but not this fast.

We ain't got time to think, you know what I mean?"

There was a swirl of dark smoke centered in the opening for a moment, like an eye pressed up against the glass of a window.

"You said you were pumping smoke, Tyrone. That smoke's still up there. The whole world can see it."

He shrugged. "Don't matter. Chan's got this place so hexed that even with everyone out there falling over themselves to help, they're begging not to know what it is they're helping with."

"Maybe. But DoD's going to find out sooner or later we've got their research. You know that, don't you?"

"Hell, they *know* we got their research. Your lady-friend's smarter than you think."

"They *what*?"

"Yes, sir. According to the great Department of Defense computer in the sky, this here island is Defense Advanced Research Project Agency's number-one mission—hands-off, die-on-sight, no expense too revolting. The way Chan's got it rigged, DARPA's missing scientist fellow was found after all, by the very fine and loyal 42nd Engineers—that's us—and to keep that self-same scientist a lot more dedicated to the cause this time, DARPA's got him shut up on this island. Heavy defensive weapons seriously required by 42nd Engineers to defend it, thank you, along with lots of MI and manufacturing tools. So—not only does the military think their little power cell is in their hands, they're taking real good care of us while we build it."

"No shit?"

"No shit."

Chan flew into my arms.

"Damn it, Eddie, you were gone too long."

"Hi, Chan." I kissed her and began to let her go, but she took my hands and put them around her, then pressed herself against me and kissed me hard.

"God, Eddie, I'm glad you're back. Things aren't going so well."

"Why?"

"We're moving too fast. Someone was killed this morning."

"Who?"

"One of the cutting crew—I watched them pull her up. She was hit with a heater."

"Jesus."

Chan dropped down in front of a battered screen on the floor, wrapping herself in a blanket. We were in a corner of the cavern lit by a dim bulb, surrounded by packing crates.

"Why are we doing this, Eddie? We'd be okay here, wouldn't we, the two of us? We could get work, a place in Alaska. It wouldn't be so bad."

"We can do better, Chan."

"By getting away from everything you hate, you mean? You used to come to me when you got like that, Eddie. I liked that. I made it better for you."

"We may not be going, anyway."

She looked up.

"It's not the cells—we can build those. And the cells can power the space tunnel, and the old ships can still be built—though like we thought, the world's going to go broke building them for us. It's the drones. This EI business is way out of our grasp. And the drones have to go up soon—the minute the tunnel's ready if they're going to have time to turn around."

Chan nodded and looked down at her screen.

"That's why I sent for you," she said.

There was a message on the screen. KATHERINE CHAN: A GOOD MACHINE TELLS ITS MISTRESS EVERYTHING. —ANNE MILLER, C.L.N.W.C.

China Lake Naval Weapons Center.

I didn't understand the message, but I knew immediately that someone had seen my work.

"Someone knows about the cells," I said.

"The cells? Probably. But look who she sent it to."

To Chan—it took a minute to sink in. If they knew to send the message to Chan...

"Someone knows what we've been doing to the DoD computers."

"You keep saying 'someone.' Don't you know who that is?"

"Anne Miller? Should I?"

"China Lake, civilian. Probably designed the system you were working on. She's also the world's foremost expert on EI."

On EI? It didn't make sense. It wasn't surprising that my interest in EI had attracted expert attention, but now that expert was sitting on a fortune and had the means to take us out of the game at the same time—and was sending us coy messages, instead.

"I called her," said Chan. "But I still don't know what she wants. She says she wants to see what we're doing. I kept asking why, and she kept saying she was just tired of everyday intelligence. Those were her words, 'everyday intelligence.' She's weird, Eddie. I don't know if she's coming to help us or stop us or what. But she's coming."

"When?"

"Today."

"So what do you think, Bolton?"

We were touring the cavern in an electric cart, and we'd stopped to watch the crews testing the blast doors over the elevators. There was nothing I could do about Anne Miller until she was there.

"I think it's quite possibly defensible," said Bolton. He was leaning on the wheel, wearing just his white uniform shorts and a t-shirt, gazing at the flying work platforms.

"You know what I mean. About ransoming the power cells."

He started the cart and nodded toward the opening. Cargo helicopters were easing up over the rim one at a time and filing toward us along the wall, so far away we could barely see them. The opening was clear of smoke.

"Looks like you could reach out and pinch them between your fingers, doesn't it? Like insects." He nodded toward David Rosler hurrying across the apron to his jump-jet, bent forward at the waist with his black hair slapping against his forehead. "Our Mr. Rosler is enjoying himself rather too much, don't you think?"

"It's occurred to me."

"What I think, lad," said Bolton, "is that we are burning our bridges."

"So? What's here that we need?"

"True, and I *am* coming with you. Nonetheless, I do have people at home, and I find I'm not proud of grasping for the ring while they stay behind. I have a younger sister somewhere, you know, and she's not quite right, and I don't even know if someone's caring for her. And a brother in the North who drives lorries and drinks. I think about them sometimes, and I can't help but think that bitter and unpleasant as it's become, it's the belly of our own civilization we are carving our way free of. It troubles me that our freedom may never lose the mark of that passage."

The jump-jet's engines spun up. Rosler twisted around to look out his side window, trying to see behind him.

"Everything *I* can think of," I said, "I'd just as soon leave behind."

"Mm," said Bolton.

With a roar the jump-jet lifted free and rose into the air, then rotated to face back the way it had come. It leaned forward and accelerated fiercely until it was free of the cavern and disappearing into the sky.

Suddenly the cavern burst into light from a lamp high above, leaping into stark highlights and shadows, as though a play had ended and the house lights had finally switched on to the applause.

"It would have been clever of them," said Bolton, "to have gotten them working *before* all our mucking about in the dark."

"Who got killed, Polaski?"

"Some grunt."

We were on a catwalk along the cavern wall, looking down at the elevator cables as they un-spooled.

"We didn't say anything about bringing in regulars."

"You said to do whatever it takes, Torres."

"Not this fast. We're going to be here a long time, Polaski, and morale has to start out better than it is."

"Most of these guys would have been dead if we'd left them where they were. We're doing them a favor. So, all right, Torres. We need to open the elevators and secure the place. You want to move nice and slow on that, too?"

I thought about the coming arrival of Anne Miller, and about her message.

"How secure are we?"

"Not very."

"Then no. Chan may have us classified in the Army's books, but that's just a signal for everybody else to slip people in here to see what the U.S. is up to. And we're in too deep to have it blow open. Get the best security people you can, Polaski, and get the place sealed."

"Yes."

"No slips."

"Yes."

I found Bolton and Chan out on the apron, watching two aircraft approach the opening. From the walls came the familiar *thwack-thwack* of anti-aircraft laser solenoids engaging before locking on the aircraft. It was Rosler's jump-jet escorting a small tail-fan passenger plane along the cavern's centerline. Rosler kept his altitude while the tail-fan touched down and rolled into the light. It had U.S. Navy markings.

The little plane's engine purred to a stop. The pilot opened her door and let herself to the ground, holding a narrow briefcase and studying her surroundings. She was a slender, elegant woman, dressed in khaki. She had fine features and high cheekbones with closely cut black hair, and silver earrings against light chocolate skin. Her eyes were dark and intelligent. But Distant.

With graceful strides she walked toward us, then hesitated and looked back at the aircraft. Finally she took the last step toward Chan, holding out her hand.

"I'm Anne Miller. Ms. Chan?"

"Yes. Welcome to— Well, welcome. I guess we haven't named it yet." Chan's quick smile.

"Yes," said Anne Miller. "I'd pictured landing on a beach somewhere." She took a step past me to Bolton, who took her hand.

"Michael Bolton, Ms. Miller. I understand you'll be helping."

"I thought you might be the lieutenant." She turned to me. "And you are Eduardo Torres. You are a very persistent man, did you know that?"

A hydraulic whine came from the airplane and a set of steps slid out. When they touched the ground, the passenger door flew open with a smack and banged against its stops, propelled by an aluminum crutch in the hands of a big man in the doorway. He was looking straight down, concentrating on getting a second crutch out onto the steps. Miller made no move to help, so we stood and watched.

He was soft and heavy, dressed in a billowing white shirt and baggy trousers. We could see only the top of his head, covered with thin black hair touched with grey at the sides. The crutches were the kind that wrapped around the forearm above a grip, and when he finally had them planted on the top step he looked up.

He had strong northern Indian features with skin the color of burnt peat. His face was big with fleshy jowls and wide, generous lips, and dark eyes close to a hooked nose.

His face dissolved into a broad smile, which vanished as he looked down again to concentrate. As he worked his way down the steps, his lips pursed and his cheeks blew in and out, his face in constant motion. Finally he made it down and began a limping gait toward us, swinging his legs behind him with evident difficulty. The half-moon smile lit in his dark face and his lips worked and his head bobbed rhythmically, eyes darting from one of us to the other. He began to speak with a melodic baritone in a refined British accent.

"A good landing, my dear! Very nicely done. Yes. Thank you. Hello! I am Madhu Patel, how are you? Yes, hello! You must be Katherine Chan. What a lovely, lovely girl! I am delighted."

He pushed himself straight with an effort to leave the crutches hanging from his arms. He took her hands in his and bowed forward to kiss them. Then he straightened and grabbed for his crutches, and looked past her shoulder.

"Hello!" He pushed his way between Chan and me and limped back to the boy. No one had seen him come up. He had a clean set of bandages on his cheek, as though it had been sutured.

"Hello! I am Madhu Patel." He reached the boy and pumped his hand. "That is a fine looking flute. Yes! Perhaps you will play it for me sometime, yes? I would be most honored. Thank you, yes. And what is your name?"

The boy looked down at the flute.

"He's a kid from the islands," I said. "We don't know his name."

Patel peered intently at him. "Kip? Yes, that's a very nice name. I am pleased to meet you, Kip."

He swung around again and leaned on his crutches a few paces away from me.

"So. From your looks you are Eduardo Torres. I am told you are a determined man. I hope that that is a good thing." He stepped toward Bolton, heaving upright again to hold out a hand. "Hello! And who are you? I am Madhu Patel."

"Michael Bolton, Mr. Patel. My pleasure."

Bolton let go of Patel's hand and turned to Miller. "Perhaps you would explain."

"Yes, of course," she said. "Madhu is an economist."

"Yes!" said the man. "And a very good one, too."

A silence followed, while Bolton looked from one to the other.

"I don't understand."

Patel walked a few steps away. "You should, young man." He turned back and looked at Bolton from under heavy brows, then gazed around at his audience.

"Allow me to explain." He seemed to savor the idea before going on. "So. My colleague here tells me that you are planning to present the world with an item for which it will pay any amount of money. You are then intending, as the Americans say, to take the money and run."

His voice rose at the end of each sentence, followed by a quick bob of his head.

"Now, I am sure we all agree that one or two things are not as they should be in our poor world, but I have nevertheless some small sympathy for it, and I do not wish to see it come to harm.

"So. What you may not realize, in your haste, is that you are about to introduce a powerful drug into the arm of a most fragile patient. It is my intention to keep that patient from expiring.

"I will also"—he smiled broadly—"offer you your only chance of success." His eyebrows rose and fell as he watched each of us in turn.

"Mr. Patel," I said, "I'm not sure why you're here. We don't, in any case, mean the world any harm. We only want to get away from it."

"Ah!" His eyes flashed, then relaxed again. "No. I do wish you much success, my boy. And, if the truth were known, I rather hope to come along. But please do not think the time will come when you have all at once left your world behind. We are none of us so innocent. No, my young friend, the answers to whatever suffering this world has caused are still here, however much more suffering that is likely to bring. But enough! My business is the orderly theft of the world's riches, instead."

Bolton glanced at me. "I thought that's what you meant to avoid."

"Ah-hah. I said only that I wished to avoid killing the patient while we operate, Mr. Bolton. No, I have come with a proposal to put to Mr. Torres. And to Mr. Polaski as well? One wonders. In any case, it is this: I will arrange for you to engage the world's industry to your ends, if you will provide for others to follow. You must also leave your little secret behind." He looked solemn for a moment, then burst into a laugh, very pleased with himself. I felt sick at hearing an outsider talk about what we'd tried so hard to keep secret.

"Perhaps," said Bolton. "But as Mr. Torres has said, we're still not certain how you come to be here. Or why."

"Ah-hah. Yes. Well, I will tell you. You see, as intelligent as my colleague here is, she still chooses to tell me things." He swung his head to look at her. "And when she told me of this little adventure of hers, I left her no choice but to bring me along."

For the first time since he'd arrived, his face was still and his eyes were hard as he looked at her.

Miller returned the gaze for a moment, then broke it off and stepped toward the group. "I'm afraid I need to rest," she said. "And then Katherine and I need to begin finding some very expensive equipment. So if you'll excuse us, I need to get my clothing from the plane. Perhaps we can join you later."

"Ms. Miller," I said. She stopped. "I have a question. You told Ms. Chan you were coming to work on EI, and whatever your reasons, you seem to have left us no choice in the matter. But I don't believe you can work without the code and data you've left at China Lake. So we need to know if you plan to open a connection from here to the mainland."

In response she sank down to rest on her heels and opened her case, which she then turned toward me. Fitted neatly inside were fully thirty of the now-familiar, dull silver petabyte memory blocks.

"You see!" said Patel, beaming and nodding. "She is so efficient. That is why I let her take such good care of me!"

Miller closed her case and walked away with Chan. Patel watched them go, then leaned forward and said, "You will want to watch that one, my young colleagues. Anne Miller is a woman whose only friends, I'm afraid, were built with her own hands."

Patel said nothing more about himself or his odd companion, but he did ask to be shown around the caverns. I found that I didn't mind.

The elevators to the lower caverns weren't ready, so Bolton brought up the electric cart for a tour of the airfield. Patel had a hard time getting himself into the front seat next to Bolton, and his big face worked hard with the effort. But when he was in he smiled and banged a crutch against the floor.

"Good, good!"

Bolton glanced at him as he drove. "What's your impression of the island, Mr. Patel? Miller said it wasn't what you expected."

"True. Yes, it is very impressive. Brutal, but impressive." He turned around and surprised me by patting my knee. "I am sorry if I was harsh with you, young man. But I do not think you should hope for more than you have."

He turned back and pointed out the front. "I should like to see the view from that very big window there, if it's not too dark. I understand we are very high in the air?"

"You didn't see it as you came in?"

"Ah." He peered at a passing laser battery. "Actually, no. We heard over the radio what the gentleman in the other aircraft expected us to do, and just at that moment I remembered a book I very much wanted to finish. Hello!" he shouted to a passing soldier. "How are you?"

He turned to me in the back. "Tell me where you are from."

"Piedras Negras. In Coahuila."

"Oh. *El desierto vacío.*"

"*Sí.*"

"My little Spanish. I am sorry." I didn't know if he was sorry for his Spanish or the desert.

"No one is left," he said. "The desert moved too quickly, and no one is left. Did you know that?"

"No."

"You had family there?"

"A mother and a sister."

"Ah-hah."

We came to the edge of the world. The cart's front wheels rested close to the lip of the opening, a knife's edge that ran to the sides and then up and across the top where it became lost in the gloom.

No one left in Coahuila? I was stunned. What had happened to Graciela, and to my mother? All those years I'd tried not to remember them, tried not to remember that I'd walked away, leaving them to look for their husband and father by themselves...to find him sideways on the wires, a foolish marionette with his pants torn, his shirt pulled up around his chest...

I'd wanted to pull the shirt back down. I always remembered that, wanting to see him dressed properly. But I'd walked away, leaving my mother and Graciela to see where the barbs had cut into his face, where the bullets had torn open his side, shattered his arm...

I gripped the seat to fight off vertigo. Looking straight up was like seeing the universe sliced in two—half lit by the stars, the other half a shadowy grey inside the cavern. We were balanced on a line that divided the world.

Outside the cavern there was nothing. It was as if sky surrounded us on every side, above and below.

Then three thousand feet down, barely visible in the pale light, the great rock shelf sloped away toward the water. We were above a haze layer, looking out at the stars that floated in the deep blue over the horizon.

Patel leaned forward, looking down at the shelf.

"That is where we will leave from?"

"Yes."

He looked for a long time, then dropped back in his seat and watched the sky. We sat for a few minutes with our own thoughts, then he said, "And that is where we are going. Yes?"

"Out there someplace," I said. "Yes."

He let out a long sigh, sputtering with his lips, then sat for another few minutes with his hands across his belly.

"So. It is like we are on the top of Mount Nebo."

We didn't answer, not understanding.

"Moses went up from the steppes of Moab to Mount Nebo, and there the Lord showed him the Promised Land."

Bolton nodded and after a minute started the cart. We made the trip back in silence, then parked by Miller's plane on the brightly lit apron. Bolton and I got out.

Thwack-thwack. Thwack-thwack. Thwack-thwack. A lamp flared in the roof closer to the entrance, then another and another in rapid succession until a full mile of the cavern was lit. We stared down the runway.

Nothing. All across the two hundred acres of apron, people were getting to their feet to watch, then pointing.

A tiny aircraft entered the light. It was flying in a slip, one wing low and the nose cocked the other way. Security troops picked up guns and started out onto the apron to meet it.

The plane settled and the low wheel finally touched. Still the plane failed to straighten. Instead it pivoted on the wheel, then its strut snapped and the wing dug into the runway. The plane spun toward Miller's Navy tail-fan, then skidded under its wing and snagged the gear, bringing the larger plane down on top of it. Fire crews broke into a run.

A smack came from the little plane and a door panel flew out. A tiny figure followed, scrambling as fast as she could. It looked like a girl, with short black hair and flat Asiatic features.

Her accent matched. She spun around and shouted in a shrill voice.

"No-good-for-nothing piece-of-shit airplane! What kind of junk you do for me, hah?" She kicked it as hard as she could and another panel caved in. She spat on it.

A woman from the fire crew reached out to get her away from the wreckage. Almost too fast to see, the girl whipped around and knocked the woman's arm down, sending her to her knees.

The girl put her hands on her hips and rocked up and down on her toes. Guns trained and steadied.

"So who in charge here, hah?" She saw the three of us and started across.

She walked like a cat, scarcely touching the ground. Her eyes seemed unnaturally bright and moved rapidly from side to side, flicking from face to face, and up to the guns.

Polaski stood across the apron, watching from the shadows.

Patel spoke quietly from the cart next to us. "My goodness. There is a fire burning in that one, isn't there?" He shook his head slowly as if giving this careful thought. "It is a very dangerous thing, such a fire."

She was very young. She had a finely-drawn, pretty face and a tiny body tight with energy. Her eyes were narrow and she took short, deep breaths, nostrils flaring.

She stopped in front of Bolton.

"So. I am here to join with you." She rocked up and down on the balls of her feet.

"I see," said Bolton.

"Yes. I will show your soldiers to fight." Her eyes flashed and she bounced on her toes and looked at each of us in turn.

"Perhaps we don't need to fight," said Bolton, folding his arms across his chest.

"Hah! Everyplace you need to fight! Always you need. I help you."

"I think not." He nodded briefly to the troops moving around to the sides.

"Hah! I think you are afraid to fight, Mister. I think maybe you are too pretty to fight. I think maybe your pecker's too small, hah?" She turned away and looked at Patel. "Hi, fat man." She turned farther and looked at me. It was hard not to look away.

"Who *are* you?" I said.

"My name is Tuyet, Mister Torres. Tuyet Pham."

Chapter Five: THE SINS OF THE FATHER

It would be thirty years before I learned how she came to know my name.

Polaski insisted she stay, and put her to work right away with the troops. The security people objected, but when they looked to me for a decision I said nothing.

I was fascinated by her. I was fascinated the way we are fascinated by an almost-familiar scent in the air, a tune heard somewhere before, the peculiar cast of winter morning's light the way it used to slip in across the warming fires. She was familiar, somehow. Expected. And, strange as it seemed, I couldn't imagine going on without her.

She was in my dreams that first night. Kip stood to one side of her in the dream, while to the other stood a big, sturdy man with the face of Madhu Patel but no crutches. Anne Miller watched from the shadows. Pham stood with her hands on her hips and her feet apart, wearing a frustratingly sheer gown and laughing. It was like a dream I'd had many times before, of standing naked in a circle of people, but this was the first time they'd had faces.

During waking hours in the caverns over the coming weeks she watched me constantly, with eyes that seemed to know some secret we shared. I avoided her when I could. Several times I had the feeling she knew Kip and Rosler already, though I couldn't imagine how that could be.

Kip made friends everywhere on the island. He took his meals around the cooking fires in the upper cavern, then after dinner played the soldiers with a deck of cards I'd given him. He never said a word. Polaski ignored him, although I hadn't forgotten his reaction to Kip that first day. I couldn't tell whether Kip had forgotten or not.

At night Kip played his flute, and sometimes I rode up in the elevators to listen. His music had a power beyond his years, melancholy and sad in the chilly air. He would start with a slow lament that drifted out across the cavern, then gently answer its echoes with the lullabies I always thought I knew.

"Wake up."

A whisper next to my ear.

"Eddie."

I woke to find Chan sitting by my cot, running a hand across my forehead.

"You slept a long time," she said.

"I should have been up."

"No, nothing's so important." She pushed her hair back and her high cheekbones caught the light from the corridor. She ran a hand down under the sheets.

I pulled the blankets higher and she put her hands back in her lap.

"Polaski wants to see us," she said.

"More table-pounding."

"You'd rather be exploding your little batteries, hm?"

"It might cheer up the dungeons some more. God knows they need it." I was looking around in the stone chamber, trying to remember what was bothering me.

"I dreamed about going home," I said at last.

"Oh. You can't, can you?"

"No, I just dream about it." I kissed the palm of her hand. "You neither."

"There's been nowhere to go, really, after my parents tried going back to Kowloon. All those years after the British, and they thought they could go home... Anyway, no."

There were times I wanted Chan so badly I could hardly breathe. I pulled her out of the chair.

"Take off your clothes."

She was soft and supple, smooth like satin, and her thighs were slick and her lips moist, and I wanted to fill her up and swallow her and crush her against me, drown in her and never come back...

We met Polaski in a corner of the south manufacturing chamber, a quarter-square-mile of barrel-vaulted rock with a string of magnesium lights on the roof. We were walled in on two sides by rock, on the others by wooden pallets that cast shadows across the table.

Polaski leaned against a wall with his hands in his pockets. Elliot, who'd taken charge of work on the island, sat where he could be in the light without having to look at it.

Madhu Patel sat wrapped in an Army blanket, frowning and blinking into the light. Chan and I sat at the far end from Polaski. I was bouncing an old rivet on the table, wanting to get it over with.

Bolton didn't come to the meetings, staying with his new teams instead. It wasn't clear what the teams were for, except that he'd staffed them with Special Operations troops from among the Shorts. They kept to themselves.

Pham came and went and was difficult when she was there. Polaski had assigned her to improving the troops' hand-to-hand combat skills, though no one really believed they'd be needed. She was very good at it, in any case.

Anne Miller came if the mood suited her. She spent most of her time with the computers she and Chan had appropriated. But that morning she came and began speaking even as she walked in.

"I'd like to start, so I can finish."

She sat down in the shadows and continued without looking up.

"I have test drones out—you'll see them in the corridors. Keep them from flying into the elevators, please, because they'll become confused by the motion and hit the floor and ceiling."

This was all delivered with abrupt condescension. She stared at the far wall and drummed her fingers. She made us uneasy, and she had yet to explain her reasons for being there. But she was building the drones.

Elliot slid his chair forward to see her better.

"That doesn't sound real smart," he said.

"They are extremely intelligent. They simply haven't been trained yet."

"So? How smart are they? As smart as our other MI?"

"Don't ever compare them to computers, Mr. Elliot! They are survey drones, and they have human intelligence."

"I thought MI was smarter than humans."

"It is *not*. MI is useless. The drones will be far more power-ful—because they'll have the one trait that makes us human and gives us our own power. I believe Mr. Torres can tell you what that is, from his time at China Lake?"

"Awareness," I said. "Come on, Anne, let's keep it moving."

"No. Any thinking machine is aware—humans are *self*-aware, and that is technically a very much more difficult procedure to construct."

Elliot snorted. "You talk like humans are a matter of getting the wires plugged in right. You don't just construct people, lady."

"Mr. Elliot, if I go into a lab and assemble DNA according to the human map, grow it in a womb, and bring it out as a child and nurture it to adulthood, is that natural or manufactured intelli-gence?"

"It's never been done."

"It will be very soon. Well?"

"Okay, it's human. It was human DNA."

"And if I construct it differently, so that the brain is identical but it comes out on wheels?"

"That's *cold*, lady."

"Well?"

"All right! I get your point."

"And if furthermore I take a pile of neurons and build a human brain? Is that an artifact, Mr. Elliot?"

"Fine!"

Madhu Patel pounded a crutch against the table.

"You've made your point, my dear. I, for one, am in awe that Allah has allowed us to see the secret behind His great mystery. He has shown us much trust, and we must be careful how we use it."

Silence.

"So how *do* you construct it?" said Elliot, interested despite himself.

"We construct it by giving the drones a memory so sensitive that it records their own internal events—unlike MI, which only records external events. Then, like us, they can record their own streams-of-consciousness for later review.

"Note that we are not aware of having thoughts as we have

them—we are too busy having the thoughts to be aware of the fact that they are occurring. But afterwards—perhaps only hundredths of a second afterwards—we can scrutinize our having had those thoughts by looking in memory, and later still we can scrutinize *that* scrutiny, and so on, until we put together a picture of the creature that must be doing the scrutinizing.

"So it is a trick—we can actually only see what we were an instant ago. But we are so fast at it that we are then able to project what we must be like *this* instant, and so we seem to see ourselves. Because of that one small twist we are able to gain new knowledge, then by knowing that that knowledge exists construct a still higher-order layer of knowledge, and so on until we are so many orders of magnitude more powerful than other devices that we seem *qualitatively* different. Hence your objection, Mr. Elliot. Do not make the same mistake with the drones."

"So," said Chan after a minute, "there wouldn't be any difference between these self-aware drones and a human being?"

"No, none."

We'd had this part of the conversation before, but this time her answer caught my attention. And left me uneasy.

"And," Chan went on, "you think you'll succeed in building this kind of human intelligence?"

"Apparently you don't understand, Katherine—I have already built it. That problem is no longer of interest. The issue is now the drones' evolution."

Patel sat up straighter. Elliot frowned.

"The drones we send out," she said, "will not be the ones that perform the work. They will be generalists: torpedo-shaped machines with good perception but few manipulators, which they will use to construct other drones better adapted to the conditions they find. Then as the need arises, that second generation will build still more."

"And what is this about evolution?"

"That should be obvious. For the first time in history, we will be in a position to witness conscious evolution."

"That's right," said Polaski, speaking up for the first time. "That's how they'll handle the alien threat, isn't that right?"

"*What?*" I stared at him. Was he mocking her? "Jesus,

Polaski, stick to politics."

"He is absolutely right," said Miller. "The drones' goal is to secure habitats, and they will need to be extremely aggressive in its pursuit. Especially in the face of a threat. It is that quality, of course, which made us successful ourselves."

She stood up to leave.

"So, Mr. Elliot. For all your squeamishness, building intelligent drones is not an issue. It is what they will become that is interesting."

She left.

The silence that followed was broken by a shrill voice across the chamber.

"So what happen to you, Ice-Lady? They throw you out, hah?"

Pham's sandals slapped against the stone floor and she slid past Polaski to drop down in a chair at the table. She began shaking a foot under the table, so that her head jogged rhythmically as her eyes roamed around the room. She was in some ways a stunning young woman, with full lips and penetrating black eyes set in angular features. She'd cut her hair back from her face and her neck all the way around, leaving herself looking strikingly naked and open.

The roar of an explosion ripped through the chamber. The table skidded on the floor and the pallets swayed. ·

No one reacted except Patel, who for an instant looked helpless and afraid.

An acrid stench filled the air.

"Torres," said Elliot. "What the hell you blowing up down here, anyway?"

"Power cells." He stared. "We can't let anyone see the insides of those things, Tyrone, and no matter how strong I make the cases people are going to cut them open. So I'm seeding the cores to blow if they're breached. The engineers have a contest to see who can get in. No go."

Patel rapped on the table.

"You will make it perfectly clear on the outside of this thing what will happen if it is opened, Eduardo. This will not be a game for the poor auto mechanic in Mali who wishes to build one for his family."

"In forty-two languages, plus pictograms, all in red."

"Yes."

"Even if it blows up they'll figure it out," said Chan. "No expense is going to be spared reverse-engineering the thing."

"True," I said, "but even if they do, I've built another surprise into them that'll buy us another year or two when we need it. No one here needs to know what it is, though. The red herrings are more important."

Pham was watching me. I looked away, but when I looked back a few seconds later she was still watching.

"Herrings?" said Elliot.

"Hah!" said Patel. "Fish! That is very good—'red fish.' Yes, we are being most clever. I am placing orders for every available lot of cobalt and thallium on the market, and we will continue to make a convincingly energetic effort to corner their markets entirely, even though they are desperately expensive commodities, and even though we have no use for them whatsoever." He beamed and nodded around the table.

"Then Eduardo here will sprinkle traces into his boxes, and the world will be deceived. Which reminds me, Katherine, I am going to need very large sums of cash soon..."

He went on, having changed the subject very smoothly to cover my surprise. Cobalt and thallium weren't red herrings at all: they were key components. The red herrings were bauxite and cadmium. Was Patel that cagey on principle, or was there someone at the table he didn't trust?

Polaski cleared his throat.

"All right, listen up. You people know that our deal for Patel's marketing help is to let foreigners build ships for another sixty thousand. We agreed because those sixty thousand are going to be the richest bastards in the world, and are going to end up on our side against the rest of the bastards who want to snuff us for the plans."

Pham stood up and pushed her way around the table the long way. She ran a hand across my cheek and up through my hair as she passed. Polaski raised an eyebrow at me.

I looked down and spun my rivet. I wanted to go and smack her against the wall.

"Also," said Polaski, still watching me, "we agreed to leave behind the plans to the batteries—which means there's going to be more people after the first sixty K. Which means it's not going to be the picnic people keep yapping about—someone out there's going to start pissing, and we're going to be everyone's favorite target. Which means we're going to defend ourselves, whether you like it or not.

"We've got a plan. There's things we can do that no one else can, that'll help us defend ourselves and implement a little law and order at the same time. Which ought to make Patel happy.

"Also—people are going on and on about kids. Well, kids have something to do with defense, so we're going to talk about them, too.

"The last of the grunts left this morning. So at thirteen hundred hours I want everyone in the vehicle assembly chambers. Is that all right with you, Torres?"

"Fine," I said, looking at my rivet and not having any idea what he was talking about.

Madhu and I sat in the center of an elevator's 160-foot back wall as it trundled to the surface after the meeting. When we'd come in, Patel had waved his crutches and shouted for everyone to move to the sides. Now he sat on his stool and held his crutches between his knees, and as he peered around and made his faces, he lifted the crutches and thumped them down against the floor.

"I watched you as you listened," he said. "You are just like me, you know. You were thinking to yourself: 'How can this be? How can there be this machine that is exactly like me, but which I know in my heart is not like me at all?' That is what you were thinking."

He lifted the crutches and brought them down.

"Eduardo, how much kinship do you feel with a moth?"

"Not much."

"Yes. And how much with a butterfly?"

"Yes, because it is fragile and beautiful, like you, and so you

"Maybe a little."

feel kinship and you protect it. And a chimpanzee, or dog or cat, or a dolphin? Quite a bit, I would think."

"Yes."

"Of course. And I feel much kinship with you, because we are just alike." He leaned out to touch the crutches against a spot on the floor a few feet away, then brought them back and sighed.

"Tell me, Eduardo. How much kinship do you think one of Anne's drones will feel for you or me?"

I looked at him.

"Yes. Eduardo, when Allah waggled his finger and spoke to Moses about one's neighbors, it was not a new idea—only a reminder. He had long ago put the commandment deep into our hearts: Those like yourself, take care of them, that you might survive together in the desert."

He sighed again, then suddenly twisted his neck around to look at the ceiling. He looked back down and thumped his crutches.

"Anne has told her little creatures no such thing, you know. She looks at us and she looks at her creatures, and because their minds are the same she thinks they are no different. So she thinks that they will behave as we do.

"That is what unsettles you, you see. Those creatures will be exactly like you or me, but with not one shred of compassion. They are like Anne, or like any one of us who has had stolen from him the whispers Allah spoke into our hearts before we were born."

The elevator lurched to a stop. The doors rolled sideways to expose the airfield.

"You see!" he said. "That is why I sit in just this place. For a moment it is like I am very tall, and a window is being opened just for me!"

The doors stopped, and he struggled to his feet.

"So. Be a good friend and bring my stool. I shouldn't want to lose it."

"No heavy weapons!" shouted Polaski into the cold air. "And no armed drones!"

Off through the gloom, like ghosts in the underworld, the island's one thousand troops applauded from the floor of the vehicle assemble chamber. A thousand faceless silhouettes, nearly all the same size. Only Elliot and fifty or so others were much taller.

Patel sat on his stool next to me. Polaski stood on a table.

"But you've all thought about staking claims and protecting trade, and about settling disputes over planetary distances. And you've come to the same conclusion I have: The ones that can move the fastest will win. And that means the fastest covering distance and maneuvering in space—and both of those mean high acceleration."

There was a rustling from the audience. With space tunnels to take care of the long distances, there should only have been short interplanetary runs to endure, under light acceleration.

"But everyone out there's going to have the same ships we will," said Polaski. "And those ships put out a hell of a lot of thrust. So it's not the ships—it's how much acceleration the crews can take. So when the time comes we can be like everyone else—soft from weightlessness and small planets, with helpless little children born in freefall—or we can be ready.

"Look around you. We're ahead of everybody else already. We can take higher thrust, and we can field higher-G companies than anyone else.

"But it's the next generation we should be worried about. They're the ones who're going to be fighting age when things start to get nasty. So we're going to make sure they start out the strongest, and we're going to make sure they stay that way."

Patel shook his head next to me, and spoke quietly. "No," he said, "that is not what children are for. He is not saying what he is thinking, that one."

"There are 972 of us," said Polaski. "We plan to launch 128 ships of our own, which means 1,800 people. As many of the rest should be children as possible."

A roar of approval from the audience.

Children—how many of us had given up on the idea, unwilling to bring them into the same world we'd found ourselves in? And how many years had we thought it would be before the ships were ready, before we'd completed the journey to someplace safe where children could become a reality?

Still—how many of us had heard what Polaski had really

said? I myself was increasingly uneasy. I was losing control of the mission, and it had scarcely begun.

But I also knew I would never try and stop it.

"You can conceive these children and bring them to term any way you want," said Polaski. "You can raise them yourselves, or give them away. And everyone will get his chance. But for an extremely temporary period we'll be using a high-thrust centrifuge. Those parents and donors who score highest will be allowed to conceive."

He paused to wipe a wrist across his mouth.

"We'll also be testing the children." He stepped down abruptly and walked off into the gloom.

It was a long time later before the crowd had dispersed. Patel hadn't moved, so Bolton and I stayed where we were.

Finally Patel sighed and reached for his crutches.

"And the Lord said to Moses, 'This is the land of which I swore to Abraham, Isaac, and Jacob, "I will give it to your off-spring."'"

He held the crutches in his lap and stared into the empty chamber.

I'd heard him quote from that passage several times before, yet it was to be years before I learned that there was a final line, one that he never spoke.

He got his crutches under him and stood up.

"My mother loved me very much, my friends," he said. "We were poor, and I could not walk like my sisters and brothers, so she carried me in her arms. For long hours in the day and sometimes at night, when I was awake from the pain, she held me and took me where she went. She loved me very much, and I was very happy."

He stared broodingly into the distance, then lowered his head and began his labored stumping across the chamber.

Kip didn't play his flute that night. Few people were in the upper cavern at all, because of the cold and because of what hung from the ceiling.

Polaski's security troops had found a man with a transmitter that afternoon, a young Greek-American soldier driving past the opening with it clipped to his lapel. That they had spotted the transmission at all was impressive; it would have taken the most intricate system of inward-facing antennas to pick up such brief signals. Or a well-developed network of informants.

Polaski ordered that the man be stripped naked and thrown from the opening. Two of the security troops had refused and had been removed from the force, but others had done his bidding. Men I didn't know.

Then at dusk the man's body was brought back up and hung from the roof of the cavern.

I paced on the runway for a few minutes, not looking up, then grew cold and rode back down. I felt the chill all the way to my bones, along with the uneasy turn our future was taking. I wanted my bed and my rest, but I didn't look forward to lying awake in the stone chamber. Nor to sleeping, for I'd come to dread the dreams.

The elevator doors rolled aside in the lower complex to reveal the roadway that ran to the assembly chambers, three miles away under the shelf. Parked along the sides were assorted vehicles and aircraft, along with the big cradles that would eventually hold the drone ships. I started across the open space, then paused, thinking I'd heard a sound from ahead. A sound I knew?

Nothing.

A quarter mile farther on I stepped quietly into a narrower side corridor, silent and dim in the red night lights.

Quick footsteps to one side, then Pham moving quickly around the corner. She saw me and stopped, then with only the briefest hesitation her face brightened. She started toward me and flashed a smile.

"So, Mr. Torres. I am very happy to see you. There is something I would like to say to you. Please, you listen to me?"

I waited.

"No, please, it is fine," she said. "We have a secret, okay?"

She reached my side, then put a hand on my arm and reached up to whisper something. Her lips brushed my ear.

I didn't know what she was doing, or why, and was starting to pull away when her fingers dug suddenly into my arm. They clamped down with such force it drove the breath out of me and brought tears to my eyes in an instant. Some particular spot, just above the elbow, nerves and bone ground together with extraordinary strength.

And there she held me, pressing herself close up against me. Then, very slowly, while I fought to regain my breath and hold myself frozen in place because of the pain, her other hand moved between my legs and squeezed me lightly.

"So you want to make fuck-fuck with me, hah?" Sarcastic, deliberately crude. Her fingers in my arm grinding ever harder against the bone, painful white lights stabbing up behind my eyes. Her tongue slid into my ear. "Make babies, hah?" Whispering. "Or how you like it, Mr. Torres? Maybe in back, I think, yes?"

Again I started to pull free, but this time held myself in check with an effort. Clearly she could move so fast that trying to get free would play into the game, whatever game it was. It would be something she was waiting for. But despite the pain I was hardening under her strokes, and I knew she could feel it.

"So you like me a little bit, hm? Maybe you don't hate me so much." Massaging me with the palm of her hand, pressing harder and then harder still as her tongue worked deeper into my ear. My arm, meanwhile, had gone numb from the pain.

I don't remember moving. There was just the pain, and, suddenly, mixed with the pain, movement. Pain that seemed to come from far away, but then not far away at all, suddenly very close. One of us moving—one of us, or both.

A sharp crack from her head. My hand, pressing her face against the wall, hard. Up under her chin, forcing it sideways. Blood on her temple. A sound from somewhere deep in her throat, or from mine, I couldn't tell.

I don't remember what I said. I remember my voice, someone's voice, but I don't remember what it said.

What I do remember and have always remembered is what was in her eyes at that moment. Disappointment. Frustration. Eyes turned away, toward the wall but not seeing, filling slowly with tears.

I lay in my chamber, shaking. For that one instant I'd been out of control, close to something I wanted no part of.

From what little I'd come to know of Pham, it was a kind of violence that should have belonged to her, that in fact would surely consume someone like her in the end, but not me. Yet here I was hiding from it in the darkened, chilly bowels of our fortress, thinking how to force it away, how to suffocate it in the even darker airlessness of space ahead.

Finally I threw off the blanket and sat up, unable to lie still, the movement causing the cot to screech sharply against the stone floor. I drew up my knees and stared past them at the empty opening into the corridor.

A sound was coming from close by, high up on the wall. Inside the room.

Tap. Tap. Pause. *Tap.* I stared up into the shadows.

There was something there, little more than a darker shadow against the shadows surrounding it, no larger than my hand. It floated next to the wall high up, the faint sound of blowing air coming from beneath it. It was finding its way toward the opening by tapping against the wall, making shallow, careful arcs in the air before striking it again.

Tap. Tap. Pause. *Tap.*

"Who is it?" I said, finding the challenge absurd even as I spoke it. But it stopped right away nevertheless and waited, then answered.

"Who is speaking?" it said. A cool, clear voice, not quite female.

"Torres, for Christ's sake. Who are you?" I couldn't see it any more.

"I said, who are you?"

It didn't move or speak for a long time. There was only the rasp of my own breathing and the whisper of its fan in the darkness.

The gloom shifted in the corner where it hovered.

"Yes," it said, finally. "I know you."

Tap. Tap. Tap. It had worked its way around the corner and into the opening. I'd been dismissed.

"*Who are you?*" I screamed at it, lunging forward to grab the sides of the cot. But the tiny drone had disappeared into the corridor and flown away.

Chapter Six: AND THE NATIONS WILL TREMBLE BEFORE YOU

"Ladies, Gentlemen, Drones—start your engines!"

Children shrieked with delight as twenty wobbling work platforms rose up from the south runway. The platforms jockeyed for position, tipping precariously.

"On your marks!" No one was anywhere near the marks, but it didn't matter. The boxy little companion drones, their six legs tucked under them like grasshoppers', squatted on their platforms and pulled even with the farthest forward humans, evidently deciding it must be legal.

"Get ready!" Stocky little three-year-olds jumped up and down on the seats. Parents lifted infants up to see.

"Go!"

The cavern filled with a manic giggling as the drones shot straight into the air instead of forward, shrieking and heckling and diving at their human competitors. Chan and Patel had spent days teaching them to giggle like that.

Even the delegates from the colonists' committees applauded, sitting in their little groups with their colored security badges, distracted for the time being from their bickering.

More cheers. One of the drones had crashed its platform into the runway and was pushing it vigorously toward the finish line, stopping every few paces to do a little dance on its insect-like feet. Someone had dressed it in six red tennis shoes. Toddlers tried to get away from their parents and onto the runway for a ride.

"Okay folks, here he comes...he's at the finish line...the judges are working hard on a decision...here we have it—yes! Ladies and gentlemen, another twenty-way tie! Let's hear it for the winners!"

The man next to me whistled and applauded. He was our logistics chief, a sturdy, ruddy-faced Irish loadmaster named Charlie

Peters, whom we'd coaxed away from a regular unit four years earlier. He gestured at the quiet south-side runway, speaking in his soft brogue.

"I'm glad we closed it, Eddie. It wasn't any good last time, everybody jumping each time a transport landed and the doors opened. What the hell if we get a day behind on shipments, I say. This is more important. The poor kids."

He was right about the last fair. The problem hadn't been noise from the transports—they ran quietly enough on our batteries now—it was jumpiness about security. There'd been fresh memories of attacks on the planes and on the elevator doors, and too many ugly scenes involving security people nervous about infiltrators. Having the children up for the fresh air had been hard.

Chan and Patel stood near the starting line, talking with one of the drones getting ready to play in the soccer game. It was draped in British racing green. Chan held a hand absently under her growing belly. Two more months.

"Mr. Torres to the command complex, please. Eduardo Torres, if you are on the airfield level please come to the central command complex."

I nodded to Peters, then worked my way along the stands to the elevators. Chan and Patel backed away from the two-foot-long grasshopper drone, then suddenly, with a synchronized *snick* of oiled machinery, it jackknifed high into the air. It landed less elegantly, but Chan righted it and leaned down to talk to it again.

The sounds of the fair were cut off by the elevator doors sealing shut. With a lurch and rumble the six-minute descent began.

Benches had been installed around the walls, except along the back where they'd been torn out again and replaced by truck tires and signs that read NO STANDING—KEEP CHILDREN AWAY! We learned our lessons.

At the bottom the doors opened with a pop of changing pressure, then a rush of icy air.

The roadway outside the elevator stretched away for miles to vanish in an antiseptic light and cold mist. Against both sides, stacked two high in their cradles and end to end until they disappeared in the distance, were the drone ships—sealed, silent, iced over in frost and shrouded in mist.

Vapor rose from nitrogen hoses snaking away toward Miller's chambers. Carefully separated from the hoses were the optical fibers that hour after hour fed the world's libraries into the waiting drones.

The ships were ugly, like enormous, welded steel barrels lying on their sides, with blunt ends and a dozen reinforcing ribs along the sides. The ends facing me had eight evenly-spaced hatch covers and nothing more, while the far ends with the engine exhausts were covered by the temporary ring of the fan-stage. They were 155 feet long and twenty-six wide, millimeters narrower than the hole in the torus they would hurtle through at seventy thousand miles per hour.

There were four hundred ships. Lying inside them at -203 °C, shaped like ten-foot-long, polished steel torpedoes, waited the real drones. Thirty-eight thousand of them.

I'd come many times to look at the drone ships in recent months, often at night when no one else was there. After the days of heated arguments and angry demands pouring in from around the world, the drones possessed a kind of seductive orderliness and predictability. I watched them for hours.

Now I drove a cart along the cross-island corridor toward the north wall. Cameras followed my progress.

The drone ships had actually been built elsewhere, as had the colony ships in final assembly three miles to the east. Anne Miller had programmed the actual drones, always in secret. I spied on her and Polaski spied on her, but if Polaski had learned more than I had about the drones' programming, he hadn't let on. I asked, but he never said.

The only manufacturing we did on the island was the quantum batteries. Everything else was built by industrial consortia around the world, in exchange for batteries and the right to market them. It was an arrangement Patel had designed to avoid using hard currency. Still, the consortia dragged their feet, hoping to crack the secret of the cells before having to deliver on the multi-billion dollar ships.

All the while, the supposedly independent regional colonists' committees—responsible for the extra colony ships Patel had insisted we finance—were coming under the increasing control of governments and of the consortia themselves, and were demanding greater and greater shares of the ships in exchange for minimal cooperation. At the same time, the leaders of the committees secretly sold off the batteries intended for the ships and lined their own pockets.

Patel's demands to market the batteries equitably throughout the world were openly scoffed at. Through one contrivance or another they flowed to the wealthiest nations, whose economies were thus staggering under the loss of energy-related jobs—a state of affairs for which we were then blamed and hated. The rest of the world, meanwhile, hated us for not releasing the batteries faster. The consortia hated us for our stranglehold on the technology.

The colonists themselves, finally, hated us for our control of the drones—which gave us the final, critical control over the exodus.

I made the turn to the north-wall corridor and stopped by the window of the children's infirmary. The infirmary was cut into the hundred-foot-thick outside wall of the island, as far from the vulnerable elevators as possible. Medics moved from crib to crib behind the glass.

There were too many children—sixty-eight of them now from a total of fewer than eight hundred. And at that, these were only the ones we'd been able to let live at birth. Like elsewhere in the world there were too many birth defects, often with later complications that even our best scanners and MI couldn't repair.

Still, genetic defects accounted for only half the children in the infirmary. The rest were there because of the centrifuge.

Polaski had learned that a side-effect of testing infants in the centrifuge was that the test itself allowed them to score higher on subsequent runs. So he'd ordered repeated exposure of two or three Gs for all children, without ever asking me. I'd meant to overrule him, but public resistance to the policy had waned after the attacks on the island had begun, and I'd said nothing.

Now I sat and watched the children play or cry, or just struggle to stay alive. There was no turning back, I thought. I was going to go, and Polaski was going to go, and Tuyet Pham. All of us to a place, I had once thought, where this kind of suffering would be at an end.

Children waved to me through the window, but I just watched them, as I always did. As always I felt unable to wave back, unable to respond at all.

"Mr. Torres, please!" I was taking too long.

Stopping moments later in front of the command complex windows, it was clear why I'd been called. His Excellency Chih-Hsien Chien, emissary of the Greater Chinese Peoples' Space Colonization Committee, did not look happy.

Nor did Priscilla Bates, the Air Defense room duty officer. Nor her superior, David Rosler, who was now Air Operations chief. Technicians behind them studied their consoles with conspicuous diligence. Pham was sprawled in a command chair ignoring them, watching the human-vs.-drone soccer game on the situation monitors. She was infantry chief, and shouldn't really have had any business in Air Defense.

"Ah, Mr. Torres," said Chih-Hsien. "Thank you for coming so promptly."

"My pleasure, Excellency."

"That I very much doubt. However, I do bring excellent news."

I glanced at Priscilla Bates, then at Rosler, who looked down to wipe his glasses on his shirt tail. Then back at Chih-Hsien's wizened, hard-to-read face. "I see."

"Yes. I am honored to announce that the heroic efforts by the People's Republic of China and her valiant allies to remedy the western nations' failure to complete the Kerr-mass toroidal projector have succeeded."

A long pause.

"It's been tested?"

"Yes, Mr. Torres. This morning. An object was translated through the torus at speed, in the direction of Holzstein's Star. The predicted Hawking-Rosen effect was observed—the object appeared to possess infinite length, then vanished."

It was very good news. The tunnel was ready for the drones.

"This is certainly a great success," I said, "for the Greater Chinese Peoples' Committee as well as for the People's Republic.

You've done the colonization effort a great service."

"A great service, yes. Disproportionately great, perhaps."

"I believe," I said carefully, "that our enterprise has already been disproportionately generous toward Chinese ambitions for the peaceful colonization of space. To the detriment, I might remind you, of the Africans and the Europeans."

"Pah! The Europeans! They are worthless scum. I do not know why you involve them at all."

"Oh? What do you know about the Europeans?"

"I know that they are tired of being the second-class citizens that they are, and that they are up to no good. For what other reason do you think the Commonwealth have excused themselves and asked to work with the North Americans instead of the Europeans? They want no part of the Europeans' vile plans. No, I could put the Europeans' ships to far better use, I assure you."

"We are in the best position to judge how the ships will be used."

"You are in a position to judge nothing! You are young and arrogant, you and your criminal band. You treat the suffering peoples of the world like servants. You claim to decide who will survive and who will not. And the deaths you cause with your exploding batteries are obscene! Do not speak to me of judgment!"

"You know that without harsh protection for the batteries none of us would be here."

"Perhaps. But you did not need to force us, your loyal allies, to carry more than two million of them all the way to the torus. We could have built a single one at the site, or carried a few large ones with us. You see, you do not trust even us!"

"We couldn't be sure that others wouldn't attack the torus, Excellency, and steal the design from such unprotected cells."

"The torus and the approaches to it are exceedingly well defended. No one may approach."

There was something final in his tone. Rosler put on his glasses.

So the Chinese were sealing up the Torus. Priscilla Bates shifted uncomfortably from one foot to the other, then after a minute one of the technicians called out.

"Priscilla! Unauthorized engine-start, north runway. No ID, no IFF!" His monitor showed a picture from an airfield camera trying to follow one of our tail-fans down the runway.

"Track it, Sayid! Infrared and zero in. We need to see who it is—maybe his radio is out. Let's go, lock on!"

The camera swung uncertainly back and forth past the plane as it approached the opening and rotated for take-off.

Then Pham was reaching across the technician's console. The picture snapped into focus and tracked. In quick succession she forced over a bank of switches, then pushed away the technician's hand and reached for the aiming ball. White crosshairs slid in and locked on the plane. The picture itself didn't zoom in, so the inside of the cockpit still wasn't visible. But the instant the crosshairs were centered she knocked aside a red switch canopy and jammed her hand onto the button.

The aircraft blossomed into a brilliant orange, then collapsed on the runway and smeared across it. It exploded again in a furious cloud of white flame as the battery struck the ground.

Bates grabbed for a phone. Screens up and down the consoles lit and steadied as technicians went to full alert. Pham snorted and went back to her chair. She weaved a little as she walked, smacking into a console on the way.

The soccer game had stopped. Fire crews raced for the north runway. Pilots reported in as they reached their planes.

Next to me, Chih-Hsien Chien stared at Pham's back in disgust.

"Vietnamese barbarian," he said. "And drunk, too."

Rosler hung up a microphone and gave Pham an appraising look. Priscilla Bates raised an eyebrow in my direction.

"Probably an infiltrator," I said, knowing it wasn't what she meant. "Thought we wouldn't fire during the fair."

I turned back to Chih-Hsien.

"Forgive the interruption, Excellency. But as you see, we do have reasons for concern." Uncalled for as it was, Pham's attack would serve its purpose. "You were saying, I believe, that the approaches to the tunnel are well defended. Surely such measures aren't necessary."

"Well, perhaps you are right. Nevertheless, my colleagues worry. You see, there are so many excellent Chinese scholars and scientists who are eminently qualified for this journey but who have not been able to join us, that we fear they may try to secure their places—and the tunnel—by force. This would be a great misfortune, don't you agree?"

"And do you suppose," I said, "that there might be a way to appease these very eminent Chinese scholars and scientists, and thus ensure our safe passage?"

"Well, it is possible—since you mention it—that these eminent persons and the expedition alike would benefit were they to be provided their most deserved passage along with the rest of us." He offered a very small bow.

"So if we were to provide the Greater Chinese Peoples' Committee with one more ship—at the expense, of course, of the other committees—then we would no longer have this difficulty, in your opinion?"

Chih-Hsien's face took on a looked of pained reluctance to offer bad news. He wrung his hands.

"I am afraid that the Committee might not be sufficiently motivated to make certain the extra seats went to exactly the right eminent persons, Mr. Torres. They are less, ah, reasonable than I am. Five ships."

"I see. Allow me to ask a question, Excellency. Why have you made this proposal to me, and not to Mr. Polaski?"

"Pah! I cannot deal with this self-appointed emperor of yours, Polaski. You are a much more sensible man."

More and more often I found myself asking other people what Polaski was doing.

"Very well," I said. "I will direct that one ship be delivered as you wish and placed at your disposal so that you can sell the seats at whatever price you can get. With certain conditions:

"First, the passage of the drone ships and *all* of the colonists' ships to the tunnel will be unimpeded." He nodded carefully.

"Second, the launch of the drone ships in a few days' time will be protected by the air forces of the PRC—"

"We have nothing to do with the PRC! We have no control—"

"Drop it, Chien. Your ships will be filled with PRC cadres, and it will be very much in their interest to protect the drones from launch to translation.

"Three. Those colony ships are designed to carry one hundred people. Every person you sell a seat to in excess of that means someone will die. If you sell one seat more than those ships can hold, Chien, I will kill you."

His eyes widened, then he leaned closer as though to see me better.

"I cannot be responsible—"

"Four. You're coming with us." His mouth opened in disbelief. Then, when he recovered, he drew himself up to his full five feet.

"Three ships."

"One."

"Aieee!" He hissed and turned for the door. "Sleep lightly, Mr. Torres."

"Your escort, Excellency."

He stiffened and waited for the armed guards.

Pick your enemies carefully, Patel had said. But had I?

"Bang, you're dead." Polaski sat behind a desk with a pistol aimed at the door where I stood.

I'd found him on 40-deck of Hull Zero-Zero. He no longer kept a fixed office, but moved from place to place. He wore a plain grey uniform.

Chan had come with me, walking out to the giant colony ship along a clattering catwalk over the dark assembly chamber. Arc welders and annealers in the distance provided the only light, reflecting from the white, pencil-thin ships. Six hundred feet tall but only twenty-six in diameter, they floated in the darkness like threads hanging from the ceiling.

The ships had the proportions of 450-story buildings. Yet instead of resting on their bases at one G like buildings, they were designed to "rest" on their engines under thrust at six Gs. Any flaw and they would vibrate and shatter like glass.

The catwalk ended at a seamless air lock marked "30-W". A pair of recessed handles spun in opposite directions to open it, one of the few stable movements possible in free-fall.

30-deck was empty except for coils of fiber and tools. There was a panel that curved out to encircle a lift running down through the floor and up through the ceiling. An emergency ladder ran next to it. 30-deck, half way up the ship, was the ship's lowest usable level. Below were the big induction coil, the batteries and fuel mass, and the equipment and shuttle bays.

From 30-deck we'd ridden the lift up to 40.

"Put it down, Polaski."

"Yes, sir." He set the pistol on the desk, still pointing at the door.

"The Chinese have tested the tunnel," I said. "The drones go in nine days."

"I know," he said. I glanced at Chan.

"I don't like not knowing how Miller's programmed them," I said. "We could shoot all forty thousand of them through the tunnel, and for all I know they can't even count to three. We'd wait for years for one to come back without knowing if it was the tunnel or the drones that had gone wrong. How much do you know, Polaski?"

He toyed with the gun. "Ask your friend here. She's the priest."

"I only program the little ones," said Chan, "and the fleet. All I've seen of the real drones is what she's let me see. But what I've seen is good. Almost scary, it's so good. But I agree with Eddie. We need to know more."

Polaski pursed his lips.

"And do something about Pham," I said. "She's drunk half the time."

"You do something."

It was the inevitable answer.

"What's the matter?" he said. "You got the hots for her like everybody else?"

Chan walked around the desk. Polaski had once said something to her about conceiving without first being tested in the centrifuge, and she'd never let him forget it. She leaned down now and said something in his ear, then turned and left. Polaski stroked the gun and watched her go.

"Pham's not so bad, Eddie."

Chan and I stood on the catwalk, watching the pale ships off in the dark chamber. "It's Polaski you should be watching."

"I watch him. So what about Pham?"

"We talk sometimes. She's a little like you, you know. Couldn't stand the way things were, wants to leave no matter what it takes. Hated her father. Lonely."

"I didn't hate him."

"You sound like it, sometimes. You were only ten, Eddie, it's hard to remember."

Patel was visiting Chan when I returned to our quarters on the ship that night. He sat half-buried in a pile of duffel bags on the bed, with Kip asleep next to him. Cards were spread out on the floor.

Patel peered out at me from under bushy eyebrows, then set Kip's flute down on the bed.

"Did you know, Eduardo," he said, "that this is an enchanted flute? It should be perfectly easy to play, but only our young friend here can do so."

Charlie Peters, the logistics chief, joined Chan and me for breakfast the next morning. He carried a wrapped parcel and a piece of bread.

"Forgive me, Charlie" said Chan, "but how did you get to be the size you are by eating little pieces of bread for breakfast?"

"Young Miss," he said, "you are truly a delight and a wonder, but you'd do better to ask if I came to be eating little pieces of bread by being the size I am."

Shouts came from across the mess. A tiny spider drone had flown in with a message tube clipped to its back, and the inevitable target practice had begun. A buttered roll finally slapped into its side to send it sluing off course, to the accompaniment of much cheering.

Chan clapped her hands sharply. The spider drone—which despite its name had no legs at all—dove down and stopped in front of her. Chan nursed it closer and spoke to it, too quietly for us to hear.

The drone leapt back into the air with a chirp and began bobbing and weaving along its course. Boos came from across the room.

"I keep telling them that," said Chan. "I don't understand why they forget."

· "My Lord," said Peters. He watched the drone go and ran a hand across his balding head. "So! How are you this morning, Eddie? I'm told you want that little fellow's frozen kin taken up on the lifts to the airport. You don't think that's asking a bit much? Four hundred ships in nine days?"

"Six days. Be glad they fit in the elevators at all, Charlie. Small miracles are all we get."

"My word! 'Miracles,' he says! Have you seen them fit in the elevators? No, you haven't, and neither have I. You are one of these godless drudges who believes the little numbers he writes on the backs of envelopes. Ah, there she is. Tuyet! Come and sit. I've got something for you."

Pham dumped her tray, and with only the briefest glance at Peters picked up a piece of fish in her hand.

Peters pushed the parcel across. "I couldn't help but hear you say to Katherine the other day that you liked to read poems—though I'm sure you didn't think anyone was listening." Pham paid him no attention.

"And so I thought to myself, 'Now there's a fine thing—here we are just *filled* up with machines, but no poems at all.' So I sent for this little book. I'm sure you'll find it delightful."

Pham paused in her eating and blinked at the book, then turned to Chan.

"So, China-Girl. What for you want baby, hah?"

Chan glanced at Peters, who seemed unoffended.

"I don't think life would mean much without children, Tuyet. What about you?"

"Nah. Everybody grow up, get dead. Someday kids get dead, too. So what good this meaning do for you then, hah? More important have a good time, I think." She took another bite. "But I think you lucky lady, maybe. Sometimes I wish, me too."

"Why? Have you spent time with children?"

"Nah. I tell you about shithead father. No mother. Father got junk he treat like kid, not me."

She dropped the fish, then turned to me as she reached for Peters' napkin.

"So, Mr. Torres, how much time we got before we shoot up Ice-Lady's drones, hah?"

"Nine days."

"Ah—no good. They not ready. Everybody get killed up there."

"Why?"

"Nobody practice. Pretty-Boy Bolton say no time, too dangerous. I say if too dangerous now, too dangerous later when everybody got cold foot. Pretty-Boy got weakness like that. He take big risk easy himself, but don't let other people take risk so they find out if they okay, too."

A chair scraped and laughter came from across the room, followed by David Rosler's voice and a plate banging against the table. Pham whipped around to look, then immediately turned back just as I spoke.

"Have you told Priscilla that?" I said. "She's launch safety officer."

"Hah! Shit no, Torres. I do you favor. I let you tell Miss Priscilla yourself. She pretty girl, and you got hard-on I bet, now China-Girl here all fat, hah? I know you pretty good."

I stared at her. Peters started to get up.

"What's gotten into you?" I said.

"Not you get into me, hah, Torres? I think maybe you like to sometime, but you too chickenshit. You afraid I break it off, hah?"

She shoved her chair back and knocked her plate aside so that the fish slid across the table.

"Piece of shit food!" She pushed past Peters and hurried out of the mess. But not, I noticed as I looked down at the table, before picking up the book of poems.

Chapter Seven: AND THEIR WALLS WILL CRUMBLE TO DUST

Nine days later the drones' launch window arrived.

I glanced for a last time at Anne Miller, then nodded to Rosler across the operations room. He wiped a sleeve across his mouth and flipped down his microphone.

"All stations, final checkpoint clear, no holds. Systems have timing. Personnel, clear the rails now. Fire crews, start your engines. Tanker crews, mark your pressure, recheck on decouple. Airlifters, respond—rails one through four."

"One through four."

Forty-ton airlifters moved into position on the screen, dangling grappling clamps like fists. Below them, eight pairs of rails ran the length of the airfield. The drone ships on their acceleration sleds filled the mile and a half closest to the elevators, while the helicopters moved into position over the empty mile and a half beyond, down which the sleds would race for the opening.

"Rails five through eight."

A pause.

"Five through eight."

"Too slow to respond, crew. When the time comes, you're only going to have ninety-six seconds to clear a bad launch before the next one comes down that rail.

"ExComm, advise PRC Air Defense we have a commit on six minutes. Mr. Bolton, launch-override is local."

Instrumentation monitors changed from green to amber. Bolton's crews on the runways had control of the overrides.

"Reports. Insertion."

"Winds aloft and pressures down range, no change. Icing negative. I have four hundred orbital insertions active. Looks good."

"Translation."

"Kerr projector systems report launch and tunnel motion

synchronized. 2,006 hours plus and counting."

"Engines and Boosters."

"Induction engines idling across the board. Fan-booster spin-up on number eighty-three is below the curve but recovering. All others are go."

"Mr. Elliot, get a paint-bomb on number eighty-three. Airlifter north, keep an eye on that hull. It'll be number eleven on rail three. Defense."

"All weapons, full release." Pham's voice, out by the opening.

"Range officer."

"Go."

"DataComm."

"Scanning data-links on all drones. Ms. Miller has function switch-over on loss."

Rosler hesitated. "InComm, take reports on the ground systems. Off."

He glanced at me and gestured to Miller.

"Anne," I said, "I have to say this again. We're going lose some ships—maybe a lot of them. You're going to need help reloading their missions to the survivors."

Silver earrings glittered.

"Thank you, Mr. Torres, but it will be quite simple."

"Okay, fine."

Rosler stuffed his shirt into his pants. "Three minutes now with shit to do."

"The checklist was well done," I said.

He ignored me.

Charlie Peters squinted at the screens. As logistics chief he'd had to get the ships up to the airfield, then off their cradles and onto the sleds. He was biting the nails of one hand and gripping a telephone in the other.

"I still say they'll fall off the edge," he said. "No wings. You people should know that. And space is *up*. Why do you insist on shooting things out sideways when you mean them to go up?"

Rosler blew his nose.

"Near-Earth orbit isn't up," I said. "It's out. In this case

you're right, though—these things are so un-streamlined we're going to run them straight up on the boosters till the air's thin enough,
and only then tip them over and blow the fans off. The induction
engines will throw them into orbit. As for falling off the edge—they
will. See that screen there? It's the range officer's, a side-view of the
launch area after the ships come off the rails. Watch it. Here we go."

Another view showed on the main screen, from above the
elevators looking toward the opening. The airfield cavern looked
like a train station, with eight rows of fifty cars each, all eight tracks
leading out into the sky.

"One released."

The first ship on the left-hand rails slid forward with decep-
tive grace—a closer look showed its giant fan buffeting the ship
behind it, hammering it against the next sled back. The first ship
accelerated at two thirds of a G, from zero to sixty in four seconds;
twelve seconds later it had covered a fifth of the distance to the
opening.

The first ship on track six moved.

"Two released."

They were released in a staggered sequence to provide the
greatest lateral spacing among them. Twelve more seconds and track
three released a ship.

"Three released."

Like a bullet from a gun, Number One burst from the ledge
at over four hundred miles per hour. Its sled tumbled away furiously
in the wind, to be caught by a parachute. The ship itself nosed
gracefully over toward the shelf below and fell for a second, then for
another—and then it was replaced by a searing white cloud.

"Number One rotation failure, manual destruct." The range
officer's voice, calm.

"Four released."

Three more seconds and Number Two burst from the ledge.
It sank toward the shelf and began to rotate nose-up, then twisted
sharply and tumbled. It, too, disappeared in a flash of white.

"Number Two rotation failure, manual destruct."

"Data on Number One, steering vane coupling failure."

"Five released."

I felt sick.

Anne Miller was out of her seat.

"Prepare to abort sequence."

"No!" I said. "Keep it going."

"That's right, sir." One of the controllers.

"What do you mean, 'that's right?'"

"Mr. Polaski said there were to be no aborts." She glanced backward over her shoulder. Polaski was standing by the door.

Number Three burst from the ledge. It hesitated, then rotated and arced gracefully into the sky.

"Three on profile."

"Hold abort."

"Data on Number Two, steering vane coupling failure."

"Six released."

Number Four dropped and rotated, then climbed into the sky behind Number Three. Controllers let out their breath. Charlie Peters looked down at the crushed phone in his hand.

"Seven released."

"Three-forty-two released."

"Three-three-niner on profile."

"Two-seven-seven insertion and close."

"Three-one-eight fan separation failure, auto destruct."

Miller frowned. We were inserting better than ninety percent into orbit, but she wasn't accustomed to a kind of hardware that failed.

"Are they still okay?" I said.

"Oh, yes, of course. You lost both ships carrying agricultural programs, and both ships carrying history and the arts, but all the mission-critical groups are still redundant."

There had been more permanent loses on the airfield, however. The huge fan bearings on one of the ships had oscillated when at full power and the blades had shattered, killing six of Elliot's people in the hail of shrapnel. An airlifter crew had gotten the coasting ship off the rails just in time for the next one.

The same airlifter crew had then tried to pull the troublesome Eighty-Three out of line, but the sled had caught on a pylon. The lifter crashed between the rails and burned, killing all eleven of the crew.

Another ship's nitrogen hose hadn't sealed off on decouple—it lashed about like a steaming snake and froze the tanker driver in a cloud of ice.

"Three-forty-six release."

I nodded to Rosler. "I'm going up to see the last ones off. I've got a phone. Charlie—you want to ride up with me?"

I looked for Polaski, but he wasn't anywhere in the command complex. Something was nagging me about him.

"Aye, I'll come," said Peters. "Can't take much more of this, I know."

We found a cart in the corridor.

"Eddie, the girl in there said it was two thousand hours to the tunnel. But I thought the torus was close to Venus' orbit and only twenty days away. Not eighty-something."

"Well, even less than twenty under steady thrust. And we could wait for the torus to line up between us and the sun and get there even faster.

"The problem is that Holzstein's Star is north of the plane of the ecliptic, the plane the planets orbit in—Holzstein's is above it. So we've got to go through the torus at an angle from underneath the plane aiming up. If we made a beeline from here to the torus we'd be in the plane all the way and we couldn't turn the corner.

"So what we do is break them out of Earth orbit, then fire their engines to slow their orbit around the sun, so they plunge toward it. At the same time we accelerate them hard out of the plane southward. They pass under the sun and the sun whips them back up through the torus northbound. The torus steers them in and fires one through every twelve seconds for over an hour, which is as fast as it can recharge."

"My word," said Peters.

The boosters' fury firsthand was like nothing I could have imagined. The ground shook and the wind swept back like hammer blows in the confined cavern.

The next-to-last ship shredded its steering vanes. The shock wave from its destruction pounded down the cavern with a concussive force that shook the entire island. Workers bled from their ears. Many of them stumbled as they worked, dazed from the exhaustion and the pain.

The last ship roared off of rail four, then without pause the work of clearing the wreckage and tearing up the rails began.

The first phase of the journey had begun. Our messengers had been sent, our minions cast to the heavens. Yet there was no joy in it, no release from the fear. No rest from the growing urgency. Instead their departure had only brought closer our own launch, which was something I feared nearly as much as I feared staying behind. I would go through with it, but I feared it. I would go through with anything.

I started down to the central complex to begin the long night of inspecting the orbiting ships. We would study each of them with interferometers and cameras from the neighboring ships, to make sure it wasn't damaged or out-of-round from the launch. No stray sliver of metal could be allowed to touch the torus on the way through.

I shared the elevator with a field ambulance and troops heading for their beds. But three minutes into the drop the elevator stopped.

An instant later it began accelerating back upward at many times its normal rate. It pressed us into the floor. Speakers burst into life at the same time as the massive doors rolled open in mid-shaft. Bare rock rushed by.

The ambulance driver spun his wheels and moved to one side. The pedestrians struggled against the extra weight to reach the benches. I made it to the communications panel at the front and punched for the tactical channel.

"—rim defense to withdraw! Personnel on the back wall, clear apron Foxtrot for incoming airborne. You've got ninety seconds. Calhoun, Tawali, Pham, I need you on Tac *now*. Lift three is for personnel only, people, clear it out! Outbound with hot engines, kill them now. There will be no mobile defense—repeat, no Tac-Air. Bates and Kolawski, get onto your people *now*. I want them down."

Sirens grew louder and the elevator slowed.

"*Stand* on the benches," I shouted, "*stand* on them. Get your feet up!"

The elevator was still two feet below the ledge when trucks began hurtling across the lip with their horns sounding, racing for the back wall. Other trucks hammered into their bumpers to smack them up against the tires in back. Work platforms flew in to crash down onto the trucks' roofs in a shower of sparks.

Warning horns blared and the other two elevators started their drops. Ours was only half full, and the doors stayed open. Outside on the apron waited thirty soldiers. Standing farthest from the elevator was Michael Bolton.

These were his Special Operations Engineers. Techno-commandos, the regulars called them. They'd been on the airfield to take control of the launch if the MI failed.

Helicopters beat toward us from the opening at full speed, inches off the ground. They struck the apron still moving and spun to a stop outside the elevator doors. A hundred or more men and women poured out, followed by Pham, harassing and cursing them through a megaphone. When they were inside the elevator, Bolton's troops folded in behind them, Bolton last. He motioned to the cameras and nodded to me to hit the all-clear. The elevator sank out from under us.

Pham climbed to the top of a truck and shouted at her troops.

"Okay, ladies, you listen good now. Their majesties not say why we run, but we not run too far, okay?" Shouts of approval.

"So no ready-room, no ready-talk—we stay *ready*, okay? At the doors down below, where we can move quick or someone's got to fuck with us, yes?"

"Yes Sir!"

"Yes Ma'am!"

"Yes, Sir, Sweetie!"

They were Technical Warfare graduates and no fools, but they loved Pham. She stood on the truck with her hands on her hips and her feet apart, very sleek in short hair and jumpsuit. It was made of some slick, dark material stretched tight around her thighs and hips.

Polaski said she slept indiscriminately with her troops, men and women alike.

She saw me when I tossed my phone to Bolton.

"So! Mr. No-Balls comes out of his little hole to see real world, hah?"

Bolton waved me over.

"Pay her no mind, lad. She's harmless." He frowned at the phone. "Nothing. I can hear them quite losing their little minds down there, but I can't get any of them to talk to me."

"I know. Let's make a run for it."

"Right."

The elevator crashed to a stop and we raced to Operations, stopping in front of the windows. Bolton stopped half way out of the cart.

"Good God in Heaven."

The main screen in Air Defense was painting a hundred-mile radar picture, and for a moment I thought it was covered with interference spots. But it wasn't. It was showing incoming aircraft, in staggering numbers. Air Defense was in chaos.

It didn't make sense, though. It couldn't be the Chinese— we'd watched them leave after the launch. Someone else had to have been waiting for the Chinese to go. And in these numbers it had to be a major power, or one of the consortia, ready to risk everything for the batteries. But why wait until after the drones had launched? The drones were no good to anyone without us to run them.

Nevertheless, it was clear what we would have to do. We would have to use the trap I'd laid the day the first battery rolled off the line.

I shouted for the signals coordinator.

"Give me the main screens. Patch all signals up front." He looked confused.

"*Now!*" I pushed him away from the central console and kicked the master reset underneath. Up and down the room people shouted as their screens went blank. Rosler whipped around and started toward me, Polaski behind him.

"What the fuck did you do, Torres?"

I typed INTERLOCK.

"You've taken down the airfield radar, Torres!"

The monitor on my console cleared. Code that had lain dormant for years began to scroll past.

"They won't attack the cavern," I said, "if they don't know the radar is out." I pressed a key. "Remember I said I would seed the batteries with a second trap? They're about to get trapped. Any sign of who it is?"

I picked up a light-pen and aimed it at the main overhead screen. When it was ready, it would make a bright circle that could be read by the computers.

The main screen came up with a map of the area, hollow rectangles indicating each of the approaching aircraft.

But the rectangles were empty.

I stared at the screen, disoriented. What had I forgotten? Each of the rectangles should have had one or more twelve-digit numbers inside it. If the aircraft were using our batteries.

Nothing. They *had* to be using the batteries. Every aircraft in the world used them. I looked at the code on the monitor.

Perfect. I broke out in sweat. Polaski and Rosler and the controllers watched me as the aircraft closed in. I tried to think.

I keyed for a signals trace and backed through it.

Nothing. Farther back. Nothing.

There!

"How in the hell?" It wasn't possible.

When the island had been built I'd had an extra line of antennas mounted on the ridge, and I'd tested every one of them personally. But now—nothing. Impossibly, not one of the antennas was feeding us a signal. More aircraft appeared on the horizon.

"Where's Elliot?" I said.

Then I was shouting. "Where's Elliot? Get me Elliot, now! And ridge cameras. I want to see the ridge!"

Elliot was out of breath and his clothes were black with oil and dried blood.

"Tyrone, my perimeter antennas are dead! Now, listen—all their cables feed into the main mast on the ridge, so there's something wrong at the mast. Here, look."

Beyond the heavy antenna mast on the ridge a mile above us, unmistakable shapes slid over the horizon. Frogs.

"Get us infrared, if you would, please," said Bolton.

Infrared overlays came up—no hot targets. The frogs were running on our batteries after all, no longer nuclear.

"Hell, Torres," said Elliot, "we unplugged those antennas years ago. Look at the base of the mast, here—that's the connector hanging next to the empty socket. No one knew what the hell it was for, and Polaski needed the juice for his antennas."

"*Polaski's* antennas? What fucking antennas?"

"Take it easy. You'll have to ask Polaski."

I stared at the connector on the screen, inches away from its socket. Gunships and frogs slid around the island and into position.

"Well," said Bolton. "We seem to have spiked our own cannon, haven't we?"

No one answered.

With the connector plugged back in we would knock out every one of those aircraft. Without it, nothing else would matter.

"Right," said Bolton. "If I'm to understand this, you need that small round object, there, plugged into that small round hole, there. At which point you are going to do some mysterious thing."

"Yes."

"Very well." He reached for a phone. "Roscoe, the sled. You and I and two volunteers."

He picked up a radio-telephone headset, then leaned closer. "Sailing a bit close to the wind, aren't we, Torres?" He turned for the door.

"I'll be on Tac. Follow me with the cameras, please."

The room was quiet. Technicians worked to reload the programs I'd dumped. Attackers deployed across the map. They were avoiding the eastern end of the island with the opening, putting up a wall of pickets on the other three sides, instead.

The largest rectangles on the map moved up against the north and south walls of the island. They were armored frogs, sliding in below the island's roof-line, out of sight of our cameras. Blunt pulse-lasers protruded from their armor.

In the corridor outside the lower elevator doors, Pham's troops made way for Bolton's troops bringing up the tunneling sled. It was heavy and ugly, ninety feet long, welded onto twelve flying work platforms. At the stern, like the deck-house on a barge, a cage protected the air-tight cabin. Forward of the cabin lay an invention we'd borrowed from the ill-fated Major Cole: sixty-four synchronized diggers and heaters, stripped of their housings and welded into a single tunneling gun. It had many times the power of a battle laser, but the sled was very, very slow.

Whump. The command complex shook under a heavy blow. Again. *Whump.* Equipment rattled.

"North wall, right up against us here. Tunneling in with those lasers."

While the rest held onto their chairs and listened, I went over to Polaski and hit him in the chest. I hit him again, pushing him against the wall.

"What antennas, Polaski?"

"Jesus, take it easy. They're just listening antennas, Torres. A few inside, a few outside. Nothing you needed to know about."

"And why the fuck not?"

"Why the fuck *not*? Because you would have pissed and moaned and dicked around about privacy and ethics and crap like that and wasted everybody's time making yourself feel better—*that's* why not."

"God damn it, I'm running this—"

"That's right, Torres. You're running it and you want to win so bad your prick hurts. You want your little picket fence in the sky no matter what it takes and I'm getting it for you. And that means there's going to be shit you don't want to know about, doesn't it?"

I stared at him.

"Isn't that right, Torres? You never want to know the shitty parts."

I left him standing against the wall.

Bolton had the tunneling sled into the center elevator. How was he going to reach the connector, though? Tunneling up through half a mile of rock would take hours, but his only alternative was to go out through the opening, up the eastern face, and back along the ridge. Which he couldn't do.

Up on the airfield, a frog's laser barrel slid above the lip and began aiming bursts at the middle elevator's blast door. I reached for a microphone.

"Bolton, there's a burner on the doors to your elevator shaft. When you reach the top and open your inside doors, that blast door's all that's going to be between you and the frog."

"His position?" A grid snapped onto the screen.

"Inclination zero, azimuth three decimal niner left. I say again *your* left, three decimal niner."

"And where is he targeting, please?"

"Bottom center, middle doors."

Inside Bolton's elevator, the sled floated up to the ceiling so it wouldn't slam into it when the elevator stopped. Then it moved to one side, still facing the doors.

"Open my inside doors, please." The doors slid aside to reveal the shaft speeding by.

Suddenly the elevator flared white as Bolton fired his entire bank of diggers in the confined space. The picture went blank.

Looking at the outside of the outer doors, from cameras up on the airfield, the frog was rapidly enlarging a gaping hole. Then all at once a patch at the upper corner of the doors, away from where the frog was firing, burst into flame. It grew brighter and brighter, then a bolt of fire lanced through it and down the full length of the cavern into the frog. The frog spun away.

The sled immediately pushed through the new hole and rose to the cavern roof for its run to the opening.

"Listen!" One of the controllers cocked an ear and held up a hand.

Nothing.

The room shook from another blow, but soundlessly.

"There!" A high-pitched whine, coming through the walls right after the blow.

"Heaters. They're blowing chunks out of the wall with lasers, then clearing it with heaters. How long to go through a hundred-foot-thick wall, do you think?"

"Not very long."

"How the hell do they know where to tunnel, though? That wall is six miles long and a mile high, and it all looks exactly the same from the outside."

"Someone told them."

Why, I thought. Why now?

Whump. Then the whining again, louder.

"There he goes!"

Bolton's sled was disappearing out the opening. On the range officer's screen, with its side view of the opening, the sled turned its flank to the wall and rose upward—he was gambling on the pickets' east wall blind spot. Finally the sled stopped, just below the ridge.

I turned to the console and got ready.

"All right," said Bolton over his radio. "We're going to cut a bit of a groove here. We'll need a very sharp call-out on distance to the mast, if you would. We're going to be able to see bugger all once we get started."

Finally I understood.

"Bolton! I can steer your sled from here. Set it to zero-zero—mark."

"Thank you, lad, that's very decent of you."

Whump.

"I'll give you timing by voice. You're going to leave the sled when it stops?"

"That I am, lad. All right, Roscoe, steady on."

The sled rotated to face in along the ridge toward the antenna mast. It jerked backward in a cloud of exploding rock as the beam lit up, cutting a groove in toward the mast.

The pattern of pickets changed instantly. Two gunships streaked in toward the sled, which at the very same moment vanished in a cloud of dust exploding outward from the ridge. The gunships veered away and circled, trying to probe the cloud with their radar and infrared.

"Thirty-four seconds."

WHUMP. An equipment rack crashed to the ground. The air grew hot. Another frog nosed around the edge of the opening.

"Fifteen."

WHUMP, WHUMP. Close. There had to be a frog all the way inside the hole, closing in on us.

"Five seconds." I picked up the light-pen.

"Two. One."

The sled stopped at the mast. Bolton appeared through the smoke, bent over and racing across the rock toward the mast.

But the smoke was already dissipating. One of the gunships accelerated around the edge of the cloud and shot in toward him.

"Company, Bolton."

He dropped to his stomach and groped overhead for the connector. I clicked on the light pen and tracked the gunship with it.

WHUMP. Dust fell from the ceiling. Bolton heaved the connector up toward its socket as a line of gunfire stitched toward him.

With a final lunge against the wires the connector slid home. Our battle map blossomed with numbers.

I pressed the button.

Bolton had caught an arm in the wire bundle and was trying to pull aside from the line of fire, but he was unable to get any leverage.

The gunship changed course, then abruptly tumbled downward. Its nose dug into the rock and an instant later an oily wall of flame slid across the rock close to Bolton.

"Stay where you are, Bolton." I flicked the light pen over to the other gunship and pressed. It nosed down into the ridge as well and promptly exploded.

"All right, you're clear for a minute. Get in the sled and stay there—we're going to need you on the north wall."

He finished untangling his arm.

"Pray tell, Eduardo." He was out of breath. "How exactly did you do that?"

"Stand by."

WHUMP. Rock exploded somewhere in the wall nearby, followed by a shriek of tearing metal. I moved the light-pen to each of the aircraft along the north wall, pushing the button again and again. They plummeted down the wall and into the ocean in a cloud of steam.

"All right," I said. "Someone write down those numbers on the screen. Fast."

"What's *happening*?" said Elliot. "Even the frogs are going in."

"Is someone writing down those goddamned numbers?

"What those are," I said after a moment, "they're the serial numbers of the batteries in the aircraft. Every battery has a transponder in it—when the antennas query it, it responds with its serial number. Then if I *transmit* a serial number, that battery shuts down."

I swept the pen across the pickets over the ocean.

"Look up those serial numbers—find out who we sold them to."

WHUMP.

"Bolton! Get down the north wall. There's a laser in that hole where I can't get at it."

"Aye, aye."

"Mr. Torres? Those serial numbers went to the Europeans."

"The *Europeans*? What the hell are *they* doing here? Christ, this doesn't make any sense."

The complex we were in began shaking again, vibrating, and this time it didn't stop.

"Bolton, can you see where they went in? They haven't broken through, but they're awfully damned close. They must be trying to hit the command center here."

"There's fuck all to see from here, I'm afraid. I don't know where I am. I do think I've got him, though. They've made a bloody big hole, about your level—"

"Oh my god, no! Mr. Torres!" A woman behind me.

More shouting. Another woman's voice, screaming now.

"The infirmary—" Awful sounds.

"It's the children!"

Disoriented, I raced for the door—and as soon as I was through I knew something was terribly wrong. Daylight was pouring in, a hundred yards down the corridor. I ran.

The infirmary door wouldn't move. Others were around me now, pushing, confused. I found a fire axe and tore it from the wall, then pushed my way through to the infirmary window.

And froze.

It was gone. The infirmary, utterly gone. Dust swirled over a gaping hole that sloped downward and away to daylight. The medics, the children, were all gone.

Then movement to one side caught my eye. Along one wall there remained a shattered piece of ledge, hard to see through the dust. A crib hung over the lip. Tiny hands gripped the bars and a face looked over the rail, shrieking with terror and wet with tears.

Enough of the floor remained to work my way around, if I could get through the window. The baby turned his head from side to side and cried, but from outside the window I could hear nothing but my own breathing. I stared, gripping the axe harder.

But I didn't swing it. I knew the baby could see me in the window and was screaming for me to come, but I just stood there andstared back for what seemed like an eternity, unable to move.

The axe was torn out of my hands. The baby lifted his head to cry harder and threw his arms out toward the window, tipping the crib.

The image of his face, his tiny hands reaching out to me, would stay with me through all the years I had left to live.

Chapter Eight: I HAVE LET YOU SEE IT WITH YOUR OWN EYES

Chan's baby was stillborn. Chan suffered a great deal in the months that followed, and drew into herself.

I myself provided little solace. It had, in fact, become so hard for me to remember the baby that sometimes I believed she hadn't existed. But I remembered the look in the medic's eyes, and so I couldn't put the event behind me completely.

It had been the worst of signs in a year filled with bad signs. I sat in the darkened manufacturing chamber now and thought about how the day past had brought only more.

By some reckonings it was the first day of the Year of the Snake—a poor sign in itself, the Chinese said. And the new year, by those reckonings, began with the full moon. The full moon meant that the sun and the moon were in line with the Earth, a circumstance that brought the highest tides of the month. This particular New Years marked a solstice, moreover, a time when the highest tides were to be found on the tropic of Capricorn and the tropic of Cancer, along which lay the Ganges River Delta. The conjunction of these events also came at a time when the oceans were rising because of melting ice packs, and coastal lands were subsiding because of excessive ground water pumping.

So, five and a half hours earlier, as the Year of the Snake stole westward out of Burma and the full moon rose over the Bay of Bengal, a storm had flooded the Ganges Delta. Dacca and parts of Calcutta lay under water. Forty-three million people were expected to die.

The news had chilled our own New Year's celebration, a procession arranged by Pham and the captive Chih-Hsien Chien during a rare truce between them. The parade had gone on for the children's sake, but only after bottles of rice wine had passed again and again among the adults.

I stood in the darkened doorway of the manufacturing chamber and watched. The procession was led by an enormous paper snake, lowered over the heads of Chan, Elliot, Peters and others. Pham led the way, bent over with her torso inside the snake's head. It weaved back and forth as she steered, sensuous and menacing. Lewd comments flew between her and the tail, while watchers banged noisemakers and passed bottles of the bitter wine.

Children clapped in time and jumped with excitement as the snake threw them candy. They were too young to see the edges of fear behind the merriment.

It was the snake's job to burst through three tall paper banners blocking its path. The first was a picture of the Earth, and the second the moon. The third was painted a deep, velvety black, speckled with stars. Only by bursting through these images of the Earth, the moon and the stars could the snake find its rightful place in the heavens for the new year.

It weaved from side to side and slid forward, the bearers chanting and swaying. Coming up against the banner of the Earth, Pham paused and the snake's head weaved in front of the paper, then reared up as high as it could and plunged through it.

Pham skidded to her knees. After an awkward moment she recovered her balance and stood, then the snake slithered through the banner of the Earth behind her.

Confronted with the moon a moment later, the snake slid up along the banner's face but drifted to one side, so slowly that the middle and tail began to catch up with the head and coil across the road. Still the head didn't move. The crowd grew restless. The head drifted the other way, and the body coiled tighter behind it. Finally it coiled so tightly that it forced the whole front end of the snake to smash through the banner sideways.

The crowd shouted its relief, and the snake headed drunkenly onward toward the stars.

Then suddenly the snake swept sideways across the roadway, only to whip back in the other direction a moment later. On the second swing it stopped abruptly in the center of the road with its nose against the black banner, as though transfixed by the stars. It stared and it stared, and the minutes crept by.

Then slowly the head rose upward. It rose higher and higher and the crowd held its breath, until suddenly it reared backward and, with an awful sound of crumpling paper, Pham pitched face-forward onto the ground. The snake's head crashed to the roadway and skidded forward, coming to rest with its nose inches away from the blackness, staring with empty eyes into the glittering, unconquered stars of space.

The crowd fell silent.

The body of the snake started to come apart. Elliot shrugged off the snake's middle and Chan sat down hard on top of it. Charlie Peters pulled the unconscious Pham out of the snake's head and picked her up, cradling her in his arms.

Across the roadway sat Madhu Patel on his stool, watching me. Chih-Hsien was next to him, staring down at the snake.

The procession had come to its unpromising end at four in the afternoon, and the corridors had grown quiet in the two hours since. Somewhere above us, the night and the full moon crept across the Pacific toward us.

I'd spent the last hours in the darkened manufacturing chamber, remembering its days of feverish activity, and then the day that the machines had stopped.

The Europeans had not revealed our ability to disable the batteries. Whatever their reasons, they'd limped back home and said nothing. For months afterward the world had continued to buy the priceless power cells, becoming ever more dependent on them.

Then finally the United States declared its intention to take control of the technology behind the batteries, and attacked us by both air and sea. We crippled their batteries en masse, and the attack failed. But the word was out.

A week later Charlie Peters told us that all two and a half million line items needed for launch were in inventory. Around-the-clock meetings followed.

The week after, we severed our ties to the world. And we sent out a warning, something I'd once sworn I wouldn't do. Sitting alone in the Operations room, I pressed a key and held it down for sixty seconds. For sixty seconds the world's batteries stopped.

Infamy, they called it. Sixty seconds that would be remembered for generations to come.

Three hundred seventy-eight million batteries died. Lights dimmed and went out, cars stopped, work platforms and low-flying aircraft crashed, hospitals and computer towers ground to a halt.

There had been no backups. The batteries had been perfect.

The world was stunned, then angry, as it came to understand the depth of our betrayal. The market for radio shielding soared until we announced that, from here on out, a new signal broadcast continuously by us was required periodically by the cells to keep them on—that if the signal were interfered with or our island destroyed, the cells would soon stop. We were vilified and condemned, and feared.

We sealed ourselves off and waited.

Chih-Hsien Chien had been forced to stay with us. In the end he'd been eager to do so, a fact which in itself was worrisome. We used him to communicate with the Chinese government, now at war with its own people. Through Chih-Hsien we reminded them that their ships could be stopped easily if they made a move toward the tunnel before allowing the rest of us safe passage.

We remained on civil terms with the Commonwealth and North American colonization contingent, but had lost contact with the Europeans.

As Patel had asked, we assured the world that the plans for the batteries would be transmitted from our ships just before passing through the torus. There were, in any case, whispers that Asian scientists were close to discovering the cell's principle for themselves. It wouldn't be surprising; I was, in fact, surprised it had taken so long.

In the meantime we tested the ships and retested them, and checked and rechecked the payload. On board were a combined 86,000 tons of food, heavy equipment, MI, grasshopper and spider drones, and frozen embryos. And dirt—the upper eighteen decks of each ship weren't really decks, but were a quarter-mile-long by eleven-foot-wide spiraling garden.

The dry stores and gardens could support more people than we'd originally planned. Polaski's projections of 1.5 children to each of sixty-one percent of all possible couples, to equal exactly fourteen people per ship, had come to nothing. There were fewer surviving children than planned, while at the same time there were many more adults: we'd become increasingly dependent on imported talent, especially payload experts drawn away from the consortia. There would be 2,400 of us in the end.

Children with disabilities would not be placed in institutions on Earth as we'd intended, but would be brought along in specially equipped quarters. Polaski had talked vaguely about just leaving them behind on the island, but Chan and Patel had quickly silenced any discussion of it.

"Everything else," I'd said to Bolton a while later, "we leave behind."

"Oh?" He was fishing from the lip of an opening he'd blown in the wall of the island, against all regulations. Rain spattered on his face as the wind picked up, and made a noise against his empty bucket.

"Yes," I said, "all of it. The fighting, the poverty. The banqueros. The stink of the place. There's nothing we need here any more."

"I wonder," he said, peering over the ledge at his line, "if that's really what you mean to leave behind."

I looked at the whitecaps through the rain, out across the ocean Bolton had yet to catch a fish from.

"I don't think we will, in any case," he said, and wound in the line. "Someday we'll look up to find it's still there."

I thought of the gun coming up in Major Cole's hand, and of the old man in his bungalow, of my father in the doorway of our shack with a piece of dung in his hand and tears in his eyes.

"Piss on it, Bolton," I said. "I just want to go."

Patel was out by the opening that evening, after the procession. The airfield was deserted, swept by fitful eddies of trash, lit by the dusk sky. He sat on a stool near his flying work platform, his crutches nearby. Next to him was an empty stool.

"I thought you would come," he said. He held a handkerchief in his lap and stared down at the mists lying on the water, his face wet with tears.

"What's the matter, Madhu?"

"I am doing very well, my friend. Thank you for asking."

I didn't know what to say, so I just sat and watched the mists darkening below us. Clouds gathered above.

"What is it, Madhu? You're crying."

"Ah, yes, that. Well, it is not an easy thing to explain." He dabbed at his eyes.

"But I will try. You see, Eduardo, a short time ago I was resting in my room and thinking about this terrible day, when all at once Allah spoke to me.

"He said 'Madhu'— He calls me Madhu, you know, because there are so very many Patels in the world.

"'Madhu,' He said, 'many people have died today, as you know. And among them were some who found in their lives much hardship and sorrow, but who passed away before they could weep for their own unhappiness. That is a bad thing, Madhu. For while Paradise is a fine place, it is not so good to leave behind in the world grief for which no one has wept.

"'Come give me your help,' He said. 'Come help me weep for them, before their grief finds new hearts to dwell in.'"

I was conscious of Patel's warmth beside me, and conscious of the ocean swelling and falling beneath the mists. It was at its lowest tide, just turning against us now as the moon approached from beyond the horizon.

"I think perhaps He called to you, as well, Eduardo, but you could not hear him in your gloomy room filled with machines."

"No."

Sometimes I felt like I couldn't hear anything at all. "We've been here too long, Madhu. I walk through the corridors sometimes, and I feel like I'm in a grave. I haven't seen a sunset in five years."

"Yes."

The first glimmer of moonlight touched the horizon.

"I don't know what to do, Madhu."

"Yes."

Wind licked upward from the ledge and tugged at us, then slid away again.

"Do you think the world will let us go?"

"Oh, yes. I think we are like their own children to them. We have taken all they have to give, and now they are angry with us. Yet in their hearts they wish us Godspeed. I think they will try to stop us, Eduardo, but they will let us go."

He rocked back and forth on his stool for a while, then stopped.

"Do not let it happen to you, my friend."

"What's that?"

"Do not allow your life to pass, before you have wept for your own sadness. I say this to you especially. I say it thinking of Katherine Chan, and the distance between you, just when she needs you the most."

The mists on the water began to glow. The sky turned a deeper black.

"You see, Eduardo, I believe that you are a compassionate man. But I think sometimes your compassion is lost in a sadness, and I fear that anything that speaks to you of that sadness, you will destroy. Perhaps even I should not speak to you of it, but— Well, now I have, so it doesn't matter. In any case, I think there may not be another time."

"But you're coming with us, Madhu. It won't be that long before we're somewhere else—you know that."

"Ah, my young friend. The place you are going, Allah has already let me see it with my own eyes."

He fell quiet then, worrying the handkerchief in his hands. The world outside had become nothing more than blacks and greys— an ashen glow behind the mists, a wash of moonlight on the clouds, a blackness in the distant sky.

"Do you remember a dream you once told me of, Eduardo, in which we come upon ourselves out among the stars?"

"Yes, I remember."

"Good. Because sometimes we do not recognize ourselves, out there where it is so empty. And I must tell you, Eduardo, it is an empty place Allah has shown me."

The moon climbed above the horizon. It rose in perfect silence, swollen by the mists to an immense size, a pitted, colorless grey. The haze on the water glowed, throwing a ghostly incandescence onto the clouds above.

In the dream Madhu had mentioned, dim shapes waited for us out in space, and gradually took on our own faces as we approached. But while I could find the faces of all the others, I couldn't find my own. There was only Pham, naked, smiling, beckoning. Even in my waking hours I carried that image with me, and sometimes it came between me and Chan.

For now, Patel and I sat on our stools next to each other, our shoulders touching. The moon swelled above the mists, below the clouds, pulling free of the ocean. It was huge and powerful, frozen in time, cold and grey as ash. Patel shivered.

"That is a not a good thing we are seeing, my friend."

He was quiet for a minute.

"When I was a little boy," he said, "we lived in Bilaspur, in the north of Himachal Pradesh. Himachal was a place of splendid green hills and good soil. It took its name from the Himalayas, which rose to the east of us.

"Across the great mountains lay the steppes of China. Once in a long while, in the evening when my mother carried me in her garden and sat on the bench and held me, a cold mist would settle along the Himalayas, and a full moon would rise up behind it. It looked then as it does now, like ashes on the snow. My mother would shiver and hold me tighter, then, and she would say, 'There is a grey moon over China, Madhi, and it will bring us no good.'"

He gripped the handkerchief in his lap, working it between his hands.

"I think I am a little bit afraid, Eduardo."

Chapter Nine: BUT YOU SHALL NOT CROSS THERE

Sirens woke me at three o'clock the next morning, out of dreams about Madhu and the great snake. Lights were burning in the corridor.

When I reached Air Defense, Bates and Rosler were looking down at an infrared image of the shelf, viewed from the opening. It was covered with blurs of light.

"Twenty thousand, maybe," said Bates. I could hardly hear her.

"Troops. Heavy equipment. None of it powered by batteries. Americans—came in by ship. Shot out our east-wall defenses before we even knew they were there. Jammed our radar."

I stared down at the image.

The shelf—troops were on the roof of our launch chamber, and in all our planning we'd never even thought of it. Such a simple and obvious mistake, and now we were trapped.

Rosler seemed unconcerned.

Pham came in behind him, looking sick and ashen-faced. She put a hand on his arm, but without even a backward glance he shook it off. She stood next to him, just the same, and stared unsteadily at the screen.

"So, Torres," said Rosler. "Let's see what you do about it this time."

I knew just what we were going to do, and it was something that frightened me more than anything had in all the years we'd been on the island.

You do have a choice, Chan had once said. You don't have to go.

"They're going to come up that face," I said, "and try an assault through the cavern."

Rosler cleaned his glasses. "So?"

Bates hugged herself and looked from one of us to the other.

"If we have to launch," she said, "it'll be an awfully long wait before they're all up off the shelf, won't it?"

"Yes." But maybe we didn't have to decide yet. We could take the first step, and decide when we knew more.

"Rosler. Move command to the ships—we'll monitor the shelf from there. Announce full boarding, with engine-start and launch sequence. Not a drill. I'm moving to Zero for systems start. Let's go, Pham."

The launch chamber under the shelf was blazing with mercury arc lamps. Voices rang out in the freezing air, while hammers slammed retaining pins out of the gantries. We'd practiced for a premature launch time and again, yet it was still our worst fear. It meant leaving with nowhere to go.

Pham followed me through the irradiation chamber and up the lift to decks 36/37, the double-height MI deck. Everyone else was already in position, listening to Bates reading boarding instructions over the radios.

I pushed behind Elliot's seat.

"Morning, Torres."

"Morning." I kicked my seat around to face the consoles and squeezed into it, glancing down at the frozen banks of equipment under the grating beneath us. The MI decks contained the ship's intelligence, linked to identical systems in the other 127 ships. The fleet's MI was designed to be holographic, so that the fleet could be run from any ship no matter how many others were lost.

But the deck itself was uncomfortable. There were no contoured instrument panels or subdued lighting, no carpeted aisles or doors that hissed politely aside. It was awkward and cramped, with jagged edges and exposed conduits, raw welds and bulging rivets. The consoles were bolted to a noisy metal grating over the hardware, and it all swayed and rattled and stank.

In the center of the grating stood a dense group of six consoles. We sat facing each other across them. Acceleration seats for another six were bolted to the walls behind them.

Directly across the consoles from me sat Pham, slumped in her seat, swiveling from side to side as she stared vacantly at her screens.

To my left sat Elliot, hunched over his screens and frowning at them. He was Power and Environmental Systems officer for the fleet; along with P and E officers under him in the other ships, it was up to him keep us moving and alive.

Opposite him sat Anne Miller, quiet and unreadable as her eyes flicked among her screens and her hands moved in their gloves. She would coordinate our mission with that of the drones sometime in the future. For now she assisted Chan in uploading ground systems into the fleet MI.

Chan and Polaski sat opposite each other. Chan was around to my left, on the other side of Elliot. Polaski sat to my right. He was slouched in his seat with his hands in his pockets, staring at an image of the shelf that spanned the chamber high above us.

Kip sat against the wall behind him. He was dressed awkwardly in the regulation sterile jumpsuit, swiveling from side to side as he studied a talking music box someone had given him.

Together with Peters and Patel in their quarters on 41-deck, our ship's complement came to nine—although like the others we could carry twenty-four if we needed to. We were as light as we were because we hadn't wanted families with children on the command ship, and because we didn't allow redundant expertise on any one vessel.

"Poor, stupid fools," said Polaski.

Chan looked up.

"You're not thinking of launching with all those people up there, Polaski."

"If it's time to go," he said, "it's time to go."

"They'll move off the shelf by themselves. You just want to blow them off, don't you?"

"I want to win."

"A sensible attitude," said Miller. "I'm glad to see someone along with intelligence."

"Not this again." Elliot jammed a manual into a slot. "Do we have to have robot-woman along, Torres?"

"That's enough," I said. "Let's go, Pham."

"They're not *robots*," said Miller. "They're drones. There's a difference."

"That's *enough*. Come on, Pham, let's have it."

Pham fiddled with her headset and squinted at her screens. She began reading lethargically.

"True launch procedure," she said. "Confirm this is the correct checklist."

"Confirmed."

"Communications, flights zero through seven."

The leaders of each of the sixteen-ship flights responded.

"Check."

"Personnel on board and secure."

I hesitated for a moment, not having checked the whole ship yet.

"Check."

"Systems integrity and console status, critical stations, command vessel."

"P and E," I said.

"Check," said Elliot.

"Maneuvering systems."

"Three in three," said Chan.

The checklist went on for forty minutes. Polaski broke the rules twice to go below for coffee, while Pham periodically dozed off or else lunged forward to slam her fist onto her console. It was close to five in the morning when we finished.

"Explosive canopy interlock."

I reached for the overhead panel, then stopped—we hadn't made a decision. We hadn't even talked about it. On the other hand, we couldn't afford to get sidetracked during the checklist. There would be time.

I unwound the retaining wires from the interlock lever and pulled them free, then carefully slid the locking pins out. The lever clicked into place when I turned it. Polaski matched my movements on his own overhead panel.

"Interlock disabled."

"Explode canopy."

"Hold."

I let out my breath and dropped back in the seat. For another few minutes we sat and fidgeted. The engine hummed beneath us.

Rosler's voice came through from the speakers.

"I can't tell without daylight, but I think there's activity against the face."

Screens bolted to the bulkheads still showed the thousands of blurry red dots on the shelf above us. They had concentrated around the cliff below the runway opening.

"Any signals activity, Rosler?"

"No. They've got to be using land wires."

"All right. Call if you get any." I cut him off.

"Has anyone figured out," said Polaski, "if the shelf is going to blow with the extra weight on it?"

"Yes," said Miller. "I have. It makes no difference. Our course is still clear, I would think."

"God save us from clear thinking," said Elliot.

"Come, Mr. Elliot. How is it you're so concerned about the people attacking us?"

"Well, hell," he said. "I guess the good Lord would just want me to blow them up as fast as I can, wouldn't He?"

We waited. Kip started and stopped his music box. Pham fidgeted and swore at the equipment. A whirring sound came from the lift shaft, and a spider drone floated out over the consoles, sampling the air. Polaski tried to land a ball of paper on top of it, and when it darted away from him and closer to Pham she lashed out and sent it spinning across the room to smack into an air shaft.

"At least," said Elliot, watching the drone retreat, "what I keep thinking is that maybe we're gone. Maybe I can stop waking up in the morning waiting for something else to turn bad."

"I don't know," I said. "Madhu says there's a price to pay for the way things got, and it has to be paid whether we go or not."

"You people are screwy," said Polaski. "We're winning and you know it."

Chan threw down her pencil. "You only want to win if somebody else loses, Polaski, and that makes me angry. That's not why we're doing this!"

"Somebody always wins," he said, "and somebody loses. I want us to win by getting off this planet is all, like we decided."

"As long as you're in charge. You're not fooling anyone,

Polaski. You haven't fooled anyone since your little eyes lit up at Eddie's plans five years ago."

"Come *on*, people," I said. "This is hard enough as it is. *Pham!* Jesus—stop pounding on your console. What the hell's wrong with it, anyway?"

"Piece of shit."

"You're just so hung over you can't focus on anything."

"Not like you, hah, Mr. Torres? Maybe it do you good to get a little drunk sometimes, fuck people for fun. Not like you fuck people, hah?"

We stared at the screens and waited for the Army to do something. A buzzer sounded.

"Torres, it's Rosler. Kill your infrared."

The screens lost their tint to show the light of dawn washing across the shelf. A line of platforms was moving up the cliff toward the opening.

"Okay," I said. "It's what we expected."

"No, it's not. Look close, next to the launchers on the platforms. Enhanced radiation rounds. They drop one of those down the shafts and the island's theirs, ships and all. All they have to do is scrape out the meat. Look at the troops on the shelf—radiation suits. I'd say we've got twenty minutes."

"Sweet Lord almighty."

"Still so sanguine, Mr. Elliot?" said Miller.

"Okay, Rosler. We'll think about it." I hit the switch and looked around. Sweat trickled down the back of my neck into the suit.

"We know what Polaski wants to do," said Chan.

"Come on, Chan. We need to think."

"Hah!" said Pham. "Let them fight. You just say stop 'cause if she make Polaski small, then you small, too."

"You're not helping."

"Ah, come on, Mr. Torres. All the time you whisper in Polaski's ear what to do and he get to be powerful guy and you get to be nice guy. You make him fuck everybody for you, hah? Let's see what you do now, Mister. Me, I like powerful guy."

"Is that why you let Rosler smack you around? That's pretty

powerful. All right, people, if you've got any ideas, I need them."

"Rosler not hit me! You don't say that!"

"Or he ignores you. You like that better? Now that's enough! Polaski?"

"Let's go."

"Just a minute. Anne?"

"Of course."

"Pham?"

"Hah!" Her lip curled for some new sarcasm, then she realized she was being watched. She looked down at her screens, glancing up at me only briefly.

She began jogging a foot under the console. The seconds passed. Her brow furrowed, and she looked uncertainly at Chan. Finally she gave a little nod, then looked away and shrugged.

"Chan?" I said.

Chan bit her lip. I felt a stab of pain as she moved a hand across her belly the way she had when she was carrying the baby.

"Yes, Eddie."

"Tyrone?"

"Yeah. Lord help us, Torres, but we gotta go."

I took a breath and nodded to Polaski. He twisted his lever and held it.

I snapped the communications switch on the armrest and kicked the lever that snapped the acceleration seats forward and locked them into position.

"Rosler. Flights. True launch—this is not a drill."

I reached for the lever. *God help us.* I twisted it.

The rock shelf, sprinkled with its carpet of soldiers in the early light, rose up toward the cameras like a child's balloon inflating. It swept past the platforms and crushed them against the cliff, then a cloud of vapor followed and the rock and debris disintegrated. The pictures went out.

The ship shook once, then hummed. It moved.

"MIC status."

"Um—" Elliot pulled himself closer to his console, dazed. "Seventy percent, all ships."

Voices came through from the other ships.

"Sever ground links."

"Separation and motion, all ships."

"Spacing maneuver commencing."

"We have insertion lock on all flights, Zero."

The weight grew and the pitch of the humming increased.

It's over, I thought. If nothing else, it's over. I fought off the image of the soldiers on the ballooning shelf, soldiers just like us, turning quietly to white dust. Twenty thousand soldiers.

"Eight-zero percent, all ships."

"Five hundred feet."

"Clear of gantries and housing."

"Spacing attitude."

"One thousand feet."

"Roll-over."

The new weight and the throb of the ship as it tipped toward the east were now a relief, a final release.

"Spacing complete."

"Eddie—" A new voice.

"Stand by. Checkpoint, HE pressure."

"Four thousand feet."

"Human environments go across the board."

"Rotation complete."

"Six thousand."

Faster. Faster! A litany now in my mind. Harder!

"One-zero thousand."

"NEO departure clock."

"One-five thousand at ninety percent."

"Eddie!" Charlie Peter's voice.

"You're on command channel, Charlie. Stand by."

"Three-zero thousand."

"Insertion spacing."

It was everything I'd wanted for all those years: the speed, the power, the pace of it. The freedom. The ship surged and hummed, and pressed me harder into the seat.

"One-zero-six thousand: two-zero miles."

"Power to five-five percent."

"One-two thousand per."

"Eddie, damn it—it's Madhu!"

"What is it, Charlie?"

God Almighty, don't let up now.

"He went down to warn them, Eddie! Down to the shelf! He took his platform and he was down there when it blew! Oh, Jesus, I didn't think you'd do it."

Madhu on the shelf? Madhu was in his quarters.

Pham's eyes met mine, and we became frozen together. Neither of us moved.

The weight of the launch grew, then became unbearable.

No, I thought. Not again.

Rosler's voice in the distance. "You're on command, Peters. Clear off now."

Madhu dead. Madhu a breath of dust on the white balloon, another puppet hanging from the wires.

"Checkpoint, re-entry option."

"Re-entry option canceled. Checkpoint clear."

I've killed him. I've killed him, and I can't do this without him.

Kip sat with the music box in both hands, tears streaming from his eyes.

PART TWO

AN OCEAN OF DISQUIET

Chapter Ten: THE SECOND MESSENGER

"That information isn't your private property, Polaski."

He wiped blood from the corner of his mouth, then looked down at it on his hand. I moved sideways to keep him away from the lift.

"If you've learned anything about the programs Miller's writing," I said, "you give it up."

"To just anyone?" he said.

"To me."

"Oh, so it's *your* private property."

He sounded bored, as though the outcome of the confrontation was of no particular interest. "Not to be confused with the riffraff's private property."

"Forget it, Polaski. You can drive wedges between your private little armies and keep them off balance, but don't try it between me and the crews. I'm the only one who keeps them off your back, remember?"

He'd done it too many times in the past two years, taken the ambitious and the idle among the troops and turned them against their own ships' captains. Then fanned their new-found loyalty with his visions of greatness and destiny. That the captains hadn't turned against him altogether was testimony to the depth of his own conviction that everything he did was necessary for the mission, in what he believed to be an infinitely unforgiving universe.

In that way, with his vision and his seductive singleness of purpose, he had planted his roots firmly into the flet's gaping, self-inflicted wound of Madhu Patel's death. That wound, that bottomless, sucking void of any remaining moral direction, had let loose upon the fleet an insidious air of distrust and recrimination. And in the stink of it, Polaski and his minions had thrived.

Then for the two years since launch he and I had circled each other and waited, just as the four great fleets now circled the sun and waited along with us, while Polaski and I played at our intrigues, bound together all the while by what was ultimately our common purpose.

"So what is all this, Torres?" he said. "What makes you think I suddenly know when the drones are coming back?"

"Six files were transferred out of Anne's partition on FleetSys into yours on the seventeenth. The transfer was initiated by her. What was in them?"

He started to say something, then stopped. He hadn't expected me to know. Not for the first time, he'd underestimated Chan's grip on the fleet MI.

"They were probability studies," he said. "Showing when we can expect the drones. I asked her for them."

"That's what she's been working on?"

"That's right."

"For two whole years, Polaski?"

"That's right," he said, "for two years."

It wasn't true, of course. Even though for a full year before launch Anne Miller had done no work of any kind, within days of Patel's death she had retired to her quarters and begun an all-consuming labor that had yet to end. Like the rest of us, she had found the need—or in her case, perhaps, the long-sought opportunity—to fill some part of Madhu Patel's void in her own way. Precisely with what she was filling it, however, no one but Polaski seemed to know.

"So now that you've got your probability studies, Polaski, how long are we going to wait for a drone to come back? The troops need an answer."

He shrugged, then motioned to the rag wrapped around my knuckles. I tossed it to him. He dabbed at the blood on his mouth with it.

"We wait forever," he said finally. "That was the whole point of launching the way we did, wasn't it? To get everyone's butts off the dirt and piss the Americans off so bad the chicken-shits in the fleet couldn't whine about going home again? I don't see you wanting to go back, Torres. And you let Pham worry about the troops. Just get her ass into gear, is all."

Tuyet Pham, unlike Miller, had begun no work of any kind after Patel's death. Instead, from that moment during the launch when she'd sat across from me and met my eyes, she'd said nothing at all, to anyone, on any subject, until fully a month later she'd seemed to come to some sort of decision and had begun a relentless, around-the-clock campaign of heaping abuse upon her most ardent supporter, Charlie Peters. Peters, for all we could tell, didn't mind in the least, and had seemed to find it an entirely expected development in the course of her strange affairs.

Chan had wept. For days, for weeks, even now sometimes, she wept. Whether for Patel, or for what she believed would become of us without him, it was impossible to tell.

I, on the other hand, had felt nothing.

"That's right," I said to Polaski, "we wait."

"I'm gonna be sick, Torres."

"Close your eyes."

I floated closer and looked in through Elliot's face plate, but all I could see was a reflection of the sight that was making us dizzy.

The ships of the fleet stretched away into space behind me. They were paired up on mile-long cables, hanging by their noses at the ends, revolving about one another. They were like sixty-three pinwheels, white pencils on silver threads, all of them turning about the same invisible axis. Three ships, instead of two, formed the final pinwheel. Hull One-Eight had collapsed in Earth orbit.

"You okay, Tyrone?"

"Give me another minute. And remind me never to try that again, okay?"

"All right. Hold still." I plugged a private communications fiber into his suit and killed the radios.

"I need to talk about Anne," I said.

"You need to talk about anything, boy. Hang on, I'm trying not to puke."

I looked cautiously back at the ships. They were on the cables because they needed to be under acceleration—whether through gravity, centrifugation, or thrust didn't matter. When they were unaccelerated the gardens had to be cooled down to force the insects to land, so that they wouldn't bash themselves to pieces trying to fly in freefall, but the plants couldn't handle the cold. So we spun the ships on the cables, instead.

The last time they'd been unaccelerated was when we'd reached solar orbit two years ago, when the fleet MI had begun the delicate dance that ended with the ships orbiting one other. The length of the cables had been set, on my instructions, to produce an uncomfortable 1.2 Gs at mid-decks. This was to begin training us for even higher thrusts later on. I'd taken Polaski's war-minded cautions to heart, though I wasn't certain why. I was sure only that with Madhu Patel's death, my own outlook had changed.

To travel from one ship to another we had to exit through a nose hatch, then clamp a motorized climber onto the cable and start up toward the axis of rotation. While starting the climb, the cable and the ship we'd exited from seemed to stand perfectly still, hanging from the other ship six thousand feet above. All of the other ship-pairs looked stationary as well. The sun and the stars, however, swept around us in a complete circle once every minute.

As we climbed higher on the cable we became lighter, until at the coupling in the center there was no up or down at all. The center-points of all the cables had red beacons attached to them, so that from where Elliot and I floated along the axis, the beacons on all of the cables were lined up in a sixty-mile-long string of lights.

According to the original designers' manuals, once we'd climbed a cable and reached the center point, but before we'd pushed off toward the beacon on the next cable, it was a good idea to discontinue our own cable-synchronous rotation and synchronize with the stars, instead. Otherwise, the moment we wandered at all away from the beacon-to-beacon axis, the cables' rotation and our own rotation were suddenly on different axes. That left neither the ships nor the stars frozen in space, leading to a ferocious disorientation.

But Elliot and I had tried it the wrong way, anyway.

"Okay, Torres. But let's keep going—I gotta get these soil samples to the lab."

We pushed off toward the next beacon, passing an adult

towing a class of six-year-olds, faceless in their little suits.

"What's Anne working on, Tyrone?" I said.

"Hell, Torres, I don't know. Everyone says she's getting ready to update the drones' programs, if one ever comes back."

"So why wasn't she working on it in the year before we left? What changed?"

"You know what changed, Torres."

"She wasn't sorry to see Madhu go, was she?"

"Don't pussyfoot around, boy. That woman looked like the weight of Hades came off her back when he died. Heads up, cable's coming—we gotta unplug or snag. Anyway, why don't you ask your buddy, Polaski? He's got spooks and priests all over the place."

"He says he doesn't know."

"You gotta do something about him, Torres. All these spooks and private guards and shit...he takes it serious, boy. Everyone else thinks it's a game, except for him and Miller. And you I don't know about. Anyway, what about Pham? I heard she got one of her people in working for Miller."

"Anne's wise to him. Anne's been feeding Pham fake programs—Pham showed them to Chan. All the man learned is that Miller cut some kind of deal with Polaski. He doesn't know what."

"Okay, here we go. Radios on."

I unplugged while Elliot grabbed the pinwheeling cable and snapped his climber onto it. When he started down—or out, at this point—I clipped on behind him and felt the familiar tug as the cable caught me up and started me turning.

"Anyway, Tyrone, keep your ears open."

"Yeah."

"So what's with the soil samples?"

"Soil samples, water samples, air samples, oil samples, coolant samples, you name it. I've even got a little bottle of live and kicking detrivores, here. Once a month I gotta do this."

"What's a detrivore?"

"Little crawly fella that eats bug shit and dead bug bits. Bottom of the food chain. Botany folks are always asking for them."

"Okay, we're down to a half G. Let's see if we can get the Wizard of Oz to open the air lock this time. Keep you from having to slide down on your face again."

We were halfway down the cable to the ship. We would be entering through an air lock on the rounded slope of the nose, and it was easiest to have the air lock opened from the inside, rather than us having to slide down to the handle and open it manually.

"FleetSys," I said.

The fleet MI answered promptly through our radios.

"Yes, Mr. Torres."

"Open air lock Six-One West on hull One-Fox."

"It is open already."

I looked down past Elliot. "No, it's not."

"Your words are not clear, Mr. Torres. 'Note snot?'"

"The air lock is not open."

"Yes."

I stopped to think. "'Yes,' you agree, or 'yes,' it's open?"

"Your question is not clear, Mr. Torres."

Elliot snorted. "You fucked that up pretty quick, Torres. Stuck sensor on the air lock."

"FleetSys, reset conversation."

"Yes, Mr. Torres."

"Reset all sensors on air lock Six-One West on hull One-Fox."

"Done."

"Open the air lock."

"It is open already."

"God damn it, who are you going to believe, me or your sensor?"

Elliot made a noise.

"Your question is not clear, Mr. Torres."

"FleetSys, terminate conversation. Jesus. All right, Tyrone, I guess you get to belly down and open it yourself."

"Did you ever notice, Torres, how none of the priests ever tries talking to that thing? They always find a terminal."

"Yeah. Okay, you're almost down. Start braking."

We slowed near the rounded nose of One-Fox, and vertigo set back in. It was like landing on the sloping roof of a sky-scraper, with nothing but space hanging beneath its base.

Elliot got his boots onto the hull next to the cable port, then backed up gingerly, trying to remain vertical as he let out the tether from the climber. As he backed further down the slope toward the air lock, it was harder and harder for him remain upright.

"Lean back against the tether, Tyrone."

"Easy for you to say."

"You've never done this with Pham around, have you? First time I got where you are, she kicked my feet out from under me. Sent me over the edge."

"That girl really hates you, doesn't she, Torres?"

"She does it to everyone. Makes you trust your tether."

"Uh-huh. Doesn't sound to me like you minded much."

He made it to the air lock and pushed apart the locking lugs. The door sank inward and a slender ladder slid up over the lip. Elliot grabbed it and it slid back in, then a moment later I followed.

While the lock was named after 61-deck, there was really no such deck. There was just a cramped space under the ship's nose with the locks, cable housing, forward-looking instruments, and a suiting-up area near the top of the lift, where the lift platforms flipped over from up to down. We unsuited and started down.

There was nothing to be seen from the lift while dropping past the gardens. There were, in fact, no lift-stops at all in the gardens; one had to enter at the bottom. There were also no cameras, machines, or—except for emergencies—paging speakers in the gardens. Privacy ethics had built up since launch, and the gardens were sacrosanct.

The industrial decks, however, were brightly lit and noisy. Some ships used that group of decks for entomology labs, like this one, while others contained suit manufacturing, infirmaries, electronics, fiber extrusion, bakeries, and so on.

I stepped from the lift and bumped into Elliot as he made his way around a madly spinning device that nearly filled the deck. It was a screened-in cage at the end of a moving arm, which a bearded man and two stocky children watched intently.

After a minute a solenoid slapped home and the arm stopped. The children raced up to peer inside.

"There's still three of 'em, Mr. Delgado. No, four. Five!"

"Okay," said the man, "you know what to do—five's more

than enough. Give them to the queen, now."

The girl planted her tongue between her teeth, then reached into the cage with tongs, drawing out something that she dropped into a jar the boy held out. It was clear they'd done it many times before. They're being made to grow up too fast, I thought.

Delgado glanced up.

"Hello, Mr. Elliot. Mr. Torres, nice to see you."

"Hello, Ramón." I worked my way around the machine. "What are you up to?"

"Two GBs."

"Two GBs?" It sounded like a candy, or a car.

"Ha!" said Delgado. "I've seen that look before. Listen: two...G...bees. Got it? Okay. We got a notice from Captain Rosler. Mr. Polaski wants to be able to run at two Gs without stopping, so we've got to come up with two-G pollinators. Okay, kids, take a break. Whoops, hand me that phone, please. Hello? Yes? Yes, he is, just a minute please. Mr. Torres, it's Kathy Chan."

I took the phone while Elliot unloaded his samples and Delgado logged them in.

At least a minute after I'd hung up, I was still staring down at the phone. Elliot and Delgado stopped.

"What, Torres?"

I wasn't sure what to say.

"A drone," I said finally.

They looked at me, and then down at the phone, as though hoping it might elaborate. When Delgado spoke, his mouth was so dry I could scarcely hear him.

"And...?"

I shook my head. "They're recording the transmission now. It'll take some time."

We continued to look down at the phone, all three of us now, not knowing what else to do. Ever since the launch, we'd lived with the awful fear that the drones had never even made it to Holzstein's System, or that they'd made it, but hadn't been able to build another torus to return through. And for all my bravado to Polaski, the same question had haunted every one of us all that time: How long would we wait? And if that allotted time expired, what would we do then?

But now a drone had returned, and the next, inevitable question hung in the air: Was there anywhere to go?

I cleared my throat.

"Go and tell your wife, Ramón. Just Elena, no one else. Wait for the announcement. Come on, Elliot, let's go. I want to see what the drones and their mistress have to say to one another."

People and noise were filling the MI deck when we got back—Miller, Chan, Polaski, Peters, half a dozen others. Only Pham, who hadn't been seen for days, was missing. Everyone else was squeezed into the tiny space, poring over a transcription of the drone's message.

I glanced quickly at the communications console. OUTBOUND TRANSMISSION ACTIVE flashed on the screen. Other words scrolled past on the data screen, too fast to see. Miller's new instructions, I was sure, for the drone to take back with it to feed to its fellows.

We finally moved down to the commons deck, where there was more room, and Chan summed up what we'd learned so far.

"The drones made it to Holzstein's and built a new torus. This return messenger hit our solar system very well-positioned for its turnaround for going back, meaning that their new tunnel works extremely well.

"They found three landable planets, as forecast. Limited terraforming has begun on two of them, the third being too heavy. Both of the viables are colder than expected, and will remain cold even after hydrogen conversion produces an atmosphere and water. Limited equatorial zones will be habitable, at best.

"Landable satellites were found throughout the system. No life forms were encountered.

"After the drones set terraforming in motion on the two viables, they appear to have decided there is little left for them to do in such a marginal system, and therein lies some better news.

"They have identified yet another system—coordinates given below—possessing at least one confirmed, ideal Earth-type. A perfect, already habitable planet. As soon as instructions are received via the returning messenger, they plan to rotate their new torus and send a contingent on to that other system."

A gunshot sounded. Elliot was holding a bottle of champagne, unauthorized cargo though it was, and was pouring it into cups.

I took one and looked down at the swirling liquid, feeling a mixture of relief and disappointment both. And, all the while, uneasiness about Miller and her drones. Why, I wondered. They had performed perfectly. Had they not begun terraforming as claimed? Was that it? Was Miller going to hold this other, reportedly perfect planet hostage, taking bids for passage while we rotted on planets left deliberately fallow? I hadn't trusted Anne Miller when she'd arrived on our island, and I didn't trust her now. Not her or Polaski, yet I felt them both slipping beyond my grasp.

"Where's Anne?" I said. "There—Anne!" I made a noise against the table, and lifted my cup.

"A toast," I said. "You are to be congratulated."

"Yes," she said, and raised her cup very slightly.

That was it, then the noise resumed. The specialists began calculating approach windows to the torus, to be used by us and by the three regional fleets that had made it off Earth in the past year. I slipped onto the lift.

The communications console on the MI deck indicated TRANS-MISSION COMPLETE. The transmitted data had stopped scrolling past, leaving on the screen just the tail end of the outgoing instructions.

It was in two columns, one in some highly compressed language, and the other in English with her comments, which wouldn't have been transmitted. A brief section of the comments remained:

...THUS THE CERTAINTY OF DRONE RESISTANCE TO ALIEN FORCE IS TO BECOME A UNIVERSAL CONSTANT OF COLONIZED SPACE. —END MATRIX.

"Do you find that interesting, Edward?"

Miller was standing by the lift, leaning back with her arms folded. She was just a year short of fifty now, though the skin of her face remained uncreased and her figure remained slender and graceful in her white jumpsuit. Her hair was cut very close to her head, and her eyes still sparkled along with the silver earrings. She was as elegant and poised as when I'd met her eight years ago, yet just as hard to read. I gestured to the console.

"Doesn't this seem a little grandiose to you, Anne? 'Universal constant of colonized space?' These are work drones—why this old fantasy of valiant defense against aliens?"

She took a step closer.

"Surely you're aware that our activity must have attracted attention by now," she said. "All the perturbations from the toroidal projectors? You know the odds as well as I do, Mr. Torres, and I would think you'd be glad we'll be so well protected—that there will, after all, be some absolutes in the universe."

I glanced again at the screen.

"So what rules did you send the drones in this decision matrix, Anne? What is it, exactly, that they're going to be capable of to effect this extraordinary resistance?"

"Why such concern, Edward? You know I couldn't have loaded these files for transmission without having them reviewed first by someone with password authority. I certainly haven't been granted such access to the fleet systems."

"Reviewed by whom?"

"Is it important?"

I leaned back and folded my arms. Something moved in the corner of the deck, up near the ceiling. A little spider drone, with its tiny camera, shifting position as I moved.

"Just the same," said Miller, seeming not to notice, "what I've sent them is no great secret. I'm having them teach their offspring to be resourceful, is all. Madhu would be proud of me. They'll be just like us."

Chapter Eleven: THE PROMISED LAND

"Alien force, hah! You take Ice-Lady too serious. That woman speak from her ass, and you people sniff around like pigs."

Pham was drunk. She was slumped against the wall of Charlie Peters' quarters, lecturing from behind glassy eyes. We were waiting for the final approach to the tunnel, and the subject of Miller's transmission to the drones had come up.

"Of course we take her seriously, Tuyet," said Peters with his nearly simple-minded patience. "She has our lives in her hands, yet she is very difficult to understand. That makes her dangerous, and we have every reason to worry."

Pham looked up sharply. "What for you say I don't understand, hah, Mush-Face? Just 'cause you believe bullshit she tell you?"

Suddenly she jerked her head forward, and began massaging the back of her neck.

"Ice-Lady not hard to understand," she said, rolling her head. "I tell you what she like. That woman, what she got is insides all locked up, like little-old-lady virgin. 'Alien force' maybe what she say, but inside she thinking you, me—everybody human. Maybe we alien to her, hah? She think we get inside her, maybe, fuck her in her insides, so she got to make machines that do what she say and keep us out. Same time, she want to think she okay in the head, so she got to make up story about alien people."

She snorted and threw her head against the wall with a crack that made us wince. Her eyes rolled toward the far wall and moved around it with short, jerky movements, the rest of her face slack. Her sleek features were swollen and pale.

Pham hadn't taken well to the months of confinement since we'd broken orbit and begun our sweep past the sun. The close quarters and her voracious appetite for distraction had worn at her endlessly. She was less and less poised, and her customary abuse of

Peters had soured into a small-minded hostility that grated on all of us.

"I don't know," said Elliot, scratching at his chin and squinting at his playing cards. His eyes were bloodshot from the dry air, and there was a hard black stubble on his dark face. "You make the woman sound confused, but personally I don't think she's got a mule's doubt about what she's doing." He drew out a card and set it down deliberately, cocking an eyebrow at Kip.

"That woman is squeaky clean," he went on. "She don't fart or belch or pick her nose, or lust after men. Her cause is good and her shit don't stink, you better believe it."

Kip picked up the card.

"Right," said Chan from behind her book. "She knows not what she does—the last of the great innocents."

"Hah!" Pham looked up. "Innocence," she proclaimed loudly, "lies not in ignorance of our purpose, but in its boundless celebration..."

"...*however black its nature*," finished Peters, "*or vast the ocean of our disquiet*. Aye, you're right. It's very appropriate, that." His face had lit up enthusiastically.

I, in the meantime, was feeling unaccountably bleak. As the moment of our passage neared, the exhilaration of escape had given way to a new certainty that I was in fact leaving something behind, something important and irretrievable. And, too, the cherished fantasy of paradise had now dissolved into the true reality of our predicament: nothing awaited us but barren planets, all too cold or too heavy.

"Attention," said the smooth voice of FleetSys. "Close-up roach to one cheap ass point."

Chan slapped a keyboard and glanced at a screen.

"Close approach to one-G pass-point," she said.

"You got to teach that thing a little in-*flec*-tion," said Elliot, throwing down his hand in disgust. "A little en-*thu*-siasm."

The one-G pass-point was the point at which aborting our blisteringly fast approach to the tiny hole would require turning the fleet ninety degrees—side-on to the torus—then thrusting in the new direction at one G in order to clear the outer edge of the torus without slamming into it. The ships, if not their crews, were in theory capable of aborting from as close as the six-G pass-point, but the up-coming checkpoint was generally considered the start of the committed approach.

Peters pulled his big frame out of his chair and stood up. A spider drone darted out from the corner and disappeared down the lift.

Elliot watched it go. "I wonder about them, sometimes."

"Well, all I know," said Chan, "is that they keep forgetting things. That's what I wonder about."

"I don't think you got to wonder too much, China-Girl," said Pham.

When I didn't follow the others, Chan stopped and looked at me.

What deal had it been, I was wondering, that Polaski had made with Miller? Was he the one who'd approved her final transmission to the drones? Did he know what it contained? And what had she given him in return?

"What, Eddie?" said Chan. "You don't want to watch the machines thread us through the needle?"

"No, I have to be there."

"Take a walk first?"

"All right, if you want."

The garden path spiraled upward amid flowers, vegetables, and dwarf trees, covered overhead by aerobic plants growing from the sunlight panels. Along the outer wall of the ship the gardens climbed gently, but toward the center they became steeper and then terraced, and finally cliff-like in the middle. At the very center was an open shaft filled with vines and orchids. Kip had run on ahead of us, and his skittering sounds filtered down the shaft.

"What is it, Eddie?" said Chan.

I brushed away some ferns and kept walking.

"Damn it, Eddie, I never know what you're thinking any more. And right now we're minutes away from everything you've wanted all along, and you're acting like a stranger to me again. Is it Polaski? What is it?"

"Why did he try and warn them, Chan?"

"Warn them? Oh, you mean Madhu. Oh, Eddie, not again. Look, have you ever thought that maybe Madhu had a higher purpose than our own mission?"

"The night before we left," I said, "he told me something, and then said I'd destroy him for saying it."

"I don't believe that. Look, every captain in the fleet skipped that headcount."

"I don't *get* to skip checklists." I stopped in the middle of the path, then after a moment Chan sat down.

"Do you remember," I said, "how he liked that quote from Deuteronomy? The one about Moses being shown the promised land?"

"Yes."

"Do you remember how it ends?"

She hesitated. "No, I've forgotten."

"He never told us. Pham knew, though. She came out with it the other day, all of a sudden. I don't know why. 'Moses went up from the steppes of Moab to Mount Nebo, and there the Lord showed him the promised land. And the Lord said to him, "This is the land of which I swore to Abraham, Isaac, and Jacob, 'I will give it to your offspring.' I have let you see it with your own eyes, but you shall not cross there."'"

Chan was crying. I couldn't see her face, but I could see the tears where they landed on her hands, folded in her lap.

"We need to reach the new planet, Chan. The one the drones found—"

"No, Eddie!" She spun toward me, her face wet with tears. "You can't do that again! You can't put off your whole life, and mine, and everyone else's, waiting for something better. I know you, Eddie. I know what losing Madhu did to you. You'll be dead to the world forever, just waiting for everything to be perfect. But it's good enough right now—it may be all we ever have, and there are things I want to do before it's too late."

"Chan, it won't be that long—"

"Yes it *will*! Oh, Eddie, why do you think we're doing all this—going through all these awful times? What do you think all the hardships have been for? What did Madhu die for, Eddie? And the kids? Do you even know?"

She took a breath. "Sometimes I don't think you do. It's not to build a perfect life for ourselves, Eddie, or to go out and conquer for the greater glory of Polaski and Rosler. No, don't say anything— it's not. It's for the children, Eddie. Did you know that? The kids aren't some tough little high-G soldiers, the means to some perfect end. They *are* the end, the reason we're doing all this. And I want to adopt one of the orphans, now, before we make them all grow up. I don't want to see you setting your sights again on something so far away we can't reach it, then trampling all over us in your rush to get there. Or is that why it's always too far, Eddie? So that you can never reach it?"

Looking at Chan at that moment, maybe because of the upcoming translation, she seemed suddenly far away, as though speaking from a dream, from beyond a veil. I hardly recognized her.

"Come on, Eddie, deal with it. Deal with whatever it is you keep holding back from, then settle down and take what's in front of you. You're going to end up a bitter old man if you don't, and it'll be too late."

Behind her, Kip looked on uncertainly, rubbing his bare arms as best he could while still holding his flute.

"Chan," I said. She looked up. "It's cold. Tyrone's got it cold for the fall."

Light from the passing decks swept by, turning the lift from light to dark, dark to light, then dark again. Shadows and flickering, framed images of life on the decks, over and over. I held onto the handles and thought about Chan and the child she wanted, but in the strobing light all I could see was the falling baby in the infirmary, and the children in One-Eight as their parents gave up their lives, one after another, to save them from the collapsing vessel. *Why*, I had wondered time and again. Why had those men and women done it, even for children who weren't their own, when they knew that they themselves would die? It was an act at once perfectly natural to me, yet somehow indescribably alien.

Then came an image of the tunnel, swelling before us now to swallow us whole. We would never be the same, I thought. Not I, not

Chan, not Tuyet Pham. Only Polaski would be unchanged, his sights set fixedly on the course I'd set him, unencumbered by the doubts that haunted me, unconcerned by the deaths we'd caused.

I'd come to distrust Polaski deeply, yet I knew that I would not stop him any more than I'd sever my own hand. On the threshold of our passage into the tunnel, there was now another journey to be made, and just as I wouldn't stop Pham for my fascination with her, I wouldn't stop Polaski for my need of him. I was doomed to follow behind him, I thought, hating him as I went, approving of what he did in its every detail.

The familiar voice of a news broadcaster filtered up through the lift as I descended, speaking in the clear, short cadence of the British public schools. Then all at once I was surrounded by the lights of the MI decks, and the voice became clear.

"—conceded," the man was saying, "as the fire entered its forty-seventh day, that no part of the Amazon basin is now expected to survive. That blunt assessment came even as a spokesperson for the environmental policy organization, Worldwatch Institute, announced that the institute are as of this moment unaware of any credible proposals for restoring a self-sustaining atmosphere, now with the critical loss of the rain forests."

Peters had an elbow up on the communications panel, stroking the top of his bald head as he stared at the floor. Anne Miller looked relaxed and was watching me with a hint of a smile, while next to her Pham sat hunched forward, eyes closed and face pale.

Chan sat down next to her, eyes still red and lips tight, and began to wipe a cloth across her screens. Between us sat Elliot, humming to himself through the radio broadcast.

Polaski was watching me.

"Where have you been?" he said.

"Elsewhere."

"Really? Don't go crapping out on us, Torres." *Or else.*

"In economic news," the announcer was saying, "the government of Indonesia are now prepared, according to a Ministry of Trade spokesperson, to release plans for Indonesia's newly developed quantum cell, whether or not the World Enterprise colonists, now in their final hours in the Solar System, transmit to Earth the plans and release codes for the existing batteries as promised. Indonesia's action is believed to come in response to pressure from other Pacific Organization states, and is designed to forestall renewed hostilities should the colonists remain silent. This is in light of mounting tensions between the United States and the Japanese-California coalition regarding secondary markets for the Enterprise batteries."

Mindless columns of digits passed on my screen, unnoticed as I listened to what would be our last news from home. Our former home.

"In related but tragic news today, the constabulary of Wansbeck, Northumberland, disclosed that an early morning explosion on an inter-town bus near Morpeth was the result of yet another spontaneous detonation by an Enterprise battery. Three school children were killed in that explosion. Renewed calls were heard in Commons this afternoon for reintroduction of petrol motors in civilian transport, but the Indonesian announcement earlier in the day served to postpone any debate."

I went on looking at my screen, though I knew that Pham was watching me.

"In other news, a report published today in the Chinese Journal of Microbiology states that clinical trials in the city of Tianjin have demonstrated the efficacy of monoclonal rDNA gene replacement in reversing several forms of malignant cancers. The report goes on to say that the technique is expected to address nearly all forms of the disease, and that therapeutic administration of the procedure will be available worldwide in fewer than eighteen months.

"On a different note, the government of the United States today announced stepped-up measures to stem what it referred to as an 'unstoppable tide' of Mexican boat-persons attempting to reach U.S. shores. Beginning in the early hours of this morning, according to Department of Defense sources, all unauthorized craft approaching U.S. waters are being sunk without warning by cannon or machine-gun fire from U.S. military and Coast Guard vessels, abandoning all past attempts to turn the craft away. No corroboration of the new policy's implementation has so far been obtained by the BBC."

I shut my eyes against the image of cannon fire ripping into families huddled in wooden boats.

"His Majesty today, in remarks before the Royal Archaeological Society, surprised his audience by mentioning the Enterprise colonists, broaching for the first time an issue that may temper the broad condemnation of them heard until now. His Majesty said, in part:

"'While we continue to oppose violence and the practice of economic terrorism in all its forms, we must at the same time take care not to hold too plain a view of a desperately complex issue.

"'We are given pause, then, as more and more we are told the truth of the Earth's condition, when we look upon the departing Enterprise spacecraft and at the regional fleets in their wake, with many thousands of British subjects on board, and at the fleets even now under construction, and understand that they may carry with them not only humankind's great dream of adventure, but our very seed as well. It is for that reason alone, and none other, that I now wish them Godspeed.'

"His Majesty's remarks were received with light applause.

"That is the news at this hour; Greenwich Time is one minute before midnight. BBC World Service, broadcasting on a frequency of eight point seven two five gigahertz from our transmitters in London, will resume at six a.m. tomorrow with the international morning update. Until then, good night. It is now midnight."

There was a pause, then the first deep toll of the bell at the Houses of Parliament echoed through the deck, and faded into a sea of static. Our own faces were grey in the light of our screens, which flickered intermittently around us. The bell tolled again and Chan wiped a hand over her face, her cheeks wet with new tears. Next to her Pham did something I couldn't see on her screen, as though running a finger back and forth through the dust. Her eyes were unfocused, though her jaw muscles worked under the skin.

Elliot was humming a spiritual I'd heard him sing before.

Will the circle be unbroken...

As the bell continued its slow tolling, I tried to focus on the upcoming events—the sudden freefall after the six-G pass-point, the terrifically fast plunge into the narrowing hole of the torus, our speed as we passed though it with no room to spare...none of it seemed real.

The eleventh toll of the bell.

...there's a better home awaiting, in the sky, Lord...

Midnight. The final deep toll of the bell faded away into the static. No one moved. A sob escaped from Chan, and Charlie Peters sighed and shifted in his seat. He was watching Chan, fingering a button on his old vest. Finally he spoke, in his quiet, rolling brogue.

> T'was nothing left o' Ireland, then,
> When sailed we off t' sea,
> But a row o' bloody buzzards, boys,
> A-watching from a tree;
> And a bone-cold mist that whispered, 'Lads,
> Your homes ye'll never see.'

Elliot blew out his breath and pulled himself up to his console. Polaski turned to Peters, who, as best he was able, ran our communications console.

"So did we get the movies?" said Polaski.

Peters frowned and turned to the console.

"Aye, I suppose. Nearly all of them ever made, from the looks of it—we've friends in low places, it seems. Most of the world's libraries, too, if you're interested. Now—what about the plans and release codes? It's time, I should think?"

Polaski started to answer, but I cut him off.

"Send them on a tight beam," I said. "The Chinese fleet isn't to get them."

I turned back to my own console to call up fleet status, but after a minute Peters spoke again.

"Eddie, my boy..."

Everyone was watching me.

"Oh, sorry. 'Esperanza.'"

"Beg your pardon?"

"'Esperanza.' Type it in, and FleetSys will transmit the file."

My face warmed—the code-name sounded silly to me now. Also, I didn't want to care as much as I did that I was giving up our secret. For so many years it had made us invulnerable, and giving it up, it seemed to me, would leave us naked. It only added to my bleak mood.

FleetSys began to say something, but Chan's hand moved to strangle it. A message came up on our screens, instead. CLOSE APPROACH: 4G PASSPOINT. Chan sniffed and dropped back into her seat. Elliot watched her.

"How come," he said, "all them itty-bitty spiders and grass-hoppers around here can talk as good as the girl next door, but we got more'n a hundred tons of fleet MI we can hardly talk English to?"

I glanced at the communications monitor. The file had been sent. Then almost right away I looked at it again...something on the screen had changed. I studied it from across the deck, but couldn't think what.

"Let me ask you this," Chan said. "Would you want a spider drone threading us through the torus at 113,000 kilometers per hour?"

"No, ma'am," said Elliot.

I began to count lines of information on the monitor, thinking maybe that the number of them had changed, and nothing more.

"No," said Chan, "you wouldn't. FleetSys is conventional MI, with no flair for language. No guessing, no judgment calls, no compromises—no assumptions about what you meant to say, no faith that you'll puzzle out what it says to you. On the other hand, the spiders are little packets of EI. All flair, quick with everyday judg-ments, but risky little bimbos when it comes to the hard stuff."

"You'll enjoy meeting the real drones, Mr. Elliot," said Miller. "They are very much like us, you know. And backed up by extraor-dinary computational power, as well. Perfect creatures—unlike Ms. Pham's opinion of me, I might add." So the little spider drone had been listening when we'd been talking about Miller an hour ago.

I counted the lines a second time and leaned closer, a warn-ing sounding inside my head.

"What about Bella?" said Elliot. "Cole's MI. She sounded like the girl next door, too, but she was controlling an air operations zone."

"Charlie?" I said. But I'd spoken too quietly, and my words

were lost.

"Bella was canned," said Chan. "Canned knowledge and canned grammar. You couldn't have taught her to play checkers, even."

Peters himself interrupted at this point, turning impatiently to me and then to Polaski.

"Why not the other fleets?" he said. "We promised them the codes, too, including the Chinese. Didn't we?"

"Fuck 'em," said Polaski. "They can't stop us. We'd end up plastered all over their precious torus if they tried."

Peters reached for his keyboard.

"*Don't!*" I shouted. "Jesus, *that's* what that is! That's impossible! Quick, someone put the comm overhead—"

Communications status blinked onto the big screen.

"Look there. The data group in green, at the bottom—does anyone see it?"

"Tunnel telemetry," said Miller.

"Yes. Synchronization data between the torus and the fleets. Each line shows telemetry for one customer. Look at the first one— that's us, FleetSys talking to the tunnel. The characters on the left— zero-alpha-six-zero—number of seconds to translation. About forty-four minutes. Look at the next line."

"NA/C," said Chan.

"Yes. North America-Commonwealth. Six hours out, right where they're supposed to be. Next one is at niner-niner-two-eight— what's that?"

"Eleven hours," said Elliot. "Southern Hem."

"Africa and friends, right. Then bringing up the rear as agreed, sixteen hours out—GCP."

"Greater Chinese People, a.k.a. PRC," said Chan. "So who—" She cut herself off.

"Yes. So who is that?"

There was one more line.

"It came up a couple of minutes ago, at all-foxes. Eighteen hours out, right up PRC's ass. Right where no one's supposed to be."

Elliot rubbed his jaw.

"You know who that's gotta be."

"Yes, I know, and it can't be."

A squeal came from the radios, and David Rosler's voice blared onto the deck. Pham jerked up to listen.

"Torres," he said. "You got that telemetry?"

I hit One-Zero on my armrest. "Yes, we got it. Stand by, Rosler."

I hit Three-Zero. "Flight Leader Bates."

"Bates."

"Permission to talk to one of your skippers. Tawali."

"Yes, of course. Is it the new telemetry?"

"Yes." I punched Three-Bravo. "Captain Tawali."

"Yes."

"Sayid, listen. Someone's locked onto the tunnel, eighteen hours out. FleetSys has their telemetry. You've got the good radioscope people, Salfelder and Fiedler. I want to know who's back there."

"Hello, Torres, this is Fiedler. We can't do it—Southern Hem's in the way. The only ones with a clear shot are North-Am-Common and the Chinese. Which means NA/C."

"All right." I stared at the screen again. "God *damn* it, how did they get there?"

I picked a new frequency, manually this time.

"Commander Dorczak."

Carolyn Dorczak was an American, the commander of the biggest fleet—the North Americans, together with the former British Commonwealth, who'd joined them after their break with the Europeans.

"Good morning, Ed," said Dorczak. "I was expecting your call. You can't see who's come on line there, and you want us to look. Okay—we're putting out the big dish right now. We should have a hull-count pretty quick. And as soon as you've finished sending us the battery release codes, we'd be happy to pass it along."

I pushed my microphone up and nodded to Peters.

"Just them," I said. "'Esperanza-dash-NAC.' No slash." I pulled the mike back down.

"It's on its way, Commander."

"I'm sure it is, Ed."

I stabbed at the armrest.

"Bates."

"Yes."

"Tell me if I've got this right. When the drone came back a few months ago and we broke orbit, it was at least two days later before we aimed a tight beam at NA/C and gave them the information, knowing that at best they could hit the tunnel six hours behind us."

"About five," said Bates.

Chan reached for her keyboard—she'd seen what I was leading up to.

"All right, five. Then a week later, we did the same for Southern Hem, then the Chinese, stacking them six hours one behind the other."

"Yes."

"Then a *month* later we broadcast the all-clear publicly, so that anyone else who'd made it to orbit could follow. If I remember it right, no matter where they were in the system at that point, they could arrive at best eight days behind the Chinese, taking their chances that the Chinese had left the tunnel open."

Chan nodded as she typed.

"That's right," said Bates, "except that we've got someone only hours behind the Chinese. Which means someone else transmitted the all-clear, too. Except that—"

"'Except' is right. Stand by." A red light had come on next to my console.

"Yes, Commander," I said.

"Well, guess what," said Dorczak. "Those mealy-mouthed little dung beetles made it off the dirt, after all."

"The Europeans."

"The Europeans. One hundred fourteen ships' worth."

Chan and I looked at each other.

"That's not all," said Dorczak. "Our people got some pretty strange readings taking that count. I don't know what exactly— they're putting out another dish now. We'll be back."

"Thank you."

Polaski was restless. "Come on, Torres, what was that all about with Bates, before?" He looked like he really didn't know.

"Someone had to have put out the all-clear, except what?"

Chan answered without looking up.

"We would have heard it," she said.

"Begging your pardon?" said Peters.

"We would have heard it," said Chan, looking up now. "If one of the fleets had sent a broadcast in all directions, we would have heard it. Whoever gave the Europeans the information did it on a tight beam."

The deck was quiet while the idea took root.

"Which means," I said, "that someone knew exactly where the Europeans were."

The red light went on again. "Unfortunately," I said, "that's still not the half of it. Yes, Commander?"

"You're not going to believe this," she said, "but sixty-two of those ships are cold."

"Cold?" A chill crept up along my spine as I thought of the drone ships.

"Cold," she said, "as in no human life."

"Carolyn," I said, glancing at Miller, "are we talking about liquid-nitrogen-type cold? Even after the solar fly-by?"

"Hang on."

"No," she said after a minute. "Ambient temperature. A little warming from the engines, is all."

Polaski pulled down his microphone. "Maybe they all got killed," he said.

"No," said Dorczak. "We also probed for density, and those ships came back nearly solid. I mean, they are *heavy*."

"All right, Commander, thank you. Did you get the release codes for the batteries?"

"Of course."

I disconnected and looked around.

"You said," said Polaski, "that sending information to the Europeans on a tight beam was only half of it. So what's the rest? Come on."

Chan answered for me.

"It came from this fleet," she said.

"Good Lord," said Peters. "That doesn't seem very likely,

does it? Surely we'd have a record of such things?"

"Yes."

"Including what ship it came from?"

"Yes," she said. "It came from Bolton's."

Horns blared from the ceiling.

06.00 SGF PASSPOINT +00:00:07. OVERRIDE OPTION CANCELED. STAND BY FOR ZERO THRUST.

I was still watching Chan.

"*Madre de Dios,*" I said, my voice drowned out by the horns. "What's happening?" Someone on the inside was advising the Europeans, just as someone had advised them before their raid on the island, telling them where to attack.

"Hey, good buddy." Elliot was tapping a pencil against my screen, where he'd brought up the free-fall checklist.

"All right, thank you. Um—ship's drones secured..." I looked up at Miller.

"They're not *my* drones, Edward."

"Jesus. Chan?"

"Stand by."

There were forty-eight seconds left—we were way behind.

Thwack. A spider drone magnetized itself to the ceiling, while Elliot passed out paper sacks.

"*Use* them this time, boys and girls. I'm not cleaning out the filters again."

"Drones secure," shouted Chan, stuffing loose items into pouches along with the others. Peters had heaved himself across the communications console to grab for Kip's harness.

"Fluids and pumps!"

"Done," said Elliot.

"Quarters—"

We were falling.

There was no deafening siren, no wrenching maneuver, no change in sound. Our seats had disappeared, was all, and we were falling. I grabbed the edge of the console, but it didn't help. I pictured us plummeting downward, twisting in the wind, plunging closer and closer to a nightmarish impact... My knuckles turned white, and my legs tensed for the crash.

But we were, in fact, perfectly still. We weren't falling at all—the thrust from our engines had stopped, was all, and we were at rest.

I eased my grip and choked back the bile, knowing that the worst was over. The first tingling of euphoria crept into my toes and the backs of my knees.

Buckles snapped and Pham twisted her way out of her seat. She thrust herself across the deck, arching her back almost double to jackknife up into the lift. It was a stunning display of skill, remembered during all our months of confinement, with the power and grace of a cat leaping for freedom.

"Pham!" shouted Elliot. But with a flick of her arm she was gone up the ladder.

There was a rancid smell on the deck. Peters was bent double, wiping at his mouth and holding his bag between shaking fingers.

"Oh, Christ," said Elliot. "I've got a light on a suit." I looked at him, not understanding. Where had Pham gone?

"She's suiting up," he said.

We looked at the mission clocks. Five minutes. Chan looked at each of us in turn.

"I don't understand," she said.

"Six-One East," said Elliot. "Air lock cycling."

I didn't answer. Whatever Pham intended, it had all at once lit a spark of interest in me, a bright flame of anticipation against the bleak horizon of my mood, against the long months of monotony. She was, I thought, surely about to die.

I pulled down my microphone and reached out to change to suit frequency, but the motion sent me sideways and I could no longer reach.

"Pham," said Elliot into his mike.

She didn't answer.

"What the fuck is she doing?" said Polaski, agitated in his seat. "Come on, people, get her down."

"FleetSys," I said, "seal the outer locks." I was certain it was too late, but I said it anyway.

"Yes, Mr. Torres," said FleetSys.

This was followed by a long pause.

"Permanently or temporarily?" it said.

"Forget it, Torres," said Elliot. "She's out."

Four minutes left.

Peters coughed weakly. "For heaven's sake, she'll be pulled apart by fields or something, won't she?"

"No," I said. I was looking up at the empty overhead screen, wondering, even as I stared at it, why I'd looked in the first place. Pham's tiny body, I was thinking, would be crushed between the ring and the giant ship, turned to dust in the heat of its passage. Unless she got out in front.

"We won't feel any forces at all going through," I said. "The problem comes afterwards." I remembered why I'd looked at the screen.

"Let's get a picture, Chan. Forward cameras."

The image snapped to life and steadied, showing no sight of Pham. Centered starkly on the screen, however, was the torus. It filled the picture, overwhelming in its size and regularity, its white shape cut sharply across its middle by its own shadow. It was more than 1,500 miles across, yet where it tapered inward, farther and farther to diminish into a seemingly solid point at its center, there was no sign at all of the hole through which we were to pass. Yet it was rushing toward us with such nerve-shattering speed that we could only stare, scarcely able to breathe.

The ratio of the torus' overall size to the size of the still invisible hole in its center gave some clue to its power. It would deliver more energy than any device ever before built, yet that entire energy would be focused on the tiny thread of its axis, and only for the incomprehensibly brief instant we would occupy it. It would tear us out of the Solar System, I thought, sucking at our insides, ripping us bodily from our pasts...

"There she is."

Pham's space-suited figure had driftedout forward of the ship. Needles of flame from her jets glinted against the gold foil of her tether, drifting out behind her.

Three minutes.

"Pham," said Elliot.

No answer.

"Pham, listen. As soon as we're through we have to maneuver, and you're going to have to be off that tether."

The speaker crackled.

"I crazy, maybe, Mr. Elliot, but not stupid."

She sounded perfectly reasonable, and I was surprised. Anne Miller was watching me with something like amusement. Charlie Peters, face white and bathed in sweat, cast worried glances at the screen while he fussed with Kip's harness.

Two minutes.

The tapering funnel in the center of the torus filled the screen, still a thousand miles away. A faint, syncopated ticking came through the walls of the ship, as its jets adjusted our course a hundred times a second, calculating each correction to the millimeter.

Pham had reached the end of her tether and was facing into the maw of the tunnel, her arms and legs spread apart like a skydiver's. No sign of the passageway through the torus had appeared.

Then from the speakers came a wild, drawn-out scream from the bottom of her lungs, a yell of total abandon, on and on and on, scarcely human. Challenging, triumphant.

Safe inside the ship, I shrank back from the screen as the torus swallowed us with its frightening speed. Pham arched her spine and threw back her head, spreading her limbs even farther.

For an instant, then, I thought I knew what she must be feeling. It was the thrill of perfect, utter vulnerability, straining forward with all her might into the fury of her own passage. I knew it in a moment of perfect clarity, and it frightened me.

A black spot appeared in the center of the funnel.

"*Haieee!*" screamed Pham, "straight up the crack of God!"

Peters coughed, and we were inside the torus. The passage closed around us and pressed inward as if to squeeze the very life from us, hurtling past in a blur of speed beyond comprehension. The spot grew into a narrow tunnel. A light appeared at its end.

"Perhaps," whispered Peters shakily, "'tis the face of God, instead."

In an instant the light beyond the passageway had swelled like a balloon to become the surface of a star, filling the screen and blinding us, searing into its surface the silhouette of Pham and her tether, her final scream filling the air.

The star receded. Points of light near to it receded as well, and the smaller ones disappeared into the darkness altogether. It was as if a telescoping lens had been drawn suddenly back.

Then the star floated alone. It looked much too far away, and too cold.

No one spoke. Heartbeat after heartbeat passed and we stared at the star and at Pham's body, floating limply at the end of her tether, her suit barely visible in the dim light. The tunnel was gone.

Then all at once the picture in front of us was replaced by a complicated, shifting diagram of orbital vectors and trajectories, all of them leading into the center of Holzstein's Star.

"Tyrone," I said, "go and get her. Stand by for maneuvering at...one and a half Gs." I was having trouble concentrating.

"Charlie, as soon as One-Zero's through, tell Rosler I want the listeners on One-Six to identify all drone transmissions, and down-load their positions to Anne. We need to talk to them, and we don't have much time before deciding where we're going to put down. Then talk to Tawali. I want a visual of that other planet in the next system, patched through to here.

"Then when Seven-Zero's through," I said, "I want to talk to Bolton."

Chan was looking at something over my shoulder, rubbing her arms as though cold, the way she'd done in the gardens a few hours ago.

On the wall-screen behind me was a picture of the Holzstein system. The star itself hung in a corner of the screen, smaller and cooler than the sun we'd left behind. A few other stars hung in the background, but on the whole the system looked too empty.

I was about to ask her why she'd positioned the sun so far off center, when something in another corner caught my eye. Barely visible against the background was a pitted, nearly black sphere, dull and motionless against the darker space behind it. No features were visible on it beyond an uneven, lighter grey at the poles. It was Holzstein-IV, the planet the drones had believed to be uninhabitable.

"One-Six is through," said Peters. "They're reeling out the antennas now."

Elliot spoke at the same moment as Peters, his voice thin and reedy from someone else's headset. My hand shot out for the speaker switches, but the movement was too fast and I spun away again. I groped for the ALL switch on my armrest.

"Is she all right?" I said to the entire fleet.

"Take it easy," said Elliot. His voice came from every speaker. "She's fine."

"All right," I said. "Okay."

I righted myself and reset the switch. "Stand by for maneuvering."

"Three-Bravo's through," said Peters. "Radio dishes are going out."

I accepted FleetSys' proposed spacing maneuver, just as Polaski launched a pencil at an unused sick-bag floating above us. Suddenly the ship lurched forward, then rotated and lurched again, and the pencil and the bag slammed into Chan's console. Then they were floating again.

"Mr. Torres, this is Lou Fiedler. We've got a lock on the coordinates the drones gave us for the planet in the next system. Patching through on channel thirty-one, visual, color-corrected. It'll take a while, though."

It did take a while. We put the image up on the big overhead screen, to find it completely dark except for a sprinkling of dots around the edge of a large circle. Slowly it filled in.

"One photon at a time," said Fiedler. "It's like taking a picture of a flea on a searchlight. Good position, though, almost full-face. Terminator's on the upper-right."

When the circle had filled in to become a pale, even disk, it took on colors—a deep, rich blue, which in turn took on wisps of white and green.

Pham drifted down out of the lift shaft. She looked flushed and alive and was followed down by Elliot. They stopped to watch the image of the planet unfolding on the screen.

It had filled in enough now to have texture and shadows, and the snaking outlines of continents began to lace the blue oceans.

"Generous God in heaven," whispered Peters as the image grew out of the darkness, "what a thing of beauty that is."

"And how many years away," said Chan, a warning tone in her voice.

It really was beautiful, like a gem through a jeweler's glass. The oceans shaded from a deep Persian blue in their depths to a silky cerulean in the shallows, and seemed to sparkle. Mountain ranges glistened with snow. It was like the visions that grow from the unformed blackness of dreams.

I met Chan's eyes. She held my gaze for a moment, then looked down at her hands in her lap. I turned back to the blue and green sphere. I was struck by its calmness, and by how few clouds drifted across its face.

It had struck Elliot, too.

"We could call it 'Fairweather,'" he said.

"That's very common," said Miller.

"I'm very common, myself," said Elliot. He sighed. "So make it Latin or something."

"'Luciditas,'" said Peters. "Fair weather is 'luciditas.'"

"'Lucidity' for a planet?" said Polaski. A light blinked on my communications panel, but I ignored it.

"Or else 'Serenitas,'" said Peters.

We looked at the shimmering image. It was clear and perfect and new, and over a hundred-million-million miles away—at the far end of another journey not even known to be possible, even by the drones.

"Eddie," said Peters. I went on watching, not wanting to look away.

"Eddie, One-Six called. They say there aren't any drones. None, anywhere. They're all gone."

Chapter Twelve: OF KINGS AND COMMON THIEVES

"Perhaps the drones just have nothing to say." Miller's earrings glinted in the red light.

"That won't wash, Anne. We've had the antennas out all night. More than thirty thousand drones entered this system, and you're going to tell us they've had nothing to say to one another in fourteen hours?"

Her eyes darted from one of us to the other. They were glassy and bloodshot, and so uneasy that I'd begun to believe she really didn't know what had happened to her drones.

"Maybe they're on the far side of one of the planets," she said.

I sighed and rubbed at my own eyes. They stung from the bad air, which was hot and stank of vomit and sweat.

"That won't wash, either," said Chan, pulling off her headset and looking down at a scrap of paper.

"We've found the new torus the drones built, out between Holzstein-IV and -V. We queried it about activity, and it reports passing over a thousand vessels into that next system, the Serenitas system. The last one went through more than two days ago." She put the paper down.

"That's all of the original drone ships, plus six hundred that they must have built. Which is more than the 'contingent' the messenger claimed they would send."

"Oh, man." Elliot dropped his head into his arms. "We are *fucked*."

"Hey!" Polaski motioned to Pham where she was curled up in her seat. "Somebody kick her awake and send her for coffee."

"No, no," said Peters. "Let the girl have her rest. Come along, Kipper, old son, let's stretch our legs a bit, hm?"

Chan waited till they were gone, then picked up the paper again.

"The torus also reports having been rotated to send a vessel back to Earth—"

"Our messenger," said Elliot.

"—twice."

Elliot looked at her blankly. "Twice?"

"Twice."

"So we must have just missed the second one."

"No," said Chan. "It went back more than three months ago."

A grasshopper drone jackknifed itself off the lift and clattered onto the deck, carrying a cluster of coffee balloons on its back. "Bimbo," it said cheerfully. A light blinked on my console.

"Jesus," I said. "We've got to make decisions, and I don't know what's going on. We can't put NA/C off much longer." I acknowledged the call.

"Well?" said Carolyn Dorczak. Her voice was even, no longer friendly. "Are you ready to discuss your plans yet? Or are we going to stay in this parking orbit forever?"

"All right," I said, "let's see what we can work out." And figure out how not to have to lie, I thought.

"I'd like to put you up on visual," she said. "I've got quite a few people here."

In other words, Commander, you want to watch my eyes. "All right," I said. I pressed a switch and a blue light began to flash near the top of my console. Dorczak's face came up on a screen on the far wall, her eyes on something below the camera. She was a plain but competent-looking woman, with unruly dark hair and intelligent brown eyes, and a way of pursing her lips in a half-smile while she thought.

"So," she said, and looked into the camera.

"All right, here's what we've got. The latest information from the drones is that the twin planets in this system—Holzstein-II and -III—remain equally hospitable, with water and atmospheric gasses being produced at the poles. Simple algaes and minimum air pressure exist in the lower equatorial regions. Prognoses are reasonably good." It was, of course, technically true, but nothing we hadn't learned months earlier.

Dorczak looked away to listen to someone off-screen, then

turned back with her pursed lips and her cryptic smile.

"I guess the real question, Ed, is what are your intentions? Where are you going to put down?"

"I think," I said, "that we're sufficiently satisfied with the drones' accuracy that we're willing to take our lead from you and the others. You know that our ultimate interest is in the next system, and it may be that Holzstein-III is a little better positioned for the jump to it, but just the same we'll let you and the others pick your landing sites first."

Dorczak relaxed visibly and gave a nod to someone off-camera.

"That's good, Ed. That's very good. I'm glad to hear you say that. So maybe we should get Southern Hem on the line?"

"Yes, but in just a minute. What about the Chinese—are you talking to them at all?"

"Not much. But we do have something of a...foreign affairs department, if you will, that feels the Chinese are only interested in their status vis-à-vis future colonists coming out from Earth, and that they expect you to head for H-III just as you said. So what we think they'll do is grab the other one for themselves, H-II." She glanced above the camera. "They just started arriving, by the way. Magic, isn't it—ships appearing out of nothing in the middle of space? Anyway, the Europeans will be right behind them. So, now you tell me: what do you think the Europeans are up to?"

"I can't help you on that one. What do your people say?"

She shrugged. "First of all, we're pretty sure their attack on your base in the Pacific was designed to get control of the drones. They didn't think they could trust you with them."

The idea took me by surprise; we'd always assumed they were after the batteries.

"Given that they failed," said Dorczak, "we believe that they've now come prepared to do their own terraforming, in order not to be dependent on anyone. We think that's what the heavy equipment is for."

"Maybe," I said. "But why their mad rush for the tunnel?"

"You said it yourself—they don't trust the Chinese not to cripple it behind them. In any case, if the Europeans are planning to take care of themselves, then we don't think they'll be a factor in where the rest of us put down. Shall we talk to Southern Hem, see if we can nudge them toward the second planet to leave H-III for us?"

"All right. Who've you been dealing with over there?"

"Sort of a revolving door with them, isn't it? A fellow named Lal Singh. 'Your Excellency' to the likes of you and me."

Another screen came to life on our far wall, showing the back of a bronze-colored head plastered with thin, oily hair. After a moment the head whipped around to show the wild, deep-set eyes of His Excellency Lal Singh, who coughed once sharply and then stared first down at his own screen, then at a point somewhere above the camera. A second face, broad and very black, bobbed in and out, trying to insert itself into the picture.

"So *there* you are, Madame," said Singh finally. "And Admiral Torres. You have kept me waiting a very long time."

"But you've just now come through—" I started, but Dorczak cut me off.

"Yes, Your Excellency," she said, "we have. We wanted to be sure you'd had ample time to survey the system for yourselves, so that you might give us your insight on the best landing sites."

Singh glared above the screen for several seconds. "Just so," he said finally, drawing himself up with an air of newly-discovered importance. "Before we announce our findings, however, it would at the very least be amusing to know what your own drones have had to say, Admiral Torres." He glowered at the tops of our heads.

"They tell us first of all, Your Excellency, that there is more than enough room for us, and for North America and Commonwealth, and for Southern Hemisphere as well—"

"I would wish you to note, Gentlemen," said Singh, either overlooking or dismissing Dorczak's sex, "that India is first of all a member of the Commonwealth of Nations, and is secondly not at all in the southern hemisphere. So I will assume that the fleets to which you refer are those of the English-Speaking Peoples and of the Great Southern Continents. Very well, then. Tell me, Admiral—where exactly do you intend to settle?" He blinked rapidly several times.

"We will be happy to discuss—" I said, but Dorczak cut me off again.

"On the second planet, Excellency." She spoke with the well-oiled sincerity of a professional minion, leaning forward and folding her hands neatly on the top of her console. "While we feel that the third planet should provide a wealth of very, very good opportunities—"

"We will be the judges of that, Miss Dorczak. If Holzstein-III is such a fine place, then you should find yourselves very happy there, should you not?" He drew himself up in his seat. "Very well, Admiral. You may inform your subordinates that the people of the Great Southern Continents have claimed the second planet of the Holzstein system, including all of its satellites, drones and sensibilities."

Without another word his screen blinked out, and I was left looking into Dorczak's sincere eyes.

"Well," she said sincerely, "it seems that we lesser peoples have been relegated to H-III. *Tant pis.* See you in orbit, 'Admiral.'"

Dorczak blinked out, too, and our deck was left quiet except for Pham's snoring and the hiss of the ventilators.

"'Sensibilities?'" said Elliot.

"Do you get the feeling," I said, "that Dorczak's people are very well organized?"

"Yes," said Polaski. "Quite a challenge, isn't it? All right, listen up. Chan, work with Rosler. Program for a quarter-G while the fleet moves into landing configuration, then back up to 1.2 G for a braking course into near–H-III orbit. In the meantime, Torres and Pham—wake her up, will you, Miller—Torres and Pham and I are taking a shuttle to pay a visit to Bolton. And I don't want him to know we're coming."

The shuttle stank of burnt insulation and ozone from the power cells. We couldn't remember how to set its maximum maneuvering thrust, so it smashed us back and forth against the gratings and conduits all the way down along the fleet to Bolton's ship. Then we forgot that docking while the fleet was under thrust meant that the shuttle would roll its nose upward to place its belly against the ship's air lock, so without warning it dropped us into the after machinery compartment. By the time we stepped onto Bolton's immaculately clean commons, we were streaked with oil and graphite.

Still, throughout the ride I was preoccupied by something entirely different. We'd backed ourselves into a decision to settle on the good planets until word came from the drones, and it was a decision that left me uneasy. I knew that however much of a consensus there was for moving on to Serenitas later, settling down in the meantime would take on a certain inertia—and that inertia, I knew, would be hard to break. It was something I wanted to avoid at all costs. I took Polaski aside, leaving Pham to fidget and stare out the portholes.

"You don't give orders without my permission, Polaski," I said. He raised an eyebrow very slightly. "Especially when we haven't decided where to land."

The eyebrow came back down and interest flickered briefly across his face, before being extinguished.

"There's only three planets we can land on," he said.

"That's right."

He studied me now with no expression at all. "Maybe," he said, "we should have a temporary base somewhere. Somewhere that'll toughen up the troops a little? Keep our options open?"

"All right," I said. "If you think they need it."

A dozen of the ships' complement were lounging in Bolton's commons when we stepped aboard, all of them from the Special Operations Engineers he'd put together years earlier. Even with the time since they'd last seen combat, they were an alert-looking group, wearing t-shirts and denims or their dark green jumpsuits. Technical manuals and game boards lay on the tables, the pages leafing back and forth in the quarter-G thrust. The troops gave us a polite scrutiny.

A bright flicker of light came from the wall-sized entertainment screen to one side of the deck. It showed a view of the entire fleet, white against the black of space. The message 7F-FWD REALTIME in the corner indicated it was being taken from the aftermost ship of Bolton's flight, which was also the last ship in the fleet, and the one with the most panoramic view of all the others.

The fleet was no longer strung out in a line, but with the

firing of thousands of attitude jets it was reforming into clusters of eight ships each. The ships in each cluster had pulled even with and parallel to one another, arranged like the fence posts of a very tall, circular corral, with about sixty feet separating each ship from the one next to it around the ring. Impossibly delicate-looking trestle-work booms had cantilevered out from three places on each hull, reaching out to mate with corresponding receptacles on the next ship clockwise, thus locking each cluster into the corral shape with eight posts. This eight-point configuration was the only way the slender ships could land and remain upright.

One of the ships in the nearest cluster had what looked like a tick fastened to its side, which I soon realized was our own shuttle, fastened to the air lock next to where we stood.

The flicker of light came again. It wasn't from the attitude jets, but from arc welders in one of the other clusters.

"Flight One," said Bolton from behind us. "Second wing." He was standing in the center of the commons watching us with his hands behind his back. He still had traces of his schoolboy look about him, but his face had hardened over the past few years, and behind his calm gaze there was an unmistakable air of power and command. Next to him stood the slight, dark-haired Roscoe Throckmorton, with his sharp nose and quick, ferret's eyes.

"It has only seven ships," said Bolton, gesturing to the screen.

He was right. It was Hull One-Eight that had collapsed in Earth orbit, and now the seven-ship wing's couplings were having to be modified.

The deck shook with a *clunk*, followed by the whining of a motor. Polaski and I turned to find its source, but neither Pham nor the others moved at all.

Throckmorton nodded pleasantly toward the screen. "We're on 30-deck," he said. "Amidships."

On the screen, three booms were hinging out from our ship, the center one coming from a point near the shuttle. After watching their progress for a minute, Polaski turned to Bolton.

"We want to talk to you in private."

Bolton's eyes flickered almost imperceptibly, but other than that he showed no reaction. "We are quite private here."

Polaski glanced around. "All right," he said. "Someone's

giving the Europeans information. Information it's not in our interest for them to have."

"Yes," said Bolton.

"Someone on this ship."

This time Bolton showed no reaction at all, although after a minute he rolled up onto his toes and then slowly let himself back down.

"Indeed," he said.

No one spoke for a time. It seemed as though Bolton was staring through the walls as he thought. Then his focus returned to Polaski, and he relaxed and rocked onto his toes again.

"You think," he said, "that it was one of us."

A phone blinked. Roscoe Throckmorton picked it up, then after a moment handed it to Bolton. Bolton listened, too, then handed it back. He spoke over his shoulder without taking his eyes off of Polaski.

"Jamie, our guests' shuttle is blocking the coupling. Take it for a bit of a ride, would you, until the maneuver is done?"

A petite blond woman with lively eyes and a quick step slipped into the air lock.

Then suddenly Bolton's eyes snapped back to the screen. His move was so sudden that the rest of us spun to look as well, searching for something out of place. My first thought involved the shuttle, but as we watched, the shuttle fired its engines normally and moved away.

It was something else that had caught Bolton's attention. Sweeping in toward the distant arc welders was a column of odd, powdery light, pulsing faintly and reaching clear across the screen. It was almost like a flaw in the picture, an illusion, hard to keep in focus.

Then all at once the column of light was in among the arc welders and sweeping across one of the ships. The hull turned a brilliant white where it touched, and suddenly a cloud of gas and debris blossomed outward as the ship disintegrated.

Unable to digest what was happening, I found myself thinking idly about relative decompression rates, about whether any of the ship's emergency lift seals had shot home in time.

But now the strange light had disappeared, and my attention shifted as Jamie fired our shuttle's engines to their full thrust to clear the ships. Then the column of light was back, much nearer now and closing in on the shuttle. *Heat-seeking.* Then the shuttle was gone. too, disintegrated.

We have no defenses, I thought, and started to move. No defenses at all.

Our ship lurched and threw me to the floor. One of our sister ships glowed, and its three booms, torn loose from our ship, bent and flapped as if in a wind.

Bolton was shouting.

"FleetSys, instructions! Maneuvering, Wing One. Rotate, conical separation, three Gs four seconds, one point five indefinite. Execute!"

He was making for the lift, but the deck tilted and he was sucked down as if pushed by a giant hand. I crashed down on top of him, and for four long seconds I couldn't breathe as we clawed our way toward the lift.

The acceleration stopped and we moved to the MI decks, Bolton shouting his staccato instructions to FleetSys all the way.

The ship tilted again and Bolton shoved me into a seat. His duty officers were working on a positions display, in one corner of which a string of black dots was unraveling against the white background—our own fleet—while thousands of miles away another cluster moved rapidly by.

In between the two clusters floated a pair of small dots. An indicator arrow moved across the screen toward them, then changed shape and snapped into a rectangle around them. The screen changed to black at that moment, with the two dots now white. The picture zoomed in, re-centering again and again, and soon the dots elongated into the familiar white pencil shapes of ships.

"Bastards," said Bolton, and pulled down his microphone. The two ships were large on the screen now, blurry and jittery at the extreme magnification. Targeting markers moved in and bracketed them, labeling them T1 and T2.

"Prepare for sustained thrust," said Bolton. "FleetSys, instruction Parthian shot, targets—" he squinted at the screen "—T2 before T1. Four Gs, pulses at maximum. Stand by." He kicked at his seat-locking lever and shoved his hands into control gloves, then looked swiftly around the deck.

"Execute."

Like a hammer blow, the ship slammed into my back and crushed the breath out of me, sending a burning pain up through my neck. My arms were sucked down off the armrests like sacks of sand, while my eyes were ground into the backs of their sockets. I had a sudden sick memory of the centrifuge at the Army school, and as the pain spread out through my back I remembered, too, the blinding, all-consuming pain I'd felt after the first weeks in the crowded refugee boats.

Bolton's ship began to vibrate like a plucked string, and I pictured it shattering. My impulse was to reach for the controls and stop the giant engine, but with a feeling of sickening helplessness I understood why Bolton had become so skilled at talking to the fleet MI. I couldn't move.

The two targets grew quickly on the screen, then something else sent a chill through me and washed away the other pain. A column of light had sprung from the end of target number two, and it was turning toward us. Dorczak had been wrong. The Europeans hadn't brought terraforming equipment at all, but particle beam weapons.

The beam swept closer. From the blur of digits on the screen, we had too far to go. "FleetSys," said Bolton between his teeth. "Instruction spiral execute."

A sideways motion was added to the crush of acceleration. White spots spread across my vision. The targets began corkscrewing on the screen; we were accelerating toward them along a spiraling course the weapon couldn't track. FleetSys' calculations for the course must have been stunningly complex, I thought. Bolton had not been wasting his time.

"FleetSys broadcast," said Bolton, and his next words boomed through the ship. "Expect turnover and maximum thrust.

Maximum thrust? Surely this was it. Already I felt I couldn't take the pain any longer, as though my heart would burst from the weight of it. I wanted it to stop, no matter what the cost.

Now the target ships filled the entire screen. The apparently unarmed ship, target number one, fired its engines and moved away. An instant later the weight vanished and I was falling. My stomach heaved, and the bile sprayed out in a cloud across the deck. We pitched forward drunkenly as the ship rotated end-over-end, the turnover, and then I understood what Bolton was going to do: the Parthian shot. He had programmed the ship to burn an enemy with the ship's own engine, pulsing its hundred-mile lance of flame toward the other ship at maximum power.

Our targets swam back into view through the after cameras, then in the very next instant I was slammed backward by a hammer blow of unimaginable force, and passed out.

Blackness finally lifted, leaving an awful pain. Then I was slammed into the seat again. I came out of it one more time to find myself choking on my own blood, then the blow came again, and again, and again, until I lost all sense of time, all sense of anything but the pain.

The darkness lifted for the last time. My sleeve came away from my mouth soaked in blood. Others coughed, or retched, or gasped for breath.

Across from me sat Polaski, blood all around his eyes, turning slowly to look at the overhead screens.

The European ships drifted aimlessly. The robot ship carrying the weapon was intact, although discolored over much of its length. The other ship had been burned through. The ragged edges of its wound glowed red, fed by wisps of oxygen seeping from the ruptured seals. The severed end of the ship drifted nearby, surrounded by a cloud of debris and the twisted, dismembered corpses of the crew.

Polaski, for one of the few times I'd ever seen him do so, smiled. It was a grotesque thing—his thin lips curling upward in a face turning black from the acceleration, his eyes, red all through and seeping blood across his cheeks, the tendons in his face pulling his mouth into that rictus of a thin, self-satisfied smile.

He'd been vindicated. His prophesy, self-fulfilling though it might have been regarding the inevitability of conflict, the decisive advantage of acceleration, the high-G training—all of it had come true just as he had said. In these people's blind rush to escape from Earth, to get away from its hatred and warfare, in their willingness to use whatever means that escape required, they had only brought it along. And Polaski, finding within it fertile ground for yet another victory, misunderstanding completely our purpose, was pleased.

Yet no degree of desperation on the part of the Europeans really explained why they had brought such weapons with them, and why they had used one without provocation the minute they were through the tunnel. Clearly they hadn't meant to use them all against us, not at that time anyway, because they had sent just the one while the rest of their fleet raced by.

But whatever their reasons, they needed to be stopped.

I turned to Bolton and worked against the pain to open my mouth.

"We need to talk to survivors," I said.

"Yes," he said, "my very thought." He didn't move, but looked around. Finally he brought his microphone into position and wiggled a switch on his armrest, and blew into the mike. Sound roared from the speakers.

"Stand down, all stations. We will hold in pattern at one-quarter G. Roscoe, assemble boarding parties if you would, please. Fully armed. Take three of the shuttles, with torches for the locks. We need at least one English-speaking prisoner in good health. The others are to be neither harmed nor rescued. Ms. Pham—I assume you are still on 30-deck—you may accompany Mr. Throckmorton's party if you wish, but you are not to interfere."

He got up and leaned down next to his communications officer. I got up, too, then waited for the dizziness to pass. We needed to break out the acceleration suits, the ones with the hydraulic cuffs that stemmed the flow of blood.

"Torres," said Bolton. He beckoned me over. "It was One-Fox they hit. I'm sorry."

I looked at him for a moment, then all at once remembered the column of strange light and the disintegrating ships. And the fact that people had died.

"Captain Keller," he said. "Thirteen others. Including some

friends of yours, I believe. Delgado."

Ramón and Elena Delgado, yes. The little entomologist, and the woman who drew children's books and illustrated our manuals for us. And Teresa and Ana, their daughters.

"God help us," I said, and ran a hand across my face. "And one of your ships? Is that what happened?"

"I'm afraid so—Seven-Three. Sixteen people, plus Jamie Peterson in your shuttle. All soldiers, at least. No families."

I shook my head, bewildered, not really grasping what had happened. Twenty-four hours ago I'd been in Charlie Peters' quarters, counting the hours till escape, completely absorbed with my own, small concerns.

I pushed into the tiny head, and tried to scrub the blood from the stubble on my chin, thinking all the while about little Teresa Delgado. When I rinsed my mouth I only spat more blood, so I gave it up and turned to the business of emptying my bladder in the tiny space with so little weight. It felt as though something had torn inside—I tried not to bite through my tongue a second time.

"They're back." Someone pounded on the door to the head. The pressure changed and the walls clanged as the shuttle docked. Down on the lower commons deck, Polaski stood to one side, while Bolton stood in the center with his hands behind his back, facing the air lock as it sucked open.

Commandos stepped briskly through and moved aside, making room for a very tall man who stooped to make it through. He was propelled from behind by Pham, who dug him repeatedly in the kidneys. There was high color back in her cheeks. Her eyes flashed. She looked sleek again, and alive.

The man she drove before her towered over us, though he was no more than nineteen or twenty. He had wavy blond hair and boyish good looks, and turned his head from side to side, looking frightened and eager to please at the same time, as though hoping for some kind word. His hands were tied behind him.

When he was a few steps into the room Bolton made a gesture, and Pham pulled him to a stop.

"So, who are you?" said Bolton, his tone conversational. The man's lips worked themselves into an anxious smile, and his eyes darted from side to side.

"Margyl," he said. "Dieter Margyl." His accent was Dutch, or Flemish.

Bolton nodded thoughtfully. "You understand, Dieter, that you are far from any international court, and that your friends are not coming back." As he spoke, he drew his knife from its ankle scabbard. The man licked his lips, while Pham fidgeted impatiently.

"We would like to know," said Bolton, straightening with the knife, "why you attacked our vessels."

The prisoner's eyes widened in astonishment.

"But, I think...to make so you cannot stop us, yes?" He was watching the knife.

Pham snorted in derision, yet the man's answer had caught my attention.

"Stop you from what?" said Bolton. "Go on."

Margyl was beginning to panic. "I think you make fun of me, yes? You would stop us from landing, and—"

The knife shot out, only at the last minute flicking aside to cut open his breast pocket. He strangled on his own shout, then stood with his eyes tightly shut, taking short, hard breaths. A sour smell filtered into the room.

Bolton sliced open the rest of Margyl's pockets, finding them empty except for a radiation badge that clinked against the deck and spun to a stop. Bolton stepped back.

"Stop you from landing, and what? By all means, continue."

"From going on to the next projection machine," said Margyl. His pale face quivered. When no one answered, he opened his eyes to steal a glance around the room.

"I am not understanding," he said. "Please. You try to keep everyone from leaving Earth, then you do not tell the truth what your robots find, and now you ask—"

Pham moved too fast to follow. For a moment I thought she'd fallen to the deck, grabbing Bolton's arm for support, but then I saw that she was still on her feet, crouching, and that she had Bolton's knife in her hand, and that her right foot was coming up toward the prisoner Margyl. With all of her strength she came up, her heel striking home between his legs with an awful sound and lifting him off the deck. Even before he'd crumpled back to his side, she had a hold of his hair and was pushing his face down, landing with a knee in his kidneys and the knife against his throat.

Margyl struggled for breath, drawing his knees up and vomiting. She pressed his face into it and leaned down.

"Now," she said, "Tell us." The knife broke the skin.

"I don't...yes," he gasped, still trying for a breath. "I try...okay." His eyes rolled up to look at her. "Yes, I will tell you. Please, no, listen. When we begin to build ships, we know that you let us build them only because you need us to help you—" Pham's knee pressed harder.

"Please, it is true...we knew you would try to destroy all the ships, so that you would have everything for yourself here—we and the Chinese, we know this. Then you lie to everybody about what your robots find here. You say there is no place to live. Nothing, so for sure we have no place to go...just you. Now you hide from us *Le Paradis*, and you go there alone, and have that planet for yourself, too."

He began to shake. His eyes, white and glassy, turned away from Pham and rolled first one way and then the other, then finally chose mine to which to issue their plea. Blood trickled from around the knife. Pham leaned closer.

"If we hide these things," she said, "then how come you know them, hah?"

"Please, there is informer. In your ships. He tells us everything—"

With an almost convulsive force she drove her knee into his side. He screamed and the tendons stood out terribly in his neck. Sweat dripped from his chin and mixed with the blood and vomit around his face.

"His name," she said.

Bolton gave a sigh at that moment, and straightened.

"We know his name," he said.

Pham ignored him and twisted the knife harder. "Tell us his name," she said.

"I swear, please. We do not know his name. We have never known his name. Always we call him 'the Chinaman'..."

Then all at once I understood. How could we have missed it, I wondered. All of us had missed it, except Bolton. Chih-Hsien Chien, our Chinese guest. Watched over by Bolton's troops, on Bolton's ship. All the while feeding the Europeans lie after lie, to whatever unfathomable end.

Pham took a long, slow breath, then jerked suddenly, as though from a spasm. She stood up.

I had turned away by then, but I began to hear an odd, swishing sound, like a bellows being pumped. I looked back at Pham, then down, not understanding at first the pool of red swirling around her feet.

My stomach turned. Dieter Margyl's throat had been cut from one side to the other, the wound gaping open in a hideous leer. His eyes were empty and wide, staring directly into mine.

I took a quick step back and made a sound at Bolton, but he only put his hands in his pockets and raised an eyebrow. Pham tossed down the knife. It landed next to Margyl, in the pool of blood still pumping from his throat.

"I think we talk to Chien," she said. Her feet made a splashing sound as she moved away. Bolton said nothing. I tore my eyes from the dead man to watch her go, seeing that the old sinuous grace had returned to her as she walked, rippling through her hips and her thighs. Her feet left smears of blood behind her. *The boundless celebration of our purpose,* I thought, *however black its nature...* I was fascinated, and revolted. And in some awful way, aroused.

"34-deck," said Bolton finally, turning to follow. The rest of us fell in behind him, the trance broken.

But the sight that awaited us in Chih-Hsien's quarters brought us no comfort, nor did it bring us any closer to the truth. He sat in his big acceleration chair, facing us with his head to one side, his tiny, frail body crushed by the acceleration. Whatever reasons he might have given us for his deadly manipulation of the Europeans, they had died with him.

PART THREE

NIGHTFALL

Chapter Thirteen: THE LAMB OF GOD

The dream came that night for the first time. It began with Ramon Delgado and his family, in a scene from Teresa's third birthday party on the island. It was a great feast with drinking and two piñatas, all under a burning artificial sun in the subterranean air. The piñata for the children was a smiling burro, but for the adults there was a demon, a grotesque underworld golem with blunt horns and fangs, and deep, sunken eyes.

The adults took their turns with the blindfold and the stick, swinging helplessly as the creature bobbed and swung out of range, turning on its rope and sweeping us with its gaze. Eventually only Pham and I were left, and the others stood in a circle and beckoned me in with the blindfold. But I held back, not being in the mood, and I told them no, go ahead, let Pham have her turn. But they beckoned anyway, and the demon watched and waited until finally I was angry and I said no, please, maybe it's the drink but no, I'd rather not.

So Pham took her turn. She took a swing with the stick then threw it aside and reached for the creature with her bare hands. She embraced it tighter and tighter, and moved her body against it as though making love to it while the others whistled and cheered. The demon finally cracked, then crumbled, then vanished into pieces, leaving only the candies and nuts spilling to the ground.

I remembered all of this in the dream, just as it really happened. But then, while the others cheered Pham and her conquest, I looked down at the ground, at a piece of the thing's face, which was staring up at me with the eyes of Dieter Margyl.

That was when the rest of the dream began, the part that was to come back again and again. In it, I was trapped in an underground cavern from which a single passage led to freedom. But it led downward first, into the mountain, and I knew that somewhere along it the demon waited, the one that Pham had embraced and dispelled, but from which I, to this day, held back.

Chan and I spent the next morning tracking the European ships. What they did was more disturbing than I could have imagined. My hopes of reaching Serenitas dimmed, and my fear of becoming trapped in Holzstein's System grew.

Chan, who didn't mind the thought of staying in Holzstein's at all, brooded about the drones instead. The scientists and priests had conferred through the night and none had been able to suggest how, or why, the drones had vanished. They were sure that Miller knew, until they met with her in the morning and saw the depth of her own concern.

"It scares me a little," said Chan. "Anne thinks they may have found something. Or seen something, and it made them leave. And now the Europeans with those weapons...I don't know what's happening any more, Eddie." She put a hand out to me. "I need you. I need you to hold me like you used to."

But I'd scarcely heard her. I was thinking about the Europeans, about the new positions they were taking up. And about warfare, and years of endurance, and life on the great, empty black planet.

Chan and I made love against the machines that afternoon, suddenly and urgently, with little concern for who might pass. She wrapped herself around me and pressed as hard as she could, making no sound as I gripped her tighter and tighter. I tried to touch every part of her at once and drive away the images of the dead, of Pham walking away from me, of the blood on the ground behind her. But I couldn't.

An aide to Carolyn Dorczak called to say that their fleet had also been attacked and to ask for assistance in their future defense.

It was David Rosler who took the call. He then conferred with Polaski, and only afterwards was I informed. I left our ship to pay Rosler a visit.

I descended from the nose hatch of his ship and smelled stale air and rotting food. Lights filtered up from the MI deck, then an angry shout and a moment later a sight that held me motionless; I let the lift carry me on past without a word.

Rosler had had a sheaf of papers in one hand, while with the other he gripped Pham's hair and pressed her down into the console with all his strength, grinding her face into the switches. His voice was contemptuous.

"You'd probably enjoy it, anyway, you little bitch..."

Hurt him. The thought came from nowhere, unbidden. *You're faster than he is.* For all I detested Pham, in that instant Rosler struck me as insufferable by comparison, and I wanted to see him hurt.

"Hi," came a small voice.

Glistening metalwork was arrayed in front of me—I'd gotten off on the lower industrial deck, with its manufacturing MI and metal-working machines. Work lamps glared from the ceiling, throwing deep shadows into the deck's perimeter.

A boy's face moved in and out of the shadows. He was running a cloth back and forth across the shaft of a turret lathe, watching me solemnly out of blue eyes in a freckled face.

"Hello," I said.

He stopped. "You looking for the sick lady?"

"I don't think so. Who's the sick lady?"

"The one who's always fighting with Captain Rosler." He took up his polishing again. "She threw up on the grinder this afternoon. I had to clean it up."

"I'm sorry. Are you the only one here?"

"Yes. Everyone else is out on the couplings."

"But not you?"

"Nah." He snapped the shaft cover into place and spun the lugs with a flick of his wrist. He was no more than eight years old, but worked with the skill of an experienced machinist. He avoided my gaze.

"I'm an LTT," he said.

"What's that?"

He cocked his head. "You making fun of me?"

"No."

"I'm a Low Thrust Tolerant. At two-point-two I start to breathe funny." He came out from behind the lathe and pointed to a bench strewn with tools and rags. "That's her piece over there."

"The sick lady's?"

"Uh-huh."

On the bench was a heavy gun, black and unfinished, unlike any I'd ever seen. The chamber had been taken from a light cannon, but a custom magazine, grip and barrel had been added to it. The barrel was ugly and heavy and a good ten inches long, with a bore nearly an inch in diameter.

"Pretty neat, huh?" said the boy, his blue eyes and delicate features brightening.

"I suppose. What's she going to use with it?"

"Twenty millimeter fléchette rounds. Wait, I'll show you." He raced up the steps to the upper deck, then came down holding a brass-clad canister. "It holds four of 'em—more'n a thousand needles each."

It was a particularly nasty type of antipersonnel round, which at close quarters would take off a person's entire torso. It was also heavy—at a full G her gun would weigh a good eight pounds, loaded.

But now the boy had lost interest, and was pecking at a keyboard.

"Where'd this shell come from?" I said, hefting the fléchette round.

"Upper indy deck. There's all kinds of stuff up there."

I started up the stairs to look. I didn't remember that we'd put an armory on Rosler's upper industrial deck.

"Want to see something?" said the boy.

"What's that?"

"I wrote a program for the machines. They don't make any-thing, but they all go at once like they're dancing. I did the order just right so it kind of makes music—you want to see?"

"Later, okay? I'm pretty busy."

"*Más tarde, Eduardo.*" My father's voice. "*Estoy ocupado.*"

Side arms and rifles lined the upper deck, including a gutted 20mm cannon and a shoulder-portable laser. I walked over to an ammunition case standing open on the floor.

"Hoping to find something you like?"

Rosler stood on the top step behind me, wearing his black

waiter's pants and a soiled white shirt. Limp, black hair hung over his glasses, which were smeared with fingerprints. I couldn't see his eyes behind the glint of the lights on his glasses.

"Tell me what the Americans said, Rosler."

"NA/C? They lost a ship. Got a warning from the Europeans to stay away from the new torus. Which is where the Europeans are heading, of course. So now NA/C's all bent out of shape because they're civvies and don't have any weapons. They're belly-aching for help." He began looking through the racks of side arms.

"How did you know the Europeans are heading for the torus, Rosler?"

"Birds, Torres, birds."

"I see. So maybe your birds have told you why the Europeans attacked us?"

"Because the Chinese set us up—isn't that what your prisoner said? Chih-Hsien told the Europeans we were going to cut them out of the action, right?" He selected an old Mauser P38 and hefted it in his hand.

"You're sure the Chinese were lying?"

"I'm sure."

"Then why did they set us up?"

He shrugged. "'Your enemy's enemy isn't your friend, he's your easiest prey...' You know the Chinese." He sighted along the Mauser.

"The prisoner didn't say anything about NA/C being set up, too. So why'd *they* get attacked?"

"Don't be a dip, Torres." He tossed me the Mauser. "If you've got the advantage in firepower, pretty soon you use it."

I looked down at the little Mauser, and thought about the cannon Pham was making down below.

"So what did you tell the Americans?" I said.

He tossed me a shoulder holster and shells to go with the Mauser.

"What do you think? I said we'd be happy to handle their defense, as long as they pay."

"Hey, Charlie."

Peters and Chan were dancing to an old song about horses and rain in Harlem. It was the next morning, and we were waiting for a meeting I'd asked Polaski to hold.

"Aye, lad."

"As quartermaster, do you remember putting assault weapons on One-Zero?"

"Ah, well now. We haven't *got* such things in the fleet, you know. 'Personal defense and law enforcement armament,' aye, that we have. Then again, one simple quartermaster can't open every box, now, can he? But, yes, Eddie, there's an armory on One-Zero, and I shouldn't be surprised if our young Mr. Rosler slipped in a little something extra to help him sleep at night."

A phone blinked and I answered it, then held it out.

"Charlie."

"Voice from the heavens," he said, "voice from the heavens." He went on dancing, so I switched the phone to the ceiling speakers.

"Charlie," said the speakers, "it's Patty Kelly."

"Good morning, Patty Kelly."

"Listen," she said. "You know how there's a meeting being broadcast this morning? Well, some of us were thinking, you know how there haven't been any services yet? For all the people on the ships, you know, yesterday? So we were thinking, maybe we could do a little something for them during the meeting."

"Aye, lass. That would be a fine idea."

"And we thought maybe you could say a few words..."

Peters stopped dancing.

"Charlie? Are you there?"

"I am." He looked around and frowned, as though trying to remember something.

"Patty," he said finally, "why have you asked me to do this, and not one of the captains?"

"Oh, I'm sorry, maybe I shouldn't have? You just seemed like...I'm sorry, Charlie, we can get someone else—"

"No, child, it's all right. I'll say a few words. I only wondered, is all. Thank you for asking."

I cut off the phone and Peters looked at me for a while, though not for any reason I could think of.

"'Mysterious ways,' indeed," he said at last, and stooped

down to one of his packing cases.

"What is it, Charlie?"

"Excuse me," he said. He took out some clothes and disappeared into his little spray-shower.

"What's with him?" I said to Chan.

"I don't know," she said. "He's been funny since the tunnel."

"Do you know what an LTT is?" I said.

"Oh, yes. The way things are going, it's someone who won't ever be allowed to have children."

I thought about the boy and the look in his blue eyes. I wished I'd stayed to watch his Dance of the Machines.

Peters returned a few minutes later, scrubbed and clean-shaven, buttoning the cuffs of a clean white shirt.

"You look very nice, Charlie."

"Aye." With the palms of his hands he brushed back the tufts of hair on the sides of his head. His face had changed in the eight years, I noticed—the fleshy cheeks were tighter, and his eyes looked out from deeper sockets under greying eyebrows. He looked older and sterner.

He reached into his case, then turned to the mirror and snapped a white clerical collar into place, followed by his familiar black vest.

"Why, Charlie, you never told us."

He snapped up the vest's collar around the white.

"Aye, it always seemed like something I'd done well to put behind me, if you know what I mean."

"That's yours?" I said. "The collar?"

"Aye, lad. As a young man I was that most formidable of God's creatures, you know. An Irish Roman Catholic Priest."

"You're serious? I thought you were a U.S. Army loadmaster. How'd you get from one to the other?"

"Well. I'm not sure I can say any more."

"How long has it been?"

"Hm?" He studied his reflection in the mirror. "Oh. I took instruction in County Cork, you know."

This seemed to be enough of an explanation, so he stopped.

"Well," he said after a minute, "that was where I was ordained, anyway. To the accompaniment of much hand-wringing by my mother and carrying-on by my father. In my youthful enlightenment I was sure I'd been saved for some fine purpose, you see, but it was a far less profitable one than my father had had in mind.

"Anyway, the fine purpose my *bishop* had in mind was the saving of the dockworkers of Cork Harbor, so that's where I went to hold forth, in the town of Cobh. The problem was that the dockworkers of Cobh hadn't heard about this fine purpose, so they didn't come to visit me in my little church, but left me to the damp little old ladies who *did* come, but who I was fairly certain were saved already. So I was quite discouraged, I tell you. I decided if God wasn't going to send His children to hear my fine sermons, then I would go down and have a word with them myself."

Peters searched for something else in his case but didn't find it, then took out a clothes brush instead and used it on his shoes, stopping now and then to work at the leather with a moistened finger.

"So that I did. On Sundays I prattled on about this and that to the old ladies, but during the week I went down to the boats to help with the cargoes and talk to the sailors about their lives. Not about God's, you see, because it bored them to tears.

"Then one day I just stayed aboard, leaving God in His little box on the Bridge Road. I was quite certain by then that He'd never had any use for me in the first place.

"But I tell you, children, as I've grown older I've wondered whether He ever really was inside that little church, and whether He really sent me away at all or only called me closer. Closer all the time, you see. Until now."

He pulled on his sweater to hide all but a thin edge of the collar.

"But, if God hasn't called me, then Patty Kelly has, and I really should think of some fine-sounding words to say. I can't for the life of me remember a proper service for sailors lost at sea."

"All right, listen *up*." Polaski raised his voice to get people quiet. They'd waited a long time while Polaski and I finished a last-minute meeting with Chan and Rosler, and officers didn't like to wait. There were too many of them in one place, in any case.

"As you know—"

The air lock cycled open and Pham walked in. She had scratches and bruises on her cheek, and wore the huge pistol on her hip. She squeezed in next to Rosler.

"Now," said Polaski. "As you know, the presence of hostile forces in this system has forced us to change our plans."

Throughout the fleet, eyes would be shifting from the defense monitors to Polaski's face. Ship's crews, soldiers, civilians, all waiting to see what he and I had decided.

"It looks like we were too trusting," said Polaski—and he stopped. "Someone said we're doing formalities for the dead. Who?"

Peters hesitated, then took a step forward. "I thought I might say a few words," he said.

"Fine," said Polaski, "so go ahead." But he didn't move aside, and Peters had to try and talk around him. Pham rolled her eyes and fidgeted.

"I think—" said Peters. Then he cleared his throat and looked down at his feet. He started over. "Mr. Polaski mentioned formalities for the dead," he said. "I think the dead are in God's hands and in no need of formalities. It is we who need some comfort."

Pham belched and jammed her hands in her pockets, then suddenly yanked them out. "A *priest*?" She'd seen the collar. "A fucking *priest*? Oh, shit!" She rolled her eyes. "'*Father*,'" she drawled.

"Shut up, Pham," said Bolton. He was careful to speak quietly, so the microphones wouldn't pick it up.

"Hah! Fuck you. Shit, a priest."

Peters watched her for a minute, then went on.

"We fancy ourselves here for different reasons," he said. "Some are searching for a fine, sunny home. Others are running from their pasts, although I'll wager they've not come far. Still others are striving for power and dominion, only to have their noses bloodied the first day.

"But our companions are dead, my friends—they'll not be back. 'Tis a hard thing, I know, but no less real for being hard. God whispers what we must do, but in the clamor of flight I fear we haven't heard. We've searched the sky for machines to tell us what to do instead, or for a paradise to welcome us home, or for the perfect weapon to protect us. But He is not there, my friends. Not in the sky.

"Well. With those few words for the living, let us now bow our heads.

"Unto almighty God we commend the souls of our brothers and sisters departed, and commit their bodies to the dark in sure and certain hope of resurrection through our Lord Jesus Christ, at whose coming the darkness shall give up her dead, and the bodies of those who sleep in her shall be made whole as if they were angels to guide us on. Amen."

"Amens" trickled in from the audience, and the deck was quiet until a silken voice dropped another pleasant "amen" from the ceiling, where a spider drone bobbed in a curtsy. Peters blinked at it, then remained standing awkwardly in front of Polaski. There were no caskets to slide from the rail or ashes to scatter, no clods of dirt to toss in the grave. There was no book to close or incense burner to lift, no sash to take from his head to give to an altar boy. He just stood there by himself, unsure of what to do next.

"You finished?" said Polaski.

"Yes...yes, I suppose I am. Thank you."

"Good. All right, listen. Most of you know the European fleet has split up, and that they're taking up positions around the new tunnel and around Holzstein-III, the planet we planned to make our temporary base. We think they're going to establish themselves on H-III and wait for the drones to send back word about Serenitas, then demand a deal before letting us through.

"We think we can dislodge them from the torus. But developing the necessary skills and assault vessels is going to take a planetary base and superior soldiers, and more labor and matériel than we have. Now, as far as a base and training soldiers goes, we're all right—we can settle on the fourth planet."

Silence fell across the deck. Faces turned to masks, mindful of the precious illusion of united leadership.

How our compatriots would be hating Polaski at that moment. How their voices would be raised in anger throughout the fleet as they finally understood what he'd said. There would be no sun for their children after all, no water or trees, not even for the briefest pause after eight years of hard rock and steel: There would only be a frozen hell of lifeless black dust and crushing weight.

And how it would have been me they'd be hating, instead, if I'd taken my place in front of the cameras. Know as they might where the decision had come from, it was Polaski's face they could see.

"H-IV has a strategically useful orbit," said Polaski, for all the world as though he'd just received applause for his announcement, "and its 1.4 surface gravity will make picking the best children easier. Especially the third generation. The oldest we have now are already good material, and in just a few years they'll be proving themselves the toughest contenders in—"

"No."

It was Bolton who'd spoken, very quietly. "You don't mess with the children," he said.

"Fourteen is old enough to fight and have more children, and that will be pretty soon. I'd think you of all people would know the value of—"

Bolton's eyes drifted closed very slightly. "I said no. And you don't need fighting crews to attack those ships. You need automatics."

Polaski glared at him, then spun away to face the cameras. "There are two kinds of colonists who are going to arrive in this system," he said. "Peaceful ones, and ones who are smart enough not to be. And when there's a shortage of resources like there is, that's a recipe for war.

"Now the Europeans will reserve their strategic weapons to interdict movement toward their new planet and the torus. That will leave us, with our conventional superiority, as the major power on the majority of the planets and on the asteroids and shipping lanes. In exchange for using that superiority to maintain order, we'll receive the resources and new recruits we need.

"An assault on the torus cannot occur until the drones return. In the meantime, we will put down on the black planet of Holzstein-IV and arm ourselves and build assault ships. We will select and condition the toughest crews, and then we will wait."

Bolton's eyes were almost closed.

"Perhaps," he said.

Chapter Fourteen: WHAT SPY BE THIS WE SEND

But the drones didn't return. For eleven years we clung to the black planet and fought the colonists' wars for them, and for eleven years we grew stronger. But while we waited for some sign from the drones, some whisper from space to send us onward, none came. Time passed and we learned to live with the cold and the weight of the fourth planet, and a third generation fought its way through a difficult infancy and into the only life it had ever known. Desperate colonists poured in from Earth only to bring their wars with them, bickering for ground on the second planet or on the moons and asteroids, or else going up against the Europeans' defenses around the third planet, always failing. And always we were called upon to rescue the survivors, and always we exacted the same price: half the ships we rescued, and the youngest and strongest recruits. No one had tried to live on the black planet with us, no one returned to Earth, no one moved on, and no one dislodged the Europeans' robot ships from the mouth of the new tunnel.

I stood at the window and thought about the Europeans' ships, not for the first time. Thin, cold sunlight sliced across the complex, and cast a shadow of the dome's iron lattice onto the black dirt below. The European ships were the single unknown, the wild card in a project I'd given the last six years of my life to.

The building I looked down from was the only tall structure under the main dome, and as such it commanded a view of all of the other massive, ugly domes sprawled across the black dirt and gravel to the horizon twenty miles away. The domes were made of crude glass formed from silica we found on the surface. The glass panels were glued into a structure of iron mined and smelted out in pits between the domes.

Vehicles ground their way across the surface from dome to dome, while bleed-off from the smelters and outgassing from the domes' sealants gave the appearance of smoke drifting across coal fields. Armed ships stood in readiness across the landscape, and banks of weapons in hardened bunkers hugged the ground and waited. In the farther distance stood clusters of pale white columns—our original ships, emptied of only a few of their thousands of tons of equipment, still equipped and waiting to take us onward. The bleak scene on the freezing plains seemed appropriate for forces that had become irresistibly powerful, as Polaski had vowed they would, but who collected nothing in return but more power and yet more time to go on waiting.

An acrid stench broke into my thoughts, and I turned away from the window. The smell was from the putty we used to hold the glass into the domes; as it dried and weakened it let out an acidic stink that seeped through the air filters of the building I was in. I was standing on the building's third floor mezzanine, an unpainted iron shelf that hung over the vehicle launch bay. The mezzanine was empty now except for a spindly metal table that held my coffee cup and a few pieces of paper. Shafts of light from above the dome slanted through the window and across the bare iron, illuminating a piece of a table leg and a section of the railing at the edge of the bay. My shoes scuffed against the metal decking as I turned. The sound echoed back and forth in the huge space. The technicians had been sequestered until launch, and for the first time it was quiet in the building.

Then against the silence I heard a telltale clicking of metal against metal, and after a pause I heard it again, then all at once a mad clattering rush like the sound of a dog's toenails against a hard floor as it attacks. I made a move to save my coffee, then changed my mind in time to see the final approach of an aluminum drone—all six of its grasshopper legs pumping madly straight for the table. At the last minute it snapped all of its legs downward to hurl itself into the air. It rose more than high enough to clear the table, but its pathetic forward momentum brought it only to the near edge and it crashed downward, collapsing the table and flinging cold coffee across me and the papers. The two-foot-long drone tumbled onto the floor and landed on its back, its legs still pumping the air. The coffee cup spun to a stop on the iron floor, and the drone went still.

"Too slow by half," it said. "Don't you think?"

It was Little Bolton. One day years ago it had for reasons known only to itself attached itself to Michael Bolton and followed him for a full week, coming away with a perfect imitation of his Welsh accent. Less productively, and to everyone's great regret, it had also at one time attached itself as best it could to Chan's cat, and from that encounter it had come away proving only that grasshopper drones were better suited to the arts than to the rigors of feline flight. But with unflagging enthusiasm, it had never stopped trying.

"Telephone call for you, Sir. Shall I ring you through?" It was still on its back, seemingly quite content.

I wiped coffee up with my sleeve. "Yes, thank you." After a brief clicking, young Roddy McKenna's voice came from somewhere in the drone's middle.

"Mr. Torres?"

"Yes, Roddy, I'm here." McKenna was a blue-eyed and still freckled nineteen-year-old whom I had recently promoted to team leader for the project. He never slowed down or slept or ate much, but just kept working through all hours.

"The entry-path people want to talk with Anne Miller before launch. They say it could cut months off the probe's turnaround if they knew the drones' entry protocol. I agree." His voice was tense, waiting for me to disagree.

"No, Rod. The project's been insulated from her for six years— you know that. Why do you want to break the rules at the last minute?"

"That's exactly why, because it's the last minute. What possible influence on the probe's design could a discussion with the entry people have? The thing's built already."

I'd promoted McKenna precisely because he was one of the few people who would argue with me; he was also sharp and aggressive. And available—he would never be able to join the more prestigious fighting crews. Unfortunately he was also prone to a muted rage that simmered in the guise of injured arrogance when questioned or doubted. He was hard to manage.

"Look, Roddy, my guess is that you're right, and that you can see this better than we could at first. But the reason the rule was made was that we don't *know* whether any of her assumptions could bleed into our project and propagate some flaw that's in the drones. And we still don't. Anyway, there's a credibility issue in the eyes of the military. We're on shaky enough ground as it is."

"All right." That was it, just "all right." Little Bolton's metallic belly went on pointing at the ceiling, saying nothing more.

"Listen, Rod, about a half hour ago I saw a couple of fast troopers putting down at the LZ. Who was that, do you know?"

"Colonel Pham with the Fourth Surface-Assault Regulars—Sino-Christian boundary dispute. Establishing new borders."

More likely establishing the highest bidder for her services, I thought.

"They'll be back here at the big lock in a couple of minutes," said McKenna. If he couldn't join any of the line divisions, he studied them endlessly and followed their every movement.

"Okay, Roddy, thanks for your help."

I turned the drone right side up.

Beyond the mezzanine rail stood the rounded nose of the Serenitas probe. It was a capsule three stories high and nearly as wide, while below the launch building, below ground level, it stood atop two of the massive engines that normally drove our capital ships. Borrowing those engines had been unpopular, but only they could do what had to be done: on one single occasion, for exactly 136 seconds, they had to hurl the Serenitas probe forward at a staggering twenty-three Gs.

Access hatches stood open on the nose, revealing the sophisticated electronics inside. For each device visible there were two others like it, redundant and redundant again, built with such care that the years had crawled by unnoticed as we worked. We knew it had to work the first time, and we knew, more importantly, that we would have to *believe* it had worked even if we never heard from it again.

The vessel was painted a light grey and bore the ragged appearance and cheerful logo of the Pikes Mountain Company asteroid mining barges; and like all Pikes Mountain vessels, it had needed christening with large black letters along its bows; my engineers, with a practiced sense of double meaning, had dubbed it *S.S. Sun of*

Gabriel.

Six similar vessels, although dummies with ordinary engines, currently waited in orbit. Shortly all seven of them would be sent on an innocuous outward-bound orbit from the black planet toward the moons of H-V, passing close to the torus the Europeans still blocked, but on a course and speed that made passage through it seem out of the question. But with a sudden, compressed communication with the torus and a blindingly fast acceleration, this one ship would break course and be through it before the European pickets could even track it. We hoped.

Once through, it was to identify the third torus, if one existed, that the drones would have built in the Serenitas system, then while looping toward that torus for a return to us, it was to collect every scrap of information about the Serenitas system at every conceivable frequency, talking to the drones all the way. Depending on the existence and position of a return torus, within a year we expected to know whether the planet of Serenitas was ready for us, and why the drones were taking so long to return.

Still, not everyone supported the project. "Torres' Folly," someone had called it. As time had passed, the immediate battles and the struggles of staying alive had become all-consuming on the base, and the hope of what Elliot called "clean sheets and country music" had begun to die away.

Muted sounds came from outside. A train of troop trailers was disgorging personnel onto the black dirt of the open mall beneath the window. Whether out of good humor or foul, the mall had been named "Trinity Square"—at this end, reaching all the way to the dome like a church tower, was my tightly secured vehicle launch building, while down one side ran the unmarried personnel quarters and down the other the recreation center, both of them long, low, black-brick buildings. The soldiers pouring from the trailers dumped weapons and body armor into piles on the dirt, and stuffed their acceleration suits in through the barracks' windows amidst shouting and cheering and the arrival of plastic kegs from the rec center.

"There's another call waiting for you, Sir, if you'd care to take it."

"Oh." I hadn't heard Little Bolton announce the call. "Who

is it, do you know?"

"Me," said Chan, putting herself straight through. "Are you coming over to watch the show? I know you're close to launch, but it would be nice if you could. The kids would get a big kick out of you being here." Her voice was pleasant, out of place in the empty iron building. I looked at my watch.

"Yes, I'll be there. Um— Little Bolton's done in another table."

"Oh, dear." A pause. "You know you've got Dorczak and her delegation coming in two hours?"

"I know." Chan was stalling. "What is it, Chan?"

"Charlie's here, Eddie. If you come over, I wonder if you could talk to him a little bit. See if you could get him to go up to the station for a rest. He could go up with the children I'm sending tomorrow, but he won't listen to me any more when I bring it up."

"He doesn't listen to me either, but I'll talk to him if you want. He's pretty strong, though, Chan. I think he's okay."

"He drives himself too hard, Eddie. And for no good reason that I know of. Hang on just a second." She asked a question of someone in the background, then came back on. "Did you know we have unidentified ships inbound?"

"Carolyn's—"

"No, a couple of hours behind them, from the asteroid belt. No one knows who they are."

"The duty officer's been told?"

"They're the ones who passed the word. Rosler is out there himself, because of Pham's ships coming in. I don't like it, Eddie. Will you be here, anyway?"

"I'll be there." With a last glance at the troops out on the black dirt of Trinity Square, I headed for the iron stairwell.

"It's not at all that bad, really," said an unhappy voice behind me.

"What's that?"

"The table. 'Done in' sounds a bit grim, don't you think?"

The performance was of a never-before-rehearsed "Peter and the Wolf." When I arrived it was already underway, to the accompaniment of much giggling and cheering from the children gathered in the classroom to watch. Chan stood to one side, supervising the chaos with good-humored patience.

The children in the audience sat mostly in little wheelchairs, wearing a variety of prostheses. They were from the third generation, mostly, casualties of the high gravity or existing genetic damage. Chan planned to move some of them into weightlessness in the orbiting station the following day, a decision as painful for the parents as it was a relief from pain for the children, because once they adjusted to free fall they would never see a planet's surface again.

I slipped in next to Peters and tried to sort out the performers. The main character, Peter, was being played by a cheery four-year-old, sitting in a wheelchair and diligently gripping a rope in his right hand. He had a complicated set of braces on his legs and an angelic face, with brown eyes and rosy cheeks and moist lips open in an excited smile. If he had ever memorized his part, he had forgotten it, because the rope and noose, intended for the wolf, remained coiled in his hand to be waved around in his excitement, rocking back and forth in his chair and laughing at the wolf.

The wolf, in any case, had very little to offer in the way of the needed tail. It had only its six telltale metal feet sticking out from under its wolf costume as it padded back and forth, circling and snapping ferociously at the bird. Its coat and head looked perfectly real, with a long pink flapping tongue and glistening eyes that followed the bird's every move. The wolf also played, albeit somewhat muffled from its speakers under the coat, a perfect rendition of the wolf's theme on the French horns.

The bird—a spider drone optimistically disguised in three or four paper feathers—played its flute theme and bobbed and weaved and teased the wolf, now and then adding its own innovation of bird calls. If the cast's fidelity to the plot was imprecise, the music, at least, was perfect.

The cat...well, there were two cats. The real cat—the real *real* cat, that is, namely Chan's cat—had apparently, and without auditioning, adopted the role of the stage cat, obeying some primordial relish involving bird sounds, a relish that had survived un-dampened through its ancestors' freezing while still embryos. It raced back and forth and hurled itself up at the plastic and metal bird, leaping frantically up and down from the wolf's back to get at it. The *actor* cat, on the other hand, another grasshopper drone decked in paper whiskers and tail, sulked at the side of the stage next to the hunters' wheelchairs, unsure of what to do about being upstaged by its own understudy. It remained gracious enough, at least, to provide the sound of the cat's clarinet at the proper moments.

Charlie Peters told me confusingly and in considerable detail about each of the children, but now he changed the subject without warning.

"You know, Eddie," he said, "this reminds me, this business of the wolf up there—" He stopped to applaud, although I couldn't see at what.

"You're going to quote something," I said.

"Oh, dear, am I so transparent? No, I'm going to tell you about children. So you see? You're wrong. Something that fellow Hesse said about children and wolves. Mr. Polaski, you know. His sort." He leaned back and folded his arms.

"I've lost you, Charlie."

"Really. Well, one thinks of the wolf as so innocent, you know. Fixed on its prey, single-minded, no qualms, no guilt of sin because it knows nothing *about* sin. The perfect innocence of clear purpose, it is. Like Mr. Polaski, you see, this hollow shell of instinct, with not one shred of real feeling."

Up on the stage, the wolf had stepped on one of the cat's feet, and now with a shriek and a hiss the cat spun around and sank a claw into the costumed wolf's face. The claw stuck. Faithful to the script, however, the wolf went on with its attacks on the bird, flinging the stuck cat from side to side. The cat panicked and howled at full lung, and in a flurry of wolf's fur tried to claw its way onto the wolf's back for better purchase. The other cat—the drone with the cat's part, anyway—inched its way forward toward the center of the stage, sensing its understudy's imminent demise.

"On the other hand," said Peters, "look at that lovely, lovely child. How sweet and innocent can a creature be, I ask you? Not like the wolf at all, yet everyone's model of perfect innocence. I think of young Kipper, you know, a boy—a man, really—just filled, *filled* by his own feelings, and not an ounce of wit about him. Everything Polaski is not."

"So what about Hesse? Wolves are innocent? Or children are innocent?"

"Oh, no, neither one. Or at least, once one has learned sin, one can never regain that simple sort of innocence. Never again shed one's own feelings, you see."

The cat had made it up onto the wolf, but because one claw was still stuck in the wolf's face, it ended up perched on the wolf's nose—facing backwards into its big rolling eyes. The cat's ears went back and it hissed and tried to back away, while nearby Chan shook her head and hid her face behind a hand. The actors playing the hunters and grandfather took their cues and tried to assemble into the grand procession into the forest. The real cat, still clinging backwards to the wolf's face, hissed and spat into the wolf's ear and urinated on its nose, while the wolf pirouetted on its six legs. Taking its unexpected opportunity, the bird now shifted its attack to the cat, and the other cat, the drone-cat, snuck into line, only to stumble into the coil of rope and tangle all six of its legs.

Peters gestured at the stage and leaned closer. "What Hesse said, you see, was that the way to innocence leads on, not back—not back to the wolf or the child, but ever further into sin, ever deeper into human life."

He stood up to applaud. "Into the jungle, you see."

"So, Eddie, what's this about unidentified ships approaching from the asteroids?"

"Chan thinks you need a rest, Charlie."

"Aye, I know she does, poor lass. Here, this way." He turned into a rough alleyway between black buildings, and scuffed at the gravel as we walked. I felt another change of subject coming. "She's the one who should be resting, you know—never takes a minute for herself. It's a fine thing, her worrying over me. But my, with those children—the *wonder* in their eyes, Eddie. Did you know—"

"She thinks you won't admit the planet's hard on you, Charlie. She says it gives you a millstone, a cross to carry." I plunged all the way in. "You like to think you're carrying the weight of some holy design, Charlie, even though it's killing you."

"Oh, dear, she shouldn't have."

I thought I'd gone too far, but in fact Peters was paying me no attention at all. He was shaking his head and muttering and lumbering away.

We'd come out of the alley and into Trinity Square, now a dreary expanse of black gravel relieved only by litter and a few weaving soldiers. The lowering sun shone through the dome to cast a grid of shadows across the bleak scene, breathing a dim life into misty rays of light that cut through the dust.

Peters was flickering in and out of the beams of light and kicking up new swirls of dust behind him, crunching across the gravel toward a tiny figure wedged into a dim corner among the farthest shadows. Seeing only that a figure lay there and that Peters was intent upon reaching it, I knew it had to be Pham—passed out and left behind among the litter and the rest of the drunks.

It was indeed Pham, easily identified by the giant gun strapped to one thigh and by the clothing. She had taken to wearing a skin-tight black body suit with nothing over it, or, as far as anyone could tell, under it. It made her look even tinier and sleeker—and deadlier: not like someone passed out and collapsed in a squalid stupor, but like a spider hiding in a shadowed corner, ready to slip out and sting enemies that passed.

Peters kicked aside a blunt-looking air-syringe that lay in the dirt next to her. It was a scene of black on black in the shadows: her sleek suit with its dull sheen of dust; her close-cropped hair and high cheekbones and slack lips pressed against the dirt; her gun twisted around and pushed into the ground under her narrow waist, the barrel filled with sand and gravel. Peters leaned down.

"Leave her be, Charlie," I said. "Let her kill herself her own way."

He knelt down beside her and pulled the gun out from under her. It seemed like all he meant to do, but then he reached in under her arms.

"Charlie, you can't pick her up, for Christ's sake. Come on, you'll kill yourself." For a man of Peters' size, just standing upright in the high gravity was like carrying an eighty-pound weight at home. To lift another human being was nearly impossible. Stealing his strength, too, was the thin air—it was kept at a painfully low pressure to keep from blowing off the domes.

"Oh, I'll be all right now." He sucked his breath in through his teeth and rolled Pham upright, then with a noise in his throat he snapped from his knees onto both feet and heaved her onto his shoulder, still crouching. "Can't just leave her like a dog, you know. Someone's got to look after her." He paused to blow out his breath, then with a thrust of his thighs drove himself to his feet, boots slipping in the gravel and kicking up a new cloud of dust in the shadows. Peters' cargo handling years were two decades behind him—for a man in his fifties it was a display of extraordinary strength.

I could hear his breathing as he steadied himself. The sound carried through the dry air and echoed back and forth in the corner between the walls. Finally he turned away from the black brick and trudged across the square, in and out of the light with his head down and Pham over his shoulder. Turning off the square by the probe's assembly building, he reached the makeshift office I kept along the alley, then rolled Pham onto the sofa.

"Well! Some coffee if we might, there's a fine idea. I'll just straighten up a bit." But behind his nonchalance he was tired. I checked Pham's pulse, then sat down and watched Peters clean up.

It was a rough and lopsided little room, but the brick walls were painted with precious white paint, and I'd put in heaters and lights. On the wall above Pham was a painstakingly assembled photograph of the blue and green planet, Serenitas.

"Poor lass." Peters poked through my hardcopy books while stealing glances at Pham.

"Charlie, she's not 'poor.' She's drugged to the gills."

"Aye, I know, poor thing. Such a sweet girl, too, when she sleeps." He settled into a chair to read.

"Charlie, you're talking about a woman who's said to be slaughtering civilians and carving her initials on her prisoners."

"Aye, that's a terrible business, I know. All this killing's got to stop, Eddie. This little one here, you know, and Polaski and Anne

Miller, and that snake of Satan himself, David Rosler...all of them."
He turned the page.

"Miller? Anne Miller's sitting in the North Tower mixing
bat's dung and mumbling incantations for the drones to return. I
wouldn't say she's killing anybody, Charlie."

Peters shut the book and looked at me as though over reading
glasses. "You aren't listening to me, laddie. Polaski's taken children
and made machines out of them, and Anne's taken machines and
made humans out of them, and they're both thinking that that's all
human beings are. And in their own little ways they're filling up the
worlds with the dead."

Pham's eyes were open. She was watching me without expression, the way she had so often through the years. I watched her
back for a while, wondering at the depth of that look. Without moving
a muscle, without shifting her eyes or blinking, it was nevertheless
a seduction, a moist, hypnotic beckoning to something deep inside of
me. Like a reptile rippling the surface of a muddy pond.

But there was something new in her face now. In the tension
around her eyes and mouth there was a ghost of uncertainty, a
shadow of weariness and pain. Vulnerability.

She pushed herself upright and sat forward on the sofa,
working her head from side to side.

"Ah," said Peters, "I see you're awake. Come, rest, I'll get
you some water. How do you feel?" He turned and went off to
rummage in a box while Pham ignored him, dropping her eyes to the
floor with a flicker of irritation. "Here, here's some water. It'll make
you feel much better." He leaned down and held out a glass. Still she
didn't look up. "You know, Tuyet, when I was younger—"

With a flick of her wrist she knocked the glass out of his hand.
"*Stop it!*" She jerked her head around to one side and stared into the
corner, eyes blazing and jaw working under the skin, clearly holding
herself in check.

But then she got to her feet and pushed a hand into his chest,
forcing him to take a step back.

"Why you so *nice* all the time, hah? Why you bring me here,
eh, *father*!" She spat the word and pushed past him, making her way
unsteadily to the door and banging through it like a cat escaping into

the street. Peters looked down in confusion at the water on his hand, and for an unguarded moment he, too, seemed frail and uncertain.

I caught a ride on a mining tractor to the landing dome on the horizon. Carolyn Dorczak was just emerging from a landing transfer trailer when I arrived, stepping down behind the man who was now her superior, the man who managed the big English-speaking colony at West Lowhead on the second planet. Bart Allerton.

Polaski had carefully assembled our most presentable troops for review, all wearing their heaviest equipment and standing ramrod straight. The visitors, by contrast, were already struggling in the high gravity, nearly twice that of their own planet.

Our troops were dwarfed by the off-worlders, who were dragging themselves along the rough dirt, coughing from the dust and squinting directly into the setting sun. No other lights had been turned on, giving the scene its intended brutal atmosphere, the cold air and the silence punctuated only by the coughing and the scraping of feet in the gravel. Polaski led the way, holding a swagger stick in his left hand and sweeping the other in lavish gestures, spelling out the troops' advantages and extolling the third generation's unparalleled prospects. Carolyn Dorczak slipped away from the entourage and walked tiredly over to stand next to me.

"Stop looking so serious, Ed—you look like you've got a lemon stuck in your throat. Don't you ever have fun?"

"Hello, Commander. You look a little worn out yourself. What time is it for you?"

"Not 'commander' any more, I'm afraid. Just 'Carolyn.'" She pursed her lips. "Nighttime. You?"

"I don't know. No one pays much attention to ship's time anymore. The sunsets are thirty-three hours apart. Sorry about the charade."

"Oh, that's all right." She rubbed her arms in the cold. "It'll impress Bart." She shifted her weight and looked around at the dome. Her pleasant face had changed little since her last visit, the intelligent brown eyes as always belying a pretense of agreeable inattention, the unruly hair still cut close to keep it in line. "So where's our charming friend, Michael Bolton? The ladies were kind

of hoping to say hello—he and his merry band have quite a reputation in the system, you know."

"No, I didn't. They're all on R and R."

"Shame."

It wasn't really true: Bolton was on one of H-V's moons,
negotiating with a group that claimed to have contacts among the
Europeans.

Dorczak shrugged her coat closer around her and peered up
at the top of the dome. "I know things, Ed."

I didn't answer her.

"I know that there are some very heavy ships inbound from
the asteroids, and that you're scanning them with everything you've
got—which means you don't know who they are. We also noticed
that all your surface defenses are active. A little nervous, are you?"

"No one would try to attack us here, Carolyn."

She nodded absently. "I also hear you're going to try to send
a probe in after your drones. Which means you don't know what
happened to them, either. For all your brave talk when we entered
the system eleven years ago, you've never known."

I was trying to think of an answer when an aide slipped a note
into my hand. I read it and then handed it back, and whispered to the
aide for a moment. She left, then a minute later reappeared at the
edge of the dome and nodded to us. I turned to Dorczak.

"Well, I'll tell you what. How'd you like to visit our command post while our ships stop and board those very unidentified
vessels?"

"Entertaining thought. And?"

"And you tell me if there's anyone else in the system who
thinks we're sending a probe."

"Okay."

I caught the aide's eye and nodded toward a tractor sitting
inside the nearest air lock. "Let's slip out this way—Polaski would
shit."

We rode in the pressurized cab of the tractor while the aide
next to us drove, farther and farther across the frozen black wastes
and past the last of the ships and the last of the domes. The sun
resting on the horizon dropped suddenly below it and winked out,

leaving Dorczak to gasp and grope instinctively for a way to stop the tractor. It was suddenly so dark that we couldn't see our own hands.

"Look behind you." Again she gasped. Stretching for miles behind us was the trail of dust kicked up by our passage, still glowing in the setting sun and suspended against the featureless black, like an electric snake lancing down toward us from out of space. The driver illuminated a direction finder on the dash.

I was sure Dorczak hadn't noticed a slender pillar of flame rising upward from the horizon behind us, but I had.

"Blacked out?" I asked the aide.

"Yes, sir. You won't see much till we're inside the dome." She was right: after a few minutes the tractor slowed, with nothing more than a dim marker crawling past above the cab. The tractor rocked to a stop with a humming of motors, then it was buffeted by blasts of air from the sides. We were in the lock tunnel.

Then we were moving again and turning to the side, only to stop one more time and crawl forward through the darkness bit by bit until we stopped for the last time. Solenoids snapped home next to our heads, and with a sucking sound from the doors the smell of watered-down dirt hit us as the doors slid open.

Fifty yards off through the darkness, under the center of the dome, was the military operations command, illuminated by dim red light that reflected from a canopy suspended haphazardly above it. We climbed down from the cab and scuffed through the damp dust toward the center, really nothing more than thirty tables and consoles placed on a metal grating. Some of the consoles were partly disemboweled, while exposed bundles of cable snaked across the ground or hung precariously from the canopy's supports. Pacing impatiently among the rows of glowing consoles was David Rosler, looking as unkempt and temporary as the rest of the complex. The center's director, a competent ship's captain named Simon Plath, stood nearer to us at the back, speaking now and then in a low voice.

Technicians were down on their knees on the far side of the covered area, working quickly behind the farthest row of consoles. Bent over and hurrying back and forth among them, shining with perspiration and stripped down to his t-shirt, was the muscular form of Tyrone Elliot.

"So this is it," whispered Dorczak with mock reverence in her voice, "the pulsing nerve center of the mighty empire."

The director leaned down next to one of the console controllers, then stood and spoke in a clear voice. "Capture vessels established on default orbit, blacked out and tumbling."

He was referring to a trick we had used elsewhere with good success: the capture vessels—high-powered, piloted "dry-docks" that could open their bays to swallow smaller ships—were observing radio silence and cooling down their skins, while they tumbled slowly to mimic orbiting debris.

"All right," said Rosler impatiently, standing still now and looking down as he cleaned his glasses on his shirt-tail. "Get boarding parties ready for launch. Second and Third Marines. Colonel Pham commanding."

"The colonel's just down with Fourth Surface Assault, sir."

"I'm sure she's recovered!" snapped Rosler. "Do it." The director started to answer back, but thought better of it and turned to one of the controllers. I interrupted.

"Director," I said, "once the capture vessels have the targets, bring them up against the orbiting station and have the prisoners processed there. This base is closed until we complete other operations."

Polaski's voice rang out from the darkened periphery. "What the fuck is *she* doing here?" He was getting down from a transport and pointing at Dorczak.

He walked closer.

"Go back to your cave, Torres." He stopped in front of Dorczak.

"We don't allow civilians in here, Secretary, and that applies to your friend here, too."

Three years ago, during a regular staff meeting, Polaski had forced a vote on the issue of civilians entering secure facilities.

It was a meeting at which, curiously enough, all of his own military confidants were present, while attendance by the professionals and fleet officers was as light as usual. The meeting also followed weeks of more or less hysterical claims by the military that classified materials were being stolen from the headquarters building.

"Maybe you should stop making paper airplanes out of them," Priscilla Bates had said after the meeting opened, "or getting drunk and yelling about them across the urinals." She sat at my end of the table, facing Polaski and the dour-faced Rosler at the other. Their cronies sat with them, mostly senior officers in the marines or the base-defense units—Polaski's Palace Guard.

"Maybe we should just keep dick-jockeys and riffraff out of headquarters," said Carl Bermer, Polaski's beetle-browed chief aide. He'd forgotten for the moment that dick-jockeys included Rosler. He meant pilots of the long ships, and civilians.

"All right, enough of that," said Polaski with an air of benign neutrality. "We need to keep civilians off the military sites, is all. We don't need a pissing match about it."

"It's not on the agenda," I said.

Polaski and Rosler furrowed their brows in unison and studied the papers in front of them.

"Yes it is."

I looked down. It was there, near the bottom. It hadn't been there on the original notice.

"You've been pretty busy with the probe," said Polaski, "so maybe you missed it. Maybe you've got more to do than you can handle, Torres. It's understandable."

Bates had counted heads, and now she slipped me a piece of paper: VETO?

I shook my head. Out of context, a vote that appeared to favor lax security at a time of increased attacks would provide Polaski with more ammunition against the professional officer corps. So with some bickering over what was really meant by civilian, the resolution passed.

There was no good line between military and civilian leadership for the colony, but as the colony's head and nominal military commander, my own offices were in the military headquarters building. That was where I was the next day when Roddy McKenna called. He'd come to see me, he said, but had been turned away at the door.

Similar calls came that same day from Anne Miller and Charlie Peters, and even from Chan, who knew more military secrets than the military itself. At the same time, Priscilla Bates and other fleet officers, even engineers and administrators who were hard to construe as military, were saluted sharply at the door and allowed in.

"The last I bothered to check," said Chan, "I outrank Polaski. Where does he get off thinking anyone on this base is a civilian, anyway?"

"It's not important," I said. We were making progress on moving the capital ships' engines to the Serenitas probe, and I didn't want to get into a fight that might leave them hostage. Instead I moved my project notes to the little office on the alley by the assembly building, and went back and forth as needed.

I returned to the headquarters building one day about a week later to find Carl Bermer installed at a desk in my office. He had his gun apart on the desk and was cleaning it with a spare shirt I kept in a drawer.

"You're in my office," I said.

"General Polaski said you wouldn't mind," said Bermer.

"He's a general now?"

"Yes, sir."

"Give me my shirt."

"This is yours?"

I took the shirt and went to Polaski's office. Rosler was there with him, his feet up on the side of the desk.

"Why's Bermer in my office?" I said.

"We didn't think you'd be needing it," said Polaski.

"I see. And why did we think that?"

"We think," said Rosler, "that you don't have your eye on the ball."

"Which ball is that, Rosler?"

"*The* ball."

"He means," said Polaski, "the ball that doesn't involve taking engines out of our capital ships. If you want to finish your little project, Torres, be glad you have someplace to work at all. You might keep that in mind."

I tossed the shirt onto the desk and leaned down to look into the familiar grey eyes.

"I have my eye on someplace better than *this*, Polaski. That's why we're here, remember? That's why I let you come along fifteen years ago. It's why I made you, Polaski. That's something *you* might keep in mind."

"No, Torres, it's me that's going to get you where you want to go. But I have my eye on the realities, not the fantasy. You, on the other hand, are becoming a liability."

"Forget it, Polaski. The only reality you care about is putting a gun to the system's head."

He picked up the shirt and dropped it in a waste bucket by his chair. "Well, you *made* me, remember?"

"Polaski, if we ever get to Serenitas, you'll be disappointed as hell."

His grey eyes studied mine for a moment.

"So will you, Torres. So will you."

Now Polaski was standing in front of Dorczak in the operations dome, waiting for her to turn away and leave. Dorczak ignored him and turned instead to the director, who was still watching us.

"Hello, Simon. Nice to see you again."

"Commander." A smile flickered across Simon Plath's face. He avoided looking at Polaski.

Into the silence that followed came the scuff of feet from Elliot and his people, still working as fast as they could with their flashlights in the dark. They were following cables out to the edge of the dome where they led across the surface to the big ships and the fleet MI. Polaski turned abruptly to the director.

"Make this a full exercise, Plath. Five Gs." He stalked off toward Rosler. A surprised oath came from the controllers, then another voice cut them off.

"Incoming identified, Mr. Plath. Two vessels, IS-20 types, modified. Still not braking."

A woman at a table near us put down a phone. "Intelligence estimate, sir. Independent Mining Coalition ships. Ordnance unknown. Probably hoping to embarrass us on our own doorstep. Possibly to discredit us with Pikes Mountain Company." Next to me, Dorczak nodded her agreement.

"Excuse me, Mr. Rosler," said Plath smoothly, "five Gs seems unnecessarily—"

"Do it!"

Plath frowned and turned away. "Very well. CV Telemetry—upload five Gs and additional crew warnings. Also log a command with both capture vehicles: as soon as they come back up live, I want visuals all the way in. Bring the visuals up on monitors six and eight."

"Inbounds are stable on default orbits. No braking. Three minutes twenty to local horizon."

"Twelve seconds to CV ignition on updated profile."

The center became silent as we waited, except for the scuffling feet and muttered oaths of Elliot's people. I watched them for a second and wondered what they were working on. Everything seemed to be running well enough.

"Three seconds." We stared at the two blank monitors, then suddenly they flickered to life as the two capture vessels threw off their sheep's clothing and began transmitting. The pictures at first showed different parts of our planet's razor-sharp terminator sweeping crazily across the screens as the ships tumbled, but then with a flare of attitude jets the pictures stabilized to show a background of stars. Nothing happened for a moment after that, then suddenly on both screens a bright pair of dots appeared, streaking at tremendous speed from the top of the screen into the distance—the intruding ships entering their orbit around our planet.

It seemed as if the pair of dots would disappear in the distance completely, but when they were almost gone they seemed to slow to a stop and begin swelling in size, instead, streaking back toward the cameras. In truth, they hadn't slowed at all, but now the capture vessels were accelerating toward them at a terrific rate, their own increasing speed throwing them into higher and higher orbits to converge with the targets. It was an impressive and graceful sight, and it was hard to remember that behind the cameras, the crews on the CVs were suffering badly under the crushing acceleration.

Now the targets swelled from dots into identifiable ships rushing toward the cameras. Only seconds had passed, yet now a collision at more than a thousand miles per hour seemed inevitable. Then at the last instant the capture vessels fired their forward-facing solid rockets and the screens turned white.

When they cleared again, in front of each of the cameras hung one of the small grey Coalition ships, sliding back into the maw of the dry-docks. It had been only nineteen seconds since the capture vessels first fired their engines.

"I'm impressed," said Dorczak. "Swallow them whole and take your time smoking out the crews."

But at the last instant before being swallowed whole, something squat and heavy separated from one of the ships in a flash of exploding bolts.

"Bogey drop!"

"Tracking."

"Inbound. One minute forty-three to horizon."

"Ballistics, trajectory please."

"No, sir, not ballistic. Bogey is correcting."

"Guided bogey, folks."

"No, belay that, too—Mama's blind now, inside the CV. We have a smart bogey here, people, smart bogey. ECM..."

At that moment the voice trailed away and the center became quiet. Something was wrong. Then all at once Tyrone Elliot's voice shot out from behind the lights.

"Well, why didn't some motherfucking son of a bitch think of this a year ago?" A crash of tools came from the darkness, then another flashlight flared on and moved away. So that was it: the heavily MI-dependent electronic counter measures were down. If whatever it was that had separated at the last minute from the attacking ship was indeed steering itself in toward our base, then we needed our ECM capability—the electronic sleight of hand that would blind or mislead it.

"One minute to horizon."

"It's all right, Mr. Elliot," said Plath, "we appreciate what you're doing. Surface Defense, from the glimpse we got I'd say we've got a detonation device of some kind here, so you can try to shoot it down. Although at that speed, I don't know. Ranging, what's its profile going to be when we get line-of-sight?"

"Range at horizon will be 1,354 miles, bearing 89.2 flat, altitude 224 descending, speed 19,807, time to impact four minutes six."

"All right. Scramble any flight-ready ships you can. Get them clear. And let's not have any yahoos up there playing hero with this thing. It's too fast—"

"Belay that," said Polaski. "I want every armed vessel we've got on that thing's path. I want to see this thing shot down. No one's turning tail, is that clear?" Plath looked away—Polaski was bypassing him by talking directly to the controllers. And if I interceded against Polaski, Rosler would step in to confirm the order, and I'd have no choice but to take him down a notch in front of his reports.

"Ten seconds to horizon." Beyond the farthest row of consoles, Elliot's people were slamming circuit modules back into the open console bays.

"Okay," said a controller, "we've got the pop-up...there she is, folks, strong radar print. And man, that sucker is moving. Stand by for default POI. Kind of makes you wish we had an atmosphere, doesn't it? That'd be one crispy critter."

"All right, here we go. Can't do anything about it, but we're ID'ing the thing's targeting freq's. Okay, it's got radar...it's got active IR...it's got a radio altimeter, coming up."

"Three minutes thirty to impact."

"Default point-of-impact looks like west end, centerline. Farming domes maybe. What do you suppose it is? Radiation bomb?"

Dorczak had been getting restless, and now she stepped forward and spoke to Plath directly.

"Excuse me Director, but the machine's target acquisition frequencies—"

"Dorczak!" said Rosler. "Stow it. You don't have any business in here."

"Three minutes." Elliot and two technicians raced across the dirt.

"Launch Controller," said Plath evenly, glancing with interest at Dorczak, "you are to disregard the instructions you received earlier and direct all vessels off-range now. They are preventing us from employing static ground defenses." The launch controller glanced briefly at Rosler and Polaski, then pulled down his microphone as Plath turned back toward Dorczak.

"Yes, Commander, you were saying—"

With a crash of metal against metal Elliot and his technicians threw themselves onto the grating and slapped up row after row of circuit breakers. Sixteen years ago he'd been in another control room, light-years away, bringing up another faulty system during a similar attack. How little things had changed.

"Go, go, go! You're up!" Screens flickered to life.

"Station radar, blue shift! Show him overflight. Now!"

On the chance that the thing was sniffing its way in along our own outgoing radar signals, we would steadily increase our radar's frequency in the hope of making it think it was going faster than it was, and about to overfly its target.

"Two minutes forty. We have visual."

"Okay...target-aq, we've still got time—trail a mouse. Drag him back."

This part was trickier. We would pick up the bomb's own sensing frequencies, then feed back to it slightly altered responses, thus "moving" our base across the landscape toward it. Trailing a mouse. It was slower but more reliable than direct jamming.

"All right, mouse is moving and rising, all frequencies. Waiting for bogey to correct."

"Two minutes twenty."

"No correction."

Dorczak suddenly took a step forward and spoke in a sharp, clear voice, one I'd seldom heard her use. The center went quiet.

"If that is a Coalition device, Director, then it was built by the Japanese. If it is a Japanese device, every target acquisition and navigational frequency it uses is positioned between two stronger dummy frequencies, in the knowledge that McAllister and EDA automatics—which I have reason to believe you are using—will stop scanning at the first frequency they find."

The silence stretched out, then Plath spun back toward the room.

"You heard the woman! Manual scanning across the board!"

"Son of a bitch, she's right. Look at that! And there's another one! And there... Jesus, Simon, this is going to take a long time."

"One minute fifty."

"Jam, sir?"

"Stand by." People stole glances at the horizon through the glass dome, although the bomb was still more than five hundred miles away. Elliot leaned on a post with his head back, pouring water on his face.

"One minute ten."

"Stand by on surface units."

"Bogey's correcting, sir! Descending...hang on...sharp descent! Holding...again! And again...I think we've got her, sir! POI fifty short...sixty...eighty—"

Cheering began, but Plath held up a hand and the dome became quiet again. Elliot brought his head back down. Polaski and Rosler turned to look out the side of the dome. Dorczak came back to stand next to me and turned to look, too. Seconds ticked by.

A rhythmic squeaking came from somewhere in the dome. The lamps under the canopy swung. Then they slowed again and stopped, and Plath let out his breath and sat down on the grating. The bomb had struck.

Elliot looked at me and bowed.

"I don't suppose," said Dorczak as the cheering started up again, "that it's time for dinner?"

"It could be arranged."

"You and Kathy? And your priest, if he's still around? Father Peters? I've brought him a little something."

"For the love of Saint Anne, Carolyn, you shouldn't have!"

But there were tears in Peters' eyes as he turned a bottle of Australian Burgundy to catch the light. "What a lovely thing to do. Come, we'll share it, just the four of us. How can I ever repay you?"

"You've already repaid me, Father. You've let me sit down. Ed here kept me on my feet all afternoon, watching Batman and Robin jack off in front of the help. Excuse me, Father."

"No, no," he said equably, and poured the wine into his precious set of crystal glasses.

"Charlie called Rosler 'the snake of Satan' today," I said.

"He'd be flattered," said Dorczak, eyeing the wine skeptically. Peters had forgotten, or had been too polite, to sniff the cork.

"Charlie also called Polaski 'innocent.'"

"Umm, Eddie," said Peters distractedly, "you do my eloquence an injustice. Out of context and all." He stared at the wine in his glass while the rest of us watched him closely. His eyes darted across to meet ours several times.

"Ah, look at that!" he said finally, still not taking a sip. "The very nectar of Eden. No, what I said was, he's innocent in a way someone like you could never be. Or the girl, Tuyet."

"She's not a girl, Charlie, she's a grown woman."

"Ah...no. I don't think so. Not yet."

"And why are you always saying we're alike? It makes my skin crawl."

"You *are* alike," said Chan. She was enjoying herself. "I keep telling you, but you never listen." She slid a foot along my ankle under the table.

Dorczak was nodding. "They are, aren't they?" She sniffed at her glass as inconspicuously as she could. "Moody types with complicated pasts. You just hold yourself back, is all. You're always trying to pretend there's no one home."

Peters took a delicate sip from his glass through pursed lips, while his eyes roamed around the room as if he weren't really present.

"Christ," I said.

"This really is quite good," Peters said with evident relief.

Dorczak took a cautious sip. "Yes, it is. Though I have to say," she said, changing the subject again, "I heard altogether too much about innocence from the nuns in school."

"Oh? You? Roman Catholic or New American?"

"Oh, very New American, my family."

"Ah, well then. But aye, as you say, sin is what you've got, innocence is what you need but can't have. Although you must keep trying, of course—keeps the Church in business." He gestured at his glass on the table. "Now *that* is true innocence."

"The wine?" said Dorczak, a bit distractedly.

"Oh, my lord, no—wine is cloudy with lies, dear woman. Mild-mannered and lovely, but filled with secrets. No, no, not the wine..." He smiled a little vacantly at her. "The crystal, Carolyn—

the world flows through crystal such as this undeceived. Though, mind you, its clarity comes of being fused in a terrible heat, its imperfections fired away in a hellish crucible. That is the truest innocence, you know, being exhausted utterly of one's own sin. The most powerful thing in the world."

By this point Chan was evidently the only one who was following him. "We don't see much of that, do we?" she said.

"Aye, lass, the soul is a shy thing. It's got to be strong if it's to become so naked in the world."

Dorczak was nodding pleasantly if distantly, sipping at her wine as she looked around the room. Peters finally settled back into his chair with a self-satisfied look and began to tap his fingers gently against his glass, beaming at it. Chan stretched her arms overhead and turned her attention to Dorczak.

I was watching Dorczak, as well. "We had a deal, Carolyn," I said.

"Did we?"

"You were going to tell me how many people know about the Serenitas probe." Her eyes lit up despite herself as I confirmed her assumption.

"Oh, well," she said. "No one really knows. I was just guessing." She looked smug despite herself. "I hope I haven't delayed your plans any."

"Oh, no, not at all. In fact, I ordered it launched while I had you in the tractor on the way to the operations center. It's four million miles away by now."

She stared at me for a while, her lips starting to purse and her brown eyes narrowing. Then she threw back her head and laughed. I'd never seen her really laugh before, and it was a good sound, a clean, full-blooded American laugh.

"You son of a bastard," she said finally, and sighed. She took a drink and sighed again, and gazed at the table top, a distant look in her eyes.

Chan was watching her. "You haven't said anything about home, Carolyn. Lowhead. How's it been?

"Oh, bad. Worse than before. Too many settlers in their flimsy little ships, not enough land yet to support them. People starting to panic because there's no way out. Bastards taking charge while everybody else is busy trying to stay alive. Not good."

Chan made a face. "Pretty much the same story we get from everywhere, isn't it? The place is turning into a battleground, everyone armed to the teeth and at everyone else's throats."

Dorczak leaned forward and set her glass on the table. "Kind of apocalyptic, isn't it?"

"How's that?"

"Well, how does Revelations go, Father? Humanity loses its way and sinks further into warfare and hatred. Then a terrible host descends from the heavens and destroys all of man's works in retribution."

"Aye. *He that killeth with the sword...* But then there's one who rises up from among men, remember, with a power so pure that the terrible multitude bows down and lets her pass."

"Eddie," said Chan. "There's a call for you."

I looked around. "How do you know?"

"I just know."

"Hello?" I said into the room.

"Mr. Torres? It's Priscilla Bates, from the can." The "can" was the orbiting station. I couldn't tell where in the room her voice was coming from, but it was tired and tense.

"Yes, Priscilla."

"Listen, the Coalition ship—the one that released its bomb? We've got everyone off it. The other one still has its bomb on board— inside the capture vessel—and they're threatening to blow it if we start cutting our way in. So that might take us a few days."

"Well, that's mostly good news. Thanks for keeping me informed, Priscilla."

"Um...that's not why I called, exactly. Are you free to talk?"

I glanced at Dorczak, but she just pursed her lips and looked at the ceiling.

"Mostly."

"Okay. I've been talking to some of the prisoners, one of them in particular. An asteroid miner, used to be freelance. I think you should come up and see him."

I frowned and looked at Dorczak again. "I'm going to be tied up with a special mission for a while, 'Scilla. Can you just keep him on ice?"

"Um, I guess, but still I think you should talk to him before anyone else does."

"Okay. Can you tell me why?"

There was a long pause before she answered.

"He says he found one of the drones."

Chapter Fifteen: NOT THE WOLF NOR THE CHILD

"Two years ago, more or less."

The prisoner floated on the other side of the room and watched me closely.

"If the drone was so hard to see," I said, "how did you know it was there?"

His eyes shifted. He worked his lips back and forth across the edges of his teeth and thought.

"It was hard to find with the naked eye, see," he said, "because it had that round torpedo shape and that perfectly reflective surface. And I mean perfect—to keep it cold even when the sun was shining on it, we figured. But it wasn't hard to see on our instruments, because it was so heavy. That's what we were looking for, you know—asteroids with a lot of metal in 'em."

The man spoke as though my questions were just one of a number of things on his mind while his eyes darted around the corners of the room. He was a tough and sinewy man, with creased, gunmetal-black skin. He had a badly healed scar down the side of his face, which he rubbed now and then when he talked.

"So was it still cold?"

"Oh, shit yes. That much of it was still working, even if the damaged tail kept it from going anywhere. It'd kept itself real cold just floating out there in the asteroids all that time—how long did you say? Nine, ten years?"

I was starting to answer when suddenly he shot across the room and slammed me up against the padded wall. He wrenched me around and then bashed me with his boots as he pushed off again—my gun out of my shoulder holster and resting in his hand. He swept it around in my direction, then just as suddenly let out a snort of disgust and sent the gun spinning back across the room toward me.

"No clip. I didn't think you Mercenary Planet types would be that stupid. Shit."

I caught the gun and kicked myself right-side-up again, feet facing the green floor.

"No loaded weapons on the station. They'd go through the skin."

The whole attack had taken just seconds, and now he was back to looking around the room, running a hand through his hair. His hair was wiry with patches of grey, cut short and flat across the top. The stubble on his face was mostly grey.

"What's your name?"

He watched me and worked his bottom teeth across his upper lip for a minute. "Harry Penderson. Vancouver."

"How did you know it was still cold?"

"Hell, we couldn't work on the thing with our suits on, so we had to bring it into our cargo hold. But I tell you, that son of a bitch was so cold it just sucked down the temperature in the hold until we were working in our suits most of the time, anyway. My wife was the one—"

"Your wife?" We'd missed that.

"Dead. Couple of months ago—froze to death. Kid in her belly, too. Fucking Chinese batteries quit too soon. That's when I ended up with the Coalition—one of their ships picked me up. Lost my boy, too. Twelve."

"I'm sorry."

"Happens." He chewed on his lip, his gaunt face tense and his eyes darting to my clothing off and on. Looking for the clip.

"How did you end up out here, Mr. Penderson?"

He snorted. "Cattle car out of Saskatchewan. Gangs took our house, so we didn't have much to lose. Through the tunnel with a couple of weeks worth of air left...put into the big Russian floating colony like a slaver hitting the docks. Didn't have a whole lot of options...took up with a tin-can mining freighter trading heavy metals to the colony in exchange for batteries and food. Cheaper hauling the shit in from the asteroids than dragging it up from the surface, I guess." He looked away again and ran a finger absently along the scar. "Had to kill a woman trying to sell my son."

"You started to say something about your wife working on

the drone."

"Yeah. She's the one with the brains when it comes to electronics. Was. It was her that figured out how to talk to it, if you can call it that."

"How so?" He held a hand to the wall to stop his drifting. He looked wary again.

"Well, I'll tell you—what's your name? Torres? Dealing with that thing wasn't like in the movies, no sir. In the movies you've got these rogue computers or these aliens, and maybe they speak a different language, but pretty soon that gets straightened out and everybody starts talking. Or maybe things are really radical and they don't even use words, but use lights or smells or something. So you've got to translate. But I tell you, even in those movies ninety-nine percent of the communication process gets taken for granted. Not with this sucker. This thing was a real eye-opener. And I'm supposed to know better."

"Why's that?"

"Can I have some water?" I unclipped the squirt bottle from my belt and pushed it toward him. "Professor of Journalism. University of Vancouver." He took a drink and hung onto the bottle. "Tenured. Anyway, first of all, we had to play games with receiving and transmitting antennas for a long time just to find a medium. Finally we found out it was zapping out some kind of coherent signal on one frequency—though we never did figure out what the signal was—so we aimed back all kinds of shit on the same frequency. The only signal protocol it finally matched, though, was plain-language text—a character at a time, same thing we use all over the system. Except it didn't use English."

"You weren't transmitting in English?"

He wiped his wrist across his grey stubble and dried it on his t-shirt. "*We* were. What *it* started using was a whole mix of languages and terminology. A lot of the references were unique to this system, though, so we figured it'd sat out there all those years listening and learning the languages, although it got them all mixed up. We thought it was pretty strange that you people built the damn thing and didn't even teach it a regular language."

Didn't we?

"So you'd use English and it would answer you in something else?"

"Well, that's the first problem. It didn't answer us, period."

"I thought you said it did."

"I know, it's weird. Look, ask me a question."

"Right now, you mean? Any question?"

"Yeah, just ask me a question."

"Um, okay. So what did you do with the drone in the end?"

Penderson floated close to the far wall, his eyes glancing around the room and sometimes at my clothing, but not at my face. He didn't answer my question. I waited a full minute for him to make his point, but he never did. "So what's all this got to do with the drone?"

Still he didn't do anything.

"Look, you told me to—"

"I'm in need of location."

He wasn't looking at me when he said it; he'd drifted around so he was looking the other way. I didn't know what he meant.

"How do—"

"I'm in need of location." I'd lost him completely, so I waited. Minute after minute crawled by, then finally he pushed himself around and looked at me.

"Pretty hard to talk to, isn't it?"

He looked more frustrated than I was.

"It's breaking all the rules, isn't it? Rules like: if you ask a question, I answer it. And like we take turns, and we use the listener's context, so he understands what the hell we're talking about. And still, that's not the half of it. There's some assumptions about just being creatures that this thing didn't have. Like realizing that *it* was an object of *our* experience the same way as we were objects of *its* experience. It finally sank in to us that it didn't know that—its world existed only as part of itself. And consider this: humans always assume that actions have purposes. There's intentionality behind every act. Think about it: that's pretty basic— signals are aimed at an antenna in order that someone *do* something. The signals don't just *exist*. And not only that, but we always assume that the purposes of the actions are to make some kind of progress—

to *get* somewhere worth getting to for the individual or the species.

"What you never realize is that, in the movies, sitting across the conference table exchanging colored lights with green-speckled aliens, all those assumptions are already made. No sir. More than half a million words must have gone back and forth between us and that fucking drone, and it took that long to realize what the word 'alien' really meant. I tell you, dealing with that thing was spooky. It was like we didn't even exist, beyond serving to provide it with the one piece of information it wanted."

"Which was?" Penderson had been getting tense, and now he looked wary again, and worked at his teeth for a while with a clouded look in his eyes.

"Well, that got real complicated, see, and we went around and around trying to make sense of why it was saying what it was. But in the end it got pretty clear, and I'll tell you, we were close to deciding that this wasn't one of your drones at all."

"From your description, it had to be."

"Yeah, well. What it was saying over and over boiled down to this: 'Query: origin of signal producers.' Meaning us—and all the other people whose signals it had been listening to over the years. We explained over and over every way we knew how, and it never did understand."

"Maybe it was more damaged than you thought."

"No, sir. That thing was smart—I mean very, very smart. That wasn't the problem."

"It could have been—"

"Look, you're about to start going over the same ground we beat our heads against day after day. Don't bother. There's no way around something that got real clear in the end, and you're just going to have to take my word for it. That goddamned drone of yours— which was supposed to be out here clearing the way for humanity, as I understand it—had no fucking idea what human beings were. And it wanted to know—bad."

Somehow for the last few minutes I'd known that was what he was going to say. It was because of a memory that was coming back to me as he spoke—something that had slid past during the excitement of the drones' launch, sixteen years earlier.

I needed to talk to Miller.

"What was your interest in the drone, Mr. Penderson?"

He shrugged. "Thought we could sell it. Seemed like a good idea at the time."

"So what did you do with it in the end?"

"Hell, we got it out of there."

He sounded disgusted. "It was cooling down the bay too much, and I suppose it was getting too warm to last much longer, anyway. Can't say I minded getting rid of it, though."

"So how'd you get involved in this attack on us? You said you've only been with the Coalition a couple of months."

His leathery face tightened and his eyes narrowed as though he was going to jump me again. "You're pretty good at asking questions, aren't you, Torres? Keep on changing the subject, don't let on anything. Don't worry, I'm not going to jump you again. That was just for fun, anyway—I don't exactly have anywhere to go."

"So why the attack on us?"

He shrugged again. "I didn't have a whole lot of choice, Mister. It gets real hungry out there."

"When we've cut your friends out of the other ship," I said, "and taken a look at all of you, we're going to put you back out there in one of your two ships." His eyes narrowed a little and he turned away, as though he regretted showing his hand about being hungry.

"You want to sign on with us?" I said. His hand stopped where it was. He didn't look at me.

"Doing what?"

"I don't know."

He raised an eyebrow in my direction and then turned farther away, then began arching his back to stretch his muscles. "So what's in it for me? Black lackey to the great mercenary empire?"

"You'd be safe most of the time. Food and warmth, people."

His grizzled face was struggling between interest and caution, and he looked around at the corners of the room and tried hard to relax. Finally his shoulders dropped and he turned to face me.

"Hell, yes, I'll sign on. That sounds really fucking good." His loneliness showed through in the lines of his face for just a moment, however much he tried to hide it.

"All right, stay here. Someone'll come to get you." I groped for the edge of the wall padding to turn myself around, then pulled my way out into the central corridor. Penderson's guard was floating alongside the doorway, a young and disgruntled-looking man armed with a stun gun. When I came out he was upside-down to me, watching the empty corridor. I told him to get Penderson out of the can and escort him down to the surface to report to Chan. Although I needed to go down myself to talk to Miller about Penderson's story, I still needed to spend some time on the can.

Early that morning the Serenitas probe had made it through the torus. Before dawn all of the teams had gathered to monitor the outbound telemetry and watch the pictures coming back, and we had struggled together through the painful sight of the giant European weapons flaring into life and rotating around toward the probe's cameras. But the probe with its breathtaking acceleration had been faster, and for the second time in my life I had watched a tunnel hurl closer and swallow me whole. This time, however, the picture and the telemetry had stopped abruptly, and in the sudden silence of the control room the long, hard wait began.

The corridor that the guard and I were floating in was nearly fifty feet across, a poorly lit, cavernous tunnel of crudely welded and unpainted iron that ran down the center of the quarter-mile-long can. Like the corridor, most of the can was as unadorned as it was big, and uninsulated, scarcely heated. Only the children's quadrant had clean air, paint, and enough emergency pressure seals.

The little room behind me that Penderson had been brought to for our meeting was one of a number of changing and equipment rooms that dotted this part of the iron corridor. They in turn served an enormous room whose giant door was below us around the corridor wall, a room more than a hundred feet in each of its three dimensions, completely empty and with all six sides padded and indistinguishable from one another. It was the can's sporting room, and while any number of games had been designed to be played in it, its unshakable if unconfirmed reputation was for sexual recreation in freefall.

Neither the guard nor I had moved, both of us listening to an approaching clamor of voices and the sounds of boots slamming against the iron walls, and the hissing of jets. The jumbled wave of echoes and whispered scuffing and sharp clanging preceded a shadowy tangle of figures approaching along the corridor in the distance, with the dim shapes of people and equipment flickering in the bright jets of flame that strobed against the sides of the rust-colored tunnel. As a boy I had once watched a friend try for the border through a sewer tunnel echoing with the baying of dogs, and the feeling here was the same.

"So!" Pham had seen me before I saw her. "Mr. No-Balls—you miss all the fun, hah?" She came streaking up the corridor ahead of the crowd to catch herself on a rung partway around from where I floated. She was wearing her tight black suit along with her big gun and a stun rifle, and a portable burner strapped to her back and a heavy chest shield with a smoke mask hanging around her neck. Her face was streaked with grease and soot, and her eyes were glassy and jumpy as she looked up and down the corridor.

"Hello, Pham. Is this the other ship?"

"Yah, shit. Finally we cut these dumb-heads out. They in there with gas and fucking traps. Couple of my people not so good." Her head whipped back to watch the chain of fifty or so prisoners, bound and clipped to a cable and kept to the center of the corridor by her soldiers. She seemed agitated and her movements were jerky. She was talking too fast. "What you doing up here—you don't come up to can so much, hah?"

"Prisoner named Penderson. He signed on—stay away from him."

"Yah, okay. No problem. What the fuck I care?" She wiped distractedly at her face then suddenly twisted and launched herself down to the corridor wall below us to open the big padded door to the sporting room, then shot back up toward the approaching procession. Both Pham's troops and the prisoners looked in bad shape. Groups of medics floated along next to a dozen screaming burn victims, trying to spray the wounds and fasten on pressurized saline canisters. Pham shouted instructions at her troops and began separating out prisoners she wanted held temporarily in the sporting room, and others she wanted segregated for individual questioning. The medics tried to argue on several of her choices, but she snapped back at them irritably and threatened them, so they held their tongues and did their best. I nodded to the guard next to me to go ahead and move Penderson out.

That night I awoke suddenly, as though disturbed by a sound. The cubicle was still lit by its red nighttime lamp, and my watch showed an hour before the start of the day. I floated against my tether waiting for the sound to repeat, sniffing at the air for smoke or gas, but there was nothing.

I knew I wouldn't fall back asleep, so I dragged off the sack and pulled on just my pants and jacket, then floated out through the cubicle's opening. The can was perfectly quiet at that hour, and the air against my chest was cold. I pulled my way along the side tunnel into the dim central corridor, drifting in the empty space. Just as I reached it the sound came again, so clearly etched against the silence that it sent a chill up my spine.

Tick.

But it was only the sound of iron walls contracting—sharp and clear and harmless. My nerves settled and I pushed off toward one of the rungs in the wall, then looked down the corridor. In both directions it disappeared into the poor light on rusted walls. I picked what I thought was the longer direction, then launched myself forward as fast as I could.

The rush of air was exhilarating—a freedom and suspension of effort never found on the surface. I pictured rushing naked through outer space, then just as quickly realized the irony of feeling such freedom inside a cold iron tunnel, its impenetrable walls looming in the shadows ahead and behind. It left me with an almost painful lightness of heart, suspended between a numb and insensible past and future.

Tick.

The whisper echoed along the corridor and stole away the image, and I spread my jacket to catch the air and tumble. The end-wall loomed up in front of me and I twisted to catch it with my feet, then pushed back the other way. A rectangle of light caught my eye, then, and after a minute I made out a doorway ajar with light spilling into the corridor. For a moment I was surprised by the size of the door, then with a shift of perspective realized where I was; it was the door to the sporting chamber. I spread my jacket again and drifted to the wall, wondering why anyone would be in the giant room so early in the morning and with so few of its lights on. I caught the edge of the padded door and swung it open.

Tick.

At first I thought Pham was dead. Her body floated at the center of the empty space, turning in the poor light, and for a moment I felt exposed and alone in the presence of her death—but then I saw that her eyes were open and watching me. They were heavily lidded, but they focused on me and followed me as she drifted in languid circles.

She was completely naked. Her head was back and her arms and legs floated at her sides, the hard muscles relaxed and sleek under her skin. Her body had been oiled over every inch from her temples to her feet, and the light shone from her cheekbones and her slack lips, from her oiled breasts and the hollows of her hips, from her thighs. She looked sated, drifting without thought, yet her eyes held out the same seduction as always, pulling at me where I floated in the doorway. On her arm, a darker area showed against the olive skin, abraded from the constant air syringes.

Tick. The sound whispered up along my legs, leaving a cool trace against the skin. I felt the cold air against my chest through the open jacket.

It seemed natural, somehow, to find Pham in that room, as though I'd always known she would be there, waiting in the half-dark. I watched her turn, arched backward at the waist, head thrown back and turned to one side to watch me, the few lights glistening off her oiled skin, black hair floating free and dark eyes following me. I pulled myself in past the doorway. She didn't move or change expression, but just watched me and waited.

But a movement elsewhere in the chamber caught my eye.

Tick.

This time the sound traced across my skin like a scalpel.

A man floated in the corner of the room, someone I'd never seen before. He was naked as well and floated against the padded walls in the corner, his skin oiled like Pham's. His head bumped against the pads, pressed against his shoulder at an impossible angle. His eyes were open and empty.

Tick.

One more time the sound, like a metronome. But not counting out the time—holding it still, frozen in place.

Pham drifted so that her head pointed down, her lidded eyes still following me upside down. As I watched her drift I felt strangely reassured by the man's presence. It seemed right that he should be there and that he should be dead, as though anything less would have left her unattended and diminished.

Tick. The sound stirred in my loins and the cool air reached in through my clothing. But slowly I pushed my way back out through the door, and with an effort broke the lock of her eyes.

Tick.

I pushed my way up the corridor, leaving the sound to slide past me and race ahead along the iron walls.

Three days later I rode to the surface with Priscilla Bates, enjoying her ordinary company while I tried to shake the image of Pham. Bates was an attractive woman now in her early forties, with pale skin and light hazel eyes and long brown hair—one of the few women who still let it grow. She'd become one of our better operations commanders, but she shied away from combat, complaining of painful joints. She took duty in charge of the can whenever she could.

Back on the surface she joined me and Chan, and the wiry and cautious Harry Penderson, for a visit to Anne Miller in her quarters under the main dome. The four of us walked along the dusty black alleyways, preceded by a pair of six-legged drones who marched solemnly on opposite sides of the alley. They dragged their feet to kick up as much dust as possible and played a heavy rendition of the Funeral March from Mahler's First Symphony, plopping down their big feet in time with the music.

"I don't get it," said Penderson, eyeing the drones uncertainly. "Why do they do that? I've never seen a frivolous machine before."

"It's not frivolous to them," said Chan. "You see, they're

allowed to give themselves points for learning new things. The more
intricate and symmetrical a thing it is, the more points they add to
their score—and they're programmed to get that score up as high as
they can. So in effect they take pleasure from doing things like that."
Bates and I both sighed, knowing what was coming and having
heard the whole argument dozens of times before. I looked away and
thought again about Pham floating in the dim light.

"I wouldn't call it 'taking pleasure,'" said Penderson, frowning first at Chan and then at the drones in their clouds of dust. "Not
if they're just machines, and not if it's just the way they're programmed."

Chan sighed, too. "That's all it is with us, Harry, on some
level: neurons firing and glands squirting—the programming of
instinct. But...no, come on, don't get your feathers up. I think it's
wonderful that something like pleasure could be made out of ordinary flesh and blood. Don't look at me like that...you're not any less
alive for being real, Harry—those interactions are so many levels
removed from what you really feel that it has nothing to do with who
you are." Unlike Chan, the rest of us still balked at the idea of being
ultimately so mundane—however far removed our selves were from
those basic interactions—and we jealously guarded some threatened
sense of our own vitality. We also tended to fall unerringly into the
mistake Penderson was about to make.

"You sound like this Miller woman," he said.

The little drones stopped in unison on a rumble of tympanis,
and solemnly tapped their inside feet in time to a funereal pause
before continuing.

"No," said Chan. She was resigned. "That's not true. Anne
Miller isn't interested in how the sparkle and mystery of life is
created—she's interested in how *intelligence* is created—that tiny,
insignificant little part of us that reasons. Don't confuse our being
real and comprehensible with our being *rational*, Harry—that's the
mistake she makes. She thinks that the source of everything worth-
while is intelligence—sophisticated, compact, and effective, maybe,
but still intelligence stripped of all else. Her belief is that with
enough of the right kind of decision-making rules you've got a
human being—when all I'm saying is that with a pile of glands and

neurons and instincts, and a lifetime of being loved and cared for, you've got a living creature worth being. Like us."

The little drones timed the brooding end of the movement perfectly to make a two-column, parade-ground pivot and stop in a cloud of black dust at either side of Miller's door. Then, in a trick that had been making their rounds, they turned around and lifted themselves onto their rear legs with their front legs extended in front of them, lions rampant guarding the door. "Giddy-up," said one, and we knocked and pushed our way in.

Miller had turned sixty the year before, and her age had begun to show in her face and her hair. And as usual these days, it took us a while to interest her in our presence, and to distract her from her papers and her screens. But finally she listened long enough to hear Harry Penderson's story.

"Well," she said finally, "that particular one may not have known who we were. Not all the drones have the same knowledge, you know." She spoke a little vaguely and her eyes wandered back to her papers now and then.

"Anne," I said, "let me ask you a couple of questions. When we were back in the Solar System waiting, and the first messenger drone went back to the Solar System with the news that terraforming was under way here and that the torus was open, did it know *why* it was going back, and *why* it was delivering the news?"

Miller was shaking her head even as I asked the question.

"No. Basic programming. Unconscious instructions. 'Why' only has to do with plans they develop themselves, the methods they themselves design for carrying out the instructions they take as givens."

"Okay, then what about this: after that drone went back to the Solar System and started receiving your new instructions, where would it think those instructions were coming from?"

She frowned at the question. "Again—it wouldn't have 'thought' anything. The instructions were sent to it embedded in special communications codes that took the instructions straight into its memory, bypassing any processing."

"Then when it returned here to Holzstein's and disseminated the new instructions to all the others—where would the others have thought the information was coming from?"

"Same thing—embedded in those same special communications codes. For them, the instructions just suddenly existed."

Bates was wandering around the room blowing dust off of things.

"Like being given directions under hypnosis?" she asked.

Miller looked surprised at the idea, but nodded. "Yes. Very close."

"By the way, Anne," I said, "where are those communications codes kept? You've never mentioned them before."

She pointed to a slender metal briefcase slipped in among her books and memory blocks on the shelf.

"Okay. Now I've just got a couple more questions. Anne, would one of your drones be capable of taking a look at those European cannon ships and identifying them as weapons?"

She jerked her head up, then slowly looked back down at her papers; she knew why I was asking.

"It's possible. Not very likely, but possible."

"All right. Now let me ask you this: when we arrived here in Holzstein's System, the torus here had a record of *two* vessels being sent back to the Solar System. Remember? Not one. And the second one was sent back to the Solar System *after* the first one returned here to Holzstein's with your new instructions. Have you ever figured out why?"

Penderson was watching me intently. Very few people in the system knew how little control we'd had over the drones.

Miller didn't answer, but ran a hand absently across her papers.

"Okay, then I'll tell you what I think happened," I said. "For a long time I thought it was something about your new instructions that caused them to send another drone back to the Solar System without letting us know about it." Miller was shaking her head tiredly as I said it. She knew it wasn't true. "But what I think now is that after the first drone came back here to Holzstein's from the Solar System, and obeyed its programming and unconsciously passed along your new instructions to the others, it proceeded to describe what it had seen on its trip. Namely another system—Earth's solar

system—filled with activity and with hundreds of huge white machines breaking out of their orbits to chase it back toward the torus—
heading for what it thought of as its own home system. Remember,
not one of those drones had ever been outside of its protective ship
before it reached Holzstein's System. It's where they were born."
Chan and Bates and Penderson had stopped where they were to
watch me, but Miller went on idly rifling the edges of her papers.

"So what would the other drones do when they heard this
story? They'd send another drone back to take a close look at those
approaching ships. And when they'd gotten that look, we all know
what they did—the perfectly reasonable thing. They left. En masse,
hours before we were expected to arrive."

Miller was nodding slightly, as though she had known all of
this long ago and was tired of thinking about it. I looked at the
others. "I don't think we're ever going to see those drones back here
again, no matter how long we wait. I think they're parked in Serenitas
System, probably doing their jobs, but not about to come back here.
They may even have concluded that their 'instinctual' return to the
Solar System is what drew us toward them, and they're not about to
make that mistake again. But all of this probably also means that
there's no reason why we can't go ahead and join them—assuming
we can get at the torus. Though no matter what we do, we'd better
make damned sure the drones don't ever see huge weapons like
those coming at them again."

I looked at Miller. "You may have programmed them to be
just like us, Anne, but that may also be why we'll never see them
again." She understood what I was saying, but even then, as I
watched her, I had the feeling that she knew something more, that
somehow she'd thought this through even further than I had.

"But Ed," said Bates, "surely the messenger drone knew who
we were, and what all of our ships were for?"

Miller closed her eyes.

"Ah, Priscilla," I said. "You weren't in the Operations room
back on the island when the drones launched. There's something
Anne said, but no one heard her—"

A scrabbling sound suddenly came from the door, then it
burst open with the two little grasshopper drones tumbling in after

it and scurrying to the side. There was nothing else in the doorway except the empty alleyway and the swirling dust glowing in the sunlight—and the crunching of boots approaching through the gravel. The footsteps got louder, then all at once Michael Bolton stood in the doorway, wearing an imposing military uniform but looking dustier and more tired than I'd ever seen him. Penderson tensed and took a step toward the door.

"Easy, Harry," said Bates. "He's one of the good guys. Michael Bolton, Harry Penderson."

Bolton took a step in and leaned back against the doorway, wiping the back of his hand across his forehead.

"Pleasure's all mine," he said, not moving to shake hands.

"I thought you were off-planet," I said.

"Was. I've had a bit of a fire under my tail for a couple of days, though—just put down. Picked up a whisper and thought we'd best get back. I take it you haven't heard."

"Heard what? Did you make contact with the Europeans?"

"Would have...remarkable what these frightful togs will do. But no, it's moot now." He pushed himself off the doorpost and brushed the dust from his jacket, then stepped forward and held out his hand to Penderson. "Pleased to meet you, Penderson. You look like you could do with a stiff drink. Hello Anne, Priscilla." He gave Chan's hand a squeeze, then turned and sat down in a chair, stretching his legs stiffly in front of him. "Wretched buggers, those Europeans. They're pulling out, you know. Going through the tunnel."

We stared at him as he idly plucked pieces of something out of his gold braid. Finally he looked up again. "Seems they were a bit discomposed by your probe, Torres...took it to mean we were about to go through ourselves. Suspicious bastards, aren't they? Lou Fiedler's just confirmed it—they're abandoning the third planet. They've pulled back all their pickets, which have themselves already gone through, by the by. All those bloody big cannon of theirs."

For the first time in years, that night, I dreamed about the cavern and the passageway leading away from it. There was someone in the cavern with me, though—just behind me and to one side, watching over my shoulder and whispering in my ear.

"You see..." My mother's voice. "The demon's right in front of you now. Naked. Don't go."

"Don't you see the light, though? At the end of the passage, like the moon? I can reach it."

"You reached for love once, Eduardo, and killed your father. You reached for power once, too, and killed an old man who'd done you no harm. Then you reached for freedom, and killed Madhu. Stay here with me, where it's safe."

"But I didn't reach for the baby, and it died, too."

"Stay."

"I've already sent out the probe."

"And you see—death has followed it already."

Chapter Sixteen: THE GOSPEL ACCORDING TO *SUN OF GABRIEL*

Pham slammed her metal cup onto the table, spilling bitter liquid, and pushed it across the pitted surface to a confused Roddy McKenna.

"You want to be powerful guy? Okay, you drink that. You drink it all quick like, no pussy feets or someone fuck with you, hah?" She looked away with a frown and sucked at the liquor on her knuckles, snorting now and then as if to remind herself of McKenna's inexperience, lest his fascination with her warrant some sort of self-consciousness on her part.

The two of them sat across a table from one another at the far end of the recreation center, while Tyrone Elliot and I sat with our backs to the bar and our feet up on stools, watching McKenna struggle with the mysteries of life according to Colonel T. Pham.

"I knew a fella in Louisiana, once," said Elliot, tossing back his own drink and belching. "Followed a mule around for forty days and forty nights...figured the mule musta known something, it was so quiet and serene, like." He groped around behind him for the jar. "Finally got tired of stepping in mule shit and came back home to his wife and kids."

The four of us were the only ones in the room—Pham and McKenna at one end, and Elliot and I at the other. Afternoon light filtered through the windows that had been cut into the black walls, but otherwise the room was dark. Back in the shadows near Pham and McKenna an obese pig rooted under the tables, grunting and rummaging for scraps. No one knew where it had come from; the story was that it had wanted a drink so badly that it held its breath and ran the two miles across the surface from the farming domes.

Down at the other end McKenna suddenly doubled over, then straightened back up with an effort.

"That's pretty good stuff," he said, gripping the cup and struggling to keep the liquor down.

"Bullshit." Pham lurched across the table and snatched back the empty cup, while McKenna tried to keep his eyes off her snake-like body leaning toward him. "That stuff kill you. You telling me what you think I want to hear. The world fuck with you real quick, buddy boy, you do that. Run around being sucker, thinking maybe if you just a little bit better guy, then boss-man, or father-man or priest-man finally see you there and say Yah, okay, you good enough now. Shit." She stared into the cup and tapped it impatiently on the table, as though trying to remember whether she'd already filled it again.

Next to me Elliot sighed and re-crossed his legs. "Sad, ain't it. Spark beat out of a pretty woman like that. Even if she is so short." He scratched his chin and looked at me. "'Course, you probably agree with her, don't you? You short, depressed people always stick together, I noticed."

"I just wish she'd leave him alone, is all. He's got no business being in here."

"So? Prove her wrong. You're the boss-man, ain't you? When was the last time you told him he's doing okay? Here we got the whole system beating on us asking when the probe's coming back and are we gonna say it's safe to follow the Europeans or not, and that kid thinks it's all his fault 'cause ol' *Sun of Gabriel* ain't come back."

"*Aieee!* Fucking pig!" At the other end of the room the waddling pink shape had reached Pham's table, snuffling at the bench leg and urinating noisily into the dirt. Pham's shout didn't have any impact on it at all, so she threw back her head and drained her cup, then flung it at the pig. It clanked against the beast's forehead between its little black eyes, but still it paid her no attention and went on sniffing at the bench. McKenna pulled himself un-steadily to his feet to lean across the table and watch.

"Hah! I think maybe we have piggy for dinner, what you think?" She dragged out her huge fléchette gun and held it out in both hands. For a minute I thought the pig was finished, but instead she pointed it at the ceiling and pulled the trigger.

As strong as she was, the gun drove her bodily back along the bench she was straddling. The force of the blast swept across the room in a hot wave, and the gout of flame from the barrel reached all the way to the ceiling—which now bore a ragged three-foot hole through the brick. Mortar dust rained to the floor and a cloud of it swirled beneath the hole in the sudden sunlight coming through it. The pig hadn't seemed to notice the blast at all, but it did gradually stop its snuffling as it realized that it stood exactly in the center of a heavenly shaft of light, slanting down through the haze and spilling across its pink feet and the wet black dirt around it. Pham was sprawled back along the bench looking at it disgustedly, while the pig slowly raised its head and looked into the circle of celestial light, as though surprised that God should have shed His benevolence upon it for doing no more than urinating on the rec center floor.

Elliot scratched his chin and leaned closer. "Twenty to one she don't shoot up through that hole again."

"That's a sucker's bet, Tyrone. If she shoots up through that hole it's going to go right through the dome, and I don't live to collect."

He looked at me. "You're pretty smart for a short, depressed person, you know that?"

"I work at it. Now what?" The pig's attention had finally wandered from the hole, and now its little eyes were following something else across the room; we peered into the gloom to make out a spider drone flitting along the ceiling toward us.

"Hah!" Pham's gun swept down from where it still pointed at the hole in the ceiling and swung across the room toward the drone as it closed on us. I watched in fascination and held my breath. Just as the gun lined unsteadily up on the drone, the drone spoke in its pleasant little voice.

"Mr. Torres? Katherine Chan sends her compliments, and wishes you to know that the probe has—" With a crashing of benches the drunken Roddy McKenna lunged across the table and drove Pham's hand upward just as she pulled the trigger. The room shook with another powerful blast and a gout of flame, and after a few long seconds Elliot and I opened our eyes carefully to look up at the ceiling. Not four feet from the first hole was a new one, with swirls of dust and brick raining down onto the floor and billowing out into the air. The pig didn't even hesitate, but trotted across into the new pool of light and contentedly resumed its rooting. Pham turned and spat in McKenna's face and jerked her arm away. "Prick," she said, and sat back with a snort of disgust.

From next to me came a polite "Ahem." The spider drone hovered at my side, unfazed by its brush with death. "Ms. Chan wishes you to know that the probe has returned and has sent a communication, and that your presence is requested in the research center auditorium. Thank you."

Elliot held out his hand. "Congratulations, Torres, you done good. I never doubted you at all, hardly."

Cables from the research building tunneled under the edge of the dome to a row of dish antennas, rotating with infinite precision and patience as they listened to the whispering of the distant probe. Other cables slithered farther across the black dirt to a row of smaller antennas that pointed to our ships resting on the horizon, where the massive fleet MI worked to process the billions of pages of data collected by the probe during eight months in the Serenitas system.

Indoors, metal chairs scraped against the brick floor as senior personnel filed in and took places on one side of a long row of tables. The tables stood in the center of the auditorium, a cold iron and brick hall with a high vaulted ceiling and a meager string of lamps hanging from it. Behind where we sat at the tables the auditorium was empty, but on the wall facing us hung rows of big display screens, suspended above doors that led to the labs and offices. Between our table and the wall with the screens, the floor was covered with a metal grating on which technicians were hastily setting up desks and computer consoles, and rows of printers and monitors on portable stands.

Charlie Peters was present in his capacity as Logistics chief, looking red-faced and pleasant with Kip in tow. Chan was there, too, dragging a chair across the floor with one hand and trying to read from a slippery sheaf of papers in the other. Polaski and Miller were already seated, Miller looking agitated and worrying a tiny notebook in one hand. Bolton and Roscoe Throckmorton sat back in their chairs at one end, while on the far side of the table, among the banks of presentation equipment, Elliot stood among the screens and tables arguing quietly with Lou Fiedler's radio astronomers. The young Roddy McKenna sat ashen-faced and disconsolate at a keyboard at the back, his day in the limelight shrouded by his alcoholic haze.

Nearly forty people worked over the machines spread across the grating, beginning the Herculean task of digesting the probe's raw data even as the probe turned for its long sweep back from where it had re-entered our system. Those data were being sent back from the probe's memory in the fastest way possible, a direct, unformatted dump into FleetSys' own immense storage. But that also meant that the data needed massive processing before becoming usable. We expected to get the gross facts over a period of a few hours, but detailed interpretations could take weeks; and some facts, though discernable in theory, might never be sifted out of the hundred-trillion bits now racing toward us.

With the hiss of a hydraulic clutch and the whining spin of its electrostatic drum, a high-speed printer began spooling out fine print on sheets of erasable vellum. Lou Fiedler, the astrophysicist who had transmitted to us the first photographs of Serenitas years before, stood and aimed his shaggy head and glasses around the room, then pulled a stack of vellum from the printer and sat back down at a desk across from us, a conductor taking his place before an orchestra.

"All right," he said, "let's move this along as fast as we can. The whole system knows the probe is back, and already everyone wants to know if they should stop squabbling over the planet the Europeans left behind and start squabbling over the one they've headed for." He licked a finger and leafed through the pages. Finally he stopped and took off his glasses.

"All right, round numbers: probe entered Serenitas System eighteen degrees north of the ecliptic, at 5.3 A.U.—well outside the outermost planetoids—and corrected for a modified hyperbolic swing around the star, Serenitas Prime, with perihelion at 0.3 A.U. It looped back to hit the return torus just outside of Serenitas herself. Communication with the return torus was established immediately on entry into the system, with the torus found to be, um— Roddy? Torus communications?"

"Yeah, let's see." McKenna was having trouble focusing. "Probe requested alignment for return to Holzstein's at such and such a future time, and...what's this? Oh, okay. Torus responded it was already aligned on Holzstein's. More information followed, but that's all we've got so far."

"All right, fine. After establishing contact with the torus during its first few seconds in the system, probe discontinued all communication for several hundred hours to pursue passive observation. Very wise, Mr. Torres—a quiet little look-see before becoming an actor on its own stage, hm?"

"I still don't get," murmured Elliot with a glance at Miller, "how come we had to go spy on our own drones."

Charlie Peters, unable to pass up a reference to stages or spies, cleared his throat and leaned closer to us. "*What spy be this we send in whispered night, to steal within our sovereign's sight?*"

"Please, Father." Fiedler had heard him and now pulled down his glasses and glared at him, then reached behind him to pull more paper off the printer.

"Now, then, gross generalizations." He leafed through more pages. "Paradise herself— I'll be damned! Kate, come here and look at this." Our planetologist, Kate Salfelder, bustled her stocky form across the grating and grabbed the papers out of his hand. After squinting at the fine print for almost a minute, her cherubic face lit up and she stuffed the papers back into Fiedler's lap, then turned to look across the table at Kip, whom she treated as one of her own children and whom she preferred addressing rather than her own colleagues.

"Well, isn't that nice! The air on that planet used to be all pukey with CO_2 and nitrogen, but now those lovely drones have gone and gotten the nitrogen down to seventy-six percent and the oxygen up to over twenty. All those European people are so lucky." She leaned down to pat Lou Fiedler's hand, then bustled away. "Oh good-good-good-good!" She bustled right out through a far door, leaving Kip smiling and nodding behind her. Excited chatter came from up and down the table. Fiedler said nothing, but was carefully un-crumpling the pages and peering at them one at a time. He was frowning intently.

"What Europeans, though?" he said, without looking up. It took a while for his comment to sink in, then the room went quiet. Fiedler put down the papers and craned around to look at his colleagues behind him. "I've got infrared and deep radar of the planet here, but I'll be blasted if I see any artifacts—even though I'd have thought the Europeans would have put down on the surface right away. So let's start looking for their ships and signals out in space somewhere, hm?" He glanced up at the wall. "What's that?"

On the screen a large round image was being filled in by raster scan lines sweeping from side to side. The completed rendition ended up in perfect color, and we drew in our breaths at the stunning beauty of the blue and green planet with its gentle wisps of white cloud—seen for the first time close up and with breathtaking clarity.

"Enough of that," said Fiedler impatiently, uninterested in what Paradise looked like to the naked eye. The image was quickly re-scanned with a rendition in grey and white, then a pale yellow was painted over it on the next scan; then a third scan shifted the whole thing into what looked like a high-contrast negative. That was the way it remained, although now each subsequent scan rotated the image of the planet a few degrees, like a glowing black and white sphere turning jerkily under a strobe.

I knew that this was the playback of a deep radar probe, although I couldn't make sense of the changing patterns. Scientists worked quickly to slip bracketing cursors across the image and pull out significant surface formations for their own screens, but after only a few seconds of this the main screen cleared and the radar image moved to one side.

"Okay, here we go," said Fiedler, and turned his chair full around to face the screen as it started to fill once more. This time it filled with a complicated planar projection—a view "flattened" for the screen—of a spherical slice of the entire system, centered around the probe, a slice which then raced outward as though through larger and larger layers of an onion, until finally it represented a shell nearly a billion miles away from the sun. Then the slice snapped back down to the probe and raced outward again, and again, each time changing slightly as a new band of the electromagnetic spectrum was studied. The more massive bodies in the system left complicated vortices on the screen each time the computer-generated slice rushed passed them, and at one point someone smacked audibly at a key and froze the image, then slid a bracketing cursor in to snip a piece of it out.

"What's that?" said Fiedler.

"Nothing. I think we've got an anomaly, is all." It was Patty Kelly, sitting in the back. "Much too far out for the Europeans. Go ahead." The scan resumed and went on and on, while people began to get restless.

Finally Chan put down her own papers and leaned forward. "Lou? How long had the probe been in Serenitas System before it began this system-wide scan we're looking at?"

Fiedler glanced at a page in front of him. "One month."

Chan sat back with a frown. "So for the first few weeks the probe wasn't paying any attention behind it," she said carefully. "Because, as you know, the first European ships went through the tunnel just days after the probe did, and we know that the torus here in Holzstein's was perfectly aligned all that time. So the European ships did get to Serenitas System—and they didn't just vanish. Something happened while the probe wasn't watching."

What Chan was saying made me think of something, and I called out to McKenna. "Roddy? Can we tell if there's any chance the Europeans already took the next leg and continued on to another system?"

"No, uh-uh—they didn't. I was going to say something about that. The probe downloaded a history of all of the Serenitas torus' activity over the years since it was built, and it's never been rotated to point anywhere but back here toward Holzstein's. There's something weird about that, though... I'm still looking at it."

"What is it, Roddy?"

"Really, Mr. Torres, I think I must have made a mistake. I'm not thinking too clearly. Let me keep working on it for a minute." He seemed confused and frustrated.

"Here's something!" shouted a technician. "Coherents on VHF! Just a minute—" People rose out of their seats, then a shriek burst from the speakers.

"Wrong knob," muttered Elliot. He winced and tapped a pencil against the table.

The shrieking stopped abruptly, then instead a wall screen burst into life with streaks of black and white noise. The technician worked frantically at her keys, then gradually the screen resolved into a comprehensible image. No one spoke for a long time.

"What the devil is *that*?" said Fiedler. Churning its way across the screen, barely discernable in the grainy and unsteady picture, was an old military tank, valiantly pushing aside drifts of sand.

"Television," said Chan disgustedly. "Received by the Serenitas probe from Earth—eighty-six years later, five hundred million-million miles away. I don't believe it." The tank began an ominous turn toward the camera, then the technician killed the picture and looked down at her instruments. Eyes drifted away from the blank display and back to the screen in the middle.

"It's just as well," said Elliot. "I already seen the movie."

The scanning process on the big display was already up into the super-high frequencies, and there was still no sign of the Europeans' ships.

"Ladies and gentlemen," said Fiedler in bewilderment, "I don't know. I just don't know." He looked over at the smaller screen where a group of specialists was still studying the surface of the planet, then watched them and scratched his head for a minute.

"Kate? Kate, get in here!"

Salfelder came storming back through the door with a collection of tapes and blocks and papers under her arm and bustled forward. "Yes, Lou, you don't need to shout."

"Kate, the way the atmosphere is now on Serenitas—is it self-sustaining?"

She poured her collection of paraphernalia onto a desk and put her hands on her hips to look at him and think. "Yes, dear. I should think it is."

"Because," said Fiedler, tapping a fingernail against his teeth, "we've found that there are no artifacts on the planet at all. And that means not only no European ships, but no terraforming equipment, either. It's all been pulled off."

Salfelder continued to look at him for a minute, then took her hands from her hips and patted at her hair. "Well, I think that's very nice of the drones, don't you? Cleaning up their mess when they're done?" She winked at Kip and bustled off toward the door again.

"*Where are my drones?*" Miller was on her feet, her voice shrill as her head swung back and forth along the table. "You go on and on about these—these European *people*, and about your goddamned seeding equipment and the air on that damn planet, and no one thinks to ask where my drones are! Are you incompetent bunglers going to tell me you've got an entire system out there without a single artifact in it? Some pristine storybook planet just waiting for us in the middle of a billion miles of empty space, without the slightest sign that any creature has ever been there? More than a hundred European capital ships went into that system, you idiots, and more than a *thousand* drone ships have been out there for twelve years seeding that planet, and you're going to tell me we're looking at the garden of Eden? With proof, no less, that not one single ship has ever even *left*? You're going to tell me with a straight face, Mr. Torres, that you believe this—this *probe*—which I had nothing to do with building?" Her eyes were wild as she looked from one of us to the other.

What she had said was true: no one had said anything yet about the drones, assuming, like me, that we'd get to them eventually. But now that Miller had brought it up, it was clear that if we weren't finding the Europeans, then we weren't finding the drones, either.

She leaned on the edge of the table and fought for control of herself, while nearly everyone else in the room looked away or fidgeted with papers.

"All right, Anne," I said, "let's take this one step at a time. I'm sure we're just overlooking something. Lou? What else should we be checking? How about radiation flux and field strengths?"

I knew as well as Fiedler did what else there was to check— I had designed the probe myself—and I knew that nothing was going to make much difference when it came to finding ships and drones that should have been smearing every part of the electromagnetic spectrum with their presence.

"Yes, those," he mumbled, raising his bushy eyebrows. "Low temperature pyrometry, as well, I think." Miller watched him steadily as she eased back into her seat, while coughs and the scuffing of chairs came from along the table as people became increasingly uneasy, uncertain what was happening. Fiedler cleared his desk carefully then reached behind him for a new stack of vellum. He adjusted his glasses and licked his finger, but just as he reached out to lift the first page Charlie Peters cleared his throat and leaned over close to us again.

"And I saw when the Lamb opened the first seal; and I heard, as if it were the noise of thunder, one of the four beasts saying, 'Come and see.'"

Had he been drinking? He settled back into his seat, apparently unconcerned that his voice had carried across the room.

"Revelations 6:1," he said.

Fiedler frowned and started to say something, then held back. Peters was uncharacteristically somber, and it wasn't clear whether he was serious or not. No one else spoke.

Finally Fiedler looked down and licked his finger again, but at that instant we heard an odd, strangled sound from the back of the room. Patty Kelly was on her feet holding a sheet of paper in her hand, her face pale as she stared at it.

"What is it, Patty?" Fiedler set his glasses down on the desk and twisted around to look. Kelly just shook her head and stared at the sheet in her hand, her other hand frozen in the air next to her as though unsure what to do with it.

Fiedler groped for his glasses and got up and went to stand next to her, then after a minute his face took on an odd rigidity. He whispered, barely audible, "Not an anomaly at all, then." He pulled the sheet from Kelly's grasp and put it down on her desk, then took off his glasses and rubbed at the bridge of his nose with a thumb and forefinger. Finally he put his glasses back on and leaned over to her keyboard and began to type.

All of the wall screens went blank, then the one in the center filled with tiny glimmering stars, Serenitas Prime large in a lower corner. Then with a shift in perspective the scene snapped in closer, and the big star dropped off of the picture; Fiedler glanced up at the screen, then back at the keys. Again the picture snapped in closer—as though the viewer were traveling farther out through the system—then again, and again, until I was sure that any object in the picture would have to be hundreds of millions of miles outside of the system itself.

Chan caught her breath as the image pulled closer for the last time. There was what looked like a fine, even sprinkling of dust across the screen, each tiny grain a faintly highlighted, uniform black shape, glinting against the deeper black of space. There were thousands of them. Miller stood up and set her little notebook on the table. "The drones," she said.

Fiedler glanced at her, then reached down to pick up Kelly's sheet of paper again. He studied it for a minute, then took off his glasses and turned to Miller. "No," he said.

After a minute he leaned down again to Kelly's keyboard, then with a rapid ticking the scene flicked in closer and closer until the screen was filled with the fuzzy outline of an oddly misshapen, bullet-like object, made from some eerily reflective black material—a bronzed black, almost translucent, like black chrome.

Then the screen shifted to a black-on-white computer-generated outline of the object, which began to rotate through all three dimensions. An accompanying scale showed the thing to be big—not as big as our own capital ships, but close. Reference lines appeared and the thing was quartered and sliced, and the screen filled with fine spectrographic displays and columns of symbols. Fiedler and the other scientists watched as it evolved, then shook their heads in unison, in disbelief.

"Cobalt, selenium...*lanthanides*, for Christ's sake. What the devil is that hull made of?" The line drawings blinked out to be replaced by the red-on-blue of infrared, which then zoomed in on the hot plume behind the hull; once centered, the chemical analyses reappeared.

"That exhaust has got isotopes in it we've never even heard of. Look at that stuff! And look at this." The screen blossomed with layers of curving field lines and flickering digits. "That thing's got a magnetic field you wouldn't believe."

"Mr. Torres." It was Roddy McKenna's voice. I tore my eyes

away from the screen just long enough to see that he was still looking at his own console, apparently unaware of what was happening in the center of the room.

Anne Miller ignored him. "Perhaps the drones—" But her voice faded away as Fiedler turned his hollow eyes on her and shook his head again to cut her off.

"Those are substances neither we nor the drones could ever have made, Ms. Miller, not in hundreds of years. But it doesn't matter. Look at this." He reached for the keys and the picture switched back to infrared, and the ship steadily expanded to fill the entire screen. The image blurred as it grew larger, and details became almost indistinguishable. But what could be seen was that, under the skin of the hull, the forward two-thirds of the ship was segmented by a faint honeycomb pattern, with each of the open spaces in the honeycomb no more than a couple of feet across. And in the center of each space was a glowing shape.

"Those aren't your drones, Ms. Miller." He stared at the shapes along with the rest of us, and another minute went by. "They're warm-blooded."

A moment passed in a kind of suspended animation, then the auditorium around us felt suddenly too big. I had a sense of being on the ceiling, looking down onto the cluster of men and women huddled together in the dim light from the screens, all facing silently forward, all thinking the same word but not saying it. Minutes ticked by, and I felt sympathy for them, staring at the frozen image of the blurred ship and its warm cargo.

Miller looked uncomprehendingly from one of us to the other, her face frozen in a rictus of denial.

"Your drones are gone, Ms. Miller," said Fiedler.

She shook her head stiffly, her hand groping for the back of her chair.

"Aliens!" said Polaski.

Chapter Seventeen: THE BAYING OF WOLVES

Acceptance came slowly and at a price, paid in the coin of our own significance. Comprehension, on the other hand, lay in an uncertain future, a dubious luxury.

Again and again we resisted the facts, and every time the noose only tightened: the materials we'd seen, the designs, the engines—all of them whispered *"alien, alien, alien."* Then always the last, insurmountable fact, the one which in other circumstances should have seemed so natural, but which instead mesmerized us in image after image, ship after ship: the warmth. For where the cold of the drones had spoken of a frightening indifference, the warmth now spoke of intention.

That others existed while we humans played blindly at our intrigues, filled with our self-importance, was a knowledge that chafed like the humiliation of a drunk, remembering how incautious he'd been the night before—how unsophisticated, how undefended, how naked among strangers.

Each of us reacted in some way. Even those who were convinced of their own indifference clung to that conviction with renewed vigor. Others armed themselves more visibly, wearing weapons around the base like totems. Some took new lovers, as though spurred to intimacy by a sudden sense of mortality, while others abandoned old lovers in confusion, embarrassed by the intimacy they'd already shown. Some displayed unaccustomed generosity and even valor, while others grew sullen and mean-spirited.

All of us had at some point in our lives considered the possibility that we weren't alone. Some had studied the statistical probabilities involved, while others had researched the problems of shape or language, or speed, or evolutionary paths. Some had formed unshakable convictions and others a cherished ambivalence, yet we had all missed the starkly personal nature of the thing. We'd been like people who lie awake in the dark and wonder whether the doors are locked, and idly note the improbability of intruders, then hear the scuff of a shoe next to the bed.

Polaski wanted to fight. He may have believed it necessary, or he may simply have sought reaffirmation of who he was in the clash of sword against sword, that tonic against self-doubt that has driven men for a hundred thousand years. *"And I beheld a white horse,"* Peters said about Polaski the day we found the aliens, finishing his earlier quote from Revelations, *"and he that sat on him was given a crown, and he went forth to conquer."*

Polaski had also apparently answered for himself the question that others still avoided: What, exactly, had happened to the Europeans and the drones?

We stayed in the auditorium a long time that afternoon, numbly re-crossing the same ground through picture after picture. Most of us never noticed that Anne Miller had suffered a stroke. Only Bolton and Throckmorton saw her, and between them they helped her up and carried her to the infirmary, where the medics later reported a mild ischemia due to rheumatic fever and myocardial infarction. There was the risk of another, they said, but it didn't merit the risk of surgery. After several days they allowed her to return to her rooms to rest, and I visited her there on most evenings.

For a time I wondered whether I felt some responsibility for the events that had ended her life's work, but more and more I sensed an empathy for her, as though we shared some special knowledge about her and her drones.

On the sixth day, during the planet's night, I brought her a tray and sat by her bed as she ate.

"I've never seen you wear a hat before," she said, picking at her food and looking up with an old woman's eyes.

I took off the cap and put it in my lap. I was looking out through the bedroom door and into her workroom, at the slender metal case containing the drones' communications codes. It was like a forgotten prop, dulled suddenly by insignificance, lying on the dusty stage after the show is over.

"You said yesterday that you thought the drones were just hiding, Anne. Have you thought any more about that?" An uneven whistling drifted in through the bedroom door. Elliot had walked over with me but hadn't wanted to come in, so he sat in her outer doorway, whistling tunelessly.

"Madhu used to wear hats," she said, her fork half-raised and forgotten. "White hats, with his white suits, when he was a young man. He was very dashing." Her old eyes flickered up to mine, then down to her plate. She set the fork back down quietly.

"How long ago did you know Madhu?" I said.

"Oh," she said, lacing together her fingertips. "Since I was a girl. He pretty much raised me after my mother died." She frowned and looked down at her hands again.

"I'm sorry. What happened?"

She pushed her plate away. "Would you take my tray, please? Thank you." She smoothed the white blanket out across her lap, then stroked it with both hands as though reassuring it about something. "My mother and I lived in East Oakland, Edward. That was a very bad place at the time—I'm sure it still is. We had a single room with a curtain across the middle. The other side of it was where my mother brought her men."

Her hands stopped and she looked up with a hint of bitterness. "An awful bunch of men, men with perspiring black faces, all of them. Big faces. Mostly wearing guns, the way men in Oakland did. Some gave her money, but a lot of them just took to beating her while I listened from the other side of the curtain. Then she'd lie there for days and drink."

She gave a short laugh. "One of them finally killed her, one of those men. I didn't even know she was dead until a neighbor came for me. Mrs. Ida. She took me on a bus and begged to have me stay where she cleaned house, for a professor in the good neighborhoods."

She smiled and began picking lint off the blanket. "That was Madhu, of course. He really couldn't walk very well." She paused for a minute, then looked up.

"I don't know whether the drones are still out there or not," she said.

After that she seemed to lose track, then finally with an effort pushed herself up and reached for her water glass on the case by the bed.

"Madhu helped me into a grade school, and when I was older he let me use the terminal in his study. He used to sit for hours and watch me, then one day he moved me into a better school. I think he was a little troubled about it all, though.

"Later, when I was on my own, I worked on robotics—military drones. That worried him. When I visited him he'd tell me that if there was ever a chance of the machines hurting someone, I had to picture it being him. He told me that over and over."

Her eyes clouded. "I hated him for that. When I went to work at China Lake I tried telling him what we were doing was different, because we were defending ourselves against armed men. Men with guns. But still, I had a hard time not thinking about him being killed by each thing we built."

She looked up—Elliot was standing in her bedroom door.

"We got company," he said.

"All right." I made Miller some tea, then followed Elliot into the dark square. Under the light across from us two people were waiting in a car. We trudged across the dark square toward them.

"It seems," I said to Elliot, "that in Anne's book you're the wrong size and the wrong color."

"Not a whole lot I can do about that."

"Afraid not. Well, look at this." Slumped in the front seat of the open car were Harry Penderson and Carolyn Dorczak, gazing at the dome overhead.

"Hello, Tyrone," said Dorczak. She stuck an arm out the side. "Hi, Ed—cheer up. I like your hat."

Penderson made no move to start the car, so Elliot and I leaned on the wall next to them, under the light. "Hello, Carolyn," I said. "Harry."

"Hi." He chewed on his lip and gave Dorczak an inquiring look, then shrugged when she didn't say anything. "The lady wanted to see you guys," he said. "What can I say?"

Dorczak rolled her eyes and sighed. They acted like a married couple after a fight, though they couldn't have known each other for more than the few minutes since she'd landed.

"Well, hell," she said, "I don't know what I'm doing here.

The whole system's lost its little mind, as far as I can tell. That nut case of yours, The Mercenary Emperor himself, Polaski the First, has suddenly got this hard-on for building new toys and going in after our little alien visitors, instead of leaving well enough alone." She glanced at her watch. "And he and Bart are in thicker than fleas, so here I am, carrying Bart's briefcase and looking like I know what I'm doing."

Polaski had announced his intention of going into Serenitas after the aliens?

"Don't look so surprised, Ed, I'll bet you couldn't wait to go along—anything to slip your way in to that planet of yours, hm?"

"I'd say it's about time old Polaski was stopped," said Elliot. "Shoot, don't look at me like that. I ain't the first one who thunk it."

No one spoke for a while. Penderson tapped out a tattoo on the steering wheel, while Dorczak inspected the buildings around us in the darkness. Finally I turned to her.

"What about Lowhead, Carolyn. And the rest of the planet? Is this something people want to do?"

She shrugged. "I don't know. People are acting funny. A few of the smarter ones are saying we need to know more, but some of the others are talking about trying to go back to Earth, or else slipping into Serenity System unnoticed, with no weapons. And of course there're the usual sightings of slime-green alien fleets and what-not. The latest thing is wolf sightings."

Penderson turned in his seat. "*Wolf* sightings?"

"Yeah, I know it's a little—"

"No," he said. "It's not that." He looked at her worriedly, and chewed on his lip for a while. "It's that I've heard that story before. More than a year ago. And a *long* way from where you come from— miners out on H-V's moons." He glanced around, first at Elliot, then me. "Except that the story I heard wasn't about any ordinary wolf."

Dorczak stared at him.

"A wolf without a head," she said.

"Yes."

"Come on, you guys," said Elliot. "Those kinds of stories are all over the place, and folks drag 'em out when they get scared about something. Why, I knew a fella in Louisiana, once—"

"Tyrone," I said. "I need to talk to Roddy McKenna. Now. He started to say something in the auditorium and got cut off, and I forgot about it. Let's go—research center. Jesus, Harry, hurry."

We found the center's labs still brightly lit and crowded with scientists, working around the clock to coax information from *Sun of Gabriel*'s massive stream of data. Roddy McKenna was nowhere in sight, but I finally won Kate Salfelder's attention by standing between her and a display of Serenitas.

When I asked about McKenna she just frowned and shook her head.

"Go and find him, Eddie dear. He's gone off after that awful woman again, and I worry. He was upset, the way he gets. Said it's unfair what Mr. Polaski did to her. Said she was going to fight it, and he was going to help." She wrung her hands in front of her, unable to fathom such a thing. "Eddie...he looks up to you so much. But you don't ever say anything, and then he takes off after that woman, instead. Go and talk to him, won't you, dear?"

"Kate," I said, "the other day in the auditorium, Roddy was working on the probe's communications with the Serenitas torus, and a couple of times he started to say something. Do you know what it was, or where those records are so we can take a look?"

She shook her head sympathetically and pointed to a row of desks along the wall. Stacks of vellum were balanced everywhere, with piles of memory blocks strewn about them with meaningless notations on them. Whatever McKenna had found, only he was going to be able to tell us what it was.

"All right, Kate. I'll call you when I find him. Come on, Tyrone. Harry, you know how to drive the tractors by now and how to find the landing dome at night—you drive. That has to be where Pham went."

We drove at Penderson's breakneck speed through the black night, and I explained what Polaski had done to Pham.

She'd been summoned early one morning to a meeting of the military service chiefs and line officers. Included were the senior ship's captains—traditionally Polaski's weakest area of support—and the commanders of the space-assault Marine units. The Marines reported to Pham and lived in uneasy coexistence with the officers on whose ships they served. Conspicuously absent, however, were officers from the "Rats," Pham's fiercely loyal ground troops.

"Colonel Pham," Polaski said. He had cultivated her meticulously over the years, currying favor with her Rats and Marines, but his tone now was peremptory.

"As commanding officer of the Marine units, you are one of the few that's allowed to carry loaded weapons on shipboard, isn't that right?"

"Yah?" She was unsure of her ground.

Ship's crews were kept alive by an almost religious observance of certain rules, and one of them regulated the carrying of loaded weapons on board. Firing one in a pressurized environment meant instant death, so while in space the ground forces and even the ship's officers themselves were not allowed to carry them. Only Pham and her Marines could.

Polaski turned to me.

"Mr. Torres, were you present on the fourteenth of this month when Colonel Pham discharged a twenty-millimeter cannon in the direction of the roof of the main dome? Twice, as I understand it."

"Get to the point, Polaski," I said.

But he'd already made his point. Ever since the incident several of the ships' captains had been agitating to have Pham disciplined. But they didn't know I had been there.

"Colonel Pham," said Polaski, turning to her again, "with the concurrence of everyone present, including Eduardo Torres, you are hereby removed from command of all space-assault forces. They will from here on out report to the wing commanders of the vessels on which they serve."

"*What*?" Her eyes grew suddenly wild, and she looked like she was going to hurl herself across the table at him.

But what about the Rats, I thought. Polaski had in a single move pitted himself against the single greatest source of power we had in the system.

"You can't do that!" Pham was spitting her words in her fury. "You crazy, Mister? Hey, I ask you a question! How you like Rats in your bed, *hah*?"

Polaski stopped, perfectly still, and then, with his eyebrows raised, turned slowly around the room as though searching for something that wasn't there. And then I understood.

Polaski believed we would leave the black planet and go to Serenitas after the aliens. He believed he could persuade the colony to abandon its base and go back into space. And so he had traded the loyalty of Pham's Rats for that of the ships' officers.

But persuade us how? His plans to take the offensive against creatures we knew nothing about had been dismissed at every turn. While clearly something had happened to the drones and to the Europeans in Serenitas System, there was no evidence that the aliens were a threat to us here in Holzstein's.

I stopped Polaski later and challenged him regarding existing ground engagements and other commitments we had here in this system. Having completely alienated Pham, the brass knuckles behind our most important multilateral agreements, our international relations policy was now in a shambles. He shrugged it off.

"Let Allerton handle it."

Bart Allerton, Polaski's friend and ally. Dorczak's boss, the new head of the colony at Lowhead. What deal had they made?

From what Kate Salfelder said that night at the labs, Pham wasn't taking Polaski's decision gracefully. And if there was an occasion to make an issue of it, I knew, it involved the Marine contingents leaving that night for the now-empty third planet. The fleet was being sent to make our presence felt following the Europeans' sudden departure, and to dampen the impending chaos left by their absence and by the news from Serenitas.

The landing dome was an iron and glass vault four hundred feet long and two hundred wide, with an air lock tunnel at each end big enough to accommodate the giant tractor-drawn trailers that crawled out across the surface to the ships.

When our own tractor cleared the inner door of the nearer tunnel and pulled to one side of the dome, the scene under the domes' floodlights was starkly clear.

Ready to leave through the far air lock were two full troop trailers coupled to their tractors, pointing away from us, one nosing up behind the other. Only a few soldiers still stood outside the trailers' left-side doors, waiting to step inside at the last minute and seal them. The rest of the dome was nearly empty.

The air under the harsh lights was bitterly cold, and the soldiers' breath condensed into clouds and drifted away against the background of black glass. Far off by the left side of the dome, sitting alone among the empty waiting-benches, was the slight form of Roddy McKenna. He was watching an altercation by the tractors, close to the far air lock.

We stepped down and scuffed our way around to the front of our own tractor. Dorczak and Penderson stepped down from the other side and Penderson took off his coat to put around Dorczak's shoulders against the cold. He put his arm around her and the four of us crunched across the black ground toward the center of the dome.

The altercation McKenna was watching involved Pham— draped in a soiled fatigue jacket and rocking unsteadily on her feet— hurling obscenities at a grim-looking officer by the forward tractor. Most of their words were lost in the odd, flat acoustics of the dome.

It was an unreal scene under the powerful lights: the ponderous iron trailers with their dark portholes, the big tractors swaying and vibrating as their motors idled, the silver trim on the soldiers' uniforms flashing in the icy air—all of it finely etched by the lights against the dull, black ground and the glass. And then, a sequence of events occurred so rapidly and so suddenly that it wasn't until later that we were able to reconstruct them—although even then, we never did fully understand what had caused them.

Pham was leaning forward at the waist and screaming at the officer, when from the side of the dome near McKenna came an eerie, rippling *crack*, like the sound of ice splitting on a lake. Pham didn't hear it, but the officer and her soldiers did, and turned in unison to look.

Near the base of the dome one of the glass panels had developed an ominous white crack across it. At the same time, for just an instant, a weak light passed across the glass from the outside and then vanished.

Another *crack* ripped through the air, and a fracture line shot across the next panel over. McKenna got to his feet in confusion, while at the far end of the dome the officer motioned curtly to her troops to get on board and seal their doors.

Pham, not having noticed anything amiss until that moment, saw them boarding and abruptly stopped her shouting. McKenna looked back and forth between the cracking panels and the tractor-trailers, then began walking toward the edge of the dome to see what was wrong with the glass.

Harry Penderson reacted the fastest, taking a grip on Dorczak and Elliot and racing them toward the air lock tunnel behind us. A third panel cracked. The sound of it lashed out through the dome like a gunshot; soon the panels would start to shatter one after the other and blow outward.

Pham finally realized that the two big tractor-trailers had begun to move. In a growing fury she reached for her gun, evidently believing she had been dismissed. The forward tractor had picked up speed and the officer was pulling her foot in to close the door, when the driver saw Pham's gun and wrenched the wheel to one side.

Over at the side of the dome a fourth panel cracked in front of McKenna. He stopped walking and looked uncertainly back at the tractor-trailers.

In that instant, then, he and Pham and I all saw what was going to happen: the forward tractor was not going to correct its swerve in time, and was going to slice through the glass wall of the dome next to the lock.

Pham lowered the gun and bolted for the far air lock tunnel, then just as suddenly realized that its inner door was still closed. She turned and started back toward the one at our end. McKenna was behind her, because he'd had to make the longer trip around the benches. Penderson, Dorczak and Elliot were already making their way up the ramp and onto the iron floor of our air lock tunnel. When I'd made it in behind them, struggling for breath like the others, I turned back around to see a terrible sight.

The giant tractor-trailer slid slowly and even gracefully into the glass wall, then lifted up and jackknifed to a stop. No noise from the collision reached us against the sudden rush of air, but my ears popped from a pressure change. Then all across the floor of the dome, in eerie silence, a layer of black dust rose up from the ground and began drifting toward the breach. Pham, and McKenna some twenty paces behind her, slowed as they were forced to lean into the wind of decompression, pulling their way through the accelerating layer of dust and debris. A spotlight blew out overhead and they became outlined more sharply than ever against the dark background. The moisture in the air condensed into fog.

Inside the air lock tunnel, we were facing back through the big doorway into the dome. We stood against the left wall in order to hold onto a conduit that ran the length of the tunnel, all the way back to the opening we'd come through.

The opening was made from a heavy, precision-ground frame, with a polished steel door retracted for the moment into the opening's right side. When it closed, the door would trundle leftward like an elevator's, closing toward our left, where the door's control panel was bolted to the wall.

Elliot and Dorczak were behind me along the wall, while Penderson had already worked his way forward around me and was carefully moving toward the control panel, never letting go of the conduit lest the dome suddenly blow out. He was breathing hard in the thinning air, and shook his head sharply several times to clear his ears.

Pham hit the ramp and fought her way up it, heaving for breath, her hand still gripping her gun. Behind her, the swirling layer of dust was up to McKenna's knees. The wind and fog sucking toward the hole in the dome whipped at his hair. The rest of the spotlights blew out, and the thickening fog obscured his form almost completely.

He made it to the foot of the ramp at the same time as Pham reached the door frame. Not ten seconds had passed since the tractor had plowed into the glass wall.

McKenna looked up suddenly at Pham ahead of him. "No!"

Pham hadn't even turned around to see if anyone else behind her was trying to reach the air lock tunnel. The instant she reached the air lock, she slammed her hand back against the controls, sending the door trundling closed along its track. Penderson swore, and both he and I pushed our way toward the controls, though with no hope of reaching them in time. Pham was several paces into the tunnel and grabbing for the conduit herself when she heard McKenna's shout. Only then did she turn.

McKenna launched himself toward the narrowing doorway with a hoarse cry, forcing himself through just before it closed. But as he smashed against the moving edge of the door it spun him around before he was completely through, catching his trailing arm at the shoulder as it closed.

Penderson and I were still moving and Pham was still turning around to look when the air lock door sensed the presence of McKenna's arm and froze, pinning him to the frame.

But it froze for only an instant. Even as it stopped, it sensed the difference in pressure between the air lock tunnel and the ruptured dome outside, and obeyed a higher priority: with the full force of its motors it crushed McKenna's arm, sealing him and us almost completely into the air lock. And as his screams echoed through the iron tunnel, we dimly heard the dome's cracked panels blowing out one after the other, like distant gunfire in the arctic night.

McKenna choked off his screams to gasp for air just as Pham finished her turn toward him. And at that same instant, she and Penderson and I—and McKenna—all heard the same sound: air hissing past the air lock door, past the imperfect seal where the bone of his crushed arm was lodged. Our ears began to pop again. The tunnel's own air bottles opened and hissed into the lock, trying to maintain pressure. They would last no more than a minute.

With the same momentum that had turned her around, in what might have been no more than a blind reflex, Pham dropped her gun and lunged for the red override lever at the top of the panel, the lever that would force the door back open, blowing Roddy McKenna back into the vacuum like a cannon shot.

"Jesus *Christ!*" shouted Penderson. "What the *fuck* are you doing?"

McKenna raised his head just as she moved, and when their eyes met she froze, her hand inches from the lever. Air continued to hiss past the door. No one in the tunnel moved.

We could only see the back of Pham's head, but we could see

all of McKenna's face. Blood trickled from the corner of his mouth where he'd bitten through his tongue. His face was pale under a sheen of sweat. But his eyes were now perfectly clear as he stared at her, filled with what could only be the loathing of utter betrayal.

Pham lowered her arm.

The hiss of the air bottles dwindled, and again the pressure in the tunnel began to drop as the air hissed out past McKenna's arm. Penderson started to move again, still gripping the conduit, carefully approaching Pham from the back.

Finally McKenna broke his gaze with Pham and looked at me, now trembling from shock. Penderson reached Pham's shoulder and carefully pulled her away from the panel, then worked his way past her, never letting go of the conduit.

Yet there was little he could do, beyond getting a grip on McKenna before opening the door. Which merely left him with a near certainty of being pulled out, too; short of chains wrapped around him, it would be impossible to hold McKenna against the wall of air that would hit him if the door opened—and short of opening the door there was no way to dislodge his arm.

McKenna stared at me for a moment, then dropped his gaze and reached with his good hand into his breast pocket. His side was soaked with blood from the severed shoulder. He pulled a folded wad of paper from his pocket with a shaking hand and tossed it as far as he could along the floor toward me. It landed out of my reach, but Elliot's boot immediately slid out and held it.

McKenna glanced at me again, then one more time at Pham. The air was thin enough now that it was hard to breath. A light breeze blew against the back of my neck as the last of our air moved toward the door.

Penderson had almost reached the panel, and McKenna's eyes finally flicked toward him. Then, with all of his remaining strength, McKenna flung himself around to his full reach and slammed his good hand against the override lever.

I remember the sound of it, and I remember Penderson diving forward to close the door again. But I don't remember seeing McKenna go.

Mostly I remember him when he was eight years old, a blue-eyed and freckled boy, alone with his machines and the music that he had taught them to play. Alone, that afternoon, with a man who had no time to listen.

It was Elliot who turned me away from the door finally, gripping my arm and sitting me down on the floor to lean against the wall. Then at some point minutes or hours later, he pressed the blood-stained piece of paper into my hand.

"He was giving it to you, Torres. Maybe you ought to look at it."

The others were sitting against the walls as well, watching me and breathing slowly in the thin air. Pham sat in a huddle in the corner, her face hidden.

I unfolded the paper numbly, but only to stare uncomprehendingly at columns of times and dates. The numbers swam before me, and no matter how hard I tried I couldn't understand what it was McKenna had left me.

Then I remembered why I'd come looking for him in the first place, and suddenly I understood. And as I understood, a chill crept up my spine. The iron wall against my back suddenly seemed far too thin.

"What is it, Torres?"

Dorczak and Penderson were watching me, as well.

"The torus in Serenitas System," I said. "Remember how Roddy told us it had never been rotated to point anywhere but back here at Holzstein's? That was how he knew it couldn't have been used to send the Europeans or the drones onward to some other system."

"That's right."

I handed him the paper. "He said it had never been rotated anywhere else. But he didn't say it had never been used."

Farther down the tunnel, comprehension settled into Dorczak and Penderson's eyes at the same time.

"It *has* been used," I said, "hundreds of times. Someone's been coming back this way from Serenitas over a period that goes back years. Coming in large numbers."

Sometime later that night the rescuers finished welding a trailer against the side of the tunnel, and cut their way in. We stayed in the trailer several hours more while they worked to free the troop trailer jammed into the dome wall. Because of the officer's quick orders, both of the trailers had been sealed in time, as had the cab of the second tractor. But the officer herself, and her driver, were gone. She hadn't gotten the door closed, after all.

Charlie Peters had come with the rescuers to say the words that needed to be said, and to look after Pham. Kip had come, too. He lay on his back on the rear bench of the trailer and played his flute.

I drifted in and out of sleep as I listened, dreaming at one point about the underground cavern and its one passage.

As always I sat hunched in the cold, and as always my mother hovered over my shoulder, watching. But this time someone else was in the cavern with us.

"And I heard the second beast say 'Come and see...'"

Peters was talking to himself in the back of the trailer.

"And there went out another horse that was red, and power was given to him that sat thereon to take peace from the earth. And there was given to him a great sword."

Chapter Eighteen: A CIVILIZED AND INNOCENT MAN

"I still say there's no way she could have missed knowing McKenna was behind her. Either way, she should have looked." The ship shuddered as we dragged deeper into the atmosphere, and Elliot turned away from the porthole with a sour face as it slued sideways. The engines growled as the MI tried to correct, while in the cabin joints groaned in protest.

"It doesn't matter," I said, rechecking my harness. "Chan says Pham can hardly remember what happened that night."

"How come Pham's staying with Chan, anyhow?"

"She's not. She's in the infirmary. Rosler beat her again. With an iron pipe."

"Jesus."

"Probably thought she'd sullied his image or something." The engines whined as the transport sank and then pitched nose-low. The commandos sitting in front of us swayed impassively on their metal benches, accustomed to the abuse. All the way at the front, Bolton released his belts and leaned past the pilot, trying to see the planet's surface. Then he turned and worked his way back with a map in his hand.

"Right," he said, and squatted next to us. "Let's have a look at where this signal's coming from, shall we?" He worked to unfold the map while the ship dipped and shook in the rough air.

The ship was little more than an iron tube welded to a pair of induction engines—not at all aerodynamic or stable, kept upright only by its MI. It had crossed the ninety million miles from the black planet to the Europeans' abandoned planet of H-III in three days, at one and a half Gs all the way. It stank of sweat and bad plumbing.

"All right, here it is," said Bolton. "What we're interested in is these uplands, about five thousand square miles of high shale running along behind the mountains." The mountains he pointed to ranged across the planet's empty quarter, a massive plate of clay and shale thrust up in the planet's early years. The new settlements were all on the far side of the planet, in cultivated valleys left behind by the Europeans.

"I thought the distress signal was coming from the lowlands," I said. Elliot and I hadn't been on the planet before; Bolton and his teams had.

"Quite so—right here below the escarpment. About eleven miles out, right where no settlement ought to be. And where no one in his right mind would put one." He pointed on the map, holding onto the bench again as the ship skidded sideways. "At any rate," he said, "it's on these uplands that we'll land...about here. Then we'll work our way along to the edge for a snug little peek at whatever's out there."

"Okay. What's all this here, though?" Someone had carefully shaded in most of the highland area with fine crosshatching.

"Ah...that's nothing, actually. Nothing to do with the mission." He refolded his map.

"Bolton..."

"Hey Torres, look at this." Elliot had been watching through the porthole, and now he pulled me over to look past him.

The planet's horizon curved away in the far distance, a cracked expanse of grey softened only by the thin atmosphere. As barren as the planet seemed—*Asile*, it was called—the sight of its sunny horizon and thin blue sky stabbed with its familiarity.

But Elliot wasn't looking at the sun on the plains. He was watching the approach of a craggy range of mountains, sweeping up into the thinner blue air ahead of us. On the distant steppes beyond them, a lazy funnel-cloud snaked high into the atmosphere. Between us and the funnel, a narrow line of rain-laden clouds clung to the mountain's near flank. I turned back to Bolton.

"Cyclonic storms?"

"Um, no, not exactly. That is to say, there are storms...but I think not just where you're looking, if you see what I mean."

I didn't, but I looked back out the side just the same. Elliot made a noise of surprise and pointed to a solitary lake, glinting through a gap in the clouds like mercury against the grey steppes. I asked Bolton for the map again, remembering the crosshatching. But he didn't hand it to me. Instead, he just sighed and beckoned to Roscoe Throckmorton.

"Roscoe," he said, "I think perhaps we'll give our guests a quick tour, after all, hm? Show them our little project? Have Stephanie give us a bit of a drive-about, would you?" Throckmorton hesitated, then worked his way back up to the pilot. Bolton squeezed onto the bench next to me and changed the subject.

"So. Early tomorrow morning we should know what this is all about, then."

"Maybe...I noticed we're slipping in across the mountains from the side opposite the signal source. You're resisting the urge to overfly, I take it?"

"Yes. I confess I've acquired your disquiet about this whole thing. It does feel a bit as though we're being set up, and overflying seems so predictable, doesn't it?"

"Maybe not. It's a standard emergency locator beacon, after all, and telescopy does show some kind of settlement, even if the maps don't."

Neither, however, did Dorczak's intelligence network, or our own.

"Then why," said Bolton, "did you warn away every rescue team in the system? And why is it you ring home every hour to see what the lab says about the glass panels that blew out in the landing dome? What do they say, by the by?"

"Possibility of fatigue in their common cross-member."

Both Elliot and Bolton made disbelieving noises.

"Although there are signs of lattice dissolution in the glass itself, simultaneously on multiple panels. Possibly from focused microwave radiation."

"Ah-hah."

"We should have built those domes differently," I said. "I didn't know when we built them—"

"It ain't your fault he's dead, Torres!" said Elliot. "I swear to God I'm tired of telling you that." He turned back to the porthole. "It wasn't the dome that killed him."

Bolton and I watched the back of Elliot's head for a minute, then sat and brooded while the ship swayed and shook irritably in the updrafts from the mountains' flank. Finally, with a last, convulsive shudder, the ship settled into the mists and the cabin fell gloomy and dark, swallowed by clouds that a moment earlier had seemed far away and insignificant. Now the sunny plains and fine white clouds had fallen behind us like a memory from another world.

When we dropped out from under the cloudy netherworld it was to find ourselves flying low over a shadowy wasteland of grey shale. The planet's reappearance as ordinary ground beneath us seemed like a sleight of hand, a shift in perspective we had somehow missed in the clouds.

Then all at once we swept back into sunlight and the land changed from the course shale into a rich and fine soil. The lake flashed by underneath and the pilot banked. Bolton pointed out the forward windscreen. To one side of our new course lay the cracked grey rock we'd left behind, and to the other the darker, furrowed soil. And in the distance, exactly straddling the dividing line, a funnel-shaped cloud of enormous proportions roiled into the sky from behind a machine that moved along the ground, half-buried. When I finally realized what it was I glanced back at Bolton, who looked pleased with himself and a little defensive at the same time.

Originally transported to the system as the rear third of one of the drone ships, the grey cylinder plowing the highland plateau was the centerpiece of Earth's terraforming technology, manufactured years before we left but never used until the drones brought two hundred of them to Holzstein's and Serenitas. Designed to be powered by nuclear fission, but greatly compacted using our quantum cells, the fifty-foot monsters inhaled rock and ice to produce atmospheric gasses. In the case of Asile that meant mostly oxygen, to convert its hydrogen-dominant fledgling atmosphere.

But the machines had the side-benefit of producing fine soil, though with the drawback of removing, rather than adding, nitrogen to it. For that reason, and because the machines worked best on ice, they were nearly always set in motion near the poles. Bolton had evidently lifted this one and brought it down to his equatorial highlands to generate soil at a much faster than usual rate.

"Nitrogen?" I asked him.

"Surface mining to make potassium nitrate, then we fill in the gash with rain water from the ridge—that was the lake you saw."

"Why are you doing this?" The ship turned to avoid the funnel pouring from the cylinder, and Bolton nodded back out the side. Below us, tiny silver shapes worked their way along the new soil—grasshopper drones nearly a hundred abreast, following along in the furrows.

Then they were gone behind us, and after another few miles came lines of green saplings. A cluster of makeshift buildings slid beneath us, then we were settling in for a landing in the rolling hills at the far edge of the uplands.

The engines threw up a cloud of loose shale that clattered against the fuselage, then with a sharp impact on the skids the ship went silent for the first time in three days. The black-clad troops slipped out through the doors with their kits and disappeared into the afternoon shadows, letting in cool air that smelled slightly of sulfur. Bolton checked the cabin, then followed Elliot and me down the twelve-foot ladder, while the pilot pulled out a tool bag and climbed down to begin inspecting the engines and the power cell compartments under the ship.

A light breeze came up from the plateaus as the hot metal creaked and hissed. The land we had crossed stretched to the far horizon with its thin new carpet of green. "Bolton?"

"Yes."

"Yes."

For a moment I thought he'd answered twice, then I heard the air hiss between his teeth as he spun to look up at the ship's open door. Teetering precariously at the edge was a little grasshopper drone, cautiously feeling the open space with his front feet. Little Bolton.

The real Bolton was furious. "Why, you little...you little *cheat!*" He ran an exasperated hand through his hair. "You told me you were someone else, didn't you!"

"Of course I did," it said matter-of-factly, trying to tip sideways to see down the ladder. "Otherwise you wouldn't have let me come." A middle foot slipped on the edge and it backed away. "Would you, now?"

The brooding look on Elliot's face softened. With a quick glance at Bolton he pulled himself back up the ladder and grabbed the drone. It yelped once as it slid off the edge, then it started chirping cheerfully as Elliot stuck it under an arm and climbed down. It scrabbled away when it touched ground.

Bolton had turned away and was looking out across his plateau with his arms folded. Finally he turned back and stabbed a finger at the drone. "But you bloody well keep up, this time!" I had heard about Bolton's inconsolable funks when his little double was around, but I'd never seen one. "I'm not carrying you again, do you hear?" Elliot worked to keep a straight face and tossed me a pack.

With nods to the pilot, the three of us began hiking up the ravine, toward the ridge overlooking the deserted plains, accompanied by the scampering of Little Bolton's six feet across the rocks. "Do you really mean to leave her unguarded?" I asked, indicating the pilot now alone in the empty hills and the lengthening shadows. I didn't know what she'd need guarding against, but I hadn't forgotten the signal coming from the plains ahead of us.

"We have other pilots," said Bolton. He was still sulking. I glanced at Elliot, who just shrugged and eyed the nearby ridges. "Don't bother looking," said Bolton, "you won't see them. Come along, Torres, the ship's well guarded." He picked up his pace.

"Okay," I said. "So—you're busy foresting a couple million acres here on Asile, while the rest of us are worrying about how to arm the fleet and how to get to Serenitas. Why?"

He gave me a guarded look. "Look, Torres. No one's ever quite certain where you stand on things, but you do know that Polaski would get a royal bug up his arse if he heard about this. 'Misappropriating military resources' and all that chest-beating crap."

"Fair enough."

He glanced at me again, then slowed to let the drone catch up. "I turned forty this year, Torres, and I've decided I'm too old to keep pretending things are going to get better. I don't know who these buggers are out there, or if I'll wake up properly tomorrow, but I have accepted that I may never see that siren planet of yours. It seems like we're always struggling against the stream, is the thing, and here we are laying in armament again. I keep wondering if we haven't missed something along the way."

He lowered his pack to the ground. "We'll camp here. And you"—he aimed a finger at the drone—"I know you like to ring up your little friends and chat them up all night, but we *are* observing radio silence. Do you understand what that means?"

The drone belched, then turned ploddingly around and scraped a hind foot at Bolton, who frowned disgustedly and opened his pack. "Anyway, Torres, no one's throwing in the towel yet, but some of us thought we might just hedge our bets a little." He pulled the string on a rations heater and sat down to eat.

When I looked at Elliot he just raised an eyebrow, then began searching through his own pack.

I slept badly during Asile's short night, and finally woke in the darkness. I felt uneasy and restless in the thin air and the light gravity.

I climbed the slope to the edge of the cliff, and watched as the first cold flush of dawn seeped into the sky beyond the lowlands. It crept toward me across the wastes with a hard, pale light, the uncaring, shadowless light of desolation. It spoke of old losses, of incomprehensible spans of time.

The colorless sliver of Asile's greater moon drifted into the sky. I drew my coat tighter and remembered Madhu's face, wet with tears as he sat next to me and watched a different moon, heavy and full and grey.

And as I sat there on the mountains of that ancient planet, looking down on its wilderness in the chilly dawn, I remembered the face of my daughter for the first time. Tiny, and helpless, and still.

The image came unbidden, and was just as quickly replaced by the face of young Teresa Delgado, solemn and proud on her third birthday, filled to overflowing with her own future.

And then, finally, I remembered Roddy McKenna as he died.

I had always thought of myself as an admirable man. A restrained and civilized man, above all blame. Yet, sitting there on the ridge, I saw it for the lie that it was. Pham's act of cowardice had somehow peeled back the lie of my own life, and I knew that I, like David Rosler, wanted to silence her for it, escape from what she'd done. But escape meant Serenitas, and now the alien ships stood in the way, a thousand flint-black eyes glinting in the face of an un-amused god.

The outline of the great moon faded away in the greying sky, and for a moment I searched for it anxiously, feeling suddenly vulnerable. An old man, I thought, admirable and alone.

"What I like about sunup," said Elliot beside me, "is how it don't pretend to be nothing else, if you know what I mean. Here." He handed me a pair of heavy goggles and pointed out across the dark lowlands, just as Bolton settled in on my other side. "One-one-six."

I fitted on the goggles and the scene brightened, then I turned my head slowly to the right as the illuminated scale ticked off the true bearing. Tiny motors whirred as it focused. At 116‡ I stopped. Near the horizon was a thin line of darker grey against the land. Bolton's and Elliot's goggles purred next to me.

I tried several times to close my left eye without moving the right, and finally the goggles understood and zoomed in on the distant smudge. At extreme magnification the pattern of structures sorted themselves out, just as we had seen them from space. But as hard as I tried to hold my head still, the goggles couldn't completely stabilize the image, and finally I took them off. Next to me, Bolton tried for a minute longer, holding his head in both hands, then took his off, too.

"Roscoe," he said quietly. Throckmorton was nowhere to be seen. "Let's have the spyglass up here, if you would, please."

Elliot took off his goggles as well, and the three of us watched the light creep in among the shadows far below. Then came the scratching of metal feet against the rock and the little drone trudged up with a short black tube and a thin case strapped to its back.

Bolton took the tube and pulled out a tripod, then crawled a way along the cliff and balanced it on the edge, pointed roughly at the distant structures. Then he lay back down next to us and slid a screen out of its case, and folded it back to stand on its own. He swore under his breath as he tried to get his blunt fingers around the tiny controls beside the screen. I wondered whether he'd had as much trouble sleeping as I had. The screen finally lit, and the tube on the cliff swung around as Bolton centered it.

"Lord almighty!" said Elliot.

"Sweet saints of Gwynedd," said Bolton at the same time, "what in the bloody hell did that, do you suppose?" The screen had centered on a small plot of grass near the settlement. Lying in the corner of it was the cleanly severed front half of a cow. The rest of the cow was nowhere in sight. "That was a bloody big sword, did that."

Elliot looked away. "Lasers," he said. "Let's see it on infra-red." Bolton fumbled with the controls.

"I expected to find weird shit down here," said Elliot, "but not that." The screen blinked out, then remained a fuzzy grey—the cow was cold. Bolton widened the picture and several brighter spots appeared, a couple of them from animals in the foreground, and one from the barely warm outline of a vaulted building behind them.

He switched back to visual and panned across the settlement. More livestock carcasses appeared, and what looked like the sprawled form of a woman between two low buildings. A cow hobbled into view. One of its hind legs had been severed at the shank, although in the nearly sterile environment it looked as if it had healed. A riderless horse stood against one of the building walls, grazing at the sparse grass and apparently uninjured.

The view panned across the settlement's scattered buildings, then came to rest on the vaulted building that still showed some warmth. Most of the buildings were ramshackle clay structures, but this one was clean and sharp and built of metal. Bolton stared at it for a minute, then craned around toward the little drone behind us. "You—come here."

It didn't move. "I've got a name," it said. "'You' seems so government school."

"Bugger it all to hell, you little shit, you *don't* have a name! That's *my* name you've got, and I won't stand for it. Now come here!" He rubbed his eyes. "God, listen to me."

"I'm going to sulk," said the drone.

"Pray, do."

After a moment Bolton turned and slid back down to the drone. "All right. Listen—can your little flying friends transmit pictures back to us?" He held up a hand. "No, *don't* ask them. I just wonder if you know."

"No, sir, they can't," it said politely. Bolton blinked. "Ms. Chan says we don't see the same way you do."

"Indeed. But they can send voice, hm?"

"Yes, sir."

"You're being deucedly civil. All right, then, get a flying drone on its way out toward that settlement—we'll steer it in. Then get another one a mile or so up the ridge to relay signals—I don't want to be giving away our position."

"Mile?" said the drone.

"Yes, *mile*, damn it! As in mil, as in thousand, as in a thousand paces by a Roman legionnaire. One mile, five thousand feet!"

"I'm not Roman. I'm Jewish."

"You're what?"

"Mr. Patel said I looked Jewish."

"Oh, for Christ's sake! Just *do* it!"

"Stop shouting. I've already done it, if you'd only look."

A little spider drone slipped across the edge, then flew out toward the first glimmering of sun. Another one veered off to follow the edge of the escarpment, clumsily navigating along the uneven ground.

For the next half hour, via Little Bolton, we steered in the flying drone—which complained shrilly and frequently of disorientation and homesickness—and studied the distant settlement, where two things struck us increasingly as peculiar. First, it was not an ordinary agricultural station. There was too much high technology visible, and too little evidence of cultivation. And there were no ships or ground vehicles at all.

Secondly, the condition of the settlement was nothing short of bizarre. Nearly every object we could see, whether livestock, building, water tank or tree—even a mound of dirt—had been attacked. The dirt pile had a hole bored into it. The buildings had individual corners or walls removed. Even the one small tree we could see looked like it had been sliced evenly in two.

"It's as though everything's been *hobbled*," said Bolton, "lest it get away. That doesn't make a pissing lot of sense, does it? Why would you want to cripple a bloody mound of sod, for Christ's sake?"

Elliot thought he saw a door in the big building drifting closed, even though it had already been closed before. I didn't see the door close, but as I looked at the building I realized that it looked familiar, even though I couldn't possible have seen it before.

Eventually Little Bolton reported that the spider drone had reached the settlement. We instructed it to move around calling out "hello."

Now and then we saw the rising sun glinting from the little drone as it flitted between the buildings, then for a long time we didn't see it at all.

"She says someone answered," said Little Bolton.

"Put us through!" I said. "Quick—we need to talk directly."

"I think not just now...perhaps in a minute. She's under attack, is the thing."

"What? Let us listen at least, for Christ's sake." Instantly came the sound of breaking glass, then a man's frightened shouting—though in a language we didn't recognize.

"Where is it now?" I said. "The drone."

"She doesn't know where she is. You may speak, though, if you like."

"We're friends!" I shouted at Little Bolton, feeling ridiculous even as I said it. "We've come to help." The shouting stopped. Then after a minute it was followed by a question we couldn't understand.

"Mandarin?" I said.

"Shanghai, Fukien," said Bolton. "I can never quite tell. Roscoe."

Roscoe stepped out of the shadows. "Yes."

"Roscoe, have we got someone who speaks Cantonese or Mandarin, or the like? The time lag home would be too long, I'm afraid."

Throckmorton's ferret's eyes stabbed here and there for a minute while he thought. "Amoy—Wei. Johnny, get Wei up here, would you?" Throckmorton had lain down on his stomach, peering over the edge with the rest of us, and again there was no way to tell who he was talking to.

"Like magic, ain't it?" whispered Elliot to me. "These guys lie around practicing this shit, did you know that?" Nothing happened for a minute, then Little Bolton's speaker sounded with the cautious questioning again. I answered as reassuringly as I could, remembering the edge of hysteria in the man's voice when he'd been shouting. He didn't answer.

I had expected the Amoy-speaking Wei to be an older man, one who might have spoken it as a child, but instead it was a quiet, part-Chinese girl who appeared suddenly, squatting down between Throckmorton and the little grasshopper drone.

"Wei," said Bolton, "translate for Mr. Torres here."

"Tell him," I said, "that we're here to help him, and that we need to know what happened." She translated fluently into the odd, strangled sounds of the Fukien dialect, and when the man didn't answer she repeated it. Then she added something of her own, and the man suddenly spoke in English.

"Ha!" he said. "You speak Amoy pretty good. Like serving girl, maybe. What, you Nationalist dog?"

Bolton and I looked at each other.

"I bet you fuck like dog, too—what you think? You got pretty voice." He suddenly burst out with a brittle, uneven laugh, then stopped in a fit of coughing. "Who you talk for, ha?" he said with difficulty.

"Commander Michael Bolton," said Wei.

"Nah. Him I don't know."

Nothing but his labored breathing came through for a minute after that. He was probably wounded like everything else. Then he spoke a few words I couldn't understand.

"He says," said Wei, "that you don't want to know what happened—and when are you coming to get him? Then he said something about 'fire-dogs.' I don't know what he means."

"Tell us what happened," I said to the man. But there was just his breathing.

Then suddenly I remembered where I'd seen a vaulted metal building like that before.

"Bolton, Roscoe—particle and radiation imaging of that building. Can you do it?" Throckmorton nodded and slipped away. I wondered if there was anything he couldn't produce.

"Who else you talking for there, you?" said the voice.

Bolton looked at the girl and inclined his head toward me. "Eduardo Torres," she said.

"So! That true? You Engineer Torres himself?" He coughed. "One who build big ships and bang-bang battery, ha?"

"Yes," I said. The girl's eyes widened in surprise.

"Yah, okay, you I know. Everybody know. You one who butcher American Army Thirty-Nine Division. You famous boy, uh-huh. Kill round-eye Europeans, too. So you knew Chih-Hsien Chien, ha?"

Elliot and Bolton and I looked at each other in surprise. Wei didn't understand.

"Who's Chih-Hsien Chien?" she whispered.

"Be quiet," hissed Little Bolton. "They're thinking."

Finally I said to the man, "Yes, we knew him. Why do you ask?"

"'Cause he make fool out of you, just like pretty soon beasties make fools out of all of us, I think." He laughed again, then choked it off with the coughing.

"Tell us why Chih-Hsien turned the Europeans against us," said Bolton. "Do you know? We're still coming to get you, but we'd like to know."

"Ha! You don't come. I die anyway, pretty soon. Pretty soon we all die, eh? Well, I tell you. Crazy-man Chien, first he do what we Chinese tell him to. He tell round-eye Europeans a couple secrets, try to get them to blow you up pretty good there on your island. We think, after they blow you up pretty good we come in, make like good guys, everything okay, except while we smiling and all we put drones and batteries in our pockets, eh? Except bad-boy Torres, he pretty clever guy. He got little surprise in batteries, kill round-eyes instead. So we all think okay, we try something else. But Chien, he all mad like monkey. He supposed to be big guy after Europeans blow you up, but now he nothing. So he start telling Europeans lies about you to get even. He tell them that all the help you claiming to give them and the other colonists, you just faking it, and really after you leave Earth you going to cut everyone off. We all think ha-ha, pretty funny, scare Europeans a little. But we don't know crazy round-eye European snakes bring old Russian-pig weapons with them here in space. Not so funny."

"So what did you do?" I said.

"So. We do what Chinese always do. We wait. Now Europeans gone, and all your bang-bang batteries empty, so we making our own, okay. So we start thinking...but don't matter now. Little dead dragons, they make everything finished."

"Tell us what happened."

"Ha!" He laughed, then started shouting incoherently. Wei looked at me and shrugged. Finally the man drew in a hoarse breath and went on.

"They don't care! Not nothing! They crazy—they just walk around and...and...like they got to *break* everything. Not kill—different. Like they got to break. Me they break—everyone, everything."

"You said 'dead' dragons—why?" Throckmorton reappeared to set something up next to the telescope tube.

"Because they dead! They don't care! They not like you, me—they don't listen, they don't run, they don't *see* us! They just take their time, *break* everything!" He shouted angrily, then it sounded like something smacked against the listening spider drone.

"What did they look like?" I said. "You said 'fire-dogs', and then you said 'dragons.'"

But he didn't answer. After a while we realized we couldn't hear the ragged breathing or the coughing any longer. I asked Little Bolton what had happened.

"She says the person is still there, but isn't speaking."

"Jesus."

Throckmorton hunched over our little screen to set something, then suddenly he straightened up and whistled. All five of us squeezed in to see. Little Bolton yelped and backed out of the way.

On the screen at least four of the settlement's structures were glowing, with the main vaulted building showing up as a bright yellow. Along the edge of the screen were counts of free particles and radioisotopes being emitted, with radiocobalt at the top blinking on and off.

"Well, ain't that something," said Elliot. "That ain't from the little dead dragons.' That's from the Chinese, who are out here building themselves radiation weapons."

"Were."

"Yup."

"Commander?" A soldier had crept up to hand Bolton a slip of paper. Bolton looked at it and the life seemed to go out of him. He crumpled the paper up and stuffed it in his pocket.

"It seems," he said, "that one of our industrial domes has blown out without explanation, and accordingly a decision has been made to raise the fleet."

Polaski, I thought.

Bolton looked up at me. "Immediately. All forces have been recalled, and we are to meet them in orbit with dispatch. Ground forces unable to disengage will be left behind."

Polaski had gotten his way.

Chapter Nineteen: BEHOLD, I COME AS A MULTITUDE

"That oughta be a real pretty sight, Torres, but it's just plain sad, if you know what I mean."

White against the black, the fleet hung sleek and assured, in its element once again for the first time in thirteen years. One hundred eighty capital ships in a line, all of our own remaining ships plus those that had joined us. Nearly a thousand smaller ships surrounded them, a cloud of minions attending the majesty of the giants.

Riding in the fleet were more than twelve thousand souls: founders and infants, soldiers and prisoners, exiles spanning four generations.

But the fleet's majesty and history were mocked now by the uncertainty of its purpose. Gone was the promise, replaced by the tightening trap, and by the bickering, and the fear. Gone was the adventure, and gone were the gardens, replaced by monstrous weapons mounted in the upper decks.

There were ships with powerful engines, carrying giant new cannon, and ships filled with tough and solid soldiers, raised on the promise of invincibility. And there were ships filled with children who would never walk, the price paid for those few who would ride the fast ships into war—a war which, even still, only Polaski and Rosler were sure we were fighting.

"I don't know, Tyrone," I said. "What else are we supposed to do?"

"Yeah. Ain't nowhere to hide, anymore, is there, Torres?"

"No. So what does a man do, Tyrone, when there's nowhere to go, and the whole world's slipping out of his control?"

"Breakfast comes to mind."

"I'm serious."

"So am I. What makes you think it ever was under your

control?"

Near the center of the fleet, driven by a light plume of flame from its tail, was the great ship with the familiar 00 across its nose. As the little commando ship on which we rode rotated to match the larger ship's acceleration, our perspective shifted and suddenly the fleet no longer stretched off into the distance, but instead climbed straight up into a black sky, one ship high above the other.

When we coupled, Elliot pushed his way through the air lock and disappeared into the big ship's commons, and after a few last words with Bolton I followed him through.

I stopped in the center of the deck, struck by the rancid air.

"So," said Polaski behind me. He was leaning against a table in the dim light, his arms folded in front of him. "So you went running off to Asile with Bolton." I didn't know whether it was a question or not.

"Yes."

"I hear the Chinese were cut up pretty bad."

"Only a few of them, Polaski. It was just a weapons station."

He thought for a minute, then dropped his hands to the edge of the table. "We're going in after the aliens, Torres. Are you with me or not?"

"Yes."

His eyes narrowed as he thought about it, then he raised his arm with a finger extended like a gun. He pulled the trigger. "Click."

Chan and Kip were on the floor of Charlie Peters' quarters, surrounded by sacks of dirt, working to transplant seedlings into pots. There was an unfamiliar tension in Chan's face, and new grey in her hair as I leaned down to kiss her. Kip waved, glad to see me, solemn.

"Where's Charlie?" I said.

"Down with Pham and the medic." She pushed the hair out of her face with the back of a hand. "I don't know why he bothers— she hates the poor man." She handed Kip more plantings. "I swear he treats her like the next messiah or something."

"Pham's got a medic? Rosler beat her that bad?"

"No, she's all right. Bruises, dislocation. The medic's for Anne. They're keeping her sedated. Worried about her heart."

"I'm surprised she allows it."

Chan frowned. "She hasn't got a choice. She's a fleet re-source, you know, strategic property. As long as there's a chance the drones are still out there, we need her alive."

"You know she had the drones' communications codes in a case, in her workroom."

"MI deck. I moved them myself."

"All right." I looked around the room, conscious of the two-hundred-foot particle cannon overhead where the gardens had once been. "Chan, how many ships had been fitted with cannon before the weapons dome blew out?"

She gave me a puzzled look. "All of them. It wasn't the weapons dome that blew."

I was confused for a minute; I'd been sure it was the weapons dome that blew, although I couldn't remember why I thought so. "Which one was it?"

"Wheel assemblies and trailers. Farming tools."

There was something wrong. I brushed off my hands and moved around the room, trying to concentrate, but in the end something else caught my eye, instead. Near the top of one of Peters' cases was a photograph of a much younger Chan, down on one knee and smiling into the camera. She was posing next to a little grasshopper drone draped in British racing green.

"Chan?"

"Hm?"

"Did you know that Bolton had a couple hundred fleet drones with him? Out on missions," I hastened to add. "Up until the recall?"

She stopped her planting and gave me a patient look. "Planting trees on Asile, you mean. Of course. He still does."

I was thinking about Chan's being privy to Bolton's project, and about his leaving it in place despite the mobilization, when I arrived in Pham's quarters to find Peters being thrown out and the medic packing her kit to follow. The medic was a competent-looking woman, attractive and alert, but clearly in no mood for abuse.

"At least Rosler got balls, Mush-Face!" Pham shouted at

Peters. "All you got's prissy little god—make you be *nice* all the time. How 'bout you fuck Miss Saintly-Patience here, go tell God how *nice* it was!"

She saw me and her head snapped around toward me, releasing Peters. "Hah! No-Balls here not even *nice*. He just dead from brain down, can't tell a teat from a cow, kill them all just the same! Shit."

She was as agitated as I'd ever seen her, leaning forward and stabbing at the air with her finger, her voice shrill and unsteady, her face a swollen, yellowish black. One arm was taped against her side, and she'd lost much too much weight.

I followed Peters back onto the lift, and we got off at the quarters Chan and I shared. Peters threw himself into a chair and ran a hand across his face and up over his balding head.

"Is she really worth it, Charlie?" I said.

"Aye, lad—she's worth everything. She's all we've got."

I still didn't understand what he meant when he talked like this. Pham was beaten. Hammered down until there was nothing left but the spit and the abuse. Peters seemed to see her at the head of some sort of legions of deliverance, but I knew she would never again have that kind of power.

"She has it now, Eddie." I looked at him. "She's got the one thing that'll save us all, in the end." But instead of going on to deliver one of his sermons as I expected, he rummaged in a kit bag to hold out a rolled piece of paper. "I'm sorry, Eddie, it was all I had time to bring." It was the blue and green photograph of Serenitas from my office wall, now worn and creased from the travel.

"Thanks." I toyed with the roll.

"What went wrong, Charlie? Do you know?"

"Aye, well you might ask. Well, they searched the planet's surface and found nothing that might have done in the dome's glass panels, but the dome had blown out just the same and people began fearing for the ships, thinking that the host was suddenly in among us—"

"That's not what I meant, Charlie." He looked at me blankly.

"Ah," he said at last. "I see. What happened before." He stroked the arm of his chair, a man accustomed to holding a cane.

"Eddie, back on Earth we inherited a civilization with a troubled past, and we tried to run. You can't do that, you know. For better or worse, what's handed us is ours, and we can't set it aside until we take it for what it is. But off we went just the same, dragging it along, killing and thieving on the way, and now the piper's at the door. *He that leadeth into captivity, shall go into captivity; He that killeth with the sword—*"

"All right, Charlie, I get your point. But even if this mess is of our own making—"

"No, Eddie. Not of our making. It was handed to us, by our fathers and masters, and we didn't take it."

"Okay, fine. But this is different, now. We've got intelligent creatures out there with intentions of their own, who have nothing to do with our pasts—or with moral retribution or karma or whatever the hell it is...things just went wrong, Charlie. And I don't know where."

"Ah, Eddie, Eddie—I love you dearly, but still you don't see." He put a hand on my arm and kept it there. "We cheated and we lied, laddie, and we drove desperate men and their weapons into space because of it. We sent robots beyond any sane man's ken to take whole systems we'd never even been to, not asking so much as a by-your-leave. Don't take me for an old fool, Eddie. I don't believe for a minute this has to do with morality."

That surprised me. "So what were we supposed to do, then, on Earth? What were we supposed to do when there was no way *to* accept what was handed us?"

"Ah, but there always is, you see. You might not like it, but it's there. And there's no changing it, or bargaining with it, or running away from it. Now, I grant you that accepting it might mean everlasting suffering, or it might mean no more than missing a cup of tea. But whatever it is, it's yours. All yours, Eddie, that's the point. That's when you're free, lad, when you accept it all as yours. That's when the one and only course truly open to you is revealed.

But as much as we might have chosen to accept our lives as they now stood, we had the futures of twelve thousand others to consider, and the eyes of another million watching to see if we would take on the alien fleet in Serenitas, or wait to be destroyed in our own homes with the rest. And so we voted to go—believing, most of us, that the aliens had decided to attack not only a Chinese nuclear weapons station, but a harmless landing dome on the black planet with Pham and me in it, and a farming equipment dome with no one in it at all. The fact that in one case laser-bearing animals of some kind had arrived to cripple indiscriminately every animate and inanimate object in sight, and that in the other, radiation had been focused on our vulnerable glass panels from a great distance, was dismissed as an unknowable subtlety of alien strategy.

And yet, I thought, who *had* destroyed the domes if not the aliens? Almost certainly not the Chinese, who had put their resources into nuclear technology instead. The Europeans and their particle weapons were long gone. The independents' attacks were political, rather than military, and anonymity did them no good. And no one else had the means, except for the Americans.

Pham didn't join us on the MI deck for the vote, but remained in her quarters, hostile and drugged. Miller came, but was vague and disoriented. Kip fidgeted and Peters quoted Shakespeare. Polaski waited indulgently through it all, smart enough to keep quiet. In the end Chan and Elliot voted to go, as did Susan Perris, the medic, whom I'd asked to be present. And somewhere overhead, a spider drone voted loudly and repeatedly to stay, until Chan called it down for a talk.

The only real argument, as it turned out, was over how fast to get there. Polaski wanted to burn fuel and race for the torus under heavy thrust, while others—especially Chan and Perris—urged a months-long orbital drift for the sake of children who'd been removed from the weightless can.

"They can catch up later," said Polaski.

"Guarded by whom in the meantime?" Chan had lost all patience with Polaski.

"Well, bring them along, then. I've got to believe they can handle at least a G or two like normal people."

"They're perfectly normal people!"

"Well, all right, fine. So some of them don't make it. It's not as though they're doing us a lot of good."

Kip was becoming increasingly agitated. He tugged at something in his hand with abrupt, jerky movements, and turned his head this way and that, staring at the walls until I began to worry that he was ill. I asked Susan Perris if there was something we should do. She looked at me disbelievingly.

"He's angry, Mr. Torres."

I looked at Kip, at his slender form and his smooth, ebony face. He had on his short pants and his loose white shirt, and was lost in the big acceleration seat. I found myself surprised at the idea of him being angry.

In the end I reminded Polaski about accumulated strain on the ships because of the new cannon in their bows, so we agreed on a low, one-half-G thrust. We issued the orders and the fleet began its turn. FleetSys informed the torus of our approach, then began the painstaking maneuver of stretching the fleet into a quarter-million-mile-long line: high-G crews in the van with Marines and fast cannon behind them, followed by the capital ships, the children, and the remaining surface assault troops holding the rear.

After that day, Kip avoided Polaski entirely and spent more and more time with me.

Darkness...almost no weight. Thin sheets and cool air, Chan's skin against mine. Soft thighs, warm lips on my neck.

"I'm think I'm afraid," I said to her.

"I know," she said. Lips against my eyelids.

"Maybe we shouldn't have come. Maybe we should have stayed on Earth"

"I love you, Eddie. I want you to know that."

The ship hummed beneath us and the night slid past outside, never again to turn to day.

"Coming up on two-G pass-point, Mr. Torres."

"Very well, Mr. Plath."

When he reached his six-G point, Simon Plath in the forwardmost gunship would be committed. Our own ship was well back in the fleet, so at the same moment that Plath was committed we would still have the option to abort at only about three Gs. Nevertheless, the moment of his commitment was the moment when all of the ships would achieve final velocity relative to the torus and cut their engines, so we needed to keep abreast of his position at all times.

More desultory reports trickled in from the fleet, while those of us on the MI deck fiddled uselessly with our equipment, the actual preparations already having been made again and again during the days past. On the big overhead screen the torus began to take on definition, the size of a giant moon now, pale in the weak light from Holzstein's Star behind us.

The MI deck was dreary and cluttered and filled with stale air. The equipment was balky and in poor repair, grimy from disuse. The open grating underfoot was clogged with empty coffee balloons and Polaski's paper airplanes. Chan had long ago given up trying to keep the trash from building up in the fleet MI's ventilators underneath.

I checked the screen again and swiveled away from the console, pushing my headset to one side. Anne Miller was resting in the seat behind me, heavily sedated and trying to keep her eyes open. A short time ago she had suddenly begun talking about the drones and about Madhu Patel, although for no reason that I could tell. I thought that our approach to Serenitas had probably brought it on.

"You started to tell me again, Anne, about how Madhu tried to keep you from building fighting machines. Why? What did he think you were going to do?"

"No, he didn't. He made me think about him being hurt by them, is all. He was very clever." Her eyes drifted closed.

"He couldn't walk very well," she said finally. "You could hear him clumping and dragging along from a long ways away. That was nice."

I looked at Susan Perris nearby, but she just shrugged and shook her head. She couldn't hear us from where she sat.

"But the idea of Madhu being hurt didn't mean much after he died, did it?" I asked. "All of that would have changed?"

She looked at me vaguely. "Well, yes. I needed to protect us."

"From the possibility of aliens, you mean. After he died."

She looked puzzled, but then she nodded. "Yes, aliens." Minutes trickled by without her speaking again, her eyes on the image of the pale circle growing in the darkness ahead of us.

"China moon," she said, still staring at it.

"I'm sorry?"

"That's what Madhu said, when he visited me at the Lake. 'China moon.' Before the war. We used to go for rides at dawn, when it was cool, and once there was a full moon setting over the Sierra. He said it looked like porcelain. 'It's a china moon over China Lake,' he said. But he was glad it was setting, he said, not rising. I remember, because that was the day the Pacific War began."

Simon Plath's voice crackled in my headset. "Three-G pass-point. Pretty good shape up here—all ready for our little friends."

Elliot hunted through the system for the freefall checklist, while Chan blinked at her screens and rubbed her eyes. Next to Pham's and Miller's empty seats, under a drooping mass of exposed cables, Peters and Kip sat by the communications console. Polaski sprawled to my right with an overlay marker in his hand, drawing little creatures of some kind on his screens. I turned back to Miller.

"Is that why you changed your instructions to the drones, Anne? Because Madhu was gone?"

"I suppose."

"Finishing work you'd wanted to do at China Lake? Arming them so much that they drew the wrath of these aliens?"

She tensed. "It *should* have worked! This is *exactly* what they were for!" She gripped the armrest. Perris motioned for me to cut it out.

"Five-G pass-point, Mr. Torres," came Plath's voice, "if you concur. One-way tunnel to serenity, here we come...at least they can't see us coming, eh? We'll just pop up somewhere in their back yards like gophers."

Chan nodded and pointed at her screen. My own read 02.00 SGF PASSPOINT +00:01:14. Our ship was into the final approach, although we could still quit at about two Gs—three Gs more gently than Plath in the lead.

"We concur, Mr. Plath. We're on the clock now, no need for further call-outs. Good luck." The great, pale grey torus grew on our screen, with the curving line of our ships disappearing up toward the maw of the terrific device.

"What's he mean, 'pop up like gophers?'" said Peters. "Surely they're watching the torus from that big fleet of theirs."

"No, Charlie, they can only see the torus at *Serenitas*. Each tunnel is just one-way, remember. We'll pop out at some unpredictable spot in Serenitas System, somewhere unrelated to their own torus, and unrelated to wherever the last set of ships appeared."

Perris was behind me doing something with Miller, while Elliot reached out to get her to sit back down. He passed out the space-sickness vacuum bags.

Overhead, the sight of the slender thread of ships disappearing up toward the torus was mesmerizing. Elliot tapped his pencil against my screen.

"Torres."

"Right. Okay, here we go. Ship's drones secured."

"Done," said Chan.

"Hey, Torres," said a voice from a speaker.

"Hurry it up, Rosler, what is it?"

"Take it easy. You've got a message coming in."

Peters at the communications console was ignoring the flashing light as he methodically unfolded his sickness bag. He was already pale and beginning to sweat with anticipation. The incoming signal was being recorded by the MI, a communication sent from somewhere in the system behind us where the five- or ten-minute lag would make conversation impossible.

"Forty seconds to freefall and fleet commit."

"Okay. Fluids and pumps." We'd listen to the message later.

"Done."

"Quarters and—"

"*Oh my God, get—*" Plath, screaming in my headphones, voice choked off in mid-sentence.

"Jesus Christ, Torres!" shouted Elliot. Peters was struggling to get out of his seat, trapped by his harness.

"*Abort, abort!*" Chan sat frozen at her keys, staring in horror at the big screen.

"Abort!" I shouted, not understanding why but feeling the rush of adrenalin. My headset came alive with voices, and finally I looked up at the screen, while at the same time a confused memory shouted at me along with the other voices. Having called for the abort, something else was supposed to be happening—and it wasn't.

Sirens. 03.00 SGF PASSPOINT -00:00:05. STAND BY FOR ZERO THRUST. I stared at the overhead screen. *Simon says, Simon says.*

"*FleetSys*, abort!"

The screen was still filled with the great, grayish torus, with our slender line of ships still threading up toward its center. But across the expanse of the torus there was now a field of black—an impossible number of odd, glistening black shapes blocking our way.

I was falling. Then just as suddenly I was slammed against the side of the seat as our ship's jets fired to pivot us sideways. The view on the screen slid to one side and snapped to a new camera. Our own fleet's ships in the far distance had also turned side-on to the torus and had sprouted hundred-mile-long lances of flame. They began to accelerate out of the way at full thrust. The ships nearer to us accelerated less harshly, having more time, and soon there was a curving line of ships arcing away from our course, away from the tremendous black fleet in our way.

"*No*! My God, what are they *doing*?"

At first it looked like flashes from the sun glinting off our farthest ships. But then the ships were gone, disappearing like sparks in the night, flaring briefly against the round grey circle behind them.

Miller spoke.

"Again," was all she said, then our seats slammed into us as the engine reignited and tried to drive us clear of the approaching torus.

Faint shafts of light lanced out from the noses of our distant gunships, but the beams were useless unless they could turn again to face the attacking fleet—and that they couldn't afford to do.

"Turn and *face* them!" shouted Polaski. "Plath! All of you! Bring those cannon to bear! That's what we *built* them for!"

"Plath's dead," said Chan. She was straining forward against the weight and counting something on her screen.

"They *can't* turn, Polaski," I said. "They'll ram the torus."

"Well, they can take out some fucking enemy ships on the way!"

I dragged my own mike down and keyed the armrest. "Disregard," I said, and pushed the mike away. "That's insane, Polaski—sacrificing ships against unbeatable odds. Save them for later."

But some of the gunships had already begun to pivot back toward the attackers with their weapons lit. Every one of them flared and winked out before it could even finish the turn.

Our own ship began to shake. I keyed the mike again. "All vessels, best escape thrust. Gunships only: one flight of missiles each, spread your targeting specs." We needed to know what would get through and what wouldn't.

"Damn it, Torres!" hissed Polaski. "At least we can turn and use these cannon we've got back here on the dick-ships! We've still got time! Who the hell's side are you on, anyway?"

"No," said Chan. "You so much as twitch one of these big cannon and they'll take out all the capital ships instantly. You're not paying attention."

A vibration ran the length of our ship, then the MI deck began to shake from side to side; with the heavy cannon resting in the nose, six hundred feet above the engine, the slender ship was now oscillating at the center. With an ominous rending of metal, a piece of equipment above us ripped lose, and a moment later a spider drone burst from overhead like a gunshot and crashed through the deck, powered by our tremendous acceleration. The noise from the shaking was louder, and my arm was smashing from side to side; I couldn't get a grip on the controls.

"Elliot!" I said. I didn't know if I he could hear me. "More thrust! Can you reach? More thrust!"

"You're crazy!"

"Yes, more! Anything, any change—break the resonance, damn it!"

His flailing hand smashed into his keys and got a grip. But in that instant we heard an awful sound, a sound that became more and more terrible as we understood its implications. It sounded like an artillery piece at close quarters—a powerful explosion, sharp and clean amidst the roaring chaos.

It was the sound of an explosive charge slamming home a between-decks seal—the heavy guillotine blade that shot through the lift cables and the ladder and the air ducts, all of them, isolating a breached segment of the ship. It had shot home right at the top of the MI deck, between decks thirty-seven and thirty-eight. Somewhere above us, the ship was coming apart.

"*Tuyet!*" Peters had understood first, and was scrabbling at his harness to get free.

Pham was in her 38-deck quarters, on the wrong side of the seal.

I was on my hands and knees, then, trying to crawl across the thrashing grating to the ladder.

Elliot increased the thrust at that moment, sucking me down onto my belly. But the hellish shaking subsided. Something overhead pulled loose due to the added weight and smashed through the grating next to me, then the deck tipped and the lighting flickered uncertainly, finally turning to red.

I got a hand onto a rung of the ladder, trying to think ahead, trying to remember how to override the emergency seal above me.

But I couldn't do it. It had taken all my strength to crawl to the ladder, and I couldn't pull myself up it. Not with the weight of three men on my back. Peters was shouting hoarsely behind me, but his words made no sense.

Then suddenly the weight lifted and we were down to two Gs. I pulled myself up the ladder, and Elliot spoke behind me.

"I can give you forty seconds, Torres. After that the ship's my first priority."

Peters was next to me, then, pushing an oxygen bottle under my arm. Then I was up against the plate of the seal, staring at a pressure gauge inset into it. 9.6 PSI. I couldn't remember: was that the actual pressure on the far side, above the seal, or was it the difference between the pressure on the two sides of the seal, an almost non-existent pressure above it and our own twelve pounds of pressure below?

I grabbed for the red lever inset into the ceiling and tugged. With a light hiss the plate slid open an inch. There was still some pressure above.

But the plate stopped where it was. I stared at it and tried to think, feeling the seconds ticking away.

The lever was a crank handle. The bones in my fingers were grinding into the rung of the severed ladder, straining to hold my weight as I began to crank with all my strength. Air rushed past me and then I was sucked through, the bottle banging against the metal and the mask catching on the way.

The plate shot home again below me and sealed tight.

I remember crawling past the privacy panel on 38-deck, wondering why it was so dark, wondering why I was growing faint even when I was breathing, finally remembering my oxygen mask.

A hand in front of me—Pham stretched out on the floor, reaching for her escape, her skin darker than mine. Too dark.

Trying to get the mask on her, running out of time. Dragging her back to the ladder, reaching for the red lever. Nothing. It spun in my hand, disabled. Those unlucky enough to be on the wrong side of a seal were not allowed to open it, condemned.

Pain swelled in my gut. *There will be a swelling of stomach gasses, leading to rupture, preceded by bleeding from the eyes and ears.* Groping for the mask, vision clearing. Then the plate was open again and a big hand was reaching through, taking Pham out of my arms.

I went through the opening the wrong way, head first, and my forty seconds were up. Elliot couldn't wait any longer. He rammed the ship up to four Gs, and there was the pain of twisting awkwardly and slamming into the deck, and there was a picture on the screen: the edge of the torus sliding by, very, very close.

We were not pursued. We reassembled the fleet and limped for home, our own crippled ship coupled to Bolton's to share his precious air.

Where the attacking fleet had come from, we didn't know. It seemed impossible that it could have arrived from Serenitas at that very instant, launched through the Serenitas torus with such pinpoint accuracy and timing that it would appear in our system exactly between us and our own torus. It was more likely that they had popped up in our system sometime in the past, undetected, and had hidden behind our torus, waiting to slip out when necessary to protect the approaches to Serenitas.

Counting their ships in the recordings, the attackers represented only a part of the great alien fleet the probe had seen in Serenitas. The rest either still waited near that far planet, or else had hidden somewhere close by in Holzstein's System.

Eighty-three of our warships had flashed out of existence, and seven capital ships had shattered from the strain of the thrust. Our recordings also showed another sixteen smaller vessels and two more capital ships that for one reason or another had failed to develop enough thrust to clear the torus, and which the alien attackers had then destroyed, presumably to prevent them from smashing into the torus they themselves needed to return to Serenitas.

One of our warships had succeeded in executing a complex six-G attack, and had destroyed two attackers with its primary weapon before being destroyed itself. Another two attackers had been destroyed by fast missiles, both of them magnetic-field-seeking.

Pham's arm had been dislocated, and she had torn ligaments in it so badly that Perris believed she might never regain full use of it.

Anne Miller was dead. Her heart had stopped under the terrible weight. Susan Perris tended to her mortal remains and Peters to her soul, and as I watched from the shadows I reflected on the irony of her passing.

She had died face to face with the black, gun-laden ships of the very aliens we had thought existed only in her imagination. And her life's work, the drones that had been intended to protect her, the drones we were now sure had themselves been destroyed by the alien's fierce weapons, had come to nothing.

Many hours after our aborted attempt to reach Serenitas we remembered the message received in the final moments of the approach, and we sat huddled on the MI deck and listened, surrounded by the stench and the wreckage, numb from the failure and loss.

"Torres from Dorczak. I know you don't have time to answer, but Godspeed and good luck. We've caught one of your aliens."

Chapter Twenty: THE FOURTH SEAL

"I want you to come with me, Harry, to look at this thing they've caught. We're going to have to try and talk to it, and I'll need your help."

Penderson nodded inside his helmet and touched the faceplate, absently feeling for the scar on his cheek.

"Look at this." He shined his helmet light on a child's doll, found lying in the dirt under the main dome. It had been burned in half.

"Why that, do you suppose?" I said. "Because of its human form? So far they've been pretty unimpressed by the distinction between human and anything else."

"No, look." He twisted it to show the insides. "It's full of MI. That's what they saw. Same with all this other stuff." He tossed the doll aside.

"So, Torres, you've got the whole system staying away from this thing, waiting for you to go and see it personally."

"I need to, Harry."

"I know. Father Peters said you would need to. Still, from what Carolyn tells me, it's pretty uninteresting so far. It hasn't batted an eye since they caught it. Hasn't got eyes to bat. I hear that their people even reported it dead, until someone said if that was the case why was it still on its feet and why was it still warm. I'm not sure its guards are too bright."

"She's trying to keep down the number of people who know about it. She hasn't even been out to see it herself. I did ask her to have them monitor temperature and humidity and sound, though, from outside the cage. No change in any of them so far."

"Why sound? Why not the whole spectrum?"

"An animal that sends radio signals? Possible, I guess. I didn't think of that."

"None of the witnesses reported sounds during the attack on

Allerton's base. A couple of them described the attack as 'quiet and unhurried.' And from the mess here at our own base, it looks like they work just fine in a vacuum. Which means they communicate with something besides sound."

We had returned from the torus to find our base in a shambles. The manufacturing domes for ships' engines and armaments had been leveled, all with the same alien thoroughness we'd found on Asile. The other domes had been neatly breached, but only a few of the items we'd left in them had been selected out for attack: some desiccated livestock embryos, an inoperative searchlight, a bank of wall ovens, some of the heaps of slag out on the surface. In every case, though, even the smallest power cell or generator had been searched out and destroyed.

Yet items of far greater economic and military utility had been left untouched, such as the domes' giant oxygen separators and scrubbers, the big surface trailers, the farms' fertilizer tanks, and the smelters and rolling mills themselves.

The attack was unmistakably the same as at the Chinese station on Asile and, by all accounts, the same as the more recent one on the English-speaking base at Wallneck, on the isthmus of Lowhead—although that attack had left many more casualties. What was becoming clearer and clearer, though, as we trudged through the wreckage with our lamps, was that all of those attacks bore no resemblance at all to the earlier failures of our own two domes—the landing dome just days after the first news of the aliens, and the farming industries dome whose breach had prompted lifting the fleet.

"All right, Harry, I've seen enough. Let's get ready for the run to H-II. The ship Tyrone's outfitting with a cage ought to be ready."

"You're bringing it back?"

"Yes. I told Carolyn we had better facilities here for examining it, or whatever. Although I don't know if that's still true."

Penderson's helmet turned my way. "You know we can't set up this base, again, Torres. It's much too vulnerable now."

"We can't stay in those ships, either, damn it! There's no fuel, no air, no decent food. Everybody's at each other's throat...we've burned our bridges behind us, Harry. And these sons of bitches are burning them in front. We *have* to reopen these domes."

Not all of the fleet had returned to the black planet yet. Shortly after turning for home, back toward the base we'd abandoned, we'd had to stare helplessly through telescopes at the flickering lights and radiation bursts as our base was destroyed.

That, then, was when the indecision had set in, slinking into our midst like a wary predator. Tensions grew even as we mourned the dead, and the fleet began to tear at itself like a trapped animal.

A few fast ships had accompanied me back to the black planet, hoping to find more reassuring news. Others had drifted away from the fleet in sullen silence, striking out on new orbits for the warmth of the inner planets or the safety of the outer moons. Polaski had raced off somewhere to agitate for joint weapons production with other colonies, while Chan, Peters and Perris had stayed with the fleet, moving to the other ships to work with the scores of new orphans. In the end, the command ship had been left crippled and empty, towed in by Bolton.

But now Penderson and I were left with little reassurance to offer, beyond the fact that our support systems were still intact. The aliens had again proved thorough and powerful, and I was beginning to fear for humanity's survival anywhere in the system.

Or worse. There was something else, now, something that was never spoken of on the radios, and only whispered in conversations. Something we superstitiously avoided even in our own thoughts. Throughout the system, we'd begun quietly to erase every reference to Earth, every coordinate, every faintest allusion. We pretended that we had no origins, no past. It was a claim we'd once made in repudiation of our own planet, but made now out of an uneasy loyalty.

"So you're going to scan this thing and dissect it, and all that?"

Penderson and I trudged out across the iron floor of the air lock tunnel, out of the main dome. We crunched across the surface and passed one at a time through the tiny lock of our transparent observation boat, throwing our torches and suits down inside.

"Dissect it, you mean, so that Polaski and Rosler can find just the right nerve gas and radiation to melt them into glorious sludge? No, Harry, I don't think so. I've got a feeling our survival depends more on finding out who they are and what they're after than on how to kill them. Which isn't going to be easy. There's something about these attacks, Harry...I don't know, it's eerie, foreign. Alien. It scares the hell out of me."

"Scares you and the surviving witnesses, both. Some of them still aren't talking, yet there's not a scratch on them. You know what that one pilot is supposed to have said? The colonel? He said it would have been better if he'd at least been wounded. If he'd just lost his legs or something."

"I know, Harry, I know. Come on, let's go."

The observation boat was a peculiar vessel, little more than a sliver of a deck set into a clear bubble. Two swiveling seats forward were for the pilot and an observer. Behind them, running along the clear walls, two soft benches also served as cots. All the way aft was the air lock and a tiny galley, head and shower.

Floating out in space in the transparent boats left most of us feeling anxious and overexposed, and as Penderson pulled us off the ground I caught myself reaching under my vest mindlessly to check the body armor beneath it, as though that would help. I never liked being more than a few feet off the surface in the eggshell-thin boats, and now Penderson was about to run it all the way up into orbit.

As we skimmed along the surface and began the climb, however, a figure below broke away from a cluster of lights on the surface and waved us down, so Penderson settled back in and spun the tail and its air lock toward him. There was a clumping and hissing from the lock, followed by a suit hitting the deck. I shifted around to look.

"Good afternoon, Rosler."

He kicked his suit aside and began to clean his glasses, the corner of his mouth twisted into a now-permanent smirk. I hadn't seen him since before the trip to Asile.

"All right," he said, "you can go." He didn't look up.

Penderson glanced at me and raised an eyebrow. "Thank you very much," he said. "That's very kind of you." Without turning around he twitched the controls suddenly to jerk the boat off the ground. But Rosler was already sitting down.

No one spoke during the long climb. I concentrated on the deck between my knees.

"That was quite a job you did on Pham, Rosler," I said when we reached orbit.

"Yeah, well. It's how you keep them in line."

"You really believe that bullshit?" said Penderson over his shoulder.

"What do you know, a couple of limp dicks like you? You couldn't even hold onto your own wife, Penderson."

Where had Rosler gotten a story like that? Penderson's wife had been in his arms when she died.

"Anyway," said Rosler, "the bitch likes it."

The scar on Penderson's cheek had turned a deeper purple.

"What's the matter, Rosler?" he said. "Can't satisfy a real woman? One who's not hurting so bad she needs that kind of abuse?"

Rosler wiped his nose on the back of his hand and tried to push the hair out of his eyes. "Piss off, Penderson. If I need advice from niggers and wetbacks, I'll ask for it."

"All right," I said. "That's enough. You're out of line, Rosler."

"I wouldn't talk, Torres. You're on pretty thin ice, yourself."

"I said that's enough. Now, where are we dropping you?"

"Four-Four-Two. It's a trooper, trailing aft. Meridian plus seven degrees at the hour."

"All right. Harry, if you're the better man here, let's see it in the docking. You're a professional, remember that." I knew he wanted to hurt Rosler, but I wanted to get the detour over with. Not so much for diplomatic reasons as that I wanted to get out of the fishbowl and into a well-armed vessel with opaque walls.

We dropped Rosler off without another word, then Penderson maneuvered us forward among the orbiting ships to let me off on the provisioning vessel to which Elliot had docked the modified trooper, the one I would use for transporting the alien. Then Penderson set off on the long ride forward to return the transparent boat to the orbiting can, where I would pick him up on my way to H-II.

The atmosphere-capable transport Elliot had prepared for

me was an iron tube of the same type we'd ridden in Asile with Bolton's commandos. Its outside was rusted and unpainted, and it floated gloomily in the dark, tied to the larger ship like a sulking child on a leash. Its sides were pitted with dark portholes, and its windscreens were scarred and black, like the eyes of an underwater predator.

Inside, Elliot had pulled out all but the two pilots' seats. That left a bare, forty-foot-long cylinder with iron decking and exposed conduits, ducts and vent gratings. The after end of the ship had been separated off by heavy, vertical iron bars, with a small hatch cut into the rear of the ship for loading the animal. Although Dorczak hadn't seen the animal herself when we'd last talked, she'd told us that similar caging had sufficed so far, and that no special atmosphere or other accommodations seemed to be necessary.

I assembled a personal kit from the provisioning ship's stores, then gave Elliot last-minute instructions for preparing a report on what we'd found on the surface. I hoped to be back with the specimen in less than a week, before the body of the fleet returned, and in a position to make informed recommendations before Rosler dreamed up something new for Polaski, like throwing high-G seven-year-olds into the maw of the aliens' weapons.

During the disastrous alien repulse at the torus, quick-thinking commanders had ordered spectrographs and radiation counts of the attackers' weapons—and, more importantly, on the debris from our destroyed ships. Scientists had then re-examined the data returned by *Sun of Gabriel*, looking specifically for that same radiation signature somewhere in the Serenitas System.

And they'd found it. Out near the periphery of the system, not far from where the probe had first seen the alien fleet, was a slender, thirty-thousand-mile-long cloud of hot particles, tightly aligned and pointing out toward Holzstein's System, the direction from which the Europeans had been coming. The calculated mass of the particle cloud was sufficiently close to that of the European fleet to serve as proof: wherever in space the aliens had been before the European venture, they'd known that the Europeans were coming. And they had drawn back to wait.

The next question had been quick to follow: knowing the

nature of the aliens' weapons and the composition of our original drones and their ships, could we calculate the radioactive signature that the *drones'* destruction would have left? The scientists' answer was Yes, they could; and in short order they found the drones' signature as well. Everywhere in Serenitas System that the probe aimed its instruments, the death of the drones was spelled out in expanding, cooling clouds of particles. Decay and dissipation rates gave the timing: they had died over a three-year period, beginning nearly five years before the probe's visit. The aliens had been unerringly thorough.

Except in one instance: *Sun of Gabriel* herself. No one knew why she'd been spared.

Yet for all the evidence, a controversy raged nevertheless among the MI priests, based on a computer-modeled war game that had approached the level of fantasy since Miller's death: if some of the drones had survived after all, and if they had finally learned the art of defense as Miller had tried to teach them, would they be a match for the aliens if they returned now? Mock battles were waged again and again, but always with uncertain results, and always hinging on a key unknown—would the drones, whom Miller had claimed to have made human, have understood the peculiarly human skills of stealth and deception, of feint and surprise? They would need them to wage battle against the aliens, but Miller's own records left the issue unclear.

Elliot sealed me into the cold transport. I strapped myself down at the controls, and prepared to guide the machine for the next hour along the difficult pseudo-orbit that would pull it forward along the string of orbiting vessels to pick up Penderson. The massive fleet MI, which resided on the capital ships, was still too far away to instruct my smaller ship's intelligence, so I was left with manual controls.

The cold vault of stars hung motionless outside the windscreen, in every direction the same. Glinting flecks of ice in the night, watching me, I could almost believe, waiting for me to release, to begin. Even on Earth I hadn't been a relaxed pilot, and in space I was far different from the generations that had grown up with little concern for precious up and down. I was better suited to mechanized astrogation below-decks. In these little shuttles, while in deep space, I tended to become disoriented.

I willed the clock to bring me closer to the planet's day-side before I had to release, where I would have a sense of firm ground beneath me...twenty more minutes. I blew on my hands after the cold of the controls, and slipped my headset on.

"Hey, Torres." Elliot's voice was accompanied by a pounding on the air lock behind me.

"Yes."

"I've got a passenger out here who needs a ride, just up to the can. Can you do it?"

"All right." Company would help, even for the few minutes it would take to reach the can. I released the lock and my ears popped as the pressure changed. After a while I hadn't heard anything, so I turned around to find Pham floating over the middle of the deck, holding a kit bag in her good hand and looking uncertainly at the seat next to me. She avoided my gaze. Finally she pushed herself aft to grab onto the iron bars of the cage.

With a sharp jolt through the ship Elliot retracted the big docking pins. I tugged the lever to blow the air out of the lock and start the two ships drifting apart.

"Okay, Torres," said Elliot, "you're clear. Safe trip."

"Thanks." I tried to keep my eyes down on the controls as I set up the parameters for the forced orbit, then rolled the ship upside-down relative to the planet and eased in a light thrust, glancing back to make sure Pham was oriented. When I'd watched the indicators for a full minute and was sure thrust and altitude were stable, I set the alarms and swiveled the seat away from the windscreens.

Pham had snapped loose a supply case and was sitting on it in the center of the deck, leaning her head back against the bars. She wore loose, dirty fatigues, with her injured arm out of its sleeve. The jacket's shoulder bulged from the bandages underneath. Her face was thin and pale, her hair long and unkempt. She had an air of being soiled somehow, overused. Against the background of the solid bars in particular she looked worn and unfocused as she shifted her position and tugged at her jacket, turning to look at the walls or the ceiling, at anything but me.

"How's your arm?" I said. She seemed not to hear, then finally shrugged without looking up.

Over the next hour I glanced back at her several times, hunched over on her case, silhouetted against the bars. And I remembered, in disconnected images, a woman with flashing eyes and wild tempers, with insatiable appetites that had driven her and finally consumed her. But now, as she sat and fidgeted listlessly, I sensed that whatever had animated her so mercilessly was still demanding of her one final effort, and that the vulnerable woman I'd once seen looking out of those same eyes, the woman who read Irish poets and talked of having children, was too tired to obey.

The first edge of the sun inched over the horizon ahead of us, and its weak light spilled across the deck. It crept toward Pham's feet.

A week earlier Charlie Peters had talked to me about Pham. It was the night before we tried for the tunnel, and I'd slipped out of bed and left Chan asleep, and gone up to his quarters.

"Come in, lad, come in." A night-lamp glowed between Kip's bed and Peters', where he sat blinking into the shadows. He eased his nightgowned knees off the bed and leaned forward to pat the other bed, next to where Kip was sitting.

"Sit here," he said.

"I'm sorry, Charlie, I didn't realize it was so late. I hadn't meant to wake you."

"Come, lad, that's enough of that. What's on your mind? I don't imagine you've come to discuss civilization's troubled past again, hm?"

"No. Too many dreams, Charlie."

"I shouldn't wonder."

"There's one, mostly, about a cavern. The damn thing woke me up again tonight."

"Perhaps it's where you live, hm?" His gaunt face hovered in the lamp light, deep lines in his cheeks and age spots on his forehead. He leaned forward and tapped his fingertips against my chest. "In here. So, is there a way out of this cavern?"

"Well, yes and no. There's a tunnel, with daylight at the end, I think. But first it drops down into the rock, and there's always something— I don't know, something in the way."

"Indeed. A tunnel leading out of the darkness, with something blocking the way." He sighed, and his warm breath brushed across my face. I studied the frayed edge of his nightgown under his chin, and the grey hairs spilling past it.

"I don't wonder it's you, yourself down there, Eddie, between you and the light. The past you're always pretending you don't have. Listen to me—come, you came here to listen, so listen, you who'd have us all believe you left nothing behind when you ran away from home. Well, what I think is that you left everything behind. And I think it's there in your dream.

"I want you to imagine a child, Eddie, born into terrible poverty. A child whose parents are struggling so hard to provide food that they can provide little else. A child whose father is so troubled by the truth of his life that he's unable to provide even the dignity and regard a child needs. 'Tis hurtful, Eddie. Hurtful to the child, hurtful to the parents. 'Tis the terrible price of poverty, you know, the destruction of childhood."

He ran a hand absently over his bald head, lost in thought for a moment.

"Now imagine that this child runs away from home, walking a great way and suffering hardship in a tiny boat among the wretched and poor. And imagine that this child loses a father at an early age, a father whose blessing and strength the child is still waiting for so desperately."

"Get to the point," I said.

"A child like Tuyet, for example."

He looked on sympathetically as I struggled with my confusion, then he reached out and squeezed my hand. "Or like you." On the bed beside me, Kip blew air through his flute without making any sound.

"I didn't know, Charlie."

"Of course you didn't."

How was it, I thought, that I knew so little about her?

"In the dream," I said, "someone's standing just behind my

shoulder, telling me—"

"—not to go into the tunnel. Aye, I know. I wasn't finished. Eddie, a child doesn't know what to do with so much hurt. He locks it away, along with everything else he needs because the needing of it brings him so much pain. He locks away all of the wonder and joy God gave him, all of the things that make him a child. And there's something else he locks away, too. When we're hurt too many times, Eddie, we become angry, and I tell you the anger of a child is a terrible thing. 'Tis a fire that blackens his whole world, and he believes it will destroy everything he loves.

"I'm sure your mother saw it in you, Eddie. And I'm sure she believed it was something her family couldn't survive. So she said to you, 'Don't be letting it out, boy. Take all those black things inside and lock them away forever.' Poverty robs us even of our feelings, you see, the one thing that makes us human.

"I'm sure you believed you drove your father from his house and killed him, Eddie—it's what a child believes. And I'm sure your mother's voice said in your ear all the while, 'You see! You've had your way and you've killed him!' And so you locked those things away, too, and off you ran. But when you do that, you put away all of the laughter and the music, too, and the wonder, and you become a secret person. Only if you are very lucky will there be someone nearby to carry those things for you, and keep them safe." Kip's arm brushed against me as he stirred; I had been gradually becoming conscious of the warmth and the smell of him as Peters talked.

"Well, all that's fine," I said, "but what about the dream?"

"Aye, well, that's what's waiting in the tunnel, you know. All of the black and troubled things, all of what we call human sin. And someday you'll have to accept them, if you want to be human. You'll have to let your grief fill you up, and you'll have to weep until you're exhausted of it. Your loss was real, laddie, and you had no choice in it, but the choice of what you do with it is yours. That's what's lying in the balance, now."

Together we listened to the humming of the engine.

"This time when I had the dream," I said, "there was some-one in there with me, raising a hand up toward me. With a gun, I thought."

"Indeed? Well, I don't know. Perhaps not a gun? I can sooner imagine a balance. You know: 'And the third beast said, "Come and see;" and I beheld a black horse, and he that sat on him held a balance in his hand.' I really do think there's no one in there but you, lad."

I tried again to picture the figure in front of me, but it remained out of sight in the gloom.

"I keep thinking we're not going to make it, Charlie."

"Through the tunnel? Well. Tuyet will, you know. And I'm thinking you'll be free to go with her, hm?"

Kip had begun a soft, slow tune, one I hadn't heard before.

I didn't understand what Peters meant. "And Chan?"

He looked at Kip, then at his hands. "She's down in your quarters, lad, waiting for you. Go."

It was a week later that I was sitting in the iron ship with Pham, watching her take a cloth from her pocket and wipe her face, shifting again to get comfortable. The things Peters had said had come to seem increasingly obscure to me, and in the days since, I'd found that I had far more immediate concerns. More than anything, I needed to see the creature that waited for me.

"Aye, I know," Peters had said when I remarked on it before leaving the fleet. "For I heard the voice of the fourth beast, and he was saying, 'Come and see'..."

But for once, like Madhu before him, he didn't finish the whole thing.

The thin light from the sun crept farther across the deck, and touched Pham's feet.

Less than two days later Penderson and I were on the second planet, drained by the glare and humidity, surrounded by the crowds and the clamor of West Lowhead—and struggling with the stink; accustomed as we were to years of cool and filtered air, we were unprepared for the texture and stench of human life. We put off the waiting officials and begged for showers.

Soon afterwards we were in the back of a converted transport racing east along the shoreline, Dorczak and Penderson and I, sitting on soft leather and watching the colony's president across from us lean forward in his seat and tell us what he believed.

If Carolyn Dorczak was the best the Americans had produced, the man who'd replaced her was the worst. Tall and athletic, with coifed white hair and practiced sincerity, Bertram "Fightin' Bart" Allerton was a man who managed perceptions. He managed the world's image of him, and, in turn, just as scrupulously managed the way in which he allowed himself to perceive his world. And in that height of American arrogance, he deeply believed that he managed the way in which others experienced their own lives, as well.

"I believe," he said, locking eyes with each of us in turn, "that this is a profound opportunity. Is there a risk? Yes, there is, there's a risk. But I believe that when the rest of the world sees that we've come to terms with this creature, they'll look to us for guidance and will recognize that we stand at the forefront of the galaxy's search for lasting peace."

Dorczak turned to watch the shacks passing outside. "We haven't come to terms with anything, Bart," she said. "The thing hasn't so much as twitched since we dropped the cage over it. And don't think the world hasn't noticed that it was our base they chose to trash the hell out of...the ranchers out there are even saying we had it coming. Ranchers on *both* sides of the wall."

For reasons long since forgotten, the planet was named Boar River. It might have had to do with its unexpected water—the drones had left the planet to the first settlers with the beginnings of a sea, a quarter-million square miles of shallow water and fertile shores.

A single great peninsula jabbed out into the sea from the eastern shore, a peninsula that the original North American and Commonwealth colonists had claimed—although they'd been able to defend it against takers only with heavy support from us on the black planet. Bart Allerton, during the colony's difficult transition from Dorczak's technical command to civil government, had claimed to be the peninsula's discoverer, and had tried to name it the Allerton Headlands, presumably thinking the name had a rugged flair. More exacting minds, however, had pointed out that a low, marshy spit of sand didn't qualify as a headland, and so the peninsula had come to be called Low Headland, and then just Lowhead—a kind of inadvertent political compromise.

Eventually, Allerton's real ticket to power had come from ending the colony's dependence on outside help to defend the peninsula's approaches, a dependence that Polaski had worked hard to foster. To combat the continual encroachment of ranchers and homeless settlers, Allerton had built a wall across the narrow neck of the peninsula, through an area now known as Wallneck. And to combat more sophisticated intrusions, he'd reorganized the colony's economy to support a defense force, with the largest units based at Wallneck.

Even then, however, Allerton had known that Lowhead enjoyed long-term security only with Polaski's and my blessing, and he'd wisely announced to us his intention to stop at a purely defensive military, and had supported treaties under which we handled the colony's international obligations in exchange for a guaranteed trade in foodstuffs and raw materials. According to Polaski and Allerton, that was where the relationship still stood—and so I was struck by Dorczak's comment about the ranchers believing that Wallneck had it coming.

"Mr. Allerton—" I said.

"'Bart,' please."

"Bart. Why do the ranchers resent the base at Wallneck? I thought they were glad to have it there."

He leaned forward with his elbows on his knees, and his face took on a look of enlightened sympathy for those less worldly than he. "Ed, you need to understand these rurals. They're good people, mind you, New Zealanders mostly, but with all the prosperity they've been privileged to enjoy they've come to take our strong posture for granted. I'm sure a man in your position understands how these sorts of people can be."

"You haven't answered my question."

"Well, I have, actually, Ed. But really, you don't need to concern yourself with internal rumors like this. I'm sure you've got much more...*cosmic* things on your mind, haven't you?" He leaned forward and patted my knee.

"Carolyn," I said, "you just said that even the ranchers on your side of the wall thought the base had it coming. Why? I assume you've been out there?"

"Now, Ed." Allerton's voice demanded my attention back. "We all know what a good administrator Miss Dorczak is. That's one good thing about many women, I'm sure you know."

Dorczak lifted an eyebrow but went on looking out the window. I knew it was only because of the influential professional and naval voting blocks that he was forced to keep her on at all.

"But," he went on, "we still have to keep things on a need-to-know basis—the cosmos isn't always such a kind and friendly place, is it?"

"No, it isn't, Mr. Allerton, and right now it's so goddamned unfriendly I don't have time for your tap dance. I need information on these attacks. Now, what's going on at Wallneck?"

"Ed, please. I'm sure you're an excellent engineer and that you can understand the limitations of rural folk who've got nothing better to do than bellyache about their water supply, but being a technical man, like our faithful assistant here"—he patted Dorczak's knee now—"I can appreciate that you aren't necessarily experienced in the subtleties of running a real operation. So you let me worry about the ranchers getting out of line, and you tell your boss that if they get to be a problem then we'll just have to take care of it." He leaned forward and his eyes widened as he said it, but the rest of his face remained a mask. He sat frozen in that position, not about to be the first one to look away.

Penderson leaned over and whispered in my ear.

"Until this alien's in your hands, Torres, I wouldn't want anyone getting too uncomfortable about our having a nice long talk with it. So let's do our sniffing around later, okay?" He turned to Dorczak.

"I guess the heat's a little hard on a couple of vacuum junkies like us, as you can tell. But listen, Carolyn, we do need to know about the attack and about this animal before we get out to the base, if we're going to make any sense of it. All we really know comes from your message: a hell of a lot of dead and wounded, and one animal that got separated from its weapon and got cornered in a cage. What else?"

As they talked I watched the passing mud flats stretching out into the shallows. They were like the backs of brown, sleeping animals in the water. The surface was a burnished silver. The sky glared white with high clouds, and now and then wild-looking swirls of grey scudded across it, while hot gusts of wind whipped across the water and rocked the fishing boats lying on the mud. Where the sky touched the horizon the clouds were grey, with sheets of heat lightning rippling through them. It seemed to add to the heat.

Like all of the colonies, Lowhead was poor. Over the years it had become even poorer, and hopes of keeping succeeding generations from sliding into poverty and ignorance had dwindled.

With the shrinking economic base, ongoing attempts to find technological solutions had come to consume a greater and greater portion of diminishing resources, in the end robbing the very poorest of the last of their surplus goods, condemning their children to the very same full-time work in the boats that they'd sought to avoid.

Long before any of us had even considered migration from Earth, colonization planners had run calculations on the minimum gene pool and industrial base needed to sustain a colony. A sufficient gene pool was needed to ensure hereditary divergence instead of convergence, and a sufficiently broad base to the industrial hierarchy was needed to support, down through subsequent levels of manufacturing, the most complex product the colony needed to be self-sustaining.

But on that second count the planners had been wrong. Staggering numbers of products and skills used to fuel Earth's industry had been taken for granted, and had come to light only when the colonists had found themselves without them. Each product or skill thus lost left some link missing in the industrial infrastructure, a problem compounded when individual workers were forced into subsistence activity as a consequence, thus falling out through the bottom of the industrial hierarchy altogether.

None of this had meant that productive and dignified life in the colonies wasn't possible. It simply meant that the dream of a post-industrial, technologically sustained civilization had faded even before the advent of the alien ships. An agrarian life with adequate cultivation of livestock, fish, and grains was possible, but it wouldn't be for many generations, if ever, that the colonies would be producing gene therapy equipment or even penicillin, or weather computers or asteroid mining ships. And what little was left of those commodities now was falling into fewer and greedier hands.

Along the shoreline lay rusted bits of space vessels turned to use as rude shacks, and, now and then, big oxygen scrubbers propped up on logs, being used for nothing more than to blow air across the fish-drying racks. On the other side of the road lay cultivated fields, occasionally with spaceship docking winches staked to the edges of the plots, dragging plows across them on cables while the farmers followed with sacks of seed, bobbing on the backs of burros. Stands of tough Eucalyptus dotted the fields, with low, spiky rows of specially-tailored Loblolly Pine between them. Gusts of hot wind whipped up top soil. The sky pressed lower.

"The wolf-like creatures weren't the only kind of animal involved in the attack," Dorczak was saying. "There were reports of some kind of bird, although no one got a very good look at them. Same charcoal-grey color, silent, no weapons. Maybe just watchers. Colonel Becker says there was something really big, too, in the background outside the hangar, although it never came in among the attackers."

"Didn't your people do them any damage at all?" said Penderson. "You must have some pretty good troops out on that base."

Allerton leaned forward and poked a finger at him. "Abso-damned-lutely. We took those mindless little bastards one-for-one, I tell you, and I'll have the hide of anyone who tells you different."

"We lost, Bart." said Dorczak. She shifted in her seat as the car left the shoreline and bounced onto the rutted road leading inland. "Harry, it's true that these things were pretty easy to put out of commission, but when they were hit with any kind of cutting weapon they just absorbed all the heat, then overheated and collapsed. Impact weapons worked, too, but again they didn't break the skin—the animals just went skidding around and smashed into things. The labs are still going through the blood, but so far it's all human. The alien carcasses are gone—these are pretty tidy animals. And Bart, it'd probably be a real good idea if you didn't confuse headless and mindless just yet."

"Carolyn," I said, "if they're so tidy, how come they left this one behind?"

"No one knows. It did get trapped behind some debris in one of the storage rooms. And it must have lost its weapon, because we couldn't find it, so it couldn't cut its way out. But if the others could find every last dead animal, you'd think they could have found a live one. Maybe it's something about the spot it's trapped in, I don't know. Is that why you insisted we leave it where it is, Ed?"

"You were going to move it?" said Penderson. "Why?"

"Well, Bart here wanted it off the base so bad his eyes were bulging pink"—Allerton shot her a look—"but then Ed got pretty nasty with him about it."

"What kind of weapon?" I asked.

"Cutting tool. Looks like a lumpy barbell, apparently. Black. Not very impressive-looking, by all accounts. They just hold them in their hands and poke around with them."

"Hands?" I said. "You mean forepaws?"

"No, hands. Four paws, two hands. The arms are attached near the bulge on their backs. No head."

Paws *and* hands? For a moment I was stunned; there was something very wrong with this description. "That's impossible," I said finally. "You didn't tell me about the hands."

"Well, yes I did, Ed. Maybe you're still picturing something else. I know someone said it looks like a wolf."

"No, that's not it." I turned to the window and watched as the car followed the rising plains, a sea of gravely sand and spiky shrubs stretching to the horizon. The wind gusted across the surface in dusty swirls and buffeted the car, while overhead wild streaks of grey gathered over the glare. The air in the car grew oppressive.

"Are all your troops accounted for, Carolyn? Do we know the attackers didn't take prisoners?"

"We're sure they didn't. In fact, it seems they couldn't have cared less about humans."

I looked at Penderson and back at Dorczak. "I don't understand. Why else were they here?"

"I'll let Becker answer that." She folded her arms and turned to look out her own window, frowning into the glass. She would say no more. Penderson and I glanced at each other, then suddenly something hard struck the window next to me.

A horse had reared up and was struggling out of the car's path. With a crash of hooves it scrambled up the lip of the road, twisting and rearing up again as the rider turned to look at us. Dotting the landscape behind her were other horses and riders among the cattle, kicking up swirls of dust into the air as they turned to watch us pass.

We were finally approaching the low silhouette of the base perimeter where it hugged the higher ground. A scattering of vehicles patrolled the scrub land around it, adding their own trails of dust to the horses', which the wind whipped into funnels reaching up toward the clouds. Tracing the horizon to the east lay the low line of Allerton's wall.

The car crunched to a stop a hundred yards from the gate. The driver remained in his seat with the engine running. Allerton and Dorczak twisted around in their seats to look out the front, where guards from the base were trying to disperse a group of nervous horses and their riders from the middle of the road. When I reached for the door handle Allerton put a hand on my arm.

"Now, Ed. As long as you're here I'm responsible for your safety, so you just wait right here in the car. I'm sure we'll be through in no time."

"I appreciate your concern." I got out and swung the door closed.

The wet scent of horses hung in the air, mixed with the unmistakable smell of dry soil before a rain. Eddies of dust swirled across the road and whipped around my feet as I walked forward past the car. The hot, jittery wind tugged at my shirt.

A confused shuffling of hooves filled the air. From the horses' nostrils came muted snorting like a whisper all around me, mixing with the dung and the dry smell of rain while the wind backed and shifted. Grey clouds slid by overhead with uneasy speed, rolling and twisting like shadows, while heat lightning flickered in the east, soundless beyond Allerton's wall.

Dust caked up inside my boots and sweat trickled down my back. Muffled voices came from the milling riders and the guards reaching for them. A car door creaked behind me.

Suddenly a spray of foam hit my face amid a crash of hooves and a blast of hot breath, as a tremendous, pale grey horse reared up next to me with a trumpet of protest. His head snapped from side to side and he fought the bit with a wild look in his eyes. He was almost pure white, with only a few flecks of grey near his mouth and mane. The rider's craggy features and thick beard were silhouetted against the glare of the sky and his face was in shadow, but his deep-set eyes watched me steadily as he forced the beast back off the road.

Other horses pounded away after him and Penderson's hand closed around my arm. The horses dispersed from the gate and the guards walked back to their posts, then Penderson dropped his arm.

"You okay?" he said.

"What do you suppose all that was about?"

"Interesting, wasn't it?"

The car pulled abreast of us at the gates, where we got in and were joined in the back seat by another man who squeezed in between Penderson and me.

"Sammy Becker." He twisted one way and then the other to shake hands. He was a pudgy man with wiry grey hair, and thick glasses perched low above a bristly mustache. He said nothing more, but sat back and watched out the front while we drove across the complex.

The base was nearly deserted. A number of buildings and vehicles had burned to the ground, while others sat askew or severed. Hobbled, as Bolton had said. A few air and space vessels stood out on the aprons, being rebuilt in a hurry by ground crews. Allerton was clearly under pressure to get a semblance of defense back into place. Long, razor-thin burn marks scarred the aprons, and a familiar, bitter odor seeped into the car.

"Power cells?" I said.

"They got every one of them," said Becker, still watching out the front.

"Tell us about the attack, Colonel."

"Sure. Why not? Easy. I'm standing with a crew in the crane hangar up there, the big one that's still standing, trying to figure out how to rebuild induction coils, okay? For the love of God we can't build the things anymore, with the shortage of—"

"Cut to the chase, Sam." Allerton folded his arms across his chest and watched Becker with a steady gaze, brooking no argument.

"Right, fine. Okay. So whatever. So suddenly we look up and the hangar is full of animals. Four legs, trunk, nothing else. Hands. Not quite waist high. You think that's strange, or what? Just wandering around. The crew bolts for it, but these things pay no attention. Me, I'm standing there pissing in my shorts, and one of them bumps into me. Just sort of *bump*, and then it turns aside. Starts burning through the coil we're working on with this black thing it's got. I hear screaming, I don't know from where.

"Then I see Topsky. She's on the seat of the tow-motor, terrified. It won't start, see. A couple of these things just wander past it, then one of them starts cutting through it. The cut goes up through the motor and then up through the wheel and then up through her face, and then the son of a bitch walks across the pieces of her head and wanders off. Some of the guys are coming back into the hangar with incendiary rounds and fléchettes, and maybe they get pieces cut off of them sooner than the others, but maybe not. This goes on an hour, two. I'm standing there saying Kaddish ten thousand times when I look around and they're gone. The place is filled with smoke and I'm standing in an inch of blood with pieces of my friends floating in it. So tell me, what do you think of that, hm? I ask you, what do you think of that?"

Dorczak put a hand on his arm, but none of us answered. Penderson looked out the far window, tapping a fingernail against his teeth while Dorczak watched him.

The car pulled up to a side door of the hangar Becker had referred to. The five of us got out and stood in the gusty wind. Visible in the distance between the buildings, outside the perimeter fence, lay a rise of ground where the riders sat on their mounts and watched.

Allerton swung up a locking bar on a metal door, then a gust of wind tore it out of his hands. It snapped inward to bang against the wall. Echoes trailed away through the hangar.

Becker was the last in. Just as I made out a single lighted area on the far side of the hangar, he reached around behind the door and snapped up breakers. Bank after bank of spotlights flared on.

"This way." said Allerton. He herded us across the enormous hangar at an angle toward the back wall, past occasional piles of debris and cleaning tools, heading for a section built out into the hangar with temporary walls and drop ceilings. Otherwise the building was empty, with the exception of the far wall, which had already been lit when we came in. There, heavy green canvas curtained off the entire wall of the hangar. Figures came and went from an opening in the canvas, dropping something into a box as they left. They were watched by uniformed troops with guns across their chests. Evidently this area had nothing to do with the captured alien.

"Now this is *real* engineering, Ed." Allerton swept his hand around the hangar. "We built this less than five years after landfall, when the first storms started to come up. I was the one who told people we really *could* do a quarter-mile freestanding arch, if we just *believed*— Where are you going?"

I was heading toward the area shielded by the canvas.

"You'll be wasting your time over there, Ed."

"That's all right. I'm not in a hurry."

"No, really, Ed, it's just logistical stuff. Not worth the time of someone important like you, believe me. It's off limits, anyway, as a matter of fact, and we really should make a show of following the rules. What do you say? Looks better for the troops, hm?"

Colonel Becker muffled a rude noise behind us. Allerton had come after me, trying not to look as though he was hurrying, one hand still in his pocket as he gestured with the other.

I didn't turn around. "Off limits to whom, specifically, Bart?"

The guards had seen us coming and now raised their guns.

"We have agreements with your people," said Allerton, "with Polaski, Ed, that involve certain courtesies, a mutual respect between equally powerful allies. I'm sure a man like you can understand how critical it is that we observe protocol at a time like this." He reached out a hand to turn me toward him, his face hard despite his words.

But I'd already seen the radiation badges in the box.

"That's a restricted area, Torres! You don't have *access*! Now let it go, or I'll have to—"

"You'll have to *what*?" I spun around. "You listen to *me*,

Allerton. Right now I have access anywhere in this system I damn well please, so save your 'equally powerful allies' crap for your ranchers out there. You survive here by my good graces, you pompous bastard, and I intend to have a good look at whatever stupidity you're hiding in there because I'm willing to bet your ass it has something to do with why you were attacked. And you'd better think twice before you let your grunts unload those bear guns at us, because that would leave only one level head standing between you and the aliens and that's the woman behind you who runs your colony when you're not looking. And I don't think that's something you could stomach, is it, Allerton? Now until I'm back you don't even *move*, is that clear?"

"Now, listen, Ed—"

"*Is that clear?*"

He clamped his jaw shut and glared at me.

I pushed aside the gun barrels and elbowed my way through the canvas flap—then for a long, uneasy minute I thought I'd made a bad mistake.

The bay was filled with nothing more than debris and equipment cradles, all of it having been pushed off the main floor into hasty piles against the wall.

But then I realized that the cradles were all of a telltale size—the size of a vessel that was just a little too small for a crew, to be specific, and much too small to be a mining or cargo robot.

The people in the bay were near the far end, working around the shattered remains of a row of RAICs—remote arm isolation chambers, otherwise known as beefed-up glove boxes. What the boxes had been used for almost didn't matter anymore—explosives, enhanced radiation, biologicals...something.

Dorczak was beside me then, standing with her hands in her pockets and surveying the scene, her lips pursed.

"No shit," she said. She was looking at the RAICs, too.

But there was something else she hadn't seen. Against the back wall, sandwiched in behind rows of cabinets, lay a number of immensely long, translucent tubes. Nearly eight feet in diameter, laced with complicated ribbing.

They were power masers. Like lasers, but used to project

intense, coherent microwave radiation over long distances.

Ordinary masers were used in communications, but power masers were intended for transmitting electrical power over a great distance, either from the surface out to distant robot ships, or from orbiting collectors down to the surface.

Or from space, aimed at domes on the black planet. *Signs of lattice dissolution in the glass,* the lab had said, *from focused microwave radiation.*

Allerton.

"I've seen enough," I said.

Why Allerton had done it was unimportant. Probably to cripple us at a time when the blame would inevitably fall to the aliens. He would never risk Polaski's wrath or mine with an outright attack.

Allerton was waiting where I'd left him, rocking up and down on his toes with his arms across his chest.

"You'd better talk to your boss before jumping to conclusions, Ed. There isn't anything in there—"

"Let it go, Bart. I'm sorry I yelled at you. Let's go see your alien."

He gave me a long, thoughtful look, then his eyes flickered away at some private thought and he turned away.

"Fine, fine," he said. He rubbed his hands together. "Carolyn? We're over here. This way."

The built-out area in back was poorly lit. It stank of wet ashes and was covered with burn marks on the walls and ceiling. Allerton led us through a maze of empty offices and storerooms to a room against the hangar's exterior wall, with a conference table in it.

The exterior wall was made from gravel poured into some kind of hard limestone and clay mixture, and had a single window cut into it for air. Bright bars of sunlight seeped around the edges of the iron shutters, and the shutters rattled and clanked sporadically from the gusts of wind.

Allerton threw his jacket onto the table and poured water into metal cups. Dorczak watched him thoughtfully, pursing her lips as she took a cup.

"All right," said Allerton, "if you're ready. The animal got itself trapped in a secure storage area down at the end of the build-out, and the troops managed to drop a cattle cage over it. They left the rest of the room the way it was, so you'll have to excuse the mess."

The narrow corridor outside the conference room widened at the end, where two armed soldiers guarded a pair of steel loading doors. They saluted and swung open the doors. "Watch your step, Gentlemen, Ma'am."

The storeroom stood on raised high-traction flooring. More steel, I noticed. So Lowhead was manufacturing carbon steel, while elsewhere we still settled for iron.

We clanked our way back through aisles of high shelving, some of it leaning drunkenly and burned, and after a minute the vertical bars of the cattle cage appeared. It was up against the outside wall, where another window let in thin shafts of light as the shutters rattled nervously.

The alien stood rigid in the center of the cage. It had dark grey, leathery skin, almost black, which tapered smoothly into four legs that ended with hard hooves. It was the size and color of a timber wolf, but the ends of its trunk were smoothly rounded, with no crease or orifice whatsoever. Its back swelled up a few centimeters in the center, and the skin along the sides of the swelling was slightly darker and porous. At the base of the swelling on each side, at the transition from flank to back, sturdy arms were folded tightly against its body. They had a single hinge and ended in bifurcated hands lined with the same gripping material as the hooves.

I looked at the creature only for a moment, then turned and pushed my way back past the others, ignoring their questions and shaking off Penderson's hand.

"What the hell's the matter with you?" he said as they followed me back into the conference room. "You act like it's your everyday farm animal or something."

I leaned against the wall, feeling the hot air from the window on the back of my neck.

"No, Harry, it's an alien all right. But it's not an animal. It's an artifact."

Chapter Twenty-one: NO BEAST SO FIERCE

Carolyn Dorczak poured herself another cup of water and watched me as she drank it. Allerton paced, while Harry Penderson leaned down with his hands on the table and blew out his breath. Colonel Becker eased himself into a chair.

"A robot, you mean?" said Becker. "I'm being killed by robots, here? How—"

"Do you mean to tell me," interrupted Allerton, spinning to face me, "that the real people are still out there *watching* us while we make asses out of ourselves with some kind of goddamned *robot*?"

"No," I said to Becker, "not a robot. An artifact."

"Come on, Torres," said Penderson, "Spit it out. What do you mean, 'artifact?'"

"Artifacts have a conscious design."

"You mean a fucking *robot*!" said Allerton. "What is going on here?"

"Listen, Bart," I said. "Let's say our planet gets covered in water. So, we modify our genetic code a little to give us gills—now we're a little bit artifact, a little bit consciously designed. And then maybe we have a hard time coding the DNA for flippers, so we just alter ourselves to give birth to offspring with no limbs at all, and we attach manufactured ones. You with me? Then maybe after a thousand years we aren't bothering with the messy part at all, but we just build new, improved offspring out of wires and bar stock. Did we cross a line there, somewhere, between animal and machine? I don't know. The only distinction I'm concerned with here is that, whether we're talking about a genetically self-modified species or an object like this table, we're talking about a conscious design."

"Ed," said Dorczak "you only looked at the thing for a second. How do you know?"

"Because," I said, pulling out a chair, "I'm an engineer. And if I were to design an animal, that's exactly how I'd do it." Across from me, Allerton was still agitated, starting to sweat. "It also happens to be a design that wouldn't, under any circumstances, evolve through natural selection."

"Oh come *on*," said Allerton, starting to pace again. "If that's all you've got, I don't for a minute believe we're not dealing with the honchos themselves, here. Anyway, everyone knows natural selection produces the best possible individuals. The *winners*, for Christ's sake." Winners like himself, he meant. "That's its whole *point*."

"That is not remotely its point, Mr. Allerton. The point of natural selection is to bind the greatest possible amount of energy into replicating forms."

"Jesus *Christ*, you two." Penderson had been pulling out a chair for Dorczak, but now he stopped. "We need to find out damn fast if this thing is ticking or not, so let's *sit* on it."

"Now, now," said Becker, "let's not be hasty." He peered pleasantly over his glasses at Allerton.

"And the unfortunate way natural selection does it," I said, finally sitting down, "always produces a dog shape."

"Not snakes?" said Becker, gazing pointedly at Allerton.

"Niche creature," I said, "not a candidate for intelligence."

"Well, *this* thing looks like a dog," said Becker. "Yes?"

"No. That thing in there is a platform designed to carry two things: hands and a brain. Whereas on the dog-shape that natural selection produces, the only things that could turn into hands are too busy holding it up, and there's no room on the neck for a bigger brain because of the neck muscles and the jaw muscles that break up its food. So the only way to get from there to here is to stand the thing up. That's because there's no way for the head to evolve up onto the back where it belongs, unless the organism already has hands—and there's no way to get hands without standing it up to begin with. There's certainly no way for the flanks to evolve a whole new pair of limbs out of nothing."

Penderson stopped tapping his metal cup against his teeth for a minute. "Why can't the head move up onto the back without hands?"

"Because then it can't get food to its mouth. No, all of Earth's candidates for dominance did it the same way. They stood up, and then the hands could be used to lift food and break it up. We evolved hands for the trees, then we were forced out onto the savannah where we had to stand up to see over the grasses.

"*But*—now we're this engineering nightmare: two legs when there should have been four, a brain that should have been down in the trunk, a mouth that should have been in the belly, an air intake that should have been on the chest, sensors that should have been on the shoulders. In other words, nothing like our perfect friend in there.

"Nor would humans ever get there. The irony of natural selection is that, as soon as a species is able to intercede in its own mortality, first-order natural selection stops. Cognitive selection takes over. And that's what we're looking at with this alien: the evolution of artifacts."

"Mr. Torres," said Becker over his glasses, "I almost hate to ask this, because I think I know the answer. But you said a while ago that we could end up reproducing by constructing our own off-spring. Do you mean *machines*? We could evolve into machines?"

"We could evolve what's called external reproduction, Colo-nel. Is that a machine? I don't know. Be careful about making distinctions where there aren't any. But yes—on Earth we were several steps in that direction already."

"But that's terrible! We'd be gone, forever. Just...gone. Re-placed by machines!"

"You and I would be gone. Our descendents would be there."

"As machines, with no soul!"

"If you say so."

"But that's abomination!"

Penderson glanced at Becker, then stood up and put his hands on the back of Dorczak's chair. "Back to the point, Torres. I take it you think this thing's brain is up under the bulge, and the sensors are in behind that porous band around it. Granted that it's consciously designed, do you think it's manufactured? Doesn't re-produce?

"I don't know, Harry. Internal reproduction, if that's what you mean, would probably need orifices for seed and issue, and growth would need orifices for fuel and waste, and I didn't see any. Just the same— Colonel, can you get us some instrumentation techs? Scanners to cover the whole spectrum? And I think we're going to need comm techs, too."

"Yes," said Allerton. "Becker, would you take care of that?"

"Absolutely. Yes, sir, Mr. President." Becker gave him a pudgy salute, then straightened his glasses and left.

"Harry," I said, "I think I know why you're asking. The next question is, if it's manufactured to size, is it manufactured as someone else's tool, or is it itself the mainline species?"

"Yeah. Or *part* of the mainline species. Becker said there were other variants present—maybe the identity of the mainline species exists simultaneously in several different forms."

"Good point. Bart? Is there hardcopy somewhere of all the witnesses' descriptions? Is that something you could get for us?"

"My pleasure, Ed." He started out, then turned back in the doorway. "You're not going to get started in the next few minutes? Talking to it or anything?"

"Not without your permission, Bart."

"Oh. Okay, that's fine, then." The door closed behind him.

Penderson sat down again next to Dorczak, and the three of us sat in the near darkness, smelling the heat from outside the window and listening to the iron shutters bang against the concrete. Lines of hazy light burned past the shutters, etching designs onto the table top like cabalistic symbols.

"Well, Carolyn? What's our old friend Bart doing out at this base with his precious defense forces?"

She gazed at her metal cup and turned it in a slow circle on the table. "Don't overestimate my position, Ed. There's not much I'm privy to anymore. But I don't think it's news that Bart's ambitious. He gets his rocks off on competition, you know. As long as he wins." She turned to Penderson.

"What you didn't see in there, Harry, is that we seem to be building a weapons delivery system. Interplanetary, probably. From the funding stuff I've seen come across my desk, and from the ranchers' complaints about their livestock dying, my guess is that it's biologicals with a nuclear dispersant. Something nice and fast to help him in his grab for territory. Just exactly what the system needs."

"How very American," said Penderson. "Shit. So what about Becker, Carolyn? He's got to know what's going on."

"Becker's got kids he wants to see get an education."

"So what do we do about it?"

"Hell, Harry," she said. "You're way ahead of me. I'm still staring at the fact that I've just become a serious liability to Bart Allerton."

"Maybe not just yet," I said. "Allerton's first concern is to see whether he can wring any advantage out of this alien."

She sighed. "Did you know, Ed, that nearly everyone on Lowhead thinks your drones are going to return and fight back against the aliens? That all we have to do is hold on and wait?"

"The drones are gone, Carolyn. We found their debris. So unfortunately that's just wishful thinking. Tell me about the masers, Carolyn."

She looked blank. "What about them?"

"What's Lowhead doing with power masers?"

"Oh. 'Allerton's Folly'. He bought them from Singh's people way back, in exchange for embryos or something. They were supposed to be for orbiting collectors, but the collectors never got built. As far as I know, they've never been used for anything. The Boar River Press calls them 'Allerton's erections.'"

Dorczak looked around at that moment to see Becker and Allerton standing in the doorway. "Hello, Bart."

Allerton twisted the ring on his little finger for a minute, then ignored her. "All right, the transcripts are on the way. The techs and the equipment are here, if you people want to get started."

The alien was alive.

We had welders tack the cattle cage down to the flooring to keep it from slipping, then we slid a truck jack in under that section of the flooring and tipped it up. When it reached a steep enough angle the creature snapped to the uphill side and with a clean snick latched onto a bar with a hand. It was an incredibly sudden, precise movement. The creature didn't move again, so we let the flooring back down.

A magnetic resonance scan of the creature showed densities that were too high to be organic, and an infrared scan showed that all of its heat was concentrated at one end of the trunk. The rest of it was at ambient temperature, except for the joints it had used during its movement—which were a fraction of a degree higher—and an area under the bulge on its back that was warm all of the time. It also turned out that the creature was emitting an infrared sensing frequency of its own, from the porous area around the bulge.

Efforts to talk to it were fruitless. It was Penderson who finally remembered his own comment about radio communications.

"It may be talking this whole time, on some frequency we can't hear," he said.

"I don't think it even thinks we're something that bears talking to," I said.

"I didn't say it was talking to us."

We looked at each other.

"Is that why it got left behind, do you suppose?"

So we had the technicians go up on top of the room's drop ceiling and lay out antennas, then start scanning the entire spectrum for signals coming from inside the room. There was none.

"Maybe it doesn't have anything to say at the moment," said Penderson. "Maybe we'll have to give it something."

So the technicians rigged up a forklift with a canister of liquid nitrogen strapped to one end and a burning space heater at the other, knowing it would leave a powerful infrared signature. A young woman then came roaring into the storeroom riding on top of it, smashing her way down a row of shelves and past the cage, then back out the other door.

A comm tech burst through the door moments later.

"Got—"

"Quiet!"

Penderson herded everyone out of the room and into the hangar, where the vans full of communications equipment stood.

"I take it you got something?" he said.

"Yes, sir. A powerful squirt, way up in the EHF band. Extremely High Frequency. Real clear. Super-compressed, though, so I've got no idea what was in it."

"Jesus, no one uses EHF. Serenitas probe wasn't even *listening* on EHF."

"Hot *damn!*" A head poked out of the van. "Someone answered. And not only that, but we've got traces of that same frequency all over the system, now that we're looking for it."

"Son of a bitch," said Penderson. "Time to find out if they know English."

We asked the vans' clocks to set themselves to our watches exactly, then while the technicians began recording, Penderson and I went in and began taking detailed photographs of the alien. While we were there we talked about cameras and lighting, and about the creature's skin and its lack of orifices. The techs recorded no further transmissions during that time.

But at two minutes and six seconds past the hour, I wondered out loud to Penderson whether the aliens knew that they'd put the base's long-range weapons program permanently out of commission. And while the creature stood perfectly motionless in front of us, the techs recorded another transmission.

"But I was under the impression they didn't pay any attention to humans at all," said Dorczak.

"My guess," I said, "is that they pay enough attention to assess our function at any particular moment, but that they don't attach any special significance to us beyond that. Our significance is whatever obstacle we represent at the time, no more nor less than the significance of any other object. And the truth is that tactically we *aren't* any more significant than most of the MI or other hardware around us. They certainly don't see us the way we see human enemies. When we fight humans we hate them or resent them or envy them—we seek them out and it's our *goal* to eliminate them."

"In other words," said Penderson, "it's personal."

"Exactly. It's personal."

"That's very frightening," said Becker. "To mean so little to one's enemy. To be killed by someone who doesn't really care whether he kills you or not."

"It's worse than that. It's being killed by something that doesn't even consider you alive in the first place, who doesn't see you as any different from the tow motor you're sitting on. Which, in an absolute sense, we're not."

"I'm surprised they know English."

"Not really," said Penderson. "Spoken English in analog form is all over the system on the radio waves. A creature that can handle a hundred gigahertz transmission can certainly sort that out, and if they've been observing events in the system at all, they can cross-correlate with events for the words' meanings."

"Could they learn to speak it, do you think?"

"Again, with something that can process as fast as these transmissions indicate they can process, it wouldn't be a matter of learning a new skill, the way it is for us. Once they've got English on file, they'd simply reverse the algorithm and spit it back out. The problem is, though, whether they *think* enough like us that anything they say is comprehensible."

"Well," said Allerton. "The main thing is that he's communicating. Which is good, because I have questions I expect answers to. And some propositions I'd like to put to it."

Penderson looked tired at the thought, and rubbed a hand across his leathery face. "What makes you think *it* wants to talk to *you*, Allerton?"

"I'm the President, damn it! Leader of this planet's preeminent nation. Don't you think that's why it's here? Do you think it's a coincidence? I believe that this attack was just a negotiating ploy. That's why I instructed Ed to come and work out the technical details, so that I could negotiate with it. And remember—this animal's our prisoner, completely at our mercy. It has no choice but to talk to us. And who are you to say differently, in any case, an asteroid miner like you. Did asteroid mining teach you the finer points of trading in power?"

"No, Mr. President, I'm just an old journalist who knows that nobody reveals anything unless there's something in it for him."

We stood on the packed dirt outside the hangar and ate sandwiches, while the comm techs instructed their MI to perform a particular task

Penderson and I had requested.

There was to be an antenna placed next to the cage, through which the MI would listen for the EHF band the aliens appeared to be using. Since it would be a long time before the priests could decode the aliens' own compacted transmissions, the communications MI was to ignore those messages and listen instead for ordinary sound carried on the same frequency, and then broadcast the sound back through a speaker near the cage. It was to act as an ordinary radio, in other words, tuned to the aliens' remarkably high broadcast frequency.

The sky had lowered and blackened, and out on the rise beyond the buildings the ranchers herded their cattle toward lower ground. Heat lightning still flickered behind us in the east, and the air smelled even more strongly of dust and the coming rain than before.

Finally the device was ready and Penderson and I left the others to finish their lunches, and went in and told the alien that if it would modulate its communications frequency with human speech, it could communicate with us.

Nothing happened. We tried prompting it by asking for the hexadecimal value of pi, or for the measurement in its units of the frequency of free hydrogen, or for where it came from; but it didn't move and the speaker made no sound, and finally we gave up and went back outside.

Sometime later we were talking about how to move the alien to the ship and had decided it would be easier to have our ship brought up to the base, when a technician stuck his head out the door to report that an experimental squawk had come over the speaker.

Penderson and I went back in and ran through our questions all over again, spicing them up with vague threats and promises, but still the alien remained silent. We gave it up again and walked out into the hangar for coffee, then met the others in the conference room. Allerton came in late, saying he'd had to make calls to his office.

"I would have been surprised," said Penderson, "if it had been any different."

"Why?"

"Well, think about it. Did you notice, for instance, that out in the comm van there was a screen there in the back, flashing on and off in big red letters something about 'advise system time and status?'"

"Um—"

"Well, it was right there next to me, and I saw it, yet I didn't advise it of any such thing. Even though it wanted to know."

"Harry..." Dorczak's brown eyes studied him as she stole a sip from his coffee.

"The truth is," he said, "I couldn't have cared less whether it got its 'system time and status.' Why the hell should I have?" He took back his coffee.

"Well." Allerton smoothed back his white hair and began to pace. "I'm sure this animal realizes that it *should* care whether it answers our questions. It must know that it's in an untenable position—"

"My *guess*," interrupted Penderson, "from listening to Colonel Becker here, is that personal danger isn't even a concept to these things. There's nothing it fears from us, and nothing it needs."

"That's scary," said Becker.

"Yes," I said, "but wait a minute, Harry. There is one thing it wants, and it is something we have control over."

The technicians laid copper mesh across the entire roof of the storeroom, working quietly up under the hangar's ceiling. Then with a series of power cells they drove the mesh's potential down to a negative fifty-thousand volts. The aliens' signals could get neither in nor out. A switch to disable the shielding was placed just outside of the cage.

Numbers of us went near the cage a few times to make important-sounding statements, and in between, the technicians paraded intriguing and powerful-looking contraptions past it. The antennas picked up the alien's brief squirts of attempted transmissions, and then finally the communications MI reported that, whatever was being transmitted, the exact same thing had just been transmitted twice in a row: the alien finally knew it wasn't getting through.

Penderson and I told Allerton and the others that for the next step we would need to concentrate, and over their objections we shut them out of the storeroom and pulled chairs up to the cage. I picked up the switch that controlled the shielding.

"If you answer some questions," I said, "I can let you talk to your friends again."

Nothing happened.

Penderson leaned closer to me. "It may be real weak on some of those concepts, Torres. Let me try." He worked his teeth across his lip for a minute in thought, then spoke.

"If information is provided, communications will be open."

"Query information type," said the alien.

The words had come from the speaker without hesitation, in a thin, sharp voice, very slightly inflected. The creature itself remained perfectly still.

"No shit," said Penderson.

"How do we ask it where it's from?" I said.

He stared at the cage. "Query," he said, "your place of origin."

"Deck ninety-one," said the speaker, "communications not open."

Penderson glanced at me. "That's a big help. It had a berth on deck ninety-one. You'd better hit your switch—it expects its communications to be opened the instant it gives an answer."

"It's hardly told us anything, Harry—"

"Do it. It's the interviewer's first law, Torres: don't mess with the ground rules. Or they never talk to you again."

I hit the switch for an instant and our indicator lit up to show that the alien had transmitted something, presumably the bits of information we'd been dropping near its cage earlier.

"Query," I said, "cause of the attack against this base."

We waited for several minutes, but nothing else came from the speaker. "It's got no reason to answer," said Penderson.

"It's got the same reason as before: being allowed to transmit."

"There's nothing new it wants to send."

"Ah-hah, tit for tat." I turned back to the cage. "The attack against the Chinese weapons base on planet number three caused weapons production there to stop permanently. Query: cause of the attack against this base."

"Origin of explosions on planet six satellite three removed before remainder removed. Communications not open."

Penderson understood before I did.

"Jesus, Torres, I don't believe this. Come here a minute. No, hit the switch first. Okay, come here." He pulled me back in among the shelves and leaned down to speak quietly. "Can Allerton hear what this thing's saying?"

"Hell, no, not a chance. When the shielding's live we've got the only antenna. I'll bet he's shitting bricks, though, wondering what's going on Did you understand that last answer the same way I did?"

"Yeah. Allerton's got interplanetary delivery systems and he's testing them by dropping warheads on H-VI's third moon. Where he thinks no one will notice. Except that the aliens did, and they saw where the missiles were coming from. Torres, there's no way Allerton's going to let you back off this planet with that alien."

"He's still got Polaski to answer to. He isn't strong enough yet to rock the boat that much."

"Accidents happen."

"Let me deal with Allerton. How did you like the tail end of that last answer: 'before remainder removed'? As though removing this base was just a chore on the way to scraping humans out of the system."

"I thought they didn't care one way or the other about humans."

"Okay, on the way to scraping out of the system whatever it is they think they see here." I rubbed at my eyes and leaned out to look down the row of shelves at the grey beast frozen in its cage. "It's being damned honest about things, isn't it?"

"It may not understand deceit," he said. "It's a pretty refined art, hard to calculate. So is the mutual leaking of military information, which is what we're doing. We've got a finely tuned sense for it, developed over thousands of years. It may not."

"Well, I do. Come on." We sat back down, and I spoke again to the alien.

"The Chinese weapons production that is stopped permanently on planet three is now continuing on planet five, satellite one,
underground beneath the equatorial base on the near-planet side—"

"*Jesus*, Torres," hissed Penderson, "that's the Indian—" I
held up a hand to stop him.

"Query:" I said, "origin of fractures to environment domes
on black planet—planet number four—prior to your attack there."

"Vessels of mass three element one moving from planet five
satellite two to planet two. Communications not open."

My stomach turned. It wasn't an answer I'd expected.

I pressed the switch to allow the alien to pass along the
information about the Indian mines on H-V's moon, then shook my
head to clear it and stared around the storeroom. *Polaski*. The shutter
in the wall rattled in the wind and a rumble of thunder came in from
outside. I walked away to lean on a shelf, and Penderson followed me.

"What's going on?" he said. "You asked how they blew out
our domes?"

"No...no, that's not it." Had I? "No," I said, "I asked it who
did it."

"You asked— What's the matter, Torres, you don't look so
good."

The world had tilted on its side, and it had filled with images
of McKenna and the black domes cracking at night.

"You sick, or what?" said Penderson.

"I'm all right."

"No, you're not," said Penderson. "So what was that all
about with the alien? What's a vessel of mass three element one? Is
that what this is all about? Come on, what's going on, Torres?"

"Element one is hydrogen," I said. "The isotope of hydrogen
with a mass of three is tritium. It's produced at a plant on H V's
second moon."

"Okay, but it said tritium vessels."

"We've been shipping tritium from H-V's moon to Lowhead
on light freighters. Those are the vessels it's talking about. The
tritium was supposed to be resold here as a medical tracer."

"Supposed to be?"

"Tritium's also used to make hydrogen warheads."

"Oh. I see."

"No, you don't. The point is, we're the ones who've been shipping it. Us—the black planet. We pick it up from the mines and bring it to Lowhead on ships we lease from Pikes Mountain. It's a project of Polaski's."

"You telling me Polaski knew the tritium was for weapons instead of for medical tracers?"

I looked away.

"Wait a minute, Torres. The alien said it was the ships carrying tritium that caused our dome failures. Is that what this is all about? I mean, forget *how* they could do it, *why* would they do it? It doesn't make sense."

My hands were cold. I wanted to get moving, get somewhere else.

"Torres," said Penderson after a minute, "I've got a feeling you'd better make real sure everyone thinks that having you talk to this alien is the best thing that's ever happened to them."

"Yes."

"You know that? So what's this business about the Indian mine? You just sentenced a couple hundred miners to death."

"No, I didn't. Let's go, Harry. I've got more questions, then I want to get out of here."

I sat down in front of the alien again as the first of the rain spattered against the shutters. I felt sluggish, no longer interested in the process. Or in Serenitas, or in the attacks, or in my brief ascendancy over Allerton. The alien in its cage had become dull and colorless, unimportant.

"On the black planet," I said to the alien, "on the side farthest from the environment domes that you attacked, are deep fissures in the surface. New weapons capable of destroying your forces are being hidden in those fissures. Query: place you were *created*."

"Deck ninety-one. Communications not open."

I pressed the switch and tried a last time.

"On the anti-spinward shore of the sea of this planet, large orbital habitats are being prepared for launch. Query: place your *species* was created."

"Deck ninety-one. Communications not open."

"So maybe that's where it was built, and it doesn't know any different."

Becker put his hands in his pockets and turned to watch the rain. He and Allerton stood with us at the opening to the hangar, a step back from the streams of water that flowed across the apron. The wind had stopped and the rain poured straight down from the afternoon sky. Crews in slick coveralls worked to tow the iron ship toward the hangar through the rain, while the tractor's wheels put up a mist and the hot motors hissed from the moisture. Water poured in sheets down the sides of the brooding vessel and splashed against the apron with a monotonous sound. Behind us in the hangar, a motorized pallet-jack navigated across the building's floor, with the alien in its cage balanced carefully on the metal runners.

Allerton was restless. He folded his arms and looked down at me again with his best aristocratic look. "So, fine," he said. "We know where it comes from. What else did it say? You two were in there for a long time."

"It said they're going to attack the Indian mines on Five's first moon."

"What? It said *that*?"

"Yes."

He brushed his hair back with both palms, then jammed his hands in his pockets. He watched the rain and rocked up and down on his toes.

"I suppose," I said, "that I should warn them."

"No," said Allerton quickly. "No. You let me take care of that." He pushed his hands farther into his pockets. "So why is it telling us this, Torres?"

"I don't know, Bart. Maybe it's on our side. Maybe the attack on the base here was just a negotiating ploy like you said, and now it's trying to show good faith."

"You think so? I should talk to it. Becker, let's go talk to this fellow we caught."

Allerton stalked back through the hangar with Becker shuffling along behind. They stopped the handlers who were moving the alien, then after a discussion the technicians were called over to unpack the antenna and speaker device.

Penderson watched me from tired eyes. "You're skating pretty close to the edge here, Torres. So are you going to warn the Indians or not?"

"No, Allerton's going to do it. He'll want the system to believe he's in thick with the aliens. Or at least that he's got a source among them."

"What about the Russians? You told the alien about the habitats they're putting up."

"I already called them, a few minutes ago when I went out to check the ship. They pissed and moaned, but they agreed to evacuate the launch site. I don't think the aliens are going to do anything there, though."

"Well, whatever game you're playing, it's better you than me. Don't underestimate Allerton."

No, I thought. I hadn't underestimated Allerton at all.

We stood a while longer watching the crews turn the ship around in the bleak weather, preparing to back it up to the hangar. Becker and Allerton finally approached from behind us.

"It won't talk to me," said Allerton.

"That's too bad, Bart. Maybe being mechanical the way it is, it's more comfortable with technical people. I don't know."

"Hm. So what else did it say?"

"It said it wants to see Polaski."

"Really?" He looked at me closely in the poor light, turning his head a couple of times to glance back at the approaching cage. Finally he stuck out his hand. "All right. Ed, listen. Thanks for coming to help out. And I want to say that if you've still got any little concerns about the treaties, why don't you work them through your boss. I'm sure no one wants to overreact at a time like this. Okay? Good. He'll know what to do. Have a good trip back." He shook Penderson's hand, then touched Colonel Becker's shoulder on the way by. "It's all right, Becker," he said. He disappeared into the hangar. Becker ignored him.

The tractor pulling the ship switched on its yellow beacon as the afternoon darkened, and the reflection slid across the rain to mix with the sound of wheels hissing through the puddles. After we'd watched it for a minute Penderson took me aside. He started to say something, then turned back toward the rain and held his silence. We stood that way for several minutes.

"Listen, Torres," he said at last. "I didn't want to say anything back there. I wasn't even sure—"

"What is it, Harry?"

He hesitated. "Well, I know there's a lot going on right now, and you're not feeling well and maybe it's not a good time, but I don't think I'll be coming back with you. I'm staying with Carolyn."

I turned away to look at the ship, and studied it for a while. It was well-built, I thought, a good use of scarce resources. Something we needed more of...I would talk to Chan about it. Where was Chan, at that moment? What would she be doing? And Charlie, what would he be doing? I lifted my face to get it wet from the rain, then wiped it with a sleeve.

"Torres?"

"What, Harry?" A cold sweat broke out on my hands at the thought of flying the ship alone.

"Nothing."

"So where is Carolyn?" I said. I had evidently missed whatever there was between them.

"She left when we were talking to Allerton. One of the techs is going to drive me out to meet her."

"Why, Harry?" I turned to look at him. He tried not to look away.

"Look," he said, "I don't think there's a whole lot of time left for any of us, and I don't want to spend it in space any more. I'm grateful you took me on, but I'm tired, Torres. And Carolyn needs someone right now. She's not going back to West Lowhead, you know."

I hadn't known. "Where's she going?"

He shook his head, then turned to watch the cage being raised up to the ship's rear hatch. The prod slid forward to force the creature through. "You going to be all right flying that thing, Torres?"

"Why wouldn't I be?"

"Oh, okay. I wasn't sure." He put out his hand and looked at me, his dark face wet from the spray. "I'm sorry, Ed." He shook my hand and walked away through the hangar.

The hatch on the ship slammed and the empty cage was lowered to the ground. The pallet-jack trundled off into the hangar, with the handlers riding on the runners behind the empty cage. Colonel Becker wandered up to stand next to me and put his hands in his pockets, and the two of us watched the engineers climb down from the ship and give me a thumbs-up before walking away. The afternoon light had faded almost to night. The rain turned colder.

Inside the hangar on the far side, the two solitary guards stood at attention by the green canvas curtain. No one else was in sight. Becker and I were the only ones. We stood and watched the iron ship, a cold, indifferent husk in the rain, with the alien on board, waiting for me.

"Hah!" said Becker suddenly. It was a sharp, cynical bark, then a moment later he turned and walked away. I listened to him go, then wiped my hands on my trousers and watched the rain. I was alone with the iron ship and the alien.

The trip home was hard. The vertigo of space and the long, manual flight were made all the worse by being alone. Even in the earliest hours, the monotony and the quiet dragged at me. During moments of disorientation I considered turning back, thinking to get a good night's sleep before setting out again. But I continued on, telling myself there was nothing to fear, that the time would pass. Yet for two days I held myself awake, not wanting to sleep.

Beyond the windscreen lay the emptiness of space, with the uncaring, icy sparks of the stars watching me from the distance. For hours at a time I stared at them until the disorientation set in again, then I turned back into the ship to stare at the alien, instead. It stood impassive and silent behind its bars.

Early in the trip I'd set up the antenna and tried to talk to it again, but I hadn't had the radio shielding to use as leverage and it had said nothing.

For the next two days I stared first at the creature and then at the blackness outside, my thoughts confused, now and then gazing at the ship's readouts in what became a meaningless ritual, as I was no longer sure whether I'd ever even set them correctly.

Sometimes while I stared at the bars in the rear I remembered Pham leaning against them a week before, shifting uncomfortably on her case and pulling her jacket close around her. And once, briefly, I thought I saw both of them at the same time: Pham, worn and restless, warming herself, the alien cold and rigid, one just outside the bars and the other in, both appearing as though in a dream, as though there could be one, or the other...not both. *Choose.* I turned and looked out the front. A light sweat had broken out on my forehead.

On the first day I pulled a headset cord into the head behind the copilot's empty seat and called Polaski. He'd returned to orbit around the black planet sooner than expected, together with the major elements of the fleet. I told him that during my interrogation of the alien it had revealed a mistaken belief that targets of opportunity lay in the fissures on the back of the black planet. I suggested that dummy targets be dropped into the fissures and an ambush mounted for the aliens. He was clearly excited at this news, and after a long pause he came back on the radio and instructed me to try for more information. For the moment, it seemed, I was back in his good graces.

It was about fifty hours later that I was sitting in the pilot's seat, digging food crumbs out of the folds of my jacket, when I twisted around in the seat one more time to look at the alien. I was having trouble concentrating, and for a moment, as I looked at it, I thought I was back on Boar River with Penderson and the alien, staring at it through the bars of its cage in the storeroom.

The memory of the storeroom came back because on the base at Wallneck, something had struck me as odd when the alien first spoke. But I hadn't been able to remember what it was afterward, with all the excitement. Still, it was a compelling memory, even though it slipped away whenever I looked at it. All through the trip it had nagged at me. And now it was gone again, and instead a flood of other memories began spilling over me, from some very different place and time.

For a moment I remembered a jail I'd seen as a boy in Mexico, where a dying man lay on the floor. A rat was biting at his hand, and the jailer paid no attention.

I blinked at the windscreen and the image of the jail vanished. But now the scene out the windscreen was gone, too. There was instead a different view of space, one I'd seen years ago through another window onto the stars.

"Do you remember a dream you once described, Eduardo?"

The voice was close to me. I spun to look at the alien, thinking it must have spoken.

"A dream in which we suddenly come upon ourselves, out among the stars?"

It was Madhu Patel's voice.

I stared at the alien, then back the other way.

Madhu Patel sat in the copilot's seat next to me. He was gazing serenely out the front, his big handkerchief in his lap.

"Yes," I said. Or was it I that said it? It was my voice, I thought.

"That is good," said Patel, "because sometimes we do not recognize ourselves out here where it is so empty."

He was wearing his billowing white suit. A red rose was pinned to the lapel.

"Why are you here, Madhu?" I said.

"Why, to look after you, of course." He turned and beamed at me brightly with his half-moon smile.

I looked back at the alien. Had it created a mirage—

"No, Eduardo, no—your alien can do no such thing. It is lifeless, no more than a mirror. It is sleep you need, that is all."

I remembered his crutches and looked around for them. They weren't anywhere on the deck.

"Eduardo," he said as I searched, "while these creatures may be lifeless, you must understand that you cannot fight them any more than you can fight your shadow. That is a fool's errand, and you must leave it to the sharks and the wolves, your Mr. Allerton and Mr. Polaski. Let them tear themselves to pieces fighting their own selves—and the harder they fight, the harder they will be fought, I assure you—it is not for you. Let them be the ones to die alone."

But I wasn't listening; I had stopped looking for the crutches now, and was watching the creature behind us, still motionless in its cage. What was it that it had said—that one comment it had made back on Boar River?

"Think, Eduardo. Think what it was that it said to you and your friend. It is important."

But I couldn't. All I could think of was Charlie Peters, muttering somewhere in the background about a different beast. Or was it different?

"Madhu," I said, "is this the beast Father Peters goes on about? The fourth beast, in the fourth place I've followed it to?"

"Charles Peters, a priest? Imagine that." Patel raised his eyebrows and pursed his lips mightily.

"No, my boy," he said finally, "don't be so dramatic. Leave such hocus-pocus to the priests and storybooks. If he spoke of such a thing, I'm sure he only meant for you to think of the four horsemen, as a warning. In any case, this thing before you is surely no beast, for there is no beast so fierce as this."

Shakespeare now? Peters and the Apocalypse, and now Madhu Patel? The cabin was beginning to swim in front of me.

"It is only a creature you invented," he said. Invented? How could that be? It was right there, in the cabin. "And remember, Eduardo, creatures we invent out of fear will always turn on us. We will defend them until the very last, because after all it is we made who them, but in the end they will turn on us and destroy us. Their own makers."

"Destroy their makers?" I said. I had half remembered. "Madhu, listen. The shots that destroyed our domes—the dome I was in and the other one—they came from freighters that—"

But Patel was gone. The copilot's harness lay across the seat where it had always been, and the ship was as quiet as ever over the hum of its engines.

Of course, I thought, Richard III: *No beast so fierce but knows some touch of pity; but I know none, and so I am no beast.*

The alien still hadn't moved.

Chapter Twenty-two: A PALE HORSE

Voices from the ship's radios filtered into my sleep, like sand into a crevice. The great sweep of the planet stretched out under the ship, the color of volcanic ash in the weak sun. Messages hung on the ship's screens, warning that my navigational instructions had run their course and that new ones were needed.

The ragged wastes a thousand miles below slid by like an old man's life, I thought, passing in stark review. My dream had lasted a hundred years, a hundred thousand, all of it dim with smoke and shadows. And yet, somewhere in the dream I'd remembered: I'd remembered the words the alien had spoken on Boar River. And they were words I'd heard before, spoken in another voice, another life, decades before. And now I was on my way to see, to be sure.

Radioed instructions from the surface advised me that the fleet remained in orbit, preparing for the planet's defense, but that the main dome had been re-pressurized and key personnel were on the surface. I dropped toward the domes glinting against the plains, suddenly comfortable at the controls.

In the strange dream, Patel had said I couldn't fight the aliens. But he was wrong: I now knew exactly how to fight them.

Tractors awaited me as I skidded the heavy ship into the dirt. Tyrone Elliot was in one, while load handlers in the other prepared to re-cage the alien and move it to a spot at the rear of the main dome.

Elliot's appearance was sobering. His face was unshaven and lined with fatigue. His clothes were black with grime. Blood had dried in long gashes on his arms. His hands shook as he leaned past me to get a glimpse of the alien.

"You don't look too good, Tyrone."

"Things aren't going too good. Half the base is hung over, and the other half is busy picking fights with people. Polaski's working us around the clock to get equipment around to the other side of the planet where the cracks are, and now he's pulling grunts out of the crews to handle the surface guns. Then he's putting kids back in the ships to handle the loaders. They're up practicing at six *fucking* Gs, for Christ's sake. A girl died this morning. The troops are chewed up too bad, or can't handle the Gs these thoroughbred miracles can, so we're tossing kids into it. So much for their chance at *being* kids, for Christ's sake. Folks are saying we're throwing them away on a fight we can't win, anyway." He twisted the wheel and waited for the air lock to open. "Anyway, we spotted the aliens an hour ago. They're headed this way."

"From where?"

"H-V. They chewed the shit out of the metal mines on the inner moon. At least there, everyone got out. So now half the alien fleet is back watching the torus, and the other half is on its way here. Be here by nightfall."

"Get some radio shielding over that cage, Tyrone."

"It's on its way. It'll be in place by tomorrow. You told Polaski, remember?"

I didn't remember. "Okay. Let's hope tomorrow's not too late."

The tractor hissed through the air lock and into the watery light of Trinity Square. Elliot stopped at the barracks.

"He wants to see you."

"Okay."

He held on to my sleeve. "Listen, Torres, people are scared. I mean, really scared, okay?"

"Okay, Tyrone. Take it easy."

The barracks was in chaos. Piles of debris and bunks had been pushed against the walls to make room for stacks of equipment in the middle of the floor. Terse commands were shouted back and forth across the hall while tractors raced to move equipment to the transports. Commanders hurriedly tried to explain to their units their plan to pour firepower into the fissures while ships overhead used missiles against the aliens, along with the one maneuver known to have worked at the torus, trying to keep them away from the fleet and the surface guns.

Polaski stood in the center of the hall speaking to his base-defense commanders, looking down through the cylinder of his revolver while he cleaned it. They made room for me when I approached.

"Hello, Polaski."

"That was good work with the alien," he said.

"Yes."

He spun the cylinder. "Should make for a turning point."

"Yes. Where's Tawali and Rosler?"

"Tawali's trying to pull the can out of orbit. Your woman friend made a stink about it. She's tying up my ships."

"The aliens are going to go after the fissures, not the can."

"No? We'll see. Rosler's out trying to get Pham's ass in here. She's needed." He sighted through the barrel and pointed it at my forehead. "President Allerton's pleased with you, Torres. Let's keep it that way. Keep working on your alien."

I started to say something, then turned away. But I stopped myself again and looked back at him.

"Polaski, why were we leasing ships for the tritium shipments when we had our own freighters?"

Polaski went still. The officers who could see his face became quiet as well, waiting for him to speak.

"Bermer," said Polaski.

Carl Bermer pushed his way forward and eyed me uncertainly.

"Yes, sir."

"Carl, Mr. Torres' contact with the alien has made him a high-risk target. See that he's well-guarded."

Charlie Peters was waiting for me in Trinity Square.

"Why the cane?" I said. He was stooped and looked tired. The skin on his face sagged in the high gravity.

"Oh, well, 'tis a little thing, really. That little run-in at the torus was a bit hard, is all." He put an arm through mine and started up the alley.

"Someone should look at that leg, Charlie."

"No, Eddie, they'll be wanting to make a fuss. It's not worth the time to an old man who has little enough of it left."

Something hissed past my ear and slammed into the wall ahead of us. A shout came from behind, then a ragged form hurried past, struggling for footing in the dust.

It was Pham. She turned to look back as she ran, then stumbled and fell. She twisted around to look behind her. Her hair was tangled and her face bruised, with smears of dirt and caked blood under her nose.

She glanced up at Peters. "What you staring at, priest?" Her voice was scarcely audible. She struggled to her feet and fell again as another stone smacked into the ground next to her. Behind us, Rosler snickered.

"Come on, princess!" he shouted. "Come on, you can do it. Let's see you run!" He pushed past us and followed her down the alley. "Run from your post, run from me. Let's see how far you get, *princess*!" His next stone struck her temple and drew more blood as she limped around the corner into the square ahead.

Peters gripped my arm, but said nothing.

Ahead of us a tractor pushed the alien's cage off its dollies into the dirt, over in a far corner of the square. The creature held exactly the same position as it had all along, motionless and eyeless in the center off the cage, watching us all.

Pham and Rosler had disappeared, and the square was left deserted as the tractor pulled away. It was the square outside Miller's old quarters, where I'd stood talking to Penderson and Dorczak the night Miller had told me about Patel. The door to her quarters hung from one hinge, the gloomy workroom behind it nearly empty after the evacuation. The few remaining items had been strewn on the floor during the aliens' ransacking.

The dust churned up by the tractor hung suspended over the square, swirling through the vertical columns of weak, midday sun. Pools of the hazy light glowed on the black dirt, surrounded by the shadows from the dome. The doorways leading from the square and the alien in its cage were difficult to see.

A soldier stuck his head into the square to stare at the creature, then went back the way he'd come. Peters gave the thing a quick glance, then steered me toward the alley that led to my old office near the empty vehicle assembly building.

Voices came from the open door to the office, but just outside Peters stopped me and turned me toward him.

"Eddie. Listen to me. This is a day I've always believed would come. I thought I was ready for it, that all of us were, but suddenly I fear I don't know how it'll end."

He looked at me intently for a moment, then took my elbow and led me into the office.

Chan wrapped herself around me and held tight, a shiver running through her as she pressed against me. "God, Eddie. I'm glad you're back. Things aren't good."

I held her for a minute with my arms in under the loose jacket, then finally the trembling stopped and she pulled me out of Peters' way. Tyrone Elliot, Susan Perris and Kip were on a seat at the far end. Elliot's eyes were closed. Piles of books and debris stood against the wall, and on the wall near the door, a faded square on the wall marked the missing photograph of Serenitas.

"What's not good?" I said to Chan.

"More of our ships are leaving, Eddie. Scores of them. We moved the children to the can to try and keep them safe, but parents are refusing to be separated from them this time. They think every-one in the system's going to die, and they want to be with their kids at the end. Even on some of the fighting ships people have got their kids with them, but most of them are just taking their families and breaking out of orbit without even knowing where they're going. Eddie...some of the orphans are asking if the aliens are coming to cut off their arms and legs because they've been bad."

With an exhausted sound she sat down and buried her face in her hands. Perris stared at the floor, while next to her Kip started to cry. Elliot slept. A column of soldiers marched past outside the open door, and then it was quiet again.

From up the alley came a yell and a shout. Peters turned his head to listen. But no more sound came, until a few minutes later when a shadow crossed the door and, while his commandos waited in the alley, Michael Bolton stepped in with Priscilla Bates. Chan dried her face and Elliot opened his eyes.

Bates stopped near the door and took Peters' arm while Bolton leaned back against a wall. It was Bates that spoke first.

"The aliens are moving faster than we thought," she said.
"How long?"
"Less than two hours. More than five hundred ships."
The room became quiet again.
"I don't think they'll attack us or the civilian ships," I said.
No one answered for a few minutes.
"That's not actually why we've come," said Bolton. "It's that I've got a rather unfortunate bit of news, I'm sorry to say." He glanced at me.

"Especially for you, I'm afraid, Eduardo. I've got a chap in West Lowhead, is the thing. It seems he's sent a report, saying a colonel in the colony defense forces—Samuel Becker by name—has formally reported to the president that a light aircraft exploded yesterday while at sea. It was carrying Administrative Chief Carolyn Dorczak and one companion. There was no other word. I'm sorry."

No one stirred except for Kip, who looked even more frightened than before. Then through the silence came a scream. Pham's voice, far up the alley. Peters turned for the door.

"I'll go see," he said. He patted Bates' arm and disappeared around the corner with his head down, poking ahead with his cane and paying no attention to the troops who made way for him outside.

Another scream came, followed by angry shouting. I turned toward the door.

"There's something I need to see," I said. But it wasn't the same thing Peters had gone to see.

When I got there, Pham stood unsteadily in the middle of the square, trying to keep her balance as she wiped the blood from her nose with a hand. Rosler stood to one side with a sneer on his face, while around the periphery of the square men and women stood, having come to see the spectacle, or the alien, or both. Now and then one of them glanced uneasily up at the dome.

"You *follow* me and you *follow* me and you *follow* me!" shrieked Pham. She was bent over at the waist and gasping for breath, straightening up with an effort to shout some more. Yet it wasn't Rosler she was shouting at.

In the very center of the square, aglow in the hazy sunlight that streamed down to form a circle where he stood, Charlie Peters

In the very center of the square, aglow in the hazy sunlight that streamed down to form a circle where he stood, Charlie Peters leaned forward with both hands on his cane and watched Pham intently as she screamed at him.

In the corner, the alien still stood, blind and immobile, watching everyone.

"Everywhere I go, you *there!*" shouted Pham. "You pretend to be nice, but *nobody* nice. You just *watch* all the time. That's why you here, hah?"

I pushed past the spectators into the gloom of Anne Miller's work room. Pham's frenzied shrieks dwindled in the background. Stale dust rose from the floor to block what little light there was. I waved it away from my face and searched among the debris.

Furniture had been tipped over or pushed aside. Piles of old memory blocks and notebooks lay on the floor under a thick layer of dust. Finally in the corner there was a dim outline of light blue, a rectangle like a thousand others I'd seen on shelves in the background over the years. It was a slender binder filled with an untidy stack of paper. I worked it loose from the trash and wiped away the dust, but I was unable to read the cover in the bad light.

I stepped back out into the square. I was about to look down at the cover of the binder when I saw the gun in Pham's hands. She was down on her knees, sobbing and holding her big fléchette gun in both hands, aiming it at Charlie Peters. Peters stood quietly in his column of light, looking down at her with growing concern as he leaned on his cane. Rosler stood to one side, apparently enjoying the spectacle, while on the other side Bolton and Throckmorton inched closer to Pham.

"You call yourself *father?*" she screamed. "You make fun of me, hah?" She wiped her face on her shoulder and shook her head to clear it. "I know about fathers and priests! You turn your back and make good laugh! *You don't fuck with me! Nobody fuck with me!*" She raised the gun higher and struggled to hold it steady, screaming and sobbing at the same time. Bolton edged closer.

I thought at that moment that Peters was quietly praying to himself, but from the few words I could hear I came to understand later what he was actually saying, the line that he was finally finishing.

"*I beheld,*" he said, "*a pale horse. And his name that sat on him was Death.*" He glanced briefly over at Rosler, then quickly back at Pham. His years of composure finally seemed to have fallen away, and his fear showed through.

Rosler snorted in disgust at Peters' words. "What are you, the Second Coming or something?" He turned back to Pham. "Go ahead, you dumb little shit, pop him."

Thinking she wouldn't really fire, and unable to wait any longer, I looked down at the binder in my hands. But in that very instant the gun exploded with a horrible noise and a blinding flash of light. A sun-like wave of heat from the muzzle swept outward across the square.

And, out in the churning dust, on that strange, bare, black earth, out in the center of his now swirling column of light, Charlie Peters crossed himself quietly and looked down at the bloody remains of David Rosler.

"No," he said, "not the Second Coming at all. Just an old Irish priest."

Pham was kneeling in a huddle with her arms in front of her. She was still for a moment, then shook with a small convulsion, and then again. A hoarse sob escaped from her, and she began to rock forward and back with her head still buried against her knees. She didn't look up as Bolton carefully pulled the gun from her fingers.

When I looked back down at the binder in my hands, my own fingers were trembling—because of the explosion, because of Rosler's sudden death, and because I had already seen the words on the cover. The words I had known would be there.

HP/Digital Equipment Corporation, Programmer's Quick Reference. Model DEC-91.

Anne Miller's computer on the island. Anne Miller's voice speaking the words: Deck Ninety-One.

The creature in the cage was a child of our own drones.

Then, just at that moment, like a distant, silver thread against the awful silence, a muted cry came from far back among the alleyways. The sound of a woman at the height of passion.

How strange, I thought. Love-making at such a time as this.

A tiny life beginning, perhaps, even as Rosler died. Even as Pham wept for her own. A flicker of light in the darkness as the drones drew nearer. Returning, at last, to their makers.

There was no one here but ourselves.

PART FOUR

SERENITY

Chapter Twenty-three: AND HIS SLUMBER SHALL
BRING YOU PEACE

It was terrifying, and it was exhilarating. It was exhilarating because the scuff of the shoe by the bed in the dead of night had proved to be only our own child, and terrifying because of the glint of steel in his hand. It was terrifying in the way that only a cancer of the flesh can be, with that ultimate intimacy that preys on men's minds from within. A creature, as Patel had said, of our own imaginings.

And it was exhilarating because we had the codes that would stop them.

Through the haze in the square I watched Bolton and Throckmorton lift Pham to her feet and help her out of the square, away from the shadows and into the road that led back through the dome. Her gun lay at Peters' feet. Peters stood looking down at Rosler's body, at the rivulets of blood cutting channels in the dust, running in and out of the shadows and making a faint trickling sound thought the silence.

Though she had been holding the massive gun in hands that were shaking, and squinting through her own blood and tears as she fired a broadside of steel needles like buckshot in a crowded square, Pham had hit Rosler squarely in the center of his chest. Little of him remained.

I edged through the crowd and pushed my way past Chan, then pulled Elliot away.

"Let's go." I got him suited up and then out onto the surface outside the main dome, past the stream of matériel and troop trailers growling through the tunnel to the warships outside.

We opened our face plates in an armored shuttle and lifted off toward the orbiting fleet.

"What the hell are you doing, Torres? Here we are—Rosler's dead, Pham's gone and blown her last fuse and ain't worth a bent nickel anymore, Polaski's got balls for brains and something bad's coming down on Boar River with Carolyn gone and all, and now we got aliens an hour out—"

"They're not aliens," I said. "They're the drones."

"So the alien's have got drones, too. Right now I don't—"

"Our own drones."

"The drones are gone, Torres, dusted in the next system—"

"The originals are gone. They were destroyed by the next generation as a matter of course when it cleaned up. These are their offspring, Tyrone, generations later. They advanced faster than even Anne thought possible."

"Come on, Torres, the drones were on our side. Shit, they'd be out here protecting us."

"No. They were supposed to protect the planets, not us. Against 'alien force.' That's what they're doing."

"Damn it, Torres, you said there ain't no aliens."

"We *are* the aliens, Tyrone. They don't know who we are."

"Lord, now you've went and got strange, too. You, Pham, and Charlie..."

"You weren't in Flight Ops on the island, Tyrone, when the drones were sent up. You didn't hear what Anne Miller said after we'd lost so many of the drone ships. She said their mission would be intact no matter what—that the only shortages were from losing both ships carrying agriculture and both ships carrying history and the arts. I may have been the only one who heard her, and its significance didn't register until Harry showed up talking about the drone he found."

"So who cares if they know history?"

"They didn't know *anything* about Earth, Tyrone. They didn't even know it existed. They thought they were born right here in Holzstein's. So when they saw us coming, the Europeans with those big guns, they ran. When Anne sent her instructions about defending themselves, it never occurred to her that we were the ones they'd defend against. She knew, though, after Harry's drone."

"So let's talk to them," said Elliot. "Tell them to cool it."

"We're going to. We'll get the communications codes off the ship and then talk to them."

The fleet swung into view through the strip of windscreen. Our stomachs sagged as I dropped the thrust and rolled the shuttle onto its back to keep our weight on the floor. Elliot leaned forward with his elbows on his knees and his hands inside his helmet, rubbing his temples.

"I knew a fella in Louisiana, once," he said. "Got so confused he just sat down and died."

The crippled command ship drifted closer.

"Shit, Torres, I don't know what's going on any more, but it's time to get out of all this. Time to go find me someplace warm, and where I don't weigh so damned much."

"That's just it, Tyrone, we're going to get out. We've got control over the aliens now. Think about it—they'll just stop. They'll be powerless, and we can move on. Serenitas is sunny and light-weight like you want. Remember what it looks like, Tyrone. Remember what you said when you saw it. 'Fairweather,' you said. You named it, Tyrone."

"I don't know if I believe you any more, Torres. I just know it's time to get out."

We docked and moved into the big ship. It was floating under a light thrust among the deserted repair platforms. We tugged our way up the ladder to the MI decks, where Chan had said the case with the codes had been stowed. Among the trash and the twisted pieces of the grating, difficult to see in the red emergency lighting, we found the slender metal case strapped against one wall. I tripped the buckles and opened the case. Set into its padded bottom were two dull silver shapes, petabyte memory blocks like the ones I'd once stolen. But unlike the oblong pieces of silver that had unleashed this storm a lifetime ago, these held the key to quelling it once and for all.

"I say," came a voice, "who's mucking about in my parlor?"

Little Bolton drifted up the ladder and onto the deck. "By Jove, it's only—" He stopped in the middle of the grating, motionless and quiet. Elliot and I waited.

"I hear something," said Little Bolton.

"You hear something? Where? On the MI decks?"

"No. I hear something inside."

Elliot stared at him, then slowly turned to one of the consoles. He fiddled with it until a radar picture came to life on the wall. Hundreds of ships were closing in on us, very close.

"Damn, Torres," he said, "they're right overhead."

"Where are we, Tyrone?"

"Backside, by the cracks. Look at the bottom of the screen. All that clutter's the trap we're laying in the fissures. And we're right in the middle—Jesus, Torres, why'd you pull this stunt about laying a trap, anyway?"

"To keep Polaski busy fighting aliens, Tyrone. To give me time. He and Allerton are up to something."

"Shit, Torres, that ain't news. They're up to fighting and winning. Fighting aliens, colonists, themselves, don't make no difference. Come on, let's get the hell out of here. We're in big trouble."

"Just a minute. Little B., what is it you hear inside?"

"Just...rather like voices, like the way I myself talk inside. Except the voices don't mean anything."

"Little B., did Anne Miller ever tell you and your friends to pass along everything you heard us talk about?"

"We like Ms. Chan better. She shows us things."

"But did you tell Ms. Miller?"

There was a long pause.

"Yes."

"Why?"

The little drone squatted in silence.

"I don't know," it said at last.

"Come *on*, Torres," said Elliot. "Let's move!"

Little Bolton begged to be taken along, and when we finally thrust off from the big ship it was only to find our way blocked completely. Making a deeper black against the darkness, ghostly shapes slid out of space and toward the decoys, down toward the great fissures in the planet's surface. One of the shapes glided toward us, then all at once our windscreen was filled with the glistening, bronze-colored nose of a strange vessel. It hovered in front of us. My blood turned cold and sweat rose along the back my of neck, and I found myself sliding the metal case off my seat and down onto the deck, as though the ship, like a living thing, could see it and know what it was.

"Torres," said Elliot.

"Yes." My mouth was dry.

"Don't crap in your suit."

The vessel slid beneath us and out of sight. I was left wondering if it had really been there, if it had really seen us at all. Elliot's hand shook as he adjusted our view of the planet passing below.

Then the windshield lit up as the thousand-mile-long fissures exploded with heaters and lasers. Drone ships by the hundreds suddenly stood out in stark relief against the inferno as they struggled to escape from the deep rifts, trying to fire on the ships of ours that rolled in over the rim at their spine-crushing six Gs.

Other drone ships plunged lower into the flames to attack the decoy buildings at the bottom, while on the surface our ground troops blew the camouflage off their missile batteries and launched at the ships still descending from space. Our own ships down in the rifts spun around to race back out of the fire zone, just before it erupted into a string of sun-white clouds that sent burning drone ships tumbling high above the surface, later to crash to the ground behind the missile crews. More drone ships flew down into the fissures to take their place.

"Fusion," I said. "We're using fusion. Courtesy of Bart Allerton. Son of a bitch, we're killing our own people along with the drones."

"I wonder if they're alive," said Elliot.

"The drones?"

"The ships. I mean, if the aliens are machines—the drones, I mean—then they wouldn't even think of building ships that need crews, would they? They'd just build big, space-going animals—drones, machines, critters, whatever the fuck I'm talking about. Jesus, Torres, *are* they alive? Is anything alive—are *we* alive? I don't even know anymore. Holy mother of God, look at that!"

Beams of light slid downward from the invaders. Where the beams sliced into the surface they turned it a blinding white, and moved glowing walls of flame toward our crews. Our own crews' weapons tried without success to stop them. Hundreds of men and women were about to disappear into the flames. The drones just had too many ships, huge numbers of them that they sacrificed one after the other.

"Good going, Torres," said Elliot.

The surface went dark. In unison the remaining drone ships sprouted flame from their engines and accelerated away from the fissures. Elliot let out his breath. "Sweet land o' mercy, Torres. What scared them off, do you think?"

"I don't think anything did. I think they figured out the deception."

"You mean they figured out they'd been conned into the cracks?"

"Yes."

Elliot was quiet for a minute.

"Then I sure as hell hope," he said, "that they don't remember who did the conning. Them's some bad folks to have pissed off at a fella. And you got enough enemies as it is."

"That shielding's not on the cage yet, is it?"

"No."

"Then we're in trouble."

The windscreen blazed to life as a giant shape hurtled past. Its lance of flame burned across our shuttle and sent it tumbling. The cabin overheated, suddenly smoking from the corners and stinking of burnt insulation. The windscreen turned a charred black, and we were left to feel our way home, blind and scarcely able to breathe in the smoky air.

"The *drones*? The aliens are the *drones*? My God, Eddie, how? Why are we being killed by Anne's drones? *How long have you known*?" Chan wiped her mouth with the back of an unsteady hand.

"Only a few hours, Chan."

"Why?"

"Well, because Anne thought human minds made them human. She thought they would side with us."

"Eddie," said Peters, "they're trying to kill us."

"I *know*. The problem is that nowhere in her programming did she actually come out and tell them they weren't the only ones in the universe. They ended up like she was. That's what Pham said about her, remember—that she'd isolated herself and convinced herself there was nothing else."

"Nothing else but what?"

"Nothing but her own mind. She probably sensed there was something out there, something messy and dangerous and human, but it was so alien to her that in the end she was building machines to defend herself from it."

"That's a fine irony," said Peters. "Because in truth it wasn't humans at all she should have feared, but the weapons. And it's the weapons the drones are coming after, isn't it?"

Chan took her cat in her arms, the peculiar grey cat with the green eyes, and scratched it behind the ears. She turned to stare out through the window.

"Yes," I said. "At least that."

From the black planet the drone ships fanned out through the Holzstein system. Euphoria over their rout in the fissures faded as they went about their business, indifferent to their losses. The trap we'd set turned out to have had no lasting effect at all, except to anger the colonies even more than before as questions flew about the fusion weapons we'd used.

It also ended my pact with the drone in its cage. We hadn't replaced the shielding in time, and it had surely learned about the ambush from its fellows. It spoke not another word, no matter how doggedly we tried.

As the weeks passed and the level of fear in the system rose to the breaking point, the colonists began to marshal their forces in preparation for fighting the drones. But every time they did, the drones attacked—blind, methodical, sinking their endless, indifferent forces into the battle. The colonists fought back as best they could, not knowing what else to do. And all the while, as they came to understand what had really happened, they became even angrier.

Even the original news of the existence of aliens hadn't sent shockwaves through the system as powerful as those from the discovery that they were really our drones. None of us had thought to release the news in a controlled way, so it leaked out through military and commercial channels as soon as I'd informed our commanders.

Even then much of the system misunderstood, believing we'd known all along that the aliens were our own drones and that we were using them to remove any competition for Serenitas. I received calls from former allies, claiming to know that even the attacks on our own base were only self-inflicted for show.

But soon the recordings of the ambush were transmitted through the system and examined, and the accusations turned to bitter questions about how it could have happened in the first place. Polaski threw our own forces into the fray, as always trading them for power and yet more ships, while those of us on the base labored to restart the farming domes.

Chan and I worked to understand the drones' communications codes embedded in Miller's blocks. The blocks had turned out to contain complex communications protocols rather than merely an encryption key. Too, while at first the protocols seemed to be complete, time after time we failed to make them run through to completion in tests. We poured over Miller's old records and bullied the priests in the research labs. We ran experiments in the vehicle assembly building, time and again pulling the blocks out of their case, then carefully putting them back. But no matter how we tried, it became clear that there was some final, critical piece of information we didn't have. A password. Chan grew increasingly fearful and restless as time passed and the drones tightened their grip on the system. Eventually she became altogether uncommunicative, no longer even interested in the renewed prize of the blue and green planet.

During those uneasy nine months, while we watched the sky and waited for the attack on the base that had to come, while our lives trickled away in disappointment and frustration, I saw Pham just three times.

The first was late one evening a month after the attack, when, irritated by the poor reception I was getting of the drone's EHF communications, I went looking for help to bring a bigger antenna down from orbit. I walked back into the maze of dark alleyways into the commandos' district of the dome. It was an isolated quarter where soft light seeped under the doors and cooking smells and music filtered into the night air.

Michael Bolton, at first furious when he learned we were being murdered by our own survey drones, later became tight-lipped and uncooperative, refusing to commit his teams to Polaski's campaign of head-on warfare. Instead he held the commandos back for the defense of the remaining civilians on the base, trying to keep both his troops and the civilians alive for as long as possible. The teams kept mostly to themselves while they waited, but I'd seen an occasional one of their ships taking off or landing. I also knew, from a conversation I'd overheard between Chan and a grasshopper drone, that the commandos' forestry work on the highlands of Asile still continued.

On the night I went looking for help with the antenna, I was searching for Roscoe Throckmorton. I didn't know exactly where he lived. I stopped at one door and knocked, then stood in the black alley and waited, shifting my feet in the cold and picking out the smells on the air. The door swung open and light poured into the alley, while a young pilot, Stephanie Teal, stood on the threshold. She wore a robe and slippers, and held the stub of a pencil in her hand.

In the room behind her, curled up in an armchair and looking up to see who was at the door, was Pham. She sat by a light and held a book in her hands. She was freshly scrubbed. Her hair was trimmed and wet from the shower, and she wore a white robe and a pair of reading glasses I'd never seen before. Her face was pale and tired, though, and she peered into the darkness outside with a little uncertainty.

Teal sent me to another building, and after a last glimpse of Pham watching from the chair, the door was pushed gently closed and I was left in the darkened alley.

The next time I saw her was four months later, while Chan and I worked on the iron mezzanine of the vehicle assembly building. We were transmitting one possible permutation of the missing password after another to FleetSys. The giant fleet MI was then struggling to simulate the unpredictable, blindingly fast intuitive leaps and self-modifying twists of the drones' intelligence, and so respond as they would. Even though we had the communications protocols for the drones, we didn't dare transmit to them directly until we had the password, for fear they'd stop listening altogether if they received a forgery. Or else attack.

"It's no use, Eddie," said Chan. "Even if Anne instructed the drones to hand the password down from generation to generation—which I'm sure she did—we're not going to fool them by cramming a million re-tries down their throats. You worked with her on the power-cell codes. You know the kind of cryptographer she was. Their definition of legitimate transmission error is going to be pretty conservative. Let's just forget it, Eddie. It's no use."

As she talked I looked out a small window set in the wall, watching Stephanie Teal. She was standing in the sun up the alley, leaning against the wall next to Charlie Peters' quarters. She'd been there for over an hour.

Chan came up beside me and we watched as Pham came out of Peters' quarters and closed the door behind her. She and Teal then turned and walked up the alley away from us. Pham's step seemed lighter. They both wore light, warm-weather jumpsuits, out of place on a base where most of us now wore armor and weapons as we waited.

"I want to leave, Eddie," said Chan.

The two women in the alleyway turned the corner.

"We talk about breaking free," said Chan, "but we're really slaves to the drones. Every day we hear about another ship lost, another colony at war. More friends gone. And we walk around waiting for the next attack to hit here. And all we do is sit around looking for a password we're never going to find. With our heads buried in books and computers, trying to find the magic letters that'll make the horror stop... Hardly anyone's left, Eddie. Carolyn and Harry are gone—"

"That wasn't the drones," I said. "That was Allerton and his toady, Becker."

"It's the same *thing*, Eddie. The wars we brought along, the bastards out there, the drones...we can't change it. Let's just go. Leave the guns behind so the drones won't come after us, and go away."

"They're going after people everywhere, Chan. There's nowhere to go."

"Only when they're armed! You know what Anne's matrix says: alien *force*. That's all they're interested in. People who don't set up defenses are being left alone. *That's* the 'known constant' of the universe now, Eddie. And no one's going to change it—live in peace and be left alone. People are even saying that unarmed boats are making it through the tunnel to Serenitas."

"Win by giving up? I find that hard to believe. A man would be crazy to go out there unarmed."

She turned away. "You never talk about Carolyn or Harry, Eddie."

It was true. I'd formed a picture in my mind of Penderson standing at the mouth of the hangar saying something, but that was all. There was spray from the rain on his face, and I couldn't hear what he was saying. Something about Dorczak or Becker. I could hear the rain, and I could see Becker in the background, but I couldn't hear what he was saying. But it had been important.

"I want to leave," said Chan, "and go to Asile. Even if I have to go alone."

"Chan—" I stopped, remembering something.

"Listen, Chan," I said. "When I came back from Asile, you already knew about Bolton's forestation project."

"I helped plan it, Eddie."

"You and Bolton?"

"Yes."

That surprised me.

"Okay, but when I got back from Asile you already knew that he'd left the grasshopper drones in place. And you hadn't talked to him yet."

"Yes. He wanted that forest on those hills, Eddie, and he didn't think we'd make it through the tunnel."

"But *how* did you know?"

She looked at me for a minute.

"From the drones, Eddie. Our little grasshopper drones."

"They tell you what they hear?"

"Yes."

"Everything?" I thought of all the little spider drones in the background over the years. Shifting for a better view as they watched...

"Yes," she said.

"And they told Anne everything, too," I said.

"Oh, yes. Although I kept telling them not to."

"But they did anyway? Why?"

"I don't know. Anne had better control of them, and she didn't trust us. She thought she had to learn everything she could from us in case she had to pass it along to her drones."

"Christ."

"There's someone else, too," said Chan.

"Someone else, what?"

"They tell someone else everything they hear."

"What do you mean? Who?"

"I don't know. All I know is they dump their records into three separate partitions on FleetSys. They've been doing it ever since we reached Earth orbit."

The last time I saw Pham during those nine months, during that lull before the great storm, was another three months after that. I was standing again in the shadows of the mezzanine in the assembly building. But Chan had gone off somewhere on the base to be alone, and now Polaski paced behind me. The hull-clamps on his boots banged against the iron as I looked out across Trinity Square, out through the front of the dome.

"I need *ships*," Polaski was saying, "not some goddamned secret message. Ships, missiles. You said you're the only one who could talk to that POW down there, but you've got nothing, so get out of here and help me *fight*, instead."

It was late in the planet's afternoon. I put a pair of binoculars to my eyes again and focused on the horizon.

"No," I said.

Polaski stopped his pacing.

That morning, Pham had walked out across the square and suited up by the lock tunnel, then she'd driven out across the surface to the wreckage of the landing dome twenty miles away. For hours, then, every time I'd put the binoculars to my eyes, she'd been stooped over and searching through the debris in the freezing vacuum. Then sometime later she'd been half a mile farther out, swinging something at the hard surface, over and over. It was a dangerous kind of exertion in a suit, especially in the high gravity, yet for hour after hour, every time I looked, she was still digging.

"What do you mean 'No?'" said Polaski.

"I haven't seen your spooks for a while," I said. "Did they get tired of following me, or have you got them all in the wards helping the radiation victims?"

"What do you mean 'No,' Torres?"

This time when I looked, whatever Pham had had in her hands was gone, and instead she was standing still next to a block of some kind she'd placed on the surface. The sunlight on the ground took on the rippling look of broken shadows, and an instant later the surface turned black to leave Pham and the object next to her lit all by themselves, floating in the darkness.

"What I mean," I said, "is that I'm not going to help you fight the drones. I'm going to find the password, at which point I'll control them. I'll set them to finish terraforming the planets, while I go on to Serenitas."

Polaski fell silent. Pham's suit lights came on and she started back toward the dome.

"What were you doing with Bart Allerton, Polaski," I said, "that Dorczak and I weren't supposed to know about?"

Still he didn't speak, but now I heard the soft, precise *snick* of rounds dropping into the chambers of his revolver.

"By the way," I said, "that was a good deal you made."

The sound from the revolver stopped. "What deal?"

"The deal you made with Anne Miller when we reached Earth orbit. Allowing her to make unsupervised transmissions to the drones, while you got access to the ship's spiders and grasshoppers to use as spies. Your officers will applaud your ingenuity, Polaski. Spider drones watching them in their bedrooms, spider drones sniffing around during their pre-vote meetings..."

For a while there was no noise at all. The sound of the safety disengaging hadn't come yet.

"We're here to win," said Polaski after a minute. His voice had a hoarse sound to it.

"To win against whom, Polaski? The other colonists? Your-self? Or is it still the aliens? Tell me something, Polaski, how many lives was it worth to you to mobilize the fleet and go after the aliens, before they were even a threat? Was it worth Pham's and mine when the landing dome blew out—"

Out on the surface Pham had reached the air lock. I lowered the binoculars.

"Yes?" said Polaski.

After a minute he turned for the door, then stopped.

"Torres," he said. "Remember that you're as expendable as Dorczak was." He left, and his hull clamps clattered against the iron of the stairs on the way down.

Nine months and two days after our only victory over the drones—the day Pham had shot David Rosler—I had become so frustrated by our failure to find the password that I finally made the decision to transmit to the drones without it.

We loaded the communications programs from the blocks into the ground transmitters for the last time, and while Elliot and Chan monitored the fleet's instruments from orbit, I drove a tractor out past the horizon, pulling a broadcast antenna far away from the base. I called Elliot.

"All right," I said, "I'm ready." The bleak landscape was starkly empty in the early light. Tiny on the horizon, back to the south, the eastern slope of the main dome glinted silver in the sun. The other side of it was still black. Along the western horizon were the twisted black remains of the landing dome, and tiny in the distance behind it the abandoned operations dome.

Glinting along the sharp line of the horizon behind the main dome were the farming and industry domes with wisps of white rising from their big converters. Like specks of dust around the main dome stood Polaski's personal flight of warships, along with the heavily armored shuttles that worked between the base and the orbiting fleet.

Nowhere across the billion square miles of frozen desert was there any sound, save for my breathing and the hissing from the radios.

"Okay, Torres," said Elliot, "we're tracking the drones' communications all over the system, and we got a visual on their biggest fleets, at the torus and out at H-VI, whatever it is they're doing out there. Chan says FleetSys is ready to pin down the password they respond to, and your system down there's been programmed to try more than a thousand of 'em. You got any last-minute bright ideas, cough 'em up."

"No, Tyrone. We've got her birth date, government ID number, system memory size, hashing seeds, launch date—every number she ever used. I'm not going to think of anything else, and we've asked every other human who ever knew her. That's it, Tyrone, it's time to try."

"Okay. You got the switch."

"How's Chan?"

"Chan says if you're gonna do it, Torres, do it."

I kicked the coupling loose from the antenna array's trailer, and with a last glance at its annunciator lights I climbed back into the cab.

When I'd driven several miles back toward the main dome, passing close to the wreck of the landing dome, I reached over and typed the start command into the terminal on the seat. COMMAND ENTERED, it said. In minutes the drones would either be back under our control, many generations later, or we would be left helpless forever.

Something on the surface caught the morning light at that moment, an object resting on the ground near my course. I climbed down to look just as Elliot's voice crackled in my headset.

"Christ, Torres, they've stopped."

My heart skipped a beat. "What's stopped?"

The frozen ground crunched under my boots as I trudged across the surface, listening to Elliot's breathing now, on top of my own.

"The drones' communications. Everywhere in the system they just stopped, the instant the first password went out."

In front of me was a gravestone, neatly carved and sunk into the ground next to a mound. Its chiseled letters caught the morning light.

"Torres?"

"Yes," I said. RODERICK CAMDEN McKENNA, 2018 – 2039.

"They're turning this way. All of them. Even the ones that were nosing around the Chinese at Asile. All of them, Torres."

Chapter Twenty-four: TRAILING CLOUDS OF GLORY

"How long until they're here?" I said.

"The closest are the ones lifting off from H-VI, and they aren't more than four hours out. They're really humping, Torres—eight Gs. And I don't think it's 'cause they heard their mama calling, either."

"All right, listen. Chan should keep trying passwords while they're on the way. In the meantime, get on to Polaski and tell him what's happening. His units are back on the base somewhere, and he's got to start evacuating. Tell him I'll meet up with him in the dome in half an hour."

"That boy's gonna take your balls off, Torres."

"No, he's not. Because if the drones are leaving H-VI unguarded, I know what he's going to do. Now get moving—I'll talk to you later."

With a last glance at Roddy McKenna's grave, I started back to the main dome. By the time I reached it, trailers were moving troops out to the ships on the surface.

Polaski was in Trinity Square, talking into a radio. He was angry.

"*Ground* assault," he said into the handset. "I want *ground* troops on those ships. I don't care if it's three Gs on H-VI. If the crews can handle it, so can the grunts... They want *what*? Mister, you tell them they answer to you, now. The colonel's not available. Here." He pushed the phone into my stomach and turned away.

"You really stuck your dick in it this time," he said as I followed him up the alley. "So let's go see what Snow White and the dwarves have to say about it."

"You haven't begun evacuating yet?"

"I'm moving *troops*, Torres."

The commandos' district was still dark and cool. Polaski

stopped at a door like all the others and kicked it open.

Inside, morning light filtered in from a courtyard in back, while in the corner a computer played Welsh folk songs. Two couples danced, either still up from the night before or up very early. The smell of breakfast came from the back.

Barefoot on the dirt floor, Pham turned in a quiet circle through the hazy light, dancing with a younger woman. She wore just her cotton pants and a white blouse, with the tails tied up in front to leave her waist bare. She scarcely glanced at Polaski when he slammed the door and jabbed a finger at her.

"You!" The other couple stopped, but Pham and her companion ignored him.

Polaski kicked the computer off of its chair.

"You're needed," he said.

A shadow fell across the room and Bolton stepped in from the courtyard in back. He carried his combat knife in one hand and a stout, half-finished walking stick in the other.

Polaski glanced at him and then back at Pham.

"We're going to the alien base on Six," he said, "and the Rats—"

"The drones," I said from the door, "are three hours out. We need to evacuate."

"We're going to *Six*, Colonel," said Polaski to Pham, "and the grunts won't get their feet wet in three Gs unless you're there to hold their dicks for them. So move it."

"No," she said. She stood quietly with her hands in her pockets, and for a minute no one spoke. Motes of dust glinted in the sun as they drifted past her.

"You're in no position to refuse," said Polaski at last. "You're the one that got thrown off our ships in the first place, and you're the one that our own clients don't want on their side any more."

"Yes," she said.

"And the drunk who gutted my operations chief. Or we wouldn't be in this mess."

"Yes."

"That's right, 'yes!' So move!"

"No."

Seconds passed.

"Evacuate people is more important," she said.

"Fucking *Christ*," he said. He turned to Bolton.

"You're needed, too, *Lieutenant*. Not for any of your fancy crap, either. I need you out there to fight."

"I expect, Sergeant Polaski," said Bolton, with just enough of a pause to let the rank sink in, "that the lady is right. There are still civilians on the surface."

"There aren't any civilians any more, Bolton."

"No? Not the children on the farms, or the ladies in the obstetrics ward? Come."

"All fucking *right*." He swore again and looked around. "So go ahead and get your dead weight off the base! At least it'll get them out of the way of my ships." He stood with his hands on his hips and watched as Pham moved toward a telephone.

"*Move!*" he said.

She stopped again and turned around. She slipped her hands into her pockets and waited. Polaski's eyes narrowed and the seconds slipped by.

Finally he spun on his heel and stalked back to the door, pushing me out of the way as he passed. The door slammed back against its hinges and he disappeared up the alley.

"So," said Bolton, stepping the rest of the way into the room. "His Lordship dares not concede the invincible foe, lest he smell the ill wind of discontent upon his own keep. Tuyet, the west lock-tunnel, I think. The cannon fodder will have the main lock quite gummed up by now. If you'll arrange for the ground transport to the shuttles as they land, I'll begin evacuating the domes. Mr. Torres— I assume your people are preparing the civilian ships for breaking orbit? Good. Then if you would have the shuttles brought down to the west lock, we should be able to catch them up in good time."

Still carrying his walking stick, he sheathed the knife and motioned his companions toward the door.

"Oh, bloody hell." Three hours later Bolton stood rooted to the center of Trinity Square in a swirling cloud of dust, leaving me to wait for a trailer to pass so I could see what he was looking at. The trailer's tail swept past to reveal Charlie Peters standing in the billowing haze on the far side, leaning on his cane and watching intently as the trailers roared toward the lock.

Bolton glanced at me in exasperation, and then back at Peters. "You were to pack yourself onto the first shuttle, Father!"

"Aye, that's what you said. But I didn't fancy myself—"

His words were cut off by another tractor grinding past. Only two more trailers were left to go, evacuating the last twenty commandos, a few bed-ridden patients from the infirmaries, and the base's medics, who had stayed until the end. Polaski and his ships were long gone.

"Good God," said Bolton.

He wasn't looking at Peters. The next trailer had passed, and he was looking up over Peters' head. The trailer made its final turn, and my own view of the dome beyond Trinity Square became clear.

A wall of shapes filled the sky. They settled toward the surface of the planet, glinting dully in the midday sun. They were descending toward a point beyond the horizon.

Then a small ball of flame tumbled toward the ground in the midst of the fleet, separating into streamers of flame. It was our shuttle that had just taken off. Filled with civilians, it had stumbled into the midst of the incoming ships with its light weapons still mounted on it.

"Hold the next flight!" shouted Bolton. "Tuyet! Ring up the pilot, get her off southbound. Slow, now, don't let her spook the incoming. Steady hands and her mind on the king, and she'll be all right. Then get those two trailer-fulls off right behind her—they'll be safer slipping away than skulking about down here. William!" He pocketed the phone.

"Everyone else not embarked yet," he said, "get into the assembly building. It's the only structure with its own air."

"Yes, sir," said a lieutenant. "But not quite everyone, sir. There's a woman in labor, and she's having some trouble. The medics don't want to move her."

"Boy or girl?" said Bolton.

"Beg your pardon, sir?" The lieutenant looked blank.

"Boy or girl?"

"Um, boy, I think, sir."

Bolton eyed the ships on the horizon. "Bad time to be born, isn't it? All right, keep someone with her and wait till our friends make a move. For now they've either made a god-awful miss, or they've stopped for tea. You, Father—Torres, you too. Let's get some tin over our heads, shall we?" He motioned toward the vehicle assembly building at the end of the square.

I didn't move. "The antennas," I said. I was still watching the distant black shapes, now hard to see on the horizon.

"How's that?" said Bolton.

"They traced the bogus password back to the antennas I left out on the horizon. That's where they've landed."

"Not for long, then. Come along."

"Poor little fellow," said Peters, looking absently around the square.

"The baby?"

"Aye. Its father was one o' those poor sods who died in the fissures, you know. Didn't want to go—Polaski had him half beaten to get him out of his wife's bed. The day that David Rosler...well, you know." He glanced at Pham.

"Enough of that," said Bolton. "By God, but you two have dreams for brains. Let's *go*."

"No, just a minute," I said. "Bolton, you've given me an idea. Charlie, you get on in—if they bring the mother in, they'll want your help. Bolton, get some of your people and follow me. As long as our visitors are just sitting out there, I think I'll offer our prisoner a deal.

Pham posted a guard in Trinity Square around the vehicle assembly building, where most of the civilians waited. Radios crackled in tense conversation with the ships in orbit. Elliot and the others on the ships were trying to come up with a way to get more shuttles down to us, even while more and more drone ships approached. Soldiers on the ground eyed the horizon or the black sky overhead, and held their weapons in sweating hands and shrugged to shift the oxygen tanks on their backs to get more comfortable.

Bolton posted a guard in Miller's square, where Rosler had died, then watched doubtfully as I approached the drone in its cage.

Bolton carried a grenade launcher on his back, but he still wore his shorts and t-shirt, and still carried the walking stick in one hand. He swung the tip against his calf over and over. Peters stood next to him, leaning on his cane and ignoring everyone's advice to get under cover.

In its nine months in the square the drone hadn't moved, nor had it made any sound through the speaker next to the cage. At least—we knew—it hadn't sent any messages to the other drones in all that time, either; once the shielding had been put into place it had never been turned off, even briefly, for fear that the drone might have picked up too much information about the base.

"I don't wholly approve, Torres," said Bolton. "Your plan makes me a little apprehensive, if the truth were known. I don't imagine this fellow's even aware there *is* a password, and I certainly don't think it would give it up if it were. Personally I'd rather take a chance and slip out on a shuttle, and just go home."

"Home, Bolton?"

"Um...yes. As you know."

I'd loaded the drones' communications codes into our transmitters one last time, and now, while the drone ships waited on the horizon and still others approached from space, I set the metal case with the codes down at my side and held the terminal in the other hand. I spoke toward the cage.

"These are the communications codes that control your species. They are what your ships have come to this planet to look for, but your friends do not know where they are. If you will tell me the password that belongs to these codes, I will open your communications."

"Yes," said the drone from its speaker.

"Well," said Bolton behind me. "You've been forgiven your little deceits regarding the fissures, it seems."

I glanced at the sky. The drone remained silent.

"Well?" I said.

"You first," it said.

The mutual leaking of military information, Penderson had said, *is a learned art.* The drone remained motionless in its shadows, hidden from the sun.

"No," I said.

Silence.

At least the drone seemed to know the password—an important step, because this was our last chance to learn it. I felt the pressure of Bolton and the others watching.

"When I open your communications," I said to the drone, "then you will say the password." A compromise.

"Yes," it said.

I looked back at Bolton and Peters. My hand was sweating on the handle of the terminal. Bolton glanced restlessly around at his troops. Peters looked mostly confused, with the lines on his old face deepened with his frowning.

"All right," I said, turning back to the drone. I reached for the switch and held it on. Then I straightened up and got ready to enter the password into the terminal. Once in, the broadcast disabling the drones would follow in seconds.

Nothing happened.

"Say the password," I said.

Still nothing.

The drone remained silent. *Deceit, too,* Penderson had said, *is a learned art.* The seconds crawled by, and turned into minutes. Bolton's stick tapped like a metronome against his calf.

"I'm afraid you've been hoisted with your own petard, Torres," he said. "Come on, give it up."

A radio crackled as tense voices came in from the distance.

"Another minute," I said. My fingers twitched on the terminal's keys. I stared at the speaker, willing it to make a sound. My ears popped, once and then again, but I paid no attention.

The minute passed. "Torres," said Bolton, his voice firmer now, "look down." I pulled my eyes away from the speaker and looked at the slate-black ground. A layer of dust had risen up and was drifting eastward.

I set the terminal down gently and groped for the handle of the codes case, unable to take my eyes off the sight at my feet.

"How long?" I said. "How long have we got?"

"From a small breach like that?" said Bolton. "We may be all right for days, if the converters stay intact. I'm more concerned with what's coming in through that breach. Let's go now, start backing out. Eyes sharp." He unslung his launcher, then something small and dark zigzagged through the air, too quick to follow.

"Wait," I said.

Bolton armed the launcher.

"*Now*, Torres! We've risked our necks for you long enough. *Now move!*" I backed away reluctantly, unable to give up on the password.

We'd turned toward the assembly building, northward, when a ripping sound began close by. The air filled with smoke, then Peters shouted. A line of flame was eating its way across the wall toward him.

Bolton moved his launcher and fired down the alley. With a *crump* and a rumbling concussion the flame went out. Someone backed into me. I fought to keep my grip on the case.

A dozen drones appeared at the end of the alley leading the other way, to the south. They were thicker and squatter than the one in the cage, and they wandered back and forth without apparent purpose, back and forth past the far entrance to the alley. Bolton fired again.

"All right, back it up. North, all of you. Torres, get a hold of Peters there and run like the devil!"

"South!" shouted another. "They're coming up from the south, too!" Tiny shapes flitted through the air.

"Get away—"

Someone fell as lances of blue flame shot into the square from the south. I grabbed Peters' arm and shook him out of his confusion, then the wall next to us exploded and crumbled. Peters' arm jerked in my hand and he stumbled. In the next instant Bolton sent us flying while something crashed to the ground where we'd been standing.

Peters dropped to his knees and groped for his cane. "Keep going," he said. He couldn't breathe properly. "Take your case and go." He looked back at Bolton. "I'll catch you up—oh Lord, laddie, no!"

He'd started to get up, but now seemed to fall again. He was bent over, clawing at a section of wall that had collapsed, barely visible under the layer of oily smoke. An arm stuck out from under the wall, just visible where the smoke parted, and a head of sandy hair. A walking stick.

"Hold up!" I shouted through the haze over the square. "We need medics!" The roar of flames and the *crump* of grenades answered out of the smoke, but no voices.

"Go," said Bolton, in a faint and unfamiliar voice.

Peters and I tried to lift the section of wall.

"No," said Bolton. "Torres, don't let him—"

Something darted past, and flames hissed in the rubble nearby. Peters wiped away the blood on Bolton's face.

It was a terrible face now, dark and contorted. The tendons stood out from the flesh as he tried to turn and see Peters.

"Colwyn," he said, or something that sounded like it. But his words were lost as more blood began to flow. He looked wildly around him for a moment, his hand groping for Peters', scrabbling in the dust like a claw. Then finally he lifted that awful, straining face upward, and there it remained.

Peters and I stared down at it, then backed away into the smoke, away from the heat. We lost sight of him as a new line of flame etched its way across the wall toward where he lay.

I stumbled into the alley leading north, one hand around Peters and the other on the case, shouting over my shoulder into the smoke behind us. "It's clear this way!" I said.

But it wasn't. Like rats sniffing along a sewer, sturdy-looking, charcoal-colored drones were approaching through the passage ahead of us. They were low to the ground and broad-backed, clearly higher-gravity models than before—either because of their base on the triply-heavy H-VI, or because earlier visitors to the black planet had recommended a sturdier design for the next attack. I eased the case around behind Peters' bent back, not knowing whether that was what they had come for—whether the drone in his cage had understood my message and described it. Peters stopped and leaned against the wall, unable to go on. Voices came from close behind us.

The drones moved toward us with a sort of elegant, fluid movement. They carried a variety of odd, compact devices in the hands extending from their backs. They must have had a policy of not incorporating their weapons into their own design, so that the weapons could be upgraded more often than the rest. In either case, it was a design and manufacturing cycle that was frighteningly short, even compared to the speed that manufacturing MI had reached on Earth.

A pair of shadows flickered through the air. One of them froze in front of us, a tiny vertical cylinder with a ring of grappling claws around its base. A gentle hissing sound—and whirlpools in the dust below it—indicated rockets or fans inside. The other one flitted on toward the commandos behind us. Watchers.

The drones up the alley ignored us. My ears popped again as pressure in the dome dropped, then suddenly an explosion lifted several of the drones into the air. Their shapes distorted wildly as they slammed into the nearby walls, but didn't rupture, as though sheathed in nanoskin. The tiny flying drone in front of us shot back up the alley toward the source of the grenade, then an instant later the remaining drones in front lit their burners even as they scrambled back to their feet.

Cries of pain and exploding masonry came from behind us. In front, between us and the vehicle assembly building, all of the headless drones, even the damaged ones, had remained upright during the grenade's explosion, stabilized by gyros, presumably. They had also fired their one, lethally accurate shot through clouds of blinding and burningly hot gas—the flying scouts were sighting for them.

"Go on, Eddie, get yourself back," said Peters. "You with your box there. Perhaps they'll let me draw them on while you slip through." Peters sank to his knees and stifled a hoarse cough as the surviving drones wandered up the alley toward us.

"No," I said. I pulled him to his feet as a drone brushed against my leg. It paid us no attention.

Larger scouts flew into the alley ahead of us and clamped themselves onto their immobilized fellows, then seconds later the alley was clear. The surviving drones walked off into the smoke and flames behind us.

Pham was the last one into the big vehicle assembly building. I pushed in just before her, dragging Peters past the crowds to the stairs, while she stood in the doorway pulling in the last of the commandos.

"Quick, quick! Inside! All you do good, but next time motion-guided, yah? Set shooters now—we go after little see-bugs next time, okay? Then we blow smoke, doggies don't see too good. Hey! You hurry up, okay? You—Tight-Buns! Move ass, maybe I let you kiss me what you think? Muzzles down—better you kill kids than you kill dome, hah?"

She slammed and bolted the door and I kicked the codes case in under the stairs, out of sight. I shifted Peters' weight and she joined me to help. She was still barefooted.

"Father Charlie!" she said, suddenly realizing he was there, "you hurt bad!" We got him up the clattering stairs and eased him down against the wall of the narrow mezzanine, where he closed his eyes.

"Michael's dead, lass," he said to her.

"No! You don't say that!"

"Aye. Saved our wretched little lives, he did, waiting out that lying bastard in its cage."

Pham turned to look at me, her eyes suddenly filling with tears. I looked away, and she knelt down next to Peters and pressed her hand against his side.

Peters gasped. "Aye, that's it, there. Took a bit o' the wall, I'm afraid. I'll be all right, though, lass, if you'll not be doing that again. Don't mind me."

The building's electric lights flickered and died, then came back on for a minute before dying out altogether. That left only the sunlight filtering through the windows, twisting with shadows as smoke rolled past.

A powerful baritone voice spoke on the floor below. "Give us room, please. We need some light, here, if you would move aside, please."

The vehicle assembly building was the one the Serenitas Probe had been launched from. It rose all the way to the dome, where it had its own retractable glass roof, a bright circle of sky high above us. The sun stood directly above it, and so shone down in a vertical shaft onto the floor below. Medics there tried to make room for a stretcher, which bore a woman with a white robe draped across her swollen belly. Drip bottles and monitors hung from the rail of the stretcher. Her hair was singed and her face bruised, injuries she'd apparently sustained during the attack.

A shrill chirping came from one of the monitors, then stopped with the slap of a switch. "I'm losing her again," said one of the medics. "She can't take any more moving around."

"All right, there...easy, now. Down easy." The baritone belonged to an enormous, black-skinned man who leaned down just then to look into her face.

"Fetal heart's down."

"Oxygen, please."

"Induce?"

"Can't afford the contractions...easy, now, there you go."

"We're going to need her back in surgery, you know that, don't you? Or some portable gear."

"You saw what it's like out there. Just hang on and wait. Let's see what happens." The woman cried out weakly, barely conscious.

Charlie Peters leaned forward with an effort and looked down at the medics in their dark green and the silent woman in white, and at the frightened faces of the farmers and clerks and machinists pressed in around them. He watched the activity in the circle of light for a moment, then leaned back against the wall.

"Father Charlie, you hurt more than you say." Pham got up. "I get medics, okay?"

"No." Peters put out a hand. "They'll be wasting their time on an old man like me. They've got more important work at hand."

Pham knelt down, and sat back on her heels with tears on her face. Whether for the mother and her baby, or for Peters, or for Michael Bolton, I couldn't tell.

For me, I couldn't believe Bolton was dead. Several times I found myself thinking he must be on the floor below, out of sight in the shadows beneath the mezzanine. But the only image I could bring to mind when I tried to think of his face was of the drone in its cage, watching as I passed through the smoke that last time.

"Do you have a radio, Mr. Torres?" A man was looking up at me from below.

"No, I'm sorry, I don't."

"We don't know what the situation is outside. We've got guns, but no radios."

"No, please." Pham moved quickly to the railing and looked down. "No guns unless no choice."

The man was skeptical. He held one hand against an arm heavily bandaged and soaked in blood. "Maybe."

Behind him a medic shielded her eyes from the sun overhead and leaned down to her instruments, then spoke quietly to the others. "We may have a choice here, guys."

"No," said the black man, cradling the woman's head in a giant hand. "She won't survive a section if we do it here. If we go ahead it's only to save the child."

"Christ. What a crummy, goddamned way to go."

"Yes. Ease her back up a little there."

Outside there was an explosion of masonry, out across Trinity Square. It wasn't clear what the drones were doing, unless they really were looking for the case hidden below. The case the prisoner had told them I had.

"Tuyet, lass." Peters had his hand clasped around the cross at his neck, and had been speaking to himself quietly. Now he opened his hand and held out to Pham a tiny, stoppered phial.

"Take this down and place a little on the woman's hand. There's a good lass. Two drops, if you would. One for the mother, and one for the child."

She took the phial and held it uneasily in her hand, and finally Peters reached out and folded her fingers around it. "Extreme unction," he said. "'Tis my duty as a priest. Go now." He leaned back against the wall and closed his eyes, then began to speak to her again. Pham stopped him.

"I know," she said. "The words, I know. Old priests in camps say them every day. Too many times." She went down the stairs and made her way through the packed bodies to the woman's side, and stepped into the circle of sunlight. She still wore only the thin white blouse tied above the waist, and her lightweight pants tied around her hips with a cotton string. She was out of place among the packed bodies with their heavy work clothes and uniforms and slung weapons.

One of the medics stopped her, not understanding what she was doing, but she spoke to him quietly and they both glanced up to where Peters sat. Then she knelt down next to the stretcher and worked a drop of the oil into the back of the woman's hand, speaking quietly. She looked at the woman for a moment then and hesitated, then returned up the steps and handed the phial to Peters.

"Not for the baby," she said.

"Well, then." He closed his eyes again.

None of us spoke for a quarter of an hour. Peters and I leaned against the outside wall while Pham knelt next to him. Indecipherable sounds came from outside, and tense voices from below. The medics were worried at some new sign of fetal distress.

"Well," said Peters quietly, "'tis a foolish life I've led, isn't it?" He lifted his head from the wall and nodded vaguely with his eyes half open. "Tramping about with a bottle o' ointment in my waistcoat, waiting for something grand. For the sound o' trumpets, a fine, blue ribbon for virtue at the close of a mean little life. But there's no ribbon out here in the black, is there? Just cold."

"Father—"

"Claiming a calling from God like some poor novice dressing up the abbot before his vows. A cowardly man is the truth, afraid to leave his mark like other men. Prattling on about fine Christian principle. 'Tis the height o' arrogance, don't you think, a man contriving a god so he can tell himself he's been chosen by him, that he's been vouched for in some high purpose? But what is it I've done, really, except meddle like an old man?"

"Father, you've done—"

But he wasn't listening.

"And here I am now with an eye against the black and my faith shriveling up like a virgin's womb, saying if there's a god, why don't I feel him, why can't I reach out and touch his face, now when I'm in need of it, when it's so cold—"

Pham had reached up to unfasten the buttons of her blouse, and now she lifted Peters' creased old hand and pushed aside her collar with it. She moved it down to rest over her heart, his palm open against her bare skin. Peters closed his eyes and leaned slowly back.

I walked to the railing to watch the medics below. One sponged the woman's forehead while another tried to fit a pressure bottle onto an air syringe. Her hands were shaking, and she couldn't get it on. A big black hand reached across to take it and finish the job.

I moved to the window. Drones wandered across Trinity Square, some of them milling around the doors to our building. Beyond the wall of the dome more ships had landed, and the black, midday sky above was filled with them as they spread farther out across the landscape. No help would be coming soon from the fleet; if it was true that the drones overlooked unarmed and non-threatening vessels, still, no one would have the courage to fly any down— and unarmed ships would do us little good, in any case. Our only chance lay in slipping out to the remaining shuttles, or waiting out the attack—assuming it would ever end. But pressure continued to drop under the dome, outside the building, and we had no suits.

A shout came from below.

"Flutter on the mother. Skip! Two...three..."

"Massage, keep it high."

"...six, seven..."

"Fetal's dropping. We're losing the baby, people."

"All right, here we go. Here to here, there's your mark. Sponge with the gown."

"You two, hold her down. There's no anesthetic."

"Longer cut...all right, there's the wall. Convulsions..."

"Baby's heart's gone! He can't take that."

"All right, get to the cord *first*, the minute you see it in here. And then you—yes, you, that whole bottle there into the mother. The minute they've got the cord. Okay, right lumbar—get ready to turn her."

Charlie Peters sat forward a little next to me so he could see.

"Eddie," he said.

I sat down and he put a hand on my arm. He didn't say anything more, but just watched the activity below.

"Got the cord—barely clamped."

"Turn the mother. All right, *now*, Atropine."

"Okay, there's the head...I don't like that color."

"A boy—did she know?"

"Yes. Suction! Again. Okay, that doesn't look too bad. Oxygen now, blow it in."

"Sixty-five seconds since he went out—he needs air..."

"There he goes! All right, son, give us another one like that one. Another breath. God Almighty, there you go. If you can keep that up you'll be all right."

"I wish those legs looked better. He isn't ever going to walk on them, I'll tell you that."

"Yeah, well, I just wish he had a mother."

"God, look at him take that air—that's enough of a miracle. One minute of life and counting."

Charlie Peters next to me shook his head. "No," he said. "No, he's always been alive. He's only waking from a dream, is all...a dream about God. 'Tis a dream he'll forget, though, as the days pass. Just like the rest of us."

A medic swaddled the baby while another lifted the stretcher's sheet up over the mother. No one else in the building spoke.

And in the middle of the floor, in the center of the circle of pale white light shining down from above, the baby struggled to open his eyes. And next to me, Peters closed his.

"A dream about God," he said again. His grip on my arm loosened and he turned a little to one side.

Charlie Peters died in Pham's arms without another word. And at that same moment, down on the floor below, the baby cried out once and then was quiet again.

I walked away. Near the window I stopped and looked back.

I looked at the baby, held now in the arms of the great black man below. I looked at Peters, quiet at last. And I looked at Pham, gazing down at him with tears in her eyes, stroking his brow.

Each of the three was alone in that great, cold building, I thought, surrounded outside by the drones and by the empty wastelands farther out still. Each was alone, and in some way not alone. And not one of the three was aware of me at all, there where I stood looking back at them from the window.

"Mr. Torres? Eddie?"

I'd fallen asleep. Peters' body had been moved into a corner and covered with a blanket. Pham stood by the window in the afternoon light, whispering to me. I watched her for a minute before answering.

"Yes?" I said.

"Come look." She made room for me at the window.

The square was empty. Smoke hung in the sunlight, indicating that there was at least some air left in the dome. The fleet of black ships still waited across the wastes, although there seemed to be no more activity near the dome.

"How long will it last?" I said. "We need to go out and find a trailer, and pull it up against the building. Then if we can load it up and slip it out through the tunnel, we can reach the shuttles. They still look intact."

"Yah, okay. Let's go." She flitted down the steps in her bare feet, then with a brief word to the nervous guards at the doors we cracked them open and she and I slipped out into Trinity Square. We were helped through by a sharp gust of air from the pressure behind.

It was strangely quiet in the aftermath of the attack. The afternoon sun slanted through the haze, and the air stank from the fires and bit our nostrils with the stench of burned power cells. Even without the smoke it was difficult to breathe; the air had become too thin by now, still leaking out faster than the converters could replenish it. If they were running at all.

"Pham, listen. I think there's a trailer behind the barracks, but if all the cells have been destroyed, then none of the tractors is going to work. We're going to have to try and bring the shuttles in through the lock, or else pull their cells out for the tractors—and either way it's going to attract attention. Otherwise we have to send everybody out to the shuttles two or three at a time in the only suits we have. Christ, what a mess." I was whispering, at the same time tightening the ablative armor under my tunic. It was too quiet.

"So, okay, we look around," she said out loud. She seemed unreasonably lighthearted.

"Look for what?"

"I don't know. The horse, maybe he learn to sing, what you think?" She started off across the square, flitting in and out of the slanting shadows, looking unbearably vulnerable in the little she wore. I moved to catch up with her, digging my boots into the dust, studying the few glimpses I could get of the waiting drone ships out past the dome.

"Tell me something, Pham," I said as I caught up. "I thought you hated Peters."

"No, I never hate him," she said. "I treat him pretty bad, though, poor guy."

"Poor guy? You seem pretty cheerful for being sorry for him."

She stopped and faced me. "He dead, Mr. Eddie. While you asleep in there maybe I cry a lot, make stupid noises, but he dead now. Before, I waste a lot of time, I think, so I say okay, but now not so much left. So come on, we see what we find."

I thought about it while we looked into the recreation center, and poked around through the piles of equipment Polaski had left behind in the barracks. Some of it was intact and some of it burned in two, but there were no undamaged power cells or suits. In the roadway leading along the dome wall to the rear of the barracks we found the empty troop trailer, apparently intact but with no tractor. "Damn it, Pham, the air in that building isn't even going to last the night; we don't have time for this. We have to find a radio that's—"

"Eddie, why we got— Look." She pointed at the control box for the air lock tunnel, where a pair of red lights glowed steadily. I'd seen them earlier, but hadn't stopped to wonder why. The tunnel's outside doors, at its far end, were open. "Come on," she said, "you stand on far side—*no*, no gun. Bad mistake. Just we get out of the way, okay?"

I moved to one side of the inner doors while she stood at the other, forty feet away, and pressed the controls to close the outer door. The lights started to blink.

"Still got full power!" she called out, and I cringed at the sound of her voice echoing through the dome. A moment later the lights went to green, and with a hissing of air the inner door trundled into its frame. When it thumped to a stop the square was finally quiet again, and we both looked carefully around the edge of the frame.

A tractor stood facing us in the center of the dimly lit tunnel, its electric motors idling quietly. One of its doors stood open, and beneath it the driver lay sprawled on the ground, suffocated in the vacuum. The passenger in the cab sat slumped against the dash. Pham walked up to me quietly and put a hand on my arm.

"Stephanie," she said. "And Robert Kune. Robert was Michael's lover, did you know? They go to Asile together, soon. Why they open tractor door when tunnel still open to the outside? Please, tell me why they do that."

"They wouldn't, Pham. In any case, the doors wouldn't have let them. The tunnel had to be sealed at the time, and they must have been getting out to trigger the manual controls."

"But who open the tunnel from outside. Drones?"

"Maybe the drones are sending out control signals now. On purpose or by accident, I don't know. Come on, we have to get their suits, and then move the tractor into the dome."

We struggled together to peel the suits from the two rigid bodies, trying not to look at their faces. Stephanie Teal had been caught under one of the tires, where she'd been blown during the explosive decompression—her eyes wide with surprise, her mouth open in her last struggle for air. In the cab, Robert Kune's eyes were closed and his face relaxed, an exquisitely handsome young man whose Nigerian parents had joined us from the Christian colony on Boar River. All I could think of as I looked at him was that now there were more visits to be made, more calls to be put through; I was beginning to feel like I was swimming through a dream, through a world of shadows and mirage where none of this had happened, where Peters hadn't died—

"Let's go, Pham, we'll check the suits later." I was also becoming more and more aware of the drones somewhere outside the air lock's thin doors. "We have to move this tractor—that outer door could open again any—"

I was cut off by a distant *whoosh* and an explosion, then the peculiar ripping sound of pulse lasers. It was coming from inside the dome, not outside. "Grenades—at close quarters! Where in the hell?"

We spun around to look back at the tall assembly building. The square in front of it was still empty, but in the alley alongside the building we could see drones moving near its far corner.

"Why they using *guns*? No!" A bluish light flickered suddenly in the building's windows, and then all at once it grew brighter as weapons began to fire back. *"Noooo!"* Pham started to run for the building, but I grabbed her arm and held her back as more drones appeared around the side of the building and wandered into the square.

"There's nothing you can do! Somebody must have seen the drones coming back and gotten nervous. Come on, we're going to be trapped in this tunnel. We have to get out of the square."

From inside the assembly building came the roaring sounds and the flickering lights of a pitched battle in the enclosed space, and as we walked quickly toward the corner of the barracks, a portion of the assembly building's first floor wall began to glow and then disintegrate.

"Please, no!" Pham leaned against a corner of the barracks and hugged herself, staring at the horrible spectacle in what had been our last sanctuary. "Everyone in there, they all die like that— *piece-of-shit bastards!*" Tears ran down her face as she hugged herself tighter and watched. "So why they do it, hah? They want your case with codes, or what?" Drones wandered toward us across the square.

"No. If they'd seen me take it in, and knew what it was, then they had their chance long before now. One of our people must have just opened the door and started firing."

A window high in the building blew out in a high-pitched shattering of glass, and heavy black smoke poured out behind it and rose to gather in the top of the dome.

"Oh, God no, nobody stay alive in there!" As she spoke, one of the drones' miniature scouts streaked toward us where we stood by the barracks and then stopped abruptly in a nearby window, gripping the sill with its tiny claws. A four-legged drone wandered up to us, its weapon held at the end of its compact arm, and Pham grabbed at my arm to stop me as I reached for my gun. But the drone just pushed between the wall and Pham's legs, and after stepping around the corner for a moment it started back the way it had come, the little flying scout taking off after it. Apparently neither of them had noticed the tractor idling inside the open lock tunnel.

At the far end of the square, drones walked out of the assembly building through the collapsed wall, followed by new clouds of smoke. Several more were carried out in the grapples of the larger flying cylinders, then after a few minutes the square was empty again.

For a long time we stood and watched the smoke trickle out of the distant building and then finally die away. Pham wiped at her eyes and turned away from the square, walking up the perimeter road past the barracks, washed in the late sun and casting a long shadow on the wall. When I caught up with her she leaned back against the wall, and faced into the sun to watch me.

"A little while ago," she said finally, "I think I want to ask you why they all come here, why you take such a big chance, why you wait too long with Michael and Father Peters, why you make such big mistakes—why all my friends dead."

I sat down on the trailer's coupling and studied her as she spoke, the dark eyes in the delicate face, the high cheekbones and the small, flat nose and full lips, the low sun bathing her skin and turning it a soft white. She wasn't expecting me to answer, and I knew there was nothing I could say, in any case.

"But I know, easy to get crazy thinking how things maybe should be different, blaming Eddie Torres because everything just the same. Long time I hate you, you know. Always I want to be just like you, strong and okay all the time, so I hate you. But nobody's fault. Friends dead, okay, very sad for me. Nobody's fault." She looked away.

We stayed like that for a time, watching the drone ships on the horizon glinting in the sun. Occasionally a ship would arrive or depart, or move along the horizon, around toward the east side of the dome.

"You want to dance?" she said. She'd moved away from the wall, and stood on her toes with her arms out, casting a sharp, clean shadow against the dusty bricks.

"No."

She began to dance nevertheless, tiny and poised, turning in slow circles as her shadow followed, her feet whispering across the ground. The sunlight glowed against her skin through her blouse, outlining first her shoulders, then her breasts and her arms as she turned. On and on she went, eyes closed, until finally she stopped and hugged herself, opening her eyes to look up at the dome.

"Hard to breathe," she said.

I followed her eyes, and after a minute looked back out across the surface at the ships. "All I wanted to do was stop them," I said.

"Well, then," interrupted a crisp, new voice suddenly, "you should have asked them nicely, shouldn't you?" It was Bolton's voice. We both spun to look.

"Up here, if you please."

"Jesus! Little Bolton." The grasshopper drone's front end hung over the edge of the barrack's roof. "What are you doing up there?"

"I'm a coward. What are you doing down there?"

"I wish we knew. How did you get up there?"

"I jumped. You know how splendidly good I am at altitude, Mr. Torres. It's only forward momentum that's a bit shy."

"Um, right. What do you mean, we should have asked them nicely?"

"Why, with the password, of course."

Pham and I looked at each other. I got to my feet slowly. "What password, Little Bolton?" My mouth was dry.

"The one Ms. Miller always used to make us do what she wanted. What other password could you mean? Surely you know."

"No. We don't. We used every number and spec there is, Little B., and this is what happened. What password?"

"China Moon."

My heart was beating too loudly. The thin air was becoming hard to suck into my lungs. "Pham, the tractor. We're going to back it up to the assembly building. Slowly, putting the suits on as we go. The case is hidden underneath the far staircase; I'm sure they didn't find it. Move quietly and try not to look at anything else. We'll leave the tractor running and both go in together. Now."

We took turns holding the wheel as we wriggled into the suits, leaving just the helmets on the seat when we stepped down quietly and pushed open the main doors into the building.

It was fortunate for us that the inside of the building was in shadow now, because from what little we could see it looked like the bloodbath Becker had described at Wallneck. The horror of it grew in me as I sensed the blood around my feet and the burned flesh and the dismembered bodies. Pham moved ahead of me, stepping gingerly among the burned masonry and the bodies, while I tried to follow in her footsteps and looked around carefully at the open doors and the holes in the walls.

"Pham—drones!" Several of them had walked quietly in through the rear door, moving idly toward the staircases. "Keep going! I'm going around over the mezzanine!"

I worked my way back as quickly as I could and raced up the steps as Pham pushed her way forward. A piece of the building's wall in front of her suddenly glowed and then crumbled inward, and more drones stepped in over the bricks. "Hurry, Pham!"

I tore my way up the stairs, tugging at the rail as I went, and then launched myself across the mezzanine, trying to keep sight of Pham as she hurried toward the back wall and the stairs. And then suddenly I twisted and fell, smashing into the railing to keep from running into half a dozen more drones that stood perfectly still in front of me, blocking my way.

"Pham! I can't get through up here. Hurry!" I clawed my way around to avoid the drones as they moved toward me, and tried to keep Pham in sight at the same time. She was moving faster than the drones down below, just a few feet away from where the corner of the case showed from under the stairs, and she was beginning to bend down to reach for it.

"You're still clear, Pham! Go! You've got it!" I scrambled backwards.

It was just as Pham's fingertips touched the case, as one of the drones raised its weapon to fire at her, that the baby cried.

Chapter Twenty-five: TEARS ON THE EARTH,
A CHILD IN THE HEAVENS

Here, I must pause in my story. For when I think back to that dark afternoon, I am overcome by the magnitude of the events that were about to occur, and by the sense of disaster that was to fall across me because of them. But I know that it was not my own story I'd meant to tell, so I collect my thoughts and tell myself I must do my best to remember the day as it truly was.

I look back, then, and see myself surrounded by those dark walls at that moment, by the iron flooring and stairs. I see the drones in front of me, waiting, I don't know what for. But they are preventing me from crossing the chamber to the stairs where the case is hidden. The railing is cold and rough in my hands.

Pham is below me. She is leaning forward a little at the waist, knees bent, and her hand is around the handle of the case.

But she is not looking at it. She is looking the other way, over her shoulder. Looking for the source of the cry. Her eyes move carefully, probing among the shapes on the floor.

Then she is moving.

"Pham," I say. I want her to return to the case, want her hand to close again around the handle of it and never let it go.

I grasp the railing with both hands and lean as far out as I can.

"Pham, the case. We have to have the case."

But she doesn't hear me. I strain forward until I'm well out over the bay, screaming at her inside. But there is nothing I can do, and my despair only grows.

In the center of the floor there is the shape of a man in a white coat. He is on his knees, bent forward. Underneath him, his great, black hand holds a breathing mask, immovable in his dying grip, around the face of the infant. Tiny hands reach around it, moving one way and then the other, looking for warmth.

Pham takes the man's arm and tries to pull it away, then glances back at the stairway. The drone has lowered its weapon.

The man's arm comes free. Pham lifts the infant, and now she is comforting it, holding it close to her.

"Come," she says. Whether to me or the infant, I do not know, but she is leaving.

The drones on the mezzanine next to me move closer. It is Peters' body I had touched, there behind them. It is no longer covered by the blanket. I back away down the stairs, careful of my footing, and turn to follow Pham.

Then I stop. I can still make it, I think. I take a step into the room, then stop again as the horror finally fills me with its full force.

The building is dark, a place out of the underworld. Smoke drifts across the corpses while the drones wander among them like sentinels over the dead. And somewhere beyond them, lost in the darkness, is the case. The one that would have brought us past the final hurdle in our journey, the one that would have finally brought us peace. The one for which I now have the password.

Pham waits for me in the doorway. She has opened her suit and placed the infant against her stomach, then closed the material around him. It is as though she means to bear the child again, herself. She holds out a hand to me.

I pushed the tractor's throttle all the way forward.

"Damn it, Pham, you could have had the case."

She adjusted the airflow to her suit. "This more important."

"More important than a million lives? Our futures were in that case, Pham."

"Futures, yah. Baby here now." She reached out to close her door, then pointed. "Look!"

Little Bolton was pumping his six legs across the square as fast as he could, while drones with their weapons moved around behind him. Others wandered toward the air lock tunnel in front of us.

"He's not going to make it," I said. "And I can't stop." I tapped the throttle lever to make sure it was all the way open. The distance between us and Little Bolton dropped to fifty yards, then forty. His blunt front end was low to the ground, all six legs pumping frantically, kicking up a trail of black dust that rushed eastward toward the breach.

Off to our other side a dim beam glowed briefly from one of the drone's weapons, aimed in our direction, then suddenly the tractor slued as one of the wheel motors froze up. Pham slammed home the seals on my helmet while I fought the tractor back on course, then just as Little Bolton disappeared under the wheels Pham reached out through her open door. There was a blur of movement and then Pham was dragging the little grasshopper drone into the cab amid a thrashing of legs and a muffled screaming I couldn't hear through my helmet. Pham pressed the door controls then turned on my suit radios.

"—of little faith! Oh, *ye* of little faith! And you thought I couldn't jump! 'Done in a table,' he says! 'How did you get up on that roof,' he says! Oh my, look at me, look at me, ten feet that must have been. Ten feet!"

I turned the wheel, and with a *thump* we rolled over one of the drones. We were into the lock tunnel.

"Eddie, look out!" Pham pointed to the rear-view screen where twin lances of flame slid across the ground toward our tunnel.

"Down!" Something burst into the cab behind us and the air filled with smoke, then in the next instant the tractor hit the outer door of the air lock at full speed with the inner door still open. The tractor staggered for an instant then lifted completely off the ground and shot forward, driven by the wall of air from the dome's decompression. Debris and equipment and drones shot past us in a cloud of freezing vapor, which turned the surface into a blinding world of white as it sparkled in the dying sun.

I groped for Pham's helmet to swing home the ring, then pulled it up against my visor so I could see her pressure readings through the mist. They steadied just as our burning motor and the crashing of the debris went silent and the mist dissipated. The tractor slued sideways one last time and rose up on its edge before settling to a stop. For an instant neither of us moved, then I was pulling Little Bolton and Pham down the ladder. She held a hand under the swell of the baby in the front of her suit.

"No, Eddie," she said, "we go this way. We need an unarmed shuttle."

Inside the supply shuttle she'd chosen she peeled off her suit while I maneuvered the craft around to the west side of the dome then gradually upward. The plains below were strewn with ships and large areas of bewildering activity. Drone ships came and went, but none paid us attention and only a few moved toward the blown-out dome to see what had happened.

The baby cried as Pham tried to get the tip of a water bottle into his mouth, then finally he was quiet as he sucked.

"We need milk," said Pham. "Eight hours old, nothing. How long we got?"

"An hour before we reach the ships."

I called Elliot and gave him the news, that I was returning with nothing more than a password, and Pham with an infant. Elliot was to have Susan Perris prepare milk and a neonatal exam, and beyond that we would talk when we reached the fleet.

The fleet, Elliot told me, the civilian fleet with the can in tow, was moving into a slow orbit toward the now-deserted inner moon of the fifth planet, where it was felt we would be safe in the abandoned Indian mines.

I pushed away the microphone.

"So," I said to Pham. "What now?"

I felt drained and bitter, scarcely interested in going on. I'd been awake for twenty-six hours with too little to eat, and too many people had died. I'd failed.

Pham had turned all of the heaters and lights on in the back of the shuttle, and now she sat in the center of the glow with the baby wrapped in a silver emergency blanket, held awkwardly against her as he sucked at the water bottle. She adjusted his position off and on, trying to hold his head up with her good arm.

"Why we got to do anything?" she said.

I looked at her.

"What about the drones?"

"Hell with drones. I know, Empty-Eyes got big plan now, I bet, all fleets, everybody new guns, try to kill little dead drones forever. But you not so stupid, hah? Got person inside, maybe. Leave

Empty-Eyes alone, Eddie, go someplace nice. West side of Boar River, nice place. Maybe you go there, hah?" ·

"You're pretty cheerful."

"Why not? I got nice company. Anyway, today maybe last day we got, and kid should have good time."

I thought about that for a while.

"What about the drones?" I said.

"What you care about drones! Drones be here forever, nothing we can do to change it."

The baby choked. In a panic Pham hit him on the back, only to set off a new round of crying.

The drones, with all their power, I thought, will indeed become a constant of colonized space. There will be nothing that can change it. But it was hard to accept.

"Life full of stupid things," she said, "and most stupid things we make, hah? Like drones. Nothing we do can change it, so what you care? Get China-Girl, go someplace nice."

"We still have to do something about the drones, Pham. Are you just going to wish them away?"

"No! Why you got to fight? You no fight, they no fight. Don't beat head on the wall all the time, hah? Maybe smart choice I make in there, leaving box behind. Now pretty soon drones make everybody stop fighting. I think not so much coincidence, Ice-Lady's little password."

"What do you mean?"

"If she picked big important number for password like everybody think, then you find it and get all hard-on powerful again, hah? But for one time in her life, Ice-Lady pick something pretty. So instead, we find baby. So, good, finished. Everybody go someplace nice. Some people even taking little farmer-boats through torus to new planet. You go there, too, maybe."

The thought of taking a ship into the maw of the drones' forces at the torus again was chilling. Especially in an unarmed trading boat. Our own past experience, together with the vestiges of the terrible destruction that had befallen the Europeans, spoke against traveling into the tunnel before the drones were completely defeated. No matter what prize waited at the other end.

"Eddie?" said Pham.

"Yes." The infant was quiet on her shoulder. His eyes were almost half open. He had a well-formed face, with olive skin and black hair, and dark eyes. His lips were moist from the water, and were opened slightly where his cheek pressed against Pham's shoulder.

"Thank you," she said.

My mind was still on the tunnel.

"Why?"

"Before," she said, "when we try to go through tunnel to Serenitas you saved my life. I pretty mad, so I not say thank you."

"Why mad?"

"Yah. You such perfect person, always okay, always important guy, then you almost get killed saving crazy person—"

"You're not—"

"No, it's okay. It's true, I pretty crazy sometimes. Stephanie, she say I got to tell you thank you, but always I say no, later. But now it's time. So, thank you."

The baby's eyes fell closed.

Hull Zero-Zero floated among the few remaining ships of the civilian fleet, heavily patched from the damage of the year before. Its engines flickered at a meager tenth of a G to save precious fuel and power cells. Nearby drifted Bolton's ships, with skeleton crews under the command of Roscoe Throckmorton. And far below us—or behind us—a ring of eight ships in their landing configuration under the command of Priscilla Bates, towed the giant orbital can, home to the orphans and now an orphan itself.

We were on a gentle five-month climb to the fifth planet, where Polaski had set up camp by the abandoned Indian mines. He'd called for a gathering of the powers in the system in order to disclose a stunning discovery he said had been made about the drones, and to implement a new plan of attack that hinged on it.

Among all of those to whom I'd had to break the news of Peters' and Bolton's deaths, Kip had surprised me by being the most upset. From that moment on, in fact, he stayed close to me, following me where I went and sleeping nearby, sometimes sitting and watching me for hours with an odd intensity. He became like a shadow to me after a time, and now and then it seemed as though, as he watched me, his face reflected thoughts I was at that very moment having. I would notice that his eyes had filled with tears, only to realize that I had myself been thinking about Charlie Peters' old face, or recalling the gentle Gaelic rhythms of his voice. Then sometimes I would wonder at an apprehension in Kip's eyes, only to realize that I'd been thinking again about drifting unarmed through the tunnel to Serenitas, the way Pham had said.

But mostly Kip just watched me, and mostly I just sat and brooded about the lost case and about the password, and about the green and blue planet we could no longer reach. Or about Polaski's plan.

At first Chan seemed less affected by the news, but after a time it seemed as though she'd finally lost whatever spark had been left in her. She still spent her time working in the children's quarter of the can, but no longer with any great interest.

Pham, on the other hand, had pretty much disappeared.

Elliot toiled unenthusiastically to keep the fleet running. He spent his spare time alone with Perris, or else in desultory radio conversations with acquaintances around the system.

"I'm leaving the fleet after the conference, Torres," he told me one day. "Me and Susan. We're going to try Boar River, helping out on a farm, maybe. Grew up on a farm." He didn't look at me as he told me, and I didn't answer him.

Later that day he was on the MI decks with his feet up and his eyes closed, and his hands behind his head. *Sweet Lord*, he sang, *come and take your angel, lyin' on the banks of Jordan....*

It was Elliot who brought me the news about the torus here in Holzstein's System.

"They've rotated it. The drones. First time in sixteen years it's pointed anywhere but Serenitas, and now they've rotated it and sent more'n six hundred ships through it—some special kind of ship they been building down on our old base."

"Rotated it where, Tyrone?"

He looked away, and in that moment he looked more tired than I'd ever seen him.

"Earth," he said.

The following day the torus was turned back toward Serenitas, as though nothing had happened. It remained under heavy guard by the drones.

Nearly a month later, after four months in space, I finally ran across Pham. One of the eight ships in Bates' ring still had its original gardens, and I found her at the very top level of them, where an open plot of grass baked under artificial sunlight, surrounded by a hedge. I'd gone to the gardens meaning only to visit the lower levels for a moment, but a lullaby was filtering down from above with a familiar tune. I started up the path to see, Kip following behind.

Your tears, you whisper, like rain
Have washed away your dreams...

Near the top of the spiraling path the bright sun above trickled down through the foliage, and Pham's voice became clearer, singing with the same minor tones and lilting inflection her speech always carried, giving the lullaby an odd and haunting sound.

So take me along with a kiss for your fears;
They're old friends and bring me no harm.

It was the same tune I'd heard more than twenty years ago, from Kip's flute, the one he still played when he thought he was alone. And finally I placed it. The tune I'd heard in the darkness after the theft, the one Pham was singing now, was a lullaby my mother had sung, too.

Tus lágrimas, como la lluvia...

Pham was sitting on the grass in the bright sunlight, leaning back against a carrying bag. She wore only the briefest of shorts and an open blouse, her eyes closed and the baby at her breast, her skin shining with oil.

She opened her eyes when we reached the head of the path.

"So," she said. "We there already?" She shifted the baby and sat up straighter, pulling the blouse a little closer around her. "No, is okay, Eddie, don't go. Sit, make company, yah? Where's China-Girl?"

I sat across from her while Kip dropped down in the grass to look at the baby. Pham watched him for a moment, then looked back at me with a hint of amusement. "So! Your face all full of 'how she do that?' I think. Needle-Lady, she make estradiol-something out of nothing, put it in all right places. Baby healthy, what you think?"

"He looks fine. No, we're not there yet. We're still a month out."

The baby heard my voice and turned around, and with a gurgle and a shriek of excitement squirmed out of Pham's arms and onto the grass, not about to be put to sleep. Under the low thrust he pushed himself onto his hands easily and pulled himself forward, his undersized legs working behind him as best they could. His dark eyes were wide and shining with the adventure, and he smiled, dribbling bits of milk as he babbled his way across to Kip. Kip put down his flute solemnly and lifted the baby into the air, soft and pink against his smooth black hands.

Pham lifted her arms over her head and stretched luxuriously, her face tanned and relaxed, framed by jet black hair cut short in front and long in the back. She leaned back on her hands and slid a foot closer to her to raise one knee, her feet bare and her blouse still open.

"So, you," she said to me. "If we still got month left, why we go all this way, chasing goose, hah? Old mines bad place, all cold."

"We have to work out a plan with the rest of the system, Pham. That's what the conference is for."

She leaned back a little further and shook her head. "Nah, you just follow Empty-Eyes all the time, like he got something. What's he got, Eddie?"

"He's learned something about the drones."

"Hah! You don't be so stupid, he just say that. You tell Polaski, go suck his own pecker, hah? Why we go all this way for shithead like him?"

She sighed and lay all the way back. "Ah, Eddie, you still got no balls."

I'd been looking for Chan when I heard Pham's lullaby, and later that day I finally found her in a berth on the can, just waking up.

No one followed ship's time any longer; the lights were simply kept half dimmed while people wandered in and out of sleep on any schedule. Especially in the cavernous can this created a sense of unreality, as flying platforms rose and fell through the dim central corridor, no longer horizontal now but a quarter-mile-deep, vertical shaft.

I'd come to ask Chan one more time if there was a chance the fleet MI could reconstruct the lost communications codes, given that it had once used them. But she wouldn't discuss it.

"Why don't you just find someone like Bolton and go back and get your codes, then," she said.

"Bolton's dead, Chan."

"I know, Eddie, I know. So are you. So are we all."

That night, for the last time, I dreamed about being in the cavern underground. The tunnel was still there, and in it the demon was still waiting. Someone still watched from my shoulder, and a figure still stood in front of me, slowly raising his hand. But the figure's face was clear this time. It was my own.

The last time I saw Pham on that trip she was standing by a porthole on one of the iron ships, with the baby asleep in her arms. She was looking out into the darkness with tears on her cheeks. For old friends, she said, and for friends she'd never had.

Then we were on the cold moon of the fifth planet, preparing for the conference. The ground shook with the roar of more ships arriving, while unfamiliar faces rushed past in the causeways interconnecting the old mining structures, carrying papers and memory blocks and terminals, some people still wearing their ship's suits and hull boots as the heaters struggled to warm the air.

Visible from the windows of the main causeway, smaller causeways snaked out across the pitted surface to the mining control towers—tall, hollow buildings with glass windows in their upper floors, from which the surface robots had once been directed. The weak light from the distant sun, now a tiny disk in the black, washed across the towers and filtered into the causeways, illuminating faded Devanagari characters at the intersections and complicated warnings in Prakrit over the air locks. Iron bars ran the length of the ceilings, welded haphazardly into place as handholds—gravity on the tiny moon was so low that without hull clamps people tended to float away from the floor and drift.

Polaski spent several days attending to his units after their return from the campaign on the sixth planet, and occasionally he met privately with Bart Allerton and the other emissaries. But we didn't meet formally until three days later. It was the first time since Boar River that I'd come face to face with Allerton.

The conference table was a long, single slab of steel, tapering near the ends, gleaming faintly in the watery light from the sun and the stars shining through the windows. Thirty chairs were pulled up to the table, one end of which was reserved for Polaski and the other for Allerton. More chairs lined the walls, set aside for aides and observers. Each place at the table was marked with a neat vellum pad, and a water decanter and cup made from real glass.

The participants milled about deciding on places, or else peering out the narrow strip of windows at the wild hills and strip mines on the surface, turning back toward the room now and then to shake hands and squint at one other in the bad light. Near the door, a boy in a grey and black uniform worked studiously on the electrical box that controlled the lighting, finally giving it up with a frown and sitting back down next to Polaski. Though nearly full-grown, the boy was less than five feet tall, heavy and broad in the shoulder, with expressionless eyes.

Polaski, dressed in a grey and black uniform like the boy's, reached for a phone and summoned a technician who came and worked futilely on the lighting box. He also gave it up, much to Polaski's disgust.

I chose a place a good three or four away from Allerton's end of the table, between Chan to my right and an impatient Lal Singh the Younger to my left. Across from me sat Elliot, who left the room for a moment to bring back an extra chair, which he squeezed in next to him for Susan Perris. Polaski glared at him.

"Piss off, Polaski," said Elliot. He looked tired, with the hair at his temples flecked with grey and his eyes restless. More and more in the past few days he'd been talking about his plans to go to Boar River with Perris, about the details of farming, but the rest of the time he fidgeted, keeping up his good humor only with an effort.

"Well! Hello there!" Allerton made his entrance and shook hands all around. "Madame Tonova, Mr. Singh, Excellency. Fine weather we're having, fine weather. Fine morning. What, no lights? We're going to play fondle-your-neighbor under the table, are we? Well, all right, sounds good. How 'bout that? Ed, good to see you!" He leaned across the table to shake hands.

I looked at the carefully groomed white hair, at the pale eyes and the sincere smile hovering in the gloomy light, then I looked away. Why was I here?

"What's the matter, boy-o, cat got your tongue? Well, that's all right, Ed, you'll sober up after a while. Take my word for it!" He took back his hand and moved to pull back his chair, carefully tugging at the knees of his trousers before sitting down. No one sat in the chairs around the corners of the table from him.

Polaski pulled a garish chrome and brass gavel from his pocket and smacked it hard against the table, then tossed it out in front of him. The impact from the blow, however, had caused him to rise up out of his seat, and he had to grip the table to stay down.

"I wish to speak!" Lal Singh the Younger stood up next to me and stared importantly at Polaski.

Polaski ignored him. "Where's Pham?" he said. "I want her present and accounted for from now on."

Singh looked around the table in confusion, thinking the question was for him.

In the meantime, decanters clinked against glasses and chairs scraped against the iron floor as they were pulled closer. Aides against the wall coughed and shuffled their papers.

"Sit down, Singh," said Allerton, brushing a hand at him in dismissal. "We've got the future of all mankind in our hands here, and we don't have time for grandstanding."

Singh remained upright.

"Maybe," I called down to Polaski, "you didn't invite her."

"So who do you think you are, Torres?" he said. "Go get her."

I went on watching him without answering. I didn't get up. After a minute the silence grew awkward. Singh sat down slowly and peered myopically around the table as the seconds dragged past.

Then finally I screeched my chair back and stood, angry at myself for doing it but at the same time not wanting to be in the room any longer. I walked around behind Allerton and pushed my way through the door. The shouting started up again as the door closed, then the door clicked shut and I was left in the quiet corridor, wondering where to start looking for Pham.

I looked into the dormitories and stood for a while in the vehicle bays, half-heartedly counting suits and tractors, not sure what it would tell me, then finally I went to the windows of the main causeway and stared out at the hellish surface.

It was while I was standing there that a motion caught my eye in one of the distant control towers. For a while when I looked I didn't see anything more, but then something white flickered in the upper windows. A full minute later it was there again. I made my way toward the narrow causeway leading out to the tower.

At the end of the twisting, windowless causeway, the dim recesses of the lowest floor of the control tower appeared at the end, emptied of equipment and abandoned. Barely visible in the center of the floor was Pham, facing away from me with her hands above her head, looking straight up. Then, by the time I reached the doorway to the tower, she was bending down with the baby in her arms, holding him near the floor.

Suddenly, with a shriek of delight from the child, she straightened up and flung him into the air. He rose higher and higher, rolling head over heels through the air in slow motion. Ten feet up he rose, then twenty, then suddenly he sailed into the sunlight spilling through the windows, catching the light as he somersaulted among the glittering motes of dust, laughing with delight. Forty, fifty feet into the air, slower and slower he tumbled, rolling through the light with his limbs waving in every direction. Then he was hanging motionless in the air, sixty feet above us, silent with awe as he faced straight down, with nothing to see in the darkness below except Pham's arms reaching out to catch him.

"Hello, Eddie," said Pham.

"Hi. Looks like fun, doesn't it?" The baby began to pinwheel slowly, starting to float back down.

"Yah. Maybe you do for me someday, hah? So, what? You tell Polaski piss off, and he throw you out?"

I didn't answer for a moment, but watched the baby picking up speed and shrieking again. "He wants you there."

"I know. Soon."

"Okay." I watched for another minute, then worked my way back up the causeway and the conference room, into a shouting match between Lal Singh the Younger and a brittle woman named Xiang, the emissary from the Chinese.

I pictured the baby floating down toward me, alive and excited. I didn't want to be at the conference. I didn't want the bickering, or Polaski's plan.

Singh was on his feet now, stabbing a manicured finger at Xiang through the gloom. "You say, Madame, that the creatures that have returned to Earth have recognized China's inherent superiority among civilized nations, and so have not attacked your homeland. I hasten to remind you, however, of the history of atrocities by the Chinese government against her people, stories about which continue to flood this system with every new refugee ship, stories that these creatures most assuredly would have heard if they heard anything at all of Earth. How do you account for this, then?"

Xiang slapped the table with the palm of her hand, making the water in her decanter jump.

"Emissary Singh. You of all people must not be so gullible as to believe these fabrications, which unscrupulous parties in this system feed back to these outlaws from Earth, telling them to present them as the truth as a condition of entry—"

Next to me Chan's eyes had narrowed at Xiang, and now she let out a hiss between her teeth. Xiang blinked in surprise, then Singh leaned across the table and poked a triumphant finger.

"Pray tell me, *Madame*, how these stories have been fed to Earth, when for sixteen years the only torus in this system has been guarded and pointed elsewhere. Earth has heard nothing from us. It has long been a measure of the desperation of settlers from Earth that they arrive in a system about whose conditions they know nothing at all, and it is a further measure of their present terror that they are fleeing to yet another system that for all they know is filled with our dead bodies and the fierce aliens that are attacking them."

"Perhaps," said Xiang. "But the fact remains, Emissary Singh, that these creatures have recognized China as the most peaceable and dedicated member of the community of nations, and that—"

"China is a member of nothing! Need I remind you, Madame Xiang, that only China and the United States, with their paralyzed economies, refused to recognize the Pacific Community of Nations, leading to *your* exclusion and to the secession of California. And even here in our new home you do not wish to participate, building instead your radiation weapons—once again, I might add, like the Americans—" He paused to glance pointedly at Allerton.

Tyrone Elliot chose that moment to stand up. He straightened to his full height with a piece of paper in his hand, and stared at Singh until the smaller man sat down.

"As of this morning," said Elliot in his soft voice, "in eight weeks, sixty million people have died on Earth from starvation, most of them on the subcontinent, in eastern Africa, and in the southern interior of China. Another four million have died in the smoke storms in Denver, central Germany, and São Paulo." He put down his paper and looked up. "And many times this number have died from the drones, all in industrial countries—including, as much as anywhere else, northern and coastal China." He sat back down and stared at his papers through the murky light, turning them in slow circles on the tabletop. No one spoke as the magnitude of the disaster sank in. Condensation dripped somewhere inside the walls, and we listened as the minutes passed.

Then the door swung open and Pham stepped through, carrying a bassinet in which the baby lay curled up, asleep. As the door closed behind her, her hand shot out and smacked into the electrical box by the door. The baby stirred briefly and the ceiling lights blazed into life, flooding the room with new light.

"What this? Everybody cheer up, hah? Hi!" Her eyes flashed a smile as she moved to the empty corner seat next to Allerton, touching Perris and Elliot on their shoulders as she passed. She set the bassinet on the corner of the table and sat down, while every eye at the table followed her, and while Allerton gave her a long look of contempt.

"What the hell is this?"

"This a baby, Mr. Barnum."

"Don't *call* me that! What the hell's it doing here?"

"Sleeping. Don't shout."

"Christ."

Someone else snickered and Allerton stared down the table, trying not to look around for who it was. He drummed his fingers on the table. Xiang leaned forward again, pale and waxen now under the bright lights.

"The Greater People's—"

"Oh, shut up, Xiang," snapped Allerton. "You're just pissing everyone off. And in the meantime these drones are attacking every innocent target they can find." He glanced at me pointedly with the word "innocent."

"Yes," said Singh. "Even our Russian friends here have been better neighbors than you, Madame Xiang, keeping to themselves like gentlemen."

"Ahem." An elderly and pudgy Marina Tonova rapped her knuckles on the table and leaned around Singh to look at me. "Mr. Singh is very kind. But still I have a question for our good friend, here, Mr. Torres." She started to say something more, but then stopped and blinked across the table at the bassinet. "My, such a sweet child! How old is he? Is a boy, yes?"

"Yes. Twenty-two weeks tomorrow."

"Ah. You are very lucky." Tonova cast her pleasant gaze on the baby for a minute, then turned back to me.

"Edvard, why it is you make Nicolai Ivanovich empty his shipyards last year, where he is building habitats, and then you say nothing? He is very good friend with you, and so he does this, but he is very confused now."

"I'm sorry. Please extend my apologies to Nicolai, Madame Tonova. It was because, at the same time that I told our captive drone of the fissures on the black planet, I told it about Nicolai's habitat construction."

"You *what*?" said Polaski.

"I had a suspicion the drones weren't interested in civilian targets," I said. I returned the look Allerton gave me. "Like the habitats, or *Sun of Gabriel*."

This was true only as far as it went. I wasn't at all sure about human-carrying vessels moving toward the torus.

"You walked up to our only captive," said Polaski, "and gave it strategic information?"

"Hardly strategic. And it wasn't a captive. It was a plant. I used it."

"You used it pretty well," said Polaski. "Half our commandos are gone now. And what about these mines? You just said they only attack military targets."

"Now, now," interrupted Allerton. "I'm the one that dug out the information about the Indian mines and warned Mr. Singh."

"They believed it was a weapons base," I said.

Polaski's eyes narrowed. "How do you *know* they believed it was a weapons base?"

I tapped my fingers on the table and looked around at the faces. Pham leaned back in her chair with her hands behind her head and a pleasant smile on her face. The baby slept, and was studiously ignored by Allerton.

"I learned it," I said, "by trading the bogus information about the fissures on the black planet." Only Penderson knew that this wasn't true, and Penderson was dead. "Now, as long as you're on your feet, Polaski, why don't you tell us about this magic discovery you've made about the drones?"

He started to answer, then folded his arms and paused for effect.

"They frighten," he said.

"They what?"

"You heard me. A sufficient show of force and they're frightened off. As well they should be. We've got an eye-witness account from the campaign on Six from Commander Todd."

He gestured to the black-uniformed boy to his left. "Commander." The boy stood up solemnly and cleared his throat, and straightened his tunic.

"During our Fourth Reserve salient flanking maneuver—"

he began.

"How old are you?" I said.

He looked at me blankly. "Fourteen. Six Gs."

"Christ."

Pham called down the table, "Hey, Todd, you got first name?"

Todd frowned and glanced at Polaski. "Jacob," he said.

"Okay," said Pham. "Jacob, I'm sure you are a very good commander. I'm sure you practice very hard. Now sit down. Sorry, I am sure what you say very important. I sorry you have to fight, too." She looked around the table. "Everybody, listen. China-Girl here, she show me in detail tactics Miller woman teach drones. Drones not frighten. They not know what frighten mean. They also not lose, ever. Like mosquito, they just change, make more mosquitoes. No matter what clever plan we got, they learn, come back more clever. They constant, now, like Ice-Lady say. Like police. Not alive, not people we can fight—they are part of the world." She reached out to adjust the blanket around the baby.

"But, Mr. Allerton," she went on. "I got question. Why you killing ranchers? And why you making radiation bombs again—"

"*What?*" Polaski stood up again, but Pham cut him off.

"And why those bombs, you aim them at black planet, hah?"

"How do you know that!" hissed Allerton. He pushed back his chair.

"Friend tell me," she said.

"What friend, you little tramp?"

"She be here soon."

"I said *what* friend?" He reached a hand past the bassinet to grip her wrist, as though to hold her attention. She glanced briefly down at the baby, but didn't move.

"I won't tell you what friend," she said. "I make promise."

He gripped her harder, now whispering to her as though aware of the spectacle he was creating. The rest of us held our breaths, waiting for her to move. "You'll tell me or I'll break you in two, do you understand me?" Spittle flew from his lips.

"When I make promises to friends, Mr. Barnum, I keep them." She watched him expressionlessly.

Polaski smacked his chrome gavel against the table, remembering to hold on this time. "What the hell is all this, Allerton? No one said you were supposed to be manufacturing weapons again—"

Allerton pushed away Pham's arm in disgust and turned back toward Polaski. "I don't tell you everything, Polaski. I'm not some fucking lackey of yours, you know."

"That not so good," continued Pham unfazed, "killing ranchers, just because they know too much, hah?"

"Don't you moralize to me, young woman. I don't go around killing people for the fun of it."

"Not Carolyn Dorczak?" I said.

He turned to stare at me. "That was an accident."

"So," said Polaski, "you were targeting your launch vehicles at us. Hedging your bets a little, Allerton?"

"It's okay," said Pham, still looking at Allerton. "Mr. Barnum here can't hit anything with them anyway. No one sell him MI and optics he need for targeting—"

"Ha!" Allerton was triumphant. "So much for your *sources,* young woman. We can sit ten million miles out in space if we want to, and look through your domes in the middle of the night and see who's *in* them—"

Polaski was on his feet and shouting. "Damn it, Allerton, shut up—"

"Let it go, Polaski," said Elliot.

But Elliot hadn't understood. Only Polaski had understood, and he already knew. And Pham? Was that why she'd brought it up? Who was this source she kept talking about?"

And I, of course, had understood as well. And finally I knew what Polaski had really done, the lengths to which he would go.

Elliot went on.

"It doesn't matter, anyway, Polaski. Tell us what your plan is for the drones, then let's get the hell out of here."

Polaski sat back down and tapped a pencil against the table for a minute, while Allerton glared at him.

"We're going to assemble every ship in this system," said Polaski. "Six thousand ships in a single wall, moving against the drone's fleet at the torus."

"Oh, shit," said Elliot. "Come on, Polaski, those drones ain't gonna back off. All you're gonna do is get your fleet up against the last passpoint, then they're gonna start shooting. *Then* what the hell are you going to do?"

"If that's the way they want it," said Polaski, "then that's fine with me, too. Because if they don't back off when they should, then our ships are going to fire in unison—ten thousand square miles of flame and missiles against that one little drone fleet."

"Jesus *Christ*, Polaski," I said. "You'd hit the torus!"

"Maybe. But either way, we get the drones."

I started to answer, but then stopped, too surprised to speak. I thought I must have misheard.

"No, Polaski," I said, "I mean the torus itself—the tunnel. You'd hit the torus. A synchronized broadside isn't selective enough. It would hit the torus, the projector."

"Who do you think you're talking to?" he said. "I know what a broadside's for."

"For Christ's sake, Polaski," I said, "we can't go to Serenitas if you hit that thing. No one can! We can't go anywhere if you hit that torus—we'd be stuck in this grave of a system for life!"

I wondered for a minute if he was joking. I looked around the table at blank or puzzled faces, feeling my own face beginning to redden.

"What's your problem, Torres?" said Polaski. "Except not having any balls?"

I felt sick to my stomach, still trying to reconcile the revelation Allerton had let slip. I looked the other way along the table at Pham, but she sat with her head back and her eyes closed, apparently no longer paying attention.

I pictured the giant torus burning, floating out in the blackness, the end to our journey tolled by its fiery death—a replacement decades or centuries away. I turned back to Polaski.

"Polaski," I said. I tried to keep my voice steady. "I thought you were trying to make it to Serenitas. I thought that was the whole point."

"I think that may be more important to you than to the rest of us," he said.

"Polaski, there are people using that torus to go on to

Serenitas. That's what it's for." Did I really believe that?

"Uh-huh. Look, our own massed cannon went up against that fleet at the torus and didn't get through, even if we did beat the pants off them. So you'd better believe no one's waltzing through by themselves. Where do you come up with this drivel, anyway?"

Next to me, Lal Singh scraped his chair around to see me better. "I'm afraid I don't understand this little disagreement, Mr. Torres," he said. "I thought that this...this 'broadside' was your plan."

I stared at him. "No. This is insanity, an attack like that. Where did you get that?"

He frowned and looked around at his counterparts and then back at me, genuinely confused.

"I don't know if you are making a joke, sir. Everywhere in this system, the events of the past twenty years are understood to have been according to your plan. Mr. Polaski's plan, Mr. Torres' plan, they are the same thing to us. When we say one, we mean the other—they are interchangeable. So naturally I assumed that this inevitable next step—"

"This expedition hasn't been mine," I said. "Polaski's the one sitting at the head of the table, isn't he? He's the one—"

"Excuse me," said Singh, "but I must notice the moment at which you are saying this. A few minutes ago we heard a most distressing account of conditions on Earth, and we know that the situation here is even worse. We are dying of hunger at an alarming rate, industries are collapsing, and these creatures are attacking us unpredictably—and now because you find distasteful the counterattack designed to rescue us from the consequences of your plan, you wish to disassociate yourself from those who all these years have faithfully carried it out?"

I looked from Singh to Polaski.

"It's not my plan, Singh." I knew my voice sounded weak. "Polaski's been driving this thing, not me."

Singh coughed discreetly into a hand and looked briefly around the table.

"Excuse me again, Mr. Torres, but I find this to be most embarrassing. You are the one, I believe, who invented the cells. And later disabled them, I might add—including the ones in the airplane of my father's brother over Madhya Pradesh. It was you who built the ships and gave so many of them to a man named Chih-Hsien Chien, a man employed by Chinese intelligence, a man who then gave those ships to the Europeans to carry their weapons. You are the one who launched your fleet, I believe, killing your own chief economist—the one man, I might add, who had been advocating greater restraint. It was you who insisted on sending a probe into the next system—a probe that incited your drones to attack us. Mr. Torres, I believe that anyone would find the events of this period to have been very much your doing."

I watched my own fingers drumming on the table. I answered without looking up.

"This isn't what I intended."

"Ah."

"So," said Polaski. "Are we done here, Torres, or do you have a better idea?"

As the others at the table watched me and waited for my answer, I looked at Pham where she sat leaning back in her chair. Kip was sitting against the wall behind her, where I hadn't seen him before. He was turned in his seat, watching Polaski with an uncharacteristic intensity.

I looked back down at my hands. I felt pressed for an answer, yet I could only call up the same old image: the drones' ships waiting between us and the tunnel, and all of them suddenly stopping as I pressed a key. The struggle ending in that single instant—the uncertainty gone, the mistakes of our past done away with in a single stroke as I entered the password. The way opened up in front of us as we sailed through the tunnel, floating on toward the shores of Serenitas' blue seas...

Polaski leaned forward in his seat.

"All right, let's—"

"I'm going back for the case," I said.

Next to me Chan turned her head away. Elliot whistled softly, but no one else uttered a sound. I stared down at my water glass.

I'd begun to suspect that Polaski might destroy us all, and I was sure now that he would destroy the tunnel leading from the system. And I knew, too, in that instant, that I didn't have the courage to stop him. Pham talked easily about standing up to him, but however much she'd changed, I hadn't seen her show that sort of courage herself in standing up to these people. Especially to the kind of person I was beginning to see in Polaski. People like Major Cole, or Bart Allerton. Tyrone Elliot had once without hesitation turned a two-barreled heater on Cole, but a battlefield at night was not the same as a conference table. Going back for the codes before Polaski could go through with his attack was the only sure course we had.

"But Edvard," said Marina Tonova, leaning forward to look at me around Singh. "It is drones' main base, now. You cannot go back there."

"I'll go in on a shuttle. They'll leave it alone." I looked at Pham as I said it, but she just opened her eyes slightly and shook her head.

Seeing her with a hand resting on the baby, I was reminded again of the darkened vehicle assembly building where she'd found him—the frozen and airless chamber filled with the dead, the drones moving like ghosts in its shadows—a black on black painting of the pit of lost souls, the pit where the treasure lay buried.

"Lord almighty," said Elliot.

"Hell, Torres," said Polaski, "you do whatever you want. Just stay out of my way."

Across from me Elliot carefully put both his hands on the table in front of him.

"Torres," he said. "You can't go back there by yourself. You can't even fly those ships worth a dog's ass—probably get lost on the way without someone to look after you." He looked down at the backs of his hands. "I'm coming with you."

"No!" Perris grabbed Elliot's shoulder. "No, Tyrone! You're not going off with that man again, to get yourself killed! You've done enough for him—more than he deserves!" She was shouting, shaking his shoulder. "You said we're getting out, Tyrone!"

Elliot stared down. "Someone's got to go with him—"

"*No!*" She spun and pointed at me, her face pale. "Don't you dare let him go, Eduardo! You tell him. *Tell him!*" She groped behind her for the door. *"Tell him, you bastard!"*

She spun around to burst out through the door and then froze, staring into the face of a man standing in the center of the doorway. He was a pudgy man, with a bristling grey mustache and thick glasses, which he peered over in confusion as his hand groped for the door handle that was no longer there.

Then I was on my feet, still reeling from Allerton's slip about identifying faces through the domes, reeling from Singh's accusations and from Perris' attack on me, and now filled with fury at the man in the doorway.

"Becker!" I shouted. "You son of bitch, you've got a nerve—"

Allerton slammed his glass onto the table. "Becker! What the hell—"

But a hand had appeared on Colonel Samuel Becker's shoulder, nudging him forward as a familiar voice spoke from behind him.

"It's all right, Ed—you can let him live another few minutes. I must say I'm flattered by your loyalties."

Carolyn Dorczak slid into the room past Becker to stand against the wall, pushing her dark hair out of her face as she looked around. She looked rested and amused, pursing her lips as she studied the room with her brown eyes, reaching back to take Harry Penderson's hand and pull him into the room behind her.

I sank back into my seat as Allerton rose out of his.

"Becker," he whispered, his face pale and his voice unsteady. "You told me—"

"That the plane crashed?" said Becker. "Yes, yes, I did, didn't I?" Becker moved away and dropped into a chair against the wall, then leaned his head back and pushed his glasses up with his little finger as though settling in for a nap.

Allerton's eyes narrowed and he lowered himself back into his seat. He was avoiding looking at Dorczak.

"I'll have your hide, Becker."

"No you won't, you schmuck. I don't work for you any more."

Polaski's grey eyes had narrowed with caution at this point. He ran the handle of his gavel slowly across his cheek. Allerton sat straight up in his chair, the fingertips of both hands placed carefully on the edge of the table, gold rings glinting in the light as he looked around the room with worried eyes, his gaze finally coming to rest on Dorczak.

"I had nothing to do with—"

"Yah," interrupted Pham, leaning back with her fingers laced together behind her head. "You did."

"How the hell do you know what I did or didn't do?" he hissed.

"Because Commander Bolton, he find out. He pretty good spy. He learn from best, hah?"

Allerton was almost whispering. "And who might that be that he learned from, in this little fantasy of yours?" His lip was trembling.

"New president, State of Lowhead," said Pham. "Carolyn Dorczak."

Allerton stared at Pham, slowly sliding his chair back. "You shut up. What's all this to you, anyway, you little junkie?"

"Truth important. You lying."

"Well then, you stay out of it!" he hissed. "You just remember that a few people at this table might be interested in *your* past, you little gook whore, and I'd hate to have to be the one—"

Pham scraped her chair back matter-of-factly and stood to address the room. "I am Tuyet-Nhung Pham. I am a coward and a liar, and a cheat, and a murderess. It is all true." She sat back down and looked at Allerton.

By the door, Penderson watched her with a raised eyebrow, then turned to give me a friendly salute.

Allerton stared at Pham, breathing rapidly and gripping his glass with both hands to keep them from shaking. Finally he took a deep breath, and with a brief glance at Dorczak he looked down the table.

"Well, I guess that tells us—"

"So, Mr. Allerton," said Pham, "you ordered Becker to kill Ms. Dorczak?"

He swatted at the air as though at a mosquito, still looking at Polaski at the other end. "I think this discussion's gone far enough," he said. "I'm as happy as anyone here to see that Mr. Penderson and—"

"You not answer question," said Pham. She leaned forward in her chair to face him. The others around the table watched without making a sound.

"Damn it!" said Allerton. "I won't stand for this! I think you've already given this assembly of honorable and *senior* representatives ample reason to doubt anything that you—"

"You still not answer question."

He gritted his teeth. "—to doubt anything that you, as a self-admitted liar, claim to have heard from a man who is conveniently *dead*. Now I think that this assembly has recently had a vivid demonstration of who's to blame for the tragedies in this system, and I'm sure that an honorable man such as His Excellency, Mr. Singh, for example, would agree that these proceedings properly concern addressing those unfortunate tragedies and working for the survival of innocent civilians, as Mr. Polaski has suggested, even though we must overlook the comments that Madame Xiang made yesterday regarding the Russian people—don't you agree Mr. Singh, given your experience in these matters?"

"Ah, well," said Singh, not understanding at all, "I suppose I most certainly do believe that, ah, under the circumstances—"

"What *about* Russian people," said Marina Tonova, "eh, Chinese witch?" She thumped the table, squinting across at Xiang.

"Yesterday?" Xiang was baffled. "What is this—"

"Excuse me! Excuse me!" Pham was on her feet again, banging a pencil against her decanter. "Mr. Allerton uses you to change subject, Madame Xiang, because he not want to answer question. That is not okay." Against the wall, Penderson and Dorczak both folded their arms and watched Allerton, who gripped the table now with white knuckles and stared at Pham.

"*What the hell is your problem?*" In a convulsive movement he flung back his chair and shot to his feet to tower over her, sweeping his glass aside to shatter against the wall. The baby startled in his bassinet and cried. "*Shut that thing up!*"

"No," said Pham. "You haven't answered question." She reached out a hand to the baby, still watching Allerton. "And stop shouting, you frighten baby."

"I don't give a flying fuck about your baby!" He stared down at the bassinet and wiped the back of his hand across the spittle on his mouth. He was shaking with anger. The baby howled louder and reached out his hands. *"I said shut that thing up!"* Allerton lifted his arm high into the air and swept it down toward the bassinet to backhand it off the table.

Bart Allerton was forced to the floor so quickly that none of us fully realized it had happened. As his hand descended toward the bassinet Pham seemed to draw away from him, but a moment later she was reaching for him as though to keep him from falling. Then she was lifting the baby, and Bart Allerton was making an odd sound from where he lay on the floor, his larynx crushed.

It was several minutes later when Susan Perris stood up from Allerton's side and told us in a shaky voice that he was not in danger, but that he had suffered wounds she wouldn't have thought someone half his size could inflict.

Then, with a last look at Allerton and a chilly glance directed at me, Perris left to summon help. Chan followed her out, though she seemed uninterested in Allerton. For a few minutes, then, the room was filled with uneasy fits of conversation, dropping away occasionally into nervous silence. Pham was gone, her departure unnoticed.

Polaski's face had closed over into a mask during the confrontation, and now, with careful looks at me and at Dorczak, and with a quick look at Allerton on the floor, he motioned to Jacob Todd and strode out of the door. He pushed a hand against Kip's chest on the way out, causing him to stumble against the chairs and fall.

Harry Penderson helped Kip up, then leaned across the table to me with his hand extended.

"How you been keeping yourself?" he said.

"Jesus, Harry, I don't believe you're here." I shook his hand, then walked around the table to embrace Carolyn Dorczak.

"Cheer up, Ed," she said.

"Damn it, Carolyn, no one knew...we thought you were dead."

She stepped back as the medics moved Allerton's stretcher through the door, his bluish face twisted with pain. Dorczak hugged herself and moved closer to Penderson, then turned back to me.

"I know that's what you thought," she said. "I'm sorry." She glanced at Allerton as he disappeared. "The girl's quick, isn't she? Scary, if she's not on your side. We heard she brought back a baby from Four. That's a change, isn't it?"

"She killed David Rosler," I said.

"I know," said Dorczak. "I can't say Harry minded any."

"How did you hear about it?" I said. "Where the hell have you two *been*?"

"Mike Bolton told us. He said Pham's been having a rough time. She's done a lot to help us out, though. We've been back on the Boar River plains, Ed—Sammy Becker's been back and forth to keep us in touch. I was sorry to hear about Mike, by the way. I kind of had an itch for him once, you know." With a wry little smile she took Penderson's hand. "He was very gracious about it."

"Bolton knew where you were?" I said. I felt the nausea coming back.

Dorczak pushed her hair out of the way and nodded uncertainly. "He wasn't sure where you stood, Ed."

"Okay." I watched her for a minute. "So you're back at the helm in Lowhead, then? Does that mean you can hold your ships back from Polaski's assault on the torus? You know about that?"

"Oh, yes, we know." All at once she looked tired. "I don't know, Ed. I may have hammered a civilian government back into place, but it's only because the military was already nervous about Allerton. I still need to be pretty careful about pissing them off. The truth is, if you were to stop people on the street in West Lowhead and ask them, they'd say they still want a strong posture against these drones. None of them's ready to have us lay down our weapons and trust in their benevolent grace. It's only the intellectuals who're saying we should, and I'm not sure even they are ready to let go and rely on faith alone. No, Ed, I can give you some time, but that's all. And maybe your defections will help. But by now I think you're the only one who can stop Polaski. I know he likes to think he wipes his feet on you these days, but without you to pump him up he'll fall apart and this whole system might have a chance to come up for air."

"Our defections?"

Penderson nodded. "Priscilla Bates is coming back to Boar River with us. With Throckmorton and all of his troops in tow, and there's a few others. What do you need more time *for*, Torres?"

I put my hands in my pockets, but neither Elliot nor I answered.

"Jeeps," said Dorczak, "you boys look like you've been caught smoking or something."

Then her face sobered. "You're not going back, are you? To try and get control of the drones again? Oh, Ed, don't!"

I'd meant to find Chan the night before Elliot and I left, but provisioning the ship seemed to grow more complicated at the last minute, and by the time we were ready to seal the locks I only had a minute to look for her. I didn't find her, but I did promise myself that I'd spend some more time with her as soon as we returned.

Elliot spent the evening with Perris, but in the morning he seemed more tired and distracted than ever.

"Harry and Carolyn said to say goodbye," he said.

"They're gone?"

"They left early. Worried about the home front. Did you know they were married?"

"No. When?"

"Back on the plains. Becker married 'em—senior officer present and all that."

I'd had to tell Kip he couldn't come. I found him in my quarters sitting against the wall, with my gun in his hands. He was turning it this way and that, looking at it from all sides. I took it away and told him he was to stay with Chan.

The only one to see the two of us off, in the end, was Pham.

The day before, the Russian Marina Tonova had silenced a move to hold Pham accountable for assault and battery against Allerton, at one point slapping Polaski publicly for suggesting that Pham's straying priorities had placed the mission in jeopardy because of it. Tonova had then dropped her official duties and closeted herself with Pham, announcing it as her intention to teach Pham how to raise a child.

Now Pham stood leaning against the wall, watching as we clattered our way into the lock for the last time, dragging our boots and oxygen bottles behind us. The baby squirmed in her arms and chattered importantly, pointing at each piece of equipment in turn and looking up at me with his big eyes each time he pointed.

"So," said Pham.

It was the last sight I had of the fleet—Pham leaning against the steel bulkhead, dark eyes and smooth skin contrasted against her black hair and white blouse, relaxed and a little sad, the baby in her arms pointing solemnly at my face in the porthole.

"Knew a fella in Louisiana, once," said Elliot, "got tired of living and went around poking in corners all the time. Looking for the plug, he said."

Elliot was sprawled in the pilot's seat, tipped back to see overhead in the direction we were moving, trying to maneuver us into orbit with his bare toes on the controls. Even as he spoke the shuttle lurched several times in rapid succession. A density finder pulled out of my hands and crashed to the deck.

"Hell, Torres," said Elliot over his shoulder, "you already checked that thing eighty-nine times. Just as well you finally set it down."

"The codes case may have been moved, Tyrone, and we're going to have to go right to it. We're only going to have one chance to get at it before the drones start deciding we're important again."

"Well, maybe, maybe not—so far no one's ever seen 'em take after a regular suit or an ordinary supply shuttle. You just smile and nod when we're down there, Torres, and don't get all uptight and start throwing rocks and waving your toys around."

"We have to have *some* advantage, Tyrone—Jesus, it makes my skin crawl, going back in there. You weren't there when it was wall-to-wall drone." My palms were sweating. The memory of the bodies, the blood, the shadowy drones drifting through the darkness, had wrapped itself around me like the stench of death itself. I had ached for a weapon then, and I couldn't imagine going back without one now.

"Your advantage is *faith*, boy, *faith*. You're gonna have to take all that being-in-charge shit and let it go." He tipped his head back to grin at me upside down, opening his fist as though letting something go. The ship twisted and dropped out from under us.

"Oops. Tricky bastard, huh?"

If the drones couldn't see a weapon, I knew, they wouldn't fire. And if they were going to fire anyway, or if they were blocking the way to the case, then it would be just as well if we had one.

The ship righted itself as the MI took over our orbit around the black planet. Elliot abandoned the controls and spun around to look at me.

"We can still turn around, Torres. Seems like a mighty fine idea, as a matter of fact. You see, I'm willing to bet a bright fella like you can talk FleetSys into shutting itself down right on Polaski's ass, and without that ol' box of wires, ain't no one attacking nothing. Might just *force* all them generals and admirals to have a little faith, don't you suppose?"

"We've been through this before, Tyrone. It takes at least two fleet officers to change FleetSys' commands, and with Rosler and Bolton gone that only leaves me and Polaski. Priscilla took herself off the list long ago."

"Well, shoot, Torres. Just forget about the whole thing, then. Learn how to dig wells or something."

The trip hadn't been easy. Day after day I'd tried to keep busy, but all the while I was plagued by the memory of Singh looking at me, and Polaski's grey eyes, and Pham's challenge about standing up to the real enemy.

"Here, look at this," I said. I brought up a picture of the surface on our screens, with our old base coming into view over the horizon. It was early in the planet's morning. Elliot tipped his seat forward and stared at it.

"Them critters is taking this pretty serious, aren't they?"

Across an area stretching for miles out from the main dome lay row upon row of new ships. Most of them were smaller than the drones' original ones. Packed in among them were complex staging areas and assembly lines, each of them leading off to the mining equipment and to some other kind of heavy equipment we didn't recognize. Every square foot was dense with activity.

"Lord almighty, look at that. Must be twenty thousand of 'em down there, all different shapes and sizes. They've got the smelters going again, huh?"

Our orbit took us over the base and Elliot pointed to an empty stretch of ground a quarter of a mile from the front of the main dome. "Right there," he said. "We'll put down on our next pass, real gentle-like. Then walk back to the dome."

"Christ, Tyrone, we'd have to walk right through the middle of the drones to get to the lock tunnel."

As the image slid off the screen and was replaced by the empty wastes, he leaned over and whispered in my ear.

"Faith," he said. He straightened and reached for his boots. "Fifty-six minutes."

But it was more faith than I had.

"Remember, Torres, back on that stinking little island in the Pacific? After Chan jinxed the air controllers and sent that poor son-of-a-bitch MP packing?"

We were suited up and sat with our feet on the instrument panel and our helmets on our laps, watching the terminator slip toward us.

"I never seen you carrying on like you done that night," he said. "Remember, you and me kept trying to get Bolton drunk and he'd just sit there saying 'No thank you,' all polite-like? With Polaski sitting on his bunk cleaning his revolver all night, and you trying to get Chan into the bushes somewhere and she was so out of it she'd just wake up and tell you it was raining and fall back asleep. It was you and me in the end there, wasn't it? Sitting out on the porch in the middle of the monsoons at three in the morning, soaking wet and popping grenades off at Polaski's truck, seeing if we could get the sucker to turn over? Shit, Torres, we had some good times there for a while, didn't we?"

"They'll be back, Tyrone. Pretty soon now, they'll be back."

"Yeah, I suppose. Hell, I can't even remember if we ever did get the truck to turn over. You were so drunk you probably don't even know what I'm talking about, do you?"

"Here we go," I said. I pulled my feet back from the panel and floated up against the harness just as the shuttle rolled and fired its engines. As it dropped to the surface I held the navigation screen's crosshairs over the tiny clearing Elliot had pointed out, and in minutes we were bumping against the ground. We held our breath and stared out through the windscreen.

For a few seconds nothing happened. Then all at once a group of the tiny drone scouts darted in to take up positions around the shuttle.

"Oh, shit."

We stared past the scouts at the banks of machinery and drones spread out in every direction, waiting for them to pick up weapons and turn them on us. The scouts hovered, and the seconds ticked by. Then just as quickly as they'd appeared, they vanished.

Nothing else happened. Fifty feet in front of us, on an assembly line, arms were being attached to rows of partially assembled drones—arms which then immediately came to life and took over the remaining assembly of their own bodies. They stood on an immaculately clean area of the surface fused to a glassy smoothness. Their movements were almost too quick to follow. None paid us the least attention.

Elliot whistled his relief and carefully reached for the buckles on his harness. I stood up and backed along the deck toward the air lock, not wanting to take my eyes off the drones as I picked up my equipment and clipped it to my suit, tired already from the high gravity.

"Okay, Tyrone. If we're going to do it, let's do it."

We locked our helmets and tested the radios, then checked the indicators on each other's suits and separated as we fastened on the last of our equipment. As I worked I found myself waiting for a shudder of the deck as the shuttle was hit, or for the roar of flames cutting through the walls.

I was also thinking about what waited for us in the vehicle assembly building. I wondered if the case was still where I'd hidden it under the stairs, and I wondered what awaited us along the quarter-mile walk to the dome, then across Trinity Square from the destroyed air lock to the silent building.

"Ready?"

"Ready."

I cycled out through the lock first, then stood on the glassy ground watching the silent and exacting activity of the drones. Hair rose on the back of my neck. From out of the midst of the equipment a machine came rushing toward me, a device like the head of a garden rake, reeling out strands of cable. It sidestepped to miss me and continued on into the distance.

"We put down in the middle of a cable run," I said to Elliot as another one raced toward us and veered aside. "At least they don't seem to mind."

"I mind, though," said Elliot. "I see what you mean about these critters. They sure as hell give me the willies. I don't know if they're alive or dead or what, but they get nearly as excited about ignoring us as they do about cutting us up into pieces, and that's spooky. Come on, let's move it along here."

I led the way across the surface, slogging past row after row of equipment running in its hurried precision, quick and silent. I tried not to think and not to imagine, and put one foot in front of the other and kept my eyes on the tunnel ahead. My breath hissed in through the regulators and out again, sucked through by the pumps, dry in my chest.

"Lord, look at that!" I jumped at Elliot's voice. "What do you suppose happened to that?" He was pointing to a burned tractor lying outside the lock tunnel. It took me a minute to recognize it.

"I was in it," I said. "Pham and I. And the baby."

"My, oh my." We clumped into the iron tunnel. "That's a real nice kid, ain't it? The baby. I think that's fine, her taking care of him like that. Hanging onto him and all."

Trinity Square was empty. Several of the familiar grey drones moved near the periphery, but otherwise our way to the assembly building was clear, and by the time we reached the center of the square I believed we would make it.

"Suit check," said Elliot behind me. I turned to look him over, then stood still as he checked my shoulder and chest plates.

"What the hell's this, Torres?" He yanked loose the grenade launcher I'd clipped under my arm, then pushed a little roughly to start me moving again. "I thought we weren't packing."

"A little insurance, is all, Tyrone."

"*Fuck*, Torres, this thing will get you *killed*. Just couldn't resist, could you? No faith at all, no sir. Swear to God, boy, I don't know what you'd do without me to look after you. I'd say you owe me, Torres."

"Hell, Tyrone, it's a just a launcher. Keep it out of sight. But all right, fine, I owe you. You'll get repaid, too, as soon as we're back in the shuttle with the codes. You'll get repaid in Serenitas, you and Susan, me and Chan, all the forests and water and open space we want. Sunshine. You'll be paid back and then some, Tyrone."

I stopped and looked at the vehicle assembly building, trying to decide on the best way in. Then I turned around.

Elliot's helmet was off. He was lying on the ground behind me, the helmet thrown aside by his fall. The launcher was still in his hand, melted in two. The cut had continued on into his side and across his back, through his heart. His mouth was open and his cheek was pressed into the dust, brown against the black, his eyes open and freezing over. I took a step toward him.

"Tyrone?"

He'd fallen forward and lay on his stomach, one leg straight and the other bent at the knee, his arms out from his sides and turned inward so that the palms faced up. Blood from the wound trickled to the ground and glistened black before it froze.

"Tyrone?" I stood still, listening to my own breath and watching his face. Minutes passed and the moisture from his last breath turned to a fine glitter of ice crystals on his lips, then I felt a warmth in the soles of my feet. It began where the frayed covering of the old boots chafed against my instep, then spread into my toes with a prickling sensation.

"It's all right, Tyrone," I said, "they just wanted the launcher."

Was I talking too loud? I couldn't tell.

Then the base of my spine was too warm, and soon after the heat swelled to burn in my loins, so that I wanted to peel off the suit and fling it aside.

His eyes were frozen, opaque, a grayish silver like the hairs on his temples. Moisture had frozen along both sides of his flat nose, in the lines that began in the corners of his eyes and gave them their warmth, the liquid frozen now in the lines like tears. The skin was burnished smooth by the cold, hardened by the stubble growing across his chin and down into the steel collar of his suit.

"Damn it, Tyrone, come on—Jesus!" The warmth moved through my belly and into my chest, an urgent thing I wanted to push away, and couldn't.

Maybe there was still air in the dome after all. Maybe he was still alive. He hadn't really seen the weapon I carried—he'd never held it in his hand at all.

But my legs were weak, and I lowered myself to my knees. I began to whisper.

"*Madre de Dios.*" I reached out and groped for Elliot's arms to turn him, but I was unable to get a grip through the clumsy gloves and unable to see him through the tears. "Oh, God, please—no." I tried to lift his head and press his face against mine, to feel his skin and squeeze life into him and hear his voice, to touch him, but my helmet pushed him away and my hands were like clubs. I could only grapple helplessly through the suit. Suddenly I felt as though I had only been able to grapple helplessly for him all my life, as though I'd never really touched him at all.

"No, please." But no matter how I held him I could only feel the lifeless rubber of my suit, engulfing me like the inside of my own skin. I lowered his head and sank down next to him, pulling him closer and burying my helmet in his side—understanding, in a sudden, final moment of clarity, that I was completely alone.

I don't know how long I stayed at his side, but I know that as the hours passed I began to grow angry. Angry at the memories of him, angry at the drones, angry at the quietness of the square. I pushed myself up and felt the suit pull at me, binding me with its bloodless skin, trapping me in with the breastplate of armor I wore and the lump of the gun I'd put under my arm, now trapped against me forever by the suit. I felt the material rubbing at my elbows, and the acceleration collars pulling at my arms and thighs...the warm spots behind the knees where heated air was pumped back in, the prickling where the helmet's headband caught my eyebrows...

"Where are you!"

My voice echoed inside the helmet.

"Which one of you bastards killed him?"

I turned from one side of the square to the other.

"It wasn't even his gun, damn you! Who the hell do you think you are? Bastards!"

But no matter which way I turned my head, I couldn't see anything. In every direction I looked the world was just as quickly erased... I reached up a hand and passed it over my faceplate. Under the touch of my glove the darkness melted and spread, smearing across my view until the world was only a hazy impression beyond the helmet. It was Elliot's blood, smeared across my gloves now and across the faceplate.

"Stop it!"

I held myself still, breathing hard.

From the bottom of my faceplate, through a blurry half-moon, I was just able to see Elliot's sprawled form, his face still pressed into the dust. I knelt down and tried to lift him, thinking to carry him back to the shuttle and the warmth. But lifting even just his shoulders took more strength than I had. His body was stiff and awkward and unwilling, and it took all my strength just to drag him a step toward the tunnel. I set him back down while my heart pounded and my lungs strained for air, then after a minute I lifted his shoulders again and took another step. My suit heated up and perspiration tickled across my skin, and as I struggled with the third step I thought of the drones somewhere beyond the blur of my faceplate, lifting their weapons to fire. A feeling like a hot knife stabbed through my chest. I took another step and thought of Elliot and the tears came back to my eyes. From the strain of carrying him, or the loss, I couldn't tell.

Every few steps I rested, and the afternoon passed. By the time I'd pulled him onto the iron floor of the tunnel and stood resting on the threshold of the wastelands, the sun's blurry glow in my faceplate told me that I'd run out of time.

I turned my helmet north and twisted my head awkwardly to look out through the tiny clear wedge at the bottom, looking for the shuttle a quarter of a mile away. The surface flared at that moment in the last light and winked into darkness. The sixteen-hour night had begun.

And the shuttle was gone.

During the night I awoke unable to breathe. There was an awful noise in my chest and my lungs were heaving for air. An alarm was buzzing in the helmet, and in the midst of a growing panic I realized that the alarm had been sounding for a long time, weaving in and out of my sleep. My air was gone. I could feel nothing but the darkness and the cold iron flooring under my shoulders.

I calmed the rising panic, whispering to myself the words from the manuals. I remembered them in Elliot's own voice, delivered during his endless training sessions. Slowly, carefully, with every sense stretched to the breaking point, I groped for the bottle on Elliot's suit and disconnected it. I fitted it to the coupling at my belly and concentrated on feeling the coupling's threads through my gloves, on feeling the tiny arrow etched on the head of the nozzle, on feeling the tiny ridges on the valve as I spun it open. On hearing the hiss of air burst into the darkness.

Then finally, one more time, I slept.

The shuttle had been moved, not destroyed. It had been lifted and then dumped carelessly against the side of the dome to get it out of the way.

One of the skids had collapsed under the impact, causing the little boat to list and crushing the engines' exhaust skirts and the forward battery compartment. The air lock in the tail still worked, and once on board I found that the rear lights, pumps and scrubbers still functioned, but that all of the forward instruments were dead and smelled of ozone and burned silicon. I wouldn't be leaving.

I stripped off my suit and washed the gloves and the faceplate, then plugged in the bottles to recharge. Then finally I ate, sitting on the sloping deck and thinking about Elliot, leaning against the wall and watching my hands as they held the food.

During the night I wept. I wept with a hurt that came up out of my deepest insides, an ache that wrapped its arms around me and squeezed the tears out of me as though out of a wound as I sat with my knees against my chest and my head in my arms.

The tears were for Elliot, I thought. They were for the chil-

dren in the infirmary, or for the families back on Earth, or Teresa
Delgado, or Charlie Peters' god. For all I wept, I was sure that the
tears were for someone else.

I have the impression now, remembering the days that followed, of washing my hands over and over, and of leaning against
the bulkhead and watching my reflection in the steel door of the food
warmer. I stared at my unshaven face and at the stiff black hair, and
ran my hands over the rough skin and the greying eyebrows, across
my cracked lips. But mostly I remember staring down at the backs of
my hands, at the tiny hairs that grew from the rough skin, at the lines
worn into the knuckles, at the darker brown of the veins and the slow
pulse beating inside them. I stared down at them and remembered
looking down at the same hands when I was a child, when they were
soft and small, and innocent.

Then sometime later I dragged all of our air bottles out and
returned to Elliot's body where it lay in the iron tunnel. I lifted his
shoulders and walked backwards, pulling him one painful step after
another away from the dome. I pulled him until the air was running
low again, and then I left him to go back for more. This I did again
and again, over many days.

The drones paid me no attention. They didn't pause in their
work at all, and through those long nights out on the surface, when
I lay on the ground awake, I could feel the vibrations of their feet as
they passed. Sometimes they brushed into me on their way by. I
would lie awake in the dark and feel them pass by on their business,
while I worked at remembering Elliot's face. Sometimes I would see
them when I sat up and turned on the flashlight, to shine it down on
Elliot to make sure I'd missed no detail, no line or hair that I'd failed
to record perfectly.

A few times, though, I couldn't recall Elliot's face at all. No
matter how I tried, the only image that would appear was Polaski's,
watching me from a distance.

"Leave me alone!" I would shout, waving my hands uselessly
in the darkness. "You've had your way, now leave me alone!"

But my voice only rang back from inside the helmet—there
was no one to hear. In any case, I knew, it was far too late: Polaski had
gone on with his destruction, while I had crept off one more time,

taking Elliot to his death.

"The thing I wanted most, Tyrone," I said one night, "was land. I've never had land of my own. There was just the desert at home, and up north there were the streets in the winter and someone else's seeds to plant in the summer. Seeds the size of your thumb, and I never got to see them grow. We just planted them, one after the other, and the *cabrónes* would give us food. But what I wanted was grown pine trees, and a wooden fence with a gate around my house. I used to lie awake at night imagining the sound of that gate, but now everyone's gone."

Most of the time when I left the shuttle, making one more trip with the oxygen bottles, some of the black scouts would fly up to look, and sometimes one of them would dart forward and land on my shoulder. It would grip the suit in its claws and watch what I watched, see what I saw. The first time it happened I froze, thinking it was a new attack, but after a time during which nothing happened I took a few cautious steps, finally deciding it meant no harm. I couldn't see it where it sat on my shoulder, even if I turned my helmet all the way to the side, and after several days I forgot about it when one was there. Only when I concentrated could I feel the light pressure against the material of the suit. They would stay in place day and night, and would leave only when I worked my way back into the shuttle's air lock. Nothing I did while one was on my shoulder seemed to cause the other drones any concern; at least none of them ever came to look.

One morning I opened my eyes to find myself looking through the legs of the passing drones at a pile of scrap metal being fed into the smelters. Along one side of the pile lay something that caught my eye, and after lying still and looking at it for several minutes I finally recognized the metal case the codes had been in. It lay open and empty, discarded on the pile.

At other times when I left the shuttle and walked out across the surface, I would discover that I'd become confused about the direction to go in and I would wander lost among the drones, sometimes stopping for hours just to watch. I watched them assemble whole ships in just a few minutes, or else watched whole production lines simply stand up and walk away when they were done.

I watched four-legged creatures take themselves apart and bolt their pieces to some greater device, thus becoming a part of some other machine.

Over the weeks I saw entire generations of drones come and go, evolving into ever more refined forms from one day to the next. It was a frightening process to watch, and after a while I laughed at the idea of ever stopping such creatures.

One day I left the shuttle with all of the air bottles and the last few days' worth of food. I also carried a sharp piece of metal and the wooden back from some musical instrument. I'd gone back into the dome to find it, the first trip back inside since Elliot's death, and I'd paused at one point to find myself looking at the headless grey drone in his cage, still standing in exactly the position it had been in when I'd last seen it through the smoke after Bolton died.

Carrying all of the bottles now and all of the food, a little ways at a time, I spent the next two days covering the twenty miles to where I'd left Elliot for the last time. It was out past the drones, out where the wastes opened up to the horizon. Getting there took the last of my strength and the last of my food.

Elliot's face had changed very little. The ice was gone from his eyes, and hundreds of capillaries had frozen and burst in the vacuum, but each time I paused from scraping out a hole in the ground with the piece of metal and looked at him, I believed that he looked just as he had during the twenty-five years we'd spent together.

The scraping passed in a blur of pain and fatigue, and often I thought that the next stroke would have to be the last. But the sun rose higher and I remained on my knees, taking stroke after stroke with my hands now frozen to the scrap of metal.

In the end, though, no matter how hard I tried, Elliot's grave looked less neat and finished than McKenna's next to it, and finally I had to stop myself from smoothing it over one more time in the midst of growing delirium and hunger.

I sat by the grave then, making sure I remembered every aspect of Elliot's face. I took the piece of wood and hammered it into the mound, then wiped it clean.

TYRONE ELLIOT, I'd scratched into it. 1995 – 2041. A GOOD FRIEND.

Sunlight leapt across the surface the next morning, lighting up the graves.

It had been a night filled with voices, so many that I'd believed at times it was the scout on my shoulder whispering in my ear.

It had been a night filled with faces, as well, floating in front of me as I stood there in the darkness. They were the faces of all the people whose deaths I'd tried to forget.

I saw my father standing on the ground between the two graves, and for the first time I saw the sadness in his eyes as he returned my gaze. I saw the old man I'd stolen the plans from, the secret plans I'd thought would set us free. Then, for a while, I couldn't tell them apart, the old man and my father.

I saw Anne Miller as a young woman, looking out of her window when she thought no one was watching. I saw Michael Bolton at his camp table, night after night, writing the letters I knew he wrote to his sister and brother, the ones he had no way to send.

I saw Charlie Peters standing on the slope of a hill, reaching out a hand to me. Then, just before dawn, I saw Chan walking away, pulling a shawl around her shoulders as she went.

The sun glinted above the horizon and the wastelands rippled with shadows and the knife's edges of light, sweeping closer and then across me from the east to the west, the land not completely real yet but no longer just imagined in the darkness. And in those few moments of half-light I saw Polaski's face filling the world, and in those moments I came to hate him. I saw his empty eyes mocking me, staring out of that pale face under his blond eyebrows, and I saw his square chin and blunt nose, his colorless lips and pale, blond hair.

And I knew then that it was the face of a man without substance, and I hated him for it. I hated him for the ambition that had driven me out to that place by the graves, and for the scorn, and the jeers and the threats.

Yet wasn't I the one who had fueled him, who had whispered in his ear at every turn? Wasn't I to be hated as well? Had the child, once huddled and trembling before the dogs in the street, turned around and sold his soul to own a wolf on a chain? Only to say, to all who passed, "There, that is the wolf, over there. Pay no attention to me."

But the wolf knew, and mocked.

Then in that brief moment of uncertain light on the black planet, I saw Polaski raise his gun one last time, and I drew in a breath and opened my mouth to shout at him, to leap forward and rip it from him and tear him apart—and in that instant the sunlight flared across the wastes and dispelled the shadows, and shattered the image of Polaski and his rising hand.

There was nothing in front of me then but the frozen gravel and the black dust of the surface, stretching out to the horizon. To my left lay Roddy McKenna's tidy grave with its carved stone, while in front of me lay Elliot's with its ragged slat of wood.

To the right of Elliot's grave was a stool, and on it sat Madhu Patel. He was still dressed in white, and the red rose on his lapel was as fresh as ever. The sun shone on him brightly from one side, lighting up his face with its crisp morning whites and shadows.

"You seem very sad," he said.

The palms of his hands rested on his thighs, and his big lips pursed sympathetically.

"Not for much longer," I said.

"Well, perhaps." He lifted his hands slightly and set them back down on his thighs. "You must eat, Eduardo."

"There's no more food."

"Ah." He nodded and looked around at the wilderness, at the drones going about their business in the distance.

"So," he said. "This is where you have chosen to live. Out where there is nothing."

I looked down at the grave, with its uneven mound of gravel.

"It's very quiet," I said.

"Yes, it is." He studied me for a minute. "Not a great many trees, though. You loved your friend very much."

"I don't know, Madhu. Sometimes I think I just used him."

"Pah! Such arrogance. Do you think your friend was such a simpleton? So gullible that he was taken in by your clever manipu-

lations? No, Eduardo, I'm sure he loved you because he saw in you
something to love. If you will just remember that, then that will be
his gift to you." He leaned back on the stool and rolled his eyes
downward and stretched his lips and his jowly cheeks down with an
effort, trying to see the rose as he adjusted it.

"So," he said, and looked up.

We looked around at the thin light and long shadows across
the surface, and watched a flight of drone ships easing their way
along the horizon.

"Madhu?"

"Yes."

"You said we don't always recognize ourselves, out here in
the emptiness."

"Yes."

"You meant the emptiness inside, like the emptiness in the
drones. That we would meet them again, but wouldn't look at them
and see ourselves for what we are."

"Yes."

"That we were just as empty."

"Oh, my dear fellow, no! My goodness. May Allah be patient
with you. Eduardo, you've quite misunderstood. What I wished for
was that you would look at them and see that you are not like them
at all!"

He straightened up and sighed, and let the air sputter out
between his lips.

"Eduardo, you of all people know that the line between
human beings and machines is just smoke and shadows. But what
you did not know is that it is love and death that make us different
from them—the very things you've always wished to deny. Everything you've needed has always been within your grasp, Eduardo,
everything that made you human, and that is what I wished for you
to see. Come, my friend, I see that there are tears in your eyes—but
listen. You would have done better, I think, to deny the one who has
driven you all this time."

I felt the tears on my cheeks and wished that I could reach up
and wipe them away, but I could only touch the faceplate with my
glove.

"What are you thinking?" said Patel.

"That too many of us died. That Polaski and I pushed them too hard all these years."

He drummed his fingertips on his knees for a moment and looked around, working his big lips in and out.

"Polaski?" he said. "Who is this Polaski?" He looked down again and adjusted the rose. "Are you sure there is such a person? Perhaps you have taken to imagining people who are not there, Eduardo."

Just as he said this he stopped and sat perfectly still for a moment, then his eyes went wide and he blinked several times, and his face burst into a great smile and he clapped his hands together.

"Ha! That is very good, 'imagining people who are not there!' Wonderfully good—I am such a clever man! Imagine that!"

And then he was gone.

When the sun reached the center of the sky I was still standing in the same place, watching the horizon and listening to the sun as it hissed off the ground. It had been so long since Elliot had died that I was certain Polaski had gone ahead with his awful plan, and I stood in the desert and imagined the blackened wreckage of the torus drifting in space, the fleet decimated, the last of my friends floating dead in the cold. All because I hadn't stopped him, because I'd come back for an empty box, instead.

"You're wrong, Tyrone," I said, "I do remember. And we did get his truck to turn over. What little was left of it, we turned it over. The two of us."

The air in my suit had grown stale, and the ground around me was littered with the empty air bottles, white against the ground. The planet's surface was a watery grey in the sun, and the drones moved silently along the horizon, glinting in the weak light. The silver husks of the domes lay empty on the horizon, and wisps of vapor flickered noiselessly over the smelters and disappeared. Somewhere above me, Boar River and Asile rolled through the darkness, their fleets gone, their voices silenced under the weight of the drones. Earth was a painful and distant memory.

The hissing of the regulators in my helmet faded away, the

sound that had been my constant companion finally noticed only as it died away. The horizon blurred in front of me, and a chill crept up across my feet and into my legs.

Then, at that moment, the last figure of my imagination finally appeared, facing me as it had so many times in the dream.

It was a mirror image of me in my suit, the two of us facing each other across the ground, perfectly still. I saw myself reflected back in the bronze faceplate, and it was reflected in mine in turn, one of us inside the other, over and over, indistinguishable. Twenty feet apart on the barren ground we stood, face to face, the memory of my dream now clear in my mind.

The figure blurred as the hissing of my air dwindled further. The cold crept into my belly and I drew deeply on the last of my air, feeling an icy moment of fear as my head begin to swim. Then the apparition raised its arm.

Charlie Peters had been wrong: it *was* a gun that it held in its hand, not a balance, and it was raising it up to point into my eyes. The hissing of my air stopped completely and the cold reached into my heart, and the finger on the trigger of the gun pulled tight. The gun fired, and a bolt of flame stabbed out toward me across the space between us.

Chapter Twenty-seven: THE WOMAN CLOTHED WITH THE SUN

There was a blow to my shoulder, and the little scout who'd been sitting on it smashed into my helmet and pieces of it flew past the faceplate. The figure in front of me threw the gun aside, then her voice cut into my helmet through the creeping fog of anoxia.

"Come on, we go quick now!" Pham's voice. She snapped her air bottle loose and pushed my empty one aside, then pulled me forward. The blurry image of a transparent observation boat swam in front of me as she pulled me along, and then we were inside of it.

The boat sped toward the horizon and heaved into space with a sickening surge of speed. I passed out.

There were half-conscious sensations of being bathed...lying naked on the padded benches while a sponge was worked across my skin, warm and wet, moving from my toes to my brow and back again. Strong fingers washing my hair, warm water coursing through it.

At another time, there were little hands exploring my face. Tiny fingers touched my eyelids and ran along the side of my nose, then worked their way in between my lips and explored my ears. Soft little palms patted my freshly shaved skin.

"So, hi! You awake!"

Stars were everywhere. The fiery dust of the galaxy was bright and alive in every direction.

I sat up stiffly. Silhouetted against the stars, Pham sat in the pilot's seat with the baby asleep on her shoulder. Both of them glowed from the lights of the instruments.

I was dressed in a jumpsuit and deck shoes and was scrubbed and rested, and felt strangely detached from the memory of standing on the black planet, dying.

"How long have I been asleep?"

"Ah, you been asleep long time, Eddie boy. You kinda dead there, a while." She swiveled around to face me and said it with good humor, the stars shining back out of her eyes.

"Tyrone's dead," I said.

"Yah, I know. I'm sorry. I call Susan, tell her. Pretty hard for you, too, I think."

I nodded and stood up, then looked around at the transparent vessel and at the stars, trying to judge the thrust of the engines under my feet. She had us accelerating at a good rate.

"Where are we, Pham?

She pointed down through the edge of the bubble beside her. I sat down in the other seat, and her hair brushed against my arm as I leaned past her to see.

Floating in the blackness, far behind us, was a pitted grey sphere, tiny and insignificant in the distance as it dwindled like a dark moon under a weak sun.

"So," she said. "Black planet one day behind, fleet two days in front. We move pretty quick."

"The fleet? It's still together? What's happened?"

"Nothing happen. Fleet still got two, three days before it's close enough to torus for attack. Empty-Eyes, he pretty pissed off 'cause it taking so long."

"I don't understand— Pham, how long have I been gone?"

"You don't know, hah? You pretty confused there for a while. Four weeks you been gone. All your friends, they wonder. I wonder, too, then decide to drag your dumb head back. Empty-Eyes, he hear I'm going, suddenly it's all his idea to get you. 'Get dumb-head-ass back here,' he say, 'tell him to make all these cowards stop dragging their feets.'"

We were sitting side by side in the forward seats now, and Pham had turned sideways to look at me with her knees up on the cushion and the baby curled at her waist. She wore just her brief shorts and a half-length t-shirt. Her eyes and her skin were soft in the starlight.

Four weeks. I'd thought months, lifetimes.

"What cowards is he talking about?"

"Cowards like your Russian friends, Eddie. Somehow all

their ships get wrong information by accident, go off wrong direction. Then on Lowhead, navy officers suddenly all got to go to Allerton's funeral—no one can say no, hah? But all the time, everybody wait for you, and wait. But nothing. They want you to stop Empty-Eyes and his black-shirts, Eddie."

"Allerton's dead?"

"Yah. Looks like he slip away home like dog, eat bad meat one night. By accident."

"I see. So the torus is still there?"

"Yah—good thing, I think. Lots of people, they want to take little boats and go through. They believe in stories. Me, too. But not much time—Empty-Eyes, he got two thousand officers with him, say drones got to go."

No fleet of Polaski's would stop the drones. No fleet anywhere.

"You?" I said. "You're going through the tunnel?"

"Yah, if we still got time."

"But you took the time to come back for me?"

"Maybe I owe you a little bit, Eddie. And maybe I hope you come, too."

"Chan and I? How does she feel about leaving behind—"

Pham's hand touched my arm, then she moved it down to hold my hand in hers.

"China-Girl gone, Eddie."

"Chan? She went through?"

"No. Day after you go, she pack bags and leave. She not tell anyone where she go. Nobody see her. I'm sorry, Eddie."

Pham slept against my shoulder while I held the baby in my lap. The galaxy of stars outside the bubble rolled around us and then stopped again, as we turned over to aim the engines forward at the half-way point. Pham and the baby stirred from the brief easing of thrust.

"Pham? Tuyet?"

"Mm?"

"How did you find me?"

She pulled herself a little closer and reached over to adjust the baby's blanket. "You pretty easy to find, Eddie, standing out there in the middle of the dirt like that."

"No, that's not what I mean. Back in the Pacific, when you showed up at the island. How did you know who I was, and where to find us?"

She pulled herself up and rubbed her eyes. Then she reached down to her sides and pulled the t-shirt up over her head, and let it fall to the deck behind her. She lifted the baby and put it to her breast.

"Eddie," she said, "There's something I never tell you." She looked down at the baby. "I think maybe not so good I don't tell you, selfish, maybe. But it gave me reason to hate you. You killed my father."

There was a time, I thought, when I wouldn't have heard. But now I just felt tired. The radio, and the clothes, in the back room.

"The power cell," I said. "Jesus, Tuyet, I'm sorry."

She shook her head. "No, Eddie. Good thing you kill shit-head father. Always I too afraid to kill him. But just the same, all these years I think, 'Here pretty good reason to hate perfect guy. He not so perfect now.'"

"You were with him on the island? He invented that cell, and you still hated him?"

"Hah! He invent nothing, old prick. He was just science teacher in camps. He sneak out one night, leave mother behind, don't say nothing. But I see him go and I follow. Big argument, he say go back.

"Always I want something from him, Eddie, but always he's scheming, stealing, making big plans while I got to work all the time. Go with soldiers, make money. Little-girl virgin first time, big price and all that.

"So father and I we go to Indonesia. Mother come later, he say, but when we get there I find out he working for Indonesia government all of a sudden, and soon he talking to American people all the time, too, late at night. Then we running again, then pretty soon he's big guy again at American university, got money and car and nice clothes. For him, never me. He tell me go back to mother. Then one day he not come home, but next day he's there and we running again, out to islands. He fuck with Americans, I think. Stupid."

"Yes," I said. "So you saw me there that night?"

"Both of us see you. I think, 'Here's a strong guy, stand up to my father, take what he wants.' Same time I hate you, like I got to kill you or something."

"Both you and your father?"

"Nah. Father just sit and smoke pipe till he all curled up like baby. Me and serving boy see you. Kip. Kip, he see you go away in helicopter next morning, so he run down and leave in boat same direction. I pretty mean to him sometimes, tease him about not talking, so he leave by himself without saying anything to me. But I got other boat, one with motor that we come in, so I go to big island with helicopter base. That's where I meet shit-head Rosler, cleaning airplanes. I treat him nice, find out who you are. Hang around, and one day I steal little plane and follow him when he go, because he tell me he getting transferred to secret stuff—meaning power cell project, I know."

She shifted the baby to the other breast, then glanced up.

The stars above rolled slightly as the shuttle corrected to follow the fleet. Ahead of us, still invisible beneath the shuttle, the passage to Serenitas lay no more than two days away.

There was nothing more to stop me. I could float past the drones and through the tunnel, ahead of Polaski's approaching fleet. Free at last, with the dream of land within my grasp. No one had any claims on me, and no one waited. No one had any expectations at all.

"I've lost everything, haven't I, Tuyet?"

She cradled the baby in one arm and reached out with the other to take my hand. She didn't answer, and we just sat and rode together through the darkness, listening to the baby's sucking and watching the stars.

"All right," I said. "Tell me about Polaski's fleet. Everything there is to know."

It was breathtaking in its size, a wall of ships as wide as space itself. It filled the sky above and stretched into the distance on every side, six thousand engines flickering restlessly as they waited for the word, drifting upward toward the grey torus half a million miles above.

Pham and I tipped our seats back and watched out the top as I floated the boat up under the fleet, listening to the command channels on the radio and looking for the familiar markings of Hull 00.

"We show forty-four minutes, Mr. Polaski," said a man whose voice I didn't recognize. "Cannon synchronized."

"I really care, Peeber," said Polaski from somewhere above. "What the hell are you telling me for?"

There was a long pause.

"Mr. Polaski," said someone else, picking her words carefully. "We should remind you that FleetSys will control timing starting at minus two minutes, and that after that only top-list officers can give final authorization. As fleet officer you are first on that list. Unless you take yourself off of it, you are going to need some of this information we are giving you."

"What do you think, Stedback," said Polaski in answer, "that I'm going to take a nap?"

"Very well, Mr. Polaski. Flight Fourteen, cannon synchronized."

I looked at Pham.

"Less than forty-five minutes," I said. "I think you should take your chance while you can, as soon as you drop me off. You can still make it to the torus ahead of the fleet if you start now."

"I will wait."

I studied her face for a minute.

"All right. It's up to you. But don't wait near the ship. Pull at least a thousand miles ahead. You said there are still two working shuttles on board Zero-Zero—I can take one of those to meet up with you."

"Okay. Over there! Big zero-ship. Empty-Eyes, he got big trouble now."

"Don't be so sure."

"Still, Eddie, I think you should just shoot him, or open air lock or something. Why not?"

"Because then there's another dozen officers that can give the okay, that's why. Polaski's not stupid enough to get shot, anyway."

"So, okay, tell FleetSys don't listen to shithead. You main guy more than him, anyway, no?"

"No, Tuyet, we've been through this. It takes two fleet officers to change who FleetSys obeys, and Polaski and I are the only ones left. We took you off the list back when you were waving that gun around all the time."

"Yah, okay, fine. Go see how long you can hold breath, then. You turn blue, I bet."

"Here we go."

Pham put the baby up to pat my face good-bye after I coupled the tail of the boat to Polaski's ship, but she herself held back. The air lock groaned shut, cutting her off from view.

The suit was uncomfortable, but at least I could leave the helmet off for the time being. The air on the ship was rancid, and the deck was covered with trash. The ship was hot and quiet, with only the sound of the radios coming down the lift from the MI decks.

The lift wasn't working. I couldn't pull myself up the ladder while holding onto the helmet, so I had to clip it to my side.

One more step to remember.

Rung by rung I pulled my way up the sixty feet to the MI decks, listening to the radio conversation that crackled back and forth across the giant fleet.

"Targets still not maneuvering. Bearings on sixty-two percent of the drone ships still intersect the torus. Twenty-three minutes to full thrust..."

"Inter-flight coordination on, target bracketing for first pulse. Those suckers are going to run or melt this time, boys..."

When my head rose up over the deck, Polaski was looking at me. He sat in the command chair on the far side of the equipment island, drumming his fingers on the armrests with his gun within easy reach. His grey eyes watched me out of his pale face, unblinking, unconcerned.

I walked to the communications console before stopping to face him. I resisted the temptation to unclip the helmet again. The deck was filthy and badly lit, with lamps missing and console panels lying open. The work on them had been abandoned.

"I understand you wanted to see me," I said.

"Not any more," he said. "You aren't needed."

"Was I ever?"

"You had your uses."

I glanced down at the base of the communications console.

"I had uses until when?" I said. "Until you had your aliens? Did they give you a better excuse than I did to put your boot to the world's throat like you always wanted?"

"That's right, Torres. Your little mission wasn't much use any more then, was it?"

The radio crackled overhead. "Ready for general quarters, Mr. Polaski."

He flicked a finger against the armrest. "Fine." I was trying to calculate the distance to his gun when he glanced at my helmet.

"I keep wondering why you're wearing your suit, Torres," he said. "Has Colonel Pham been giving you ideas?"

When I didn't answer he went on.

"You don't have the balls, Torres. And anyway, you always want the same thing I want, don't you? Anything I say is fine with you? That's the real truth, isn't it, Torres?"

Still I didn't answer.

"I hear you killed your buddy," he said.

"So what was it, Polaski?" I said, having decided on the distances. "Once you had your aliens you needed Pham and me out of the way? Or was it Dorczak you were trying to kill in the landing dome that night, as a little favor to Allerton. Or maybe Roddy McKenna, who knew something that made you nervous? Who was it Allerton was bragging about being able to see through a dome from a million miles out, Polaski? And whose hand was on the switch of those masers you had him mount in your leased freighters, in return for the tritium shipments?"

His eyebrow rose. "You always were too smart, Torres."

"Who killed McKenna, Polaski?"

Easy.

"But," I said, "the attack on the landing dome only got people nervous, didn't it? Not enough reason to attack the alien fleet, not yet. But the industries dome, now, that got your fleet off the ground for you, didn't it? A few civilians dead? Amazing how nothing important was hit. That's what gave you away, Polaski. That's how I knew it wasn't the same as the attack on Wallneck."

I'd moved a step closer to the communications console. *Right foot, toe down. Ten inches.*

Polaski laughed. "So you lied, didn't you, Torres? That captive alien didn't tell Allerton about the Indian mines. You told *it*, and then you told Allerton. Bought yourself a little time, didn't you?"

"That's right, Polaski. FleetSys!"

Polaski straightened.

"Yes, Mr. Torres."

"Modify authorization top-list—"

"Todd!" Polaski's hand jabbed at his armrest. "Get—"

I slammed my boot into the breakers under the communications console, and drove them through the panel with a splintering of plastic; Polaski jerked forward in his seat, then stopped as he saw that the light over his microphone was dead.

"Yes, Mr. Polaski?" said Jacob Todd. Polaski didn't try to answer, but glanced at his gun and then back at me. FleetSys' smooth voice continued from the speakers.

"Your command is incomplete, Mr. Torres."

"Modify top-list," I said, "to allow attack authorization by me only."

"*What?*" Polaski got to his feet. "You do that, Torres, and you'll authorize an attack with a gun in your ear. FleetSys, ignore him!"

"Stand by, Mr. Polaski. Mr. Torres, exclusive authorization will require the system administrator, or the administrator's password."

Polaski stopped at that point, then relaxed with the beginnings of a smirk on his face. He eased himself back into his seat. FleetSys needed its senior-most priest.

"The password," I said, "is 'Saint Catherine.'"

"Fuck!" Polaski snatched up his gun just as Todd's voice crackled over the speakers again.

"Mr. Polaski, was there something I can do for you? You're not responding."

FleetSys interrupted them. "Password is correct, Mr. Torres."

Polaski had his gun in his hand and was edging his way around the console toward me. "Concurrence is now required by one other fleet officer. I believe only Mr. Polaski is available."

Polaski stopped, while I stared blankly at the speakers.

"I don't understand," I said.

Don't overdo it. "FleetSys," I said, "it's Mr. Polaski I need to exclude."

"No sir," said Polaski. He smacked his revolver down on the console. "Too smart again, huh, Torres? That thing knows who's in charge here."

"Mr. Torres," said FleetSys, "you may authorize the use of force, or you may demand a polling of top-list officers if authorization has already been given, but that is all."

"No," said Polaski, "I don't think we want you pissing in the soup even that much, do we, Torres? Look at you. And everybody always thought you were so good with this system, thought I depended on you. Now we'll see."

The radio squawked.

"Mr. Polaski," said Stedback, "we're going to have a pretty short window for this maneuver, so if you've got a reason not to be giving the go-ahead, you need to let us know."

"Maybe he's taking that nap, after all," said Peeber.

"Stow it, Peeber," said Stedback. "Todd, you're number two on the list, so I'd suggest you call up your checklist now and be prepared to give the word."

Polaski picked up his gun again and gripped it in both hands. His face had lost expression now and his voice was flat.

"All right, Torres, here we go. Open the front of your suit." He motioned with the gun.

Not too far. Every second sealing it back up's going to count.

"All right," I said.

But far enough so it doesn't look stupid when I reach in.

"Now the automatic," said Polaski. "I know you've got it. Okay, put it down on the deck, push it away. Remember, Torres. I may put a hole in the skin, but I'll still have time to get to another deck, and I'm going to empty this revolver into you on the way. There you go, nice and easy."

Slide it as far as you can...there, over by the ladder. Can't afford to trip on it in the dark.

"Okay, Torres, straighten up. Hands where I can see them. FleetSys!"

"Yes, Mr. Polaski."

"Modify authorization top-list to allow attack orders by me only. No one else—no polling or any of that."

"Your exclusive authorization will require the system administrator, or the administrator's password, Mr. Polaski."

"Password is 'Saint Catherine.'"

"Password is correct, Mr. Polaski. Concurrence is now required by one other fleet officer. I believe only Mr. Torres is available."

"You got that right." Polaski brought the barrel around to point at my forehead. "He's right here."

"Mr. Torres?" said FleetSys. "If you wish to relinquish authorization, please state that fact in a complete sentence."

"He wishes," said Polaski. He fingered the hammer. "Don't you, Torres?"

This is the hard part.

I took a deep breath.

"I concur in granting Mr. Polaski exclusive authorization to employ fleet weapons."

Polaski's mouth twitched and his thumb slid up to pull back the hammer.

"I'm sorry, Mr. Torres," said FleetSys, "but your voice shows excessive stress. Please take your time and repeat your statement."

Polaski's eyes clouded and he leaned forward, his hands gripping the revolver more tightly than ever. Then a flicker of hesitation crossed his eyes, and he let down the hammer.

At least he's figured that much out.

"Take it easy, Torres," he said. "Just relax. But you'd better relax good."

Yes...eyes closed, deep breath. Sun hissing off the ground, a pool of clear water...the rush of pebbles in a brook, a gate standing open, an airplane arriving over the jungle—

I opened my eyes to see Polaski watching me and the revolver pointed at my forehead, just as it had been twenty-five years ago on the island. It's even the same gun, I thought; nothing has changed.

"I concur," I said, "in granting Mr. Polaski exclusive authorization to employ fleet weapons."

"Very well, Mr. Torres."

"Good for you, Torres," said Polaski. "And now I think we're through."

Yes. And now, Polaski, you're the only one in the fleet who can give orders. Not me, not your minions. It's a heavy burden, isn't it?

Radios crackled in the background. Ten minutes left.

"Isn't there something you're forgetting, Polaski?" I said.

Buy time for one last rehearsal. Drop straight down, left arm back to the levers to seal off the deck, so Polaski can't get off it. Two levers. Above-deck seal and below-deck seal. Four paces to the left—don't slip on the gun—unclip the helmet with the right hand, take a deep breath.

"And what might that be?" said Polaski. He pulled back the hammer.

Left hand on decompression safeties—remember there's three of them. That's right, Tyrone, I owe you for all the blindfold drills. Then head down—he's crazy enough to shoot blind. Final reach for the fire suppression panel and the air release lever. Thirty more seconds without air to get the suit fastened and the helmet on.

"You've forgotten," I said, "that you can't authorize anything if you can't breathe."

Simon says.

"And you can't see in the dark."

Deep breath.

"FleetSys," I said, "turn off all lights."

Polaski's eyes widened and the gun wavered as he looked around. I tensed for the drop.

But nothing happened. Sweat gathered on my forehead and my legs cramped, but the seconds crawled past and FleetSys remained silent.

The gun came back around, and then FleetSys spoke:

"'Stern awful lice,' Mr. Torres?" it said. "Your words are not clear."

I stood frozen in place. Heat spread through my bowels and nausea welled up in my stomach. Polaski's hand shook as he pulled back the hammer one last time.

"Too clever," he whispered. "Always trusting your machines, Torres, never getting your own hands dirty. Too bad."

The barrel came up and steadied, and his finger tightened.

But with the blast that followed, he himself was thrown violently up against the bulkhead and twisted as he struck, then collapsed out of sight behind the console. His gun clattered to the grating, then into the MI bays below. I could no longer see him or the gun, but from his face in that final, brief moment, I knew that he was not alive.

The blast had come from the opening to the lift. Yet the deck by the lift was empty. Only my gun was there, though not quite where I'd left it, and now with a wisp of smoke coming from the barrel. And Kip's flute, discarded on the deck nearby.

The ship was quiet. If it was Kip who had come, it was to disappear only moments later into the bowels of the ship. But why? Other than his flute he had left no sign of himself, no mark, as indeed from where I stood there was no remaining sign of Polaski, either. There was no sign of any person at all, except for me.

It was as though, in that one, final moment, Polaski and Kip had destroyed each other. Or, perhaps, as in some mysterious implosion of physics, they had in that one moment given up all illusion of substance, and had formed some new thing that I could not see at all.

Indeed, I was alone in the ship. From one end to the other there was no clue, no possessions left behind, no sign that Kip had ever been on board. No sound came to me but the radios.

"Five minutes," said Stedback.

"Mr. Polaski? We've only got five minutes."

"Todd, get ready."

"Um, okay. All right."

Pham had said that there were two shuttles on board, but there was only one.

On my last pass through the ship I stepped off the ladder to look at the familiar grey of the MI decks, at the frayed fabric on the seat where my hands had rested, at the indentation left in the back from my head. Or from Polaski's.

"Three minutes."

I backed the last shuttle out of its bay and away from the ship. A sound came from the back of the shuttle's cabin, once and then several times more, but when I went to look it wasn't Kip, after all.

Pham's tiny boat was no more than a speck on my instruments, drifting against the grey circle of the torus. A speck against the night, a tiny, transparent bubble against the wall of black ships guarding the approaches to Serenitas.

When I pulled closer, the cargo bins strapped to the bottom grew visible, the ones that would contain her tools and the seeds, and the first year's food. In the cabin, Pham sat in the middle of the transparent bubble with her shirt still off and the sun shining in across her skin. The baby suckled while she watched the growing circle of grey and the black ships ahead. The sky was filled with stars.

The radios on board hissed and crackled as I came through the lock. The voices were clipped and angry.

"Mr. Polaski, please! FleetSys is telling us you're the only one who can release all of a sudden, and our window is slipping."

"Stedback, find a priest, for Christ's sake—"

Pham turned off the radios. There was only the pulsing of the engines then, as they pushed us toward the tunnel, and the sucking of the baby. I tilted my seat back next to her and watched the torus.

"Like Madhu's moon," she said.

When I looked at her, the baby's eyes rolled up to study me in return.

"Is that who you've named him after?" I said. "Madhu?"

"No, Eddie. I name him after you. Edward."

The baby and I regarded each other for a minute as we considered this.

"Please, Eddie," said Pham. "He need a father. You come just for us, maybe?"

"I'm sorry," I said, "I can't change my mind. I've got to go back and look for Chan."

She didn't answer, then after a minute a warning came from the panel in front of us. I turned it off.

"First pass point," I said. "I have to go."

"No," she said, "pass points not so important. I won't need to turn aside."

"I know you won't, but I will."

She tilted her seat to face me, then reached out with her free arm. She put it around my neck and drew me nearer, then her lips pressed tight against mine, moist and soft, her tongue like silk as it traced the sides of my mouth. She pressed her head against the palm of my hand as I ran it across her cheek and under her hair to pull her closer. It was liquid, hypnotic, endless.

The kiss lasted for a long time, our lips wet and sliding under the stars, the baby stirring between us and her other breast pressing against me, her skin soft and warm.

Then I was back inside my shuttle and watching her through the porthole as she moved off toward the black ships—naked to the stars, her baby at her breast, a woman clothed with only the sun.

EPILOGUE

There were times, over the years that followed, when I almost believed I had fired the gun myself. Then at other times I imagined that no gun had been fired at all, that I had been alone on that deck from the beginning. But then I would set down my tea and turn away from watching the rain on the meadows, and see the flute on my writing table, and I would know that I hadn't been alone at all.

The flute had been with me since I'd picked it up from the deck and left the gun in its place, but I'd never tried playing it. I hadn't wanted to find out that I couldn't, I suppose. Or else hadn't wanted to find out that I could.

After Pham's boat disappeared toward the torus I turned my shuttle and landed on the western shores of the Boar River Sea. Asile was much too far for such a tiny vessel, and if I'd tried to reach her I would have been left with a choice between food and fuel far too soon.

From acquaintances at the Russian colony on Boar River, I learned that the great fleet had eventually fallen apart, unable to pursue its attack. Individual commanders had tried going up against the drones, but they'd been destroyed or turned aside, prevented by the drones from damaging the torus that formed their only link to Serenitas. Other commanders were called home to bolster defenses against the continuing attacks on their bases. Near the Boar River Sea, battles with the drones flared every time weapons were brought to bear—whether against other humans in regional disputes that originally had nothing to do with the drones, or else each time die-hard commanders believed they had finally found a weakness in the drones and sought to prove it.

I'd reached Boar River with few possessions. Worse, it came to dawn on me slowly that I had reached her possessing little status and few skills that the colonies required. The planet had grown poor during the wars, and its industry had collapsed from mismanagement and warfare: the subsistence economy that had taken its place left little time for anything more than farming.

The resources required for space travel had mostly been appropriated by the colonies' remaining militaries, which I found I had no desire to join. The technical academies had turned their attention to agriculture, and most engineers found themselves with little to engage them beyond civil works. I found myself, in any case, restless at the idea of working within an organization, if only because the great power and stature I had once held as the founder of the exodus now counted for little, and even brought contempt.

I worked with Nicolai Panov for several months while I made inquiries about Chan's whereabouts, helping build Panov's orbiting colonies, but without the resources to make any real progress on them neither of us could pretend that the arrangement was more than charity, and finally I thanked him and began to travel from city to city along the shore. I was anxious, in any case, to find Chan.

The months turned into years, however, and the fast vehicles and aircraft I was accustomed to eventually gave way to moving slowly from village to village on foot, as I found myself increasingly compelled to visit the poorest farmers and fishermen in their everyday lives, and to take my meals with them. But although I asked at every house and at every market, no one recognized the description I gave of Chan.

So I made my living, in those years, by moving from farm to farm and repairing machinery in exchange for food and a place to sleep. I became a tinker, of sorts, a mender of things, passing the days by walking along the shoreline under Boar River's strange sky, with little human companionship and no money at all.

During the fourth year, after I'd walked the length of the sea to Wallneck and then back out through the dismal poverty of the muddy Lowhead peninsula, I began to ask after the colony's president, Carolyn Dorczak. But my question was always received with puzzlement, and sometimes suspicion—suspicion of a stranger, I supposed, of a rough-looking man.

"The blue house," I was told at last.

The blue house stood a way back from the main road, a tidy mud house squatting on a farm outside the city of West Lowhead.

Dorczak's face was sunburned and worn and her hands callused, but her brown eyes hadn't lost their intelligence or good humor as she looked me up and down, and studied my small companion and my knapsack filled with metal and wires.

"There is no government in Lowhead," she said. "There are a few military outfits that hire on to the highest bidder, but that's about it. You see them out at Wallneck, sometimes, or on China-side."

Penderson wasn't well. He worked as hard as he could on their little farm, but he needed antibiotics for his lungs and he didn't have them, so he rested often and kept his words short. He did seem glad to have me with them, though.

"How do I get to Asile, Carolyn?" I said.

She shook her head and pulled her work shirt closer around her.

"I don't think you do, Ed. That's a rich person's game now, and there's none of us that rich. Not even the mail comes or goes."

Neither of them had had any word of Chan, and after helping to get the late crops in the ground I left again. I walked out along the muddy beaches with my feet sucking into the clay, still trying to leave behind a single, last doubt.

Had I known, when I'd returned with Elliot for the codes, that I would fail? Had I turned my back on Polaski at precisely that moment so that he could close the tunnel, after all? Had I been, all those years, a man in need of his prison?

Perhaps that was why I had allowed the wars to follow us into space in the first place, and why I'd never really forced Miller's hand regarding her intentions for the drones. And why I hadn't tried for the torus sooner, as others had. Afraid that what waited for me there might not hold me back after all, might not hold me responsible for the poverty, or for my father, or for the deaths. That it might hold me responsible for no more than myself.

It was the next year in the Christian colonies, along the sea's south shore, that I came to an adobe shanty near a grove of Eucalyptus. A little girl watched me from over the hedge, while nearby a bicycle leaned against a tree with a leather physician's bag over its handlebars.

The girl regarded me solemnly. She had light brown skin and soft eyes, and an achingly familiar look.

"Anna? Who's there?" A woman came out of the house to stand in the doorway. She wiped her hands on her apron and nodded to me.

"Yes?" she said.

I turned to face her. She was still a handsome woman, though there were lines of worry etched in her face now, much as there had been in Elliot's.

It was Susan Perris, and her child. Tyrone Elliot's child, whom he'd never gotten to see.

Perris' eyes clouded when she recognized me, then grew cold. The apron became motionless in her hands, and her face filled with a fury she had to struggle to find words for. Finally she spoke in a hoarse voice.

"These are decent people, here." It was all she said.

I'd wanted to ask her if Chan were with her, or had even written to her, but in the end I couldn't bring myself to speak and I walked away.

It was several years later that stories came to China-side about independent traders who were building ships again on Asile, and who were reopening a minimal commerce in the system. There was even said to be a small trade with Serenitas.

I returned to the Russian cities at the western end of the sea, where I'd begun, and in time I was able to find a trader who accepted my services as an instructor to her young astrogator, in exchange for passage to Asile. I left Boar River for the last time.

We put down on Asile on rough ground. The port and its valley had been burned during the trader's absence—the drones, we were told, had come to the next valley and were at that moment pushing back its last defenders. But from the smells in the air, and from the color of the smoke, I wondered if it wasn't only a wood fire that had gotten out of hand.

Just in case, we moved the ship away from the settlements for reloading, and there I said good-bye. Some days later I joined a train of carts and livestock setting out across the Empty Quarter, hoping to make it to the forested highlands.

Thirty-five years earlier, the Europeans had given Asile the only thing of theirs that remained, which was her name. It was a French word that meant 'sanctuary,' but fears had grown that the space-going ships would bring the drones and that it was safe no longer, and more and more groups were leaving the city for the distant mountains. It was a trip that took most of a year, and when we finally wound our way up the western slopes and into the trees, more than a dozen had died.

From the last rise on the trail, the plateau opened up before us, silver with its lakes and green with its millions of acres of pine. The air was cool and moist, and clouds gathered along the far ridge fifty miles away, where Michael Bolton and Elliot and I had lain together one morning and looked out on a bleak dawn.

I was to spend the rest of my life on the Bolton Uplands, yet in all those years I never found anyone who knew where the land had gotten its name. But at least the name was known.

There were a hundred small settlements on the highlands by then, mostly families raising fish and livestock, and for the next year I made my way among the villages. I told people that I was looking for a woman, and I described her, and told them that she wrote programs for machines or else looked after children. People listened and nodded sympathetically, but none knew her by my description, even though I was sure that my memory of her hadn't failed in any detail.

Then one evening I paused, as I often did, at a small, one-room wooden house left standing empty. Its people had either traveled to another town or else moved away completely. I reached it by walking up a narrow gravel road and through an old gate. The gate stood open, and had fallen to one side.

I swept out the house with a broom and fixed a meal from the food I'd brought with me, giving a little to the cat that I'd found sleeping on the porch.

The next morning there came the sound of a dairyman's bell, and I walked down the road to meet it.

Part way down the hill I stopped, though. Next to the road

was a neat clearing that I'd missed in the dusk the evening before. In the center was a gravestone, and I knelt down to look at it.

But I'd already known the night before, from the cat, with its grey fur and its green eyes.

KATHERINE MIAH CHAN, 1998 – 2054. R.I.P.

She'd died just the year before, even as I'd been climbing the road to the highlands.

And I hadn't even known her whole name.

It was during those days that the traders began coming directly to the highlands, trading scarce equipment for our wood, although they left some of us afraid that their ships would cause the drones to follow.

I sought out those traders each time I walked into town carrying my mended goods, because I knew that some had been through the tunnel to Serenitas and back, and had brought stories of its green pastures and blue oceans.

I always listened to their stories, and then I would take them aside and ask them if in their travels they had ever come across a young man by the name of Edward Pham. He was a young man, I said, who walked with crutches and might have been with his mother, a slender and pretty Vietnamese woman in her later years. But none of them ever had.

The house where Chan had lived stood near the eastern slope of the highlands, and on some of the mornings when I couldn't sleep I made my way across the meadows to the ridge, and from there I watched the dawn creep in across the desert, always seeming to hesitate for a moment as it passed a blurry scar in the distance.

At other times, once or twice each year, I walked to the ridge in the evening just as the sky turned grey. For there was a special time on Asile, the night of two moons, when her greater moon and her lesser moon drifted into the darkness together, both of them full, the small one behind the other and a little above. On the highlands it was said that the greater moon, drifting large and grey against the night, was God's soul, and that the silver jewel behind was a tear in His eye.

The afternoon had passed now since I'd woken so suddenly from my morning's reverie, and during the hours in between the clouds had finally let loose with their rain. I still sat at the table by the window, and looked out at the puddles and the widening ripples that mingled together in a blur of endings and beginnings.

I'd been reminded of Pham by an encounter in town the day before, an encounter that had brought about the decision I'd made that morning. It was a small decision, to be sure, of the sort that's available to an old man, but it was a decision nevertheless and I found that it brought me some comfort.

Outside, water from the meadows coursed down the narrow road and twisted around the posts of the old gate. It pattered against the windows, and inside left shadows of lines and circles on the creased photograph of Serenitas on the wall. A lively scrabbling sound came closer across the wooden floor, then a familiar voice.

"Do you really think she'll come?" The scrabbling stopped by my chair. "It's a bit wet, is the thing. I've just been out myself to see."

"I think she'll come," I said.

"Another log on the grate, then, do you think?"

He didn't wait for my answer, but scrabbled across to nudge another log onto the fire. He came back.

"Shall I throw out the cat?" he said.

"Are you nervous, Little Bolton?"

"Nervous? Preposterous, of course not. Now then, what next? You haven't forgotten the kettle again, have you? You always do, you know, and then there's no water."

He hurried across to check, then worked his little legs onto the porch one more time to peer down the road.

That morning, after stopping on my way back up the hill to catch my breath, I'd turned around and called out to the woman who lives across the way. She stopped, and I asked her to tea. She was as surprised as I was, I think, but she did seem pleased, and she did say she'd come.

It was a decision borne of loneliness, I suppose. Loneliness, because on the day before, I'd made my way into town to find work, and as so often I'd stopped a trader to ask him about Serenitas. And as always I'd listened as he spoke, and as always I'd asked him about the youth; a handsome and quick young man, I'd said, with his pretty mother beside him.

The trader gave my question some thought, accustomed as he was to requests for news of families, but in the end he shook his head and turned away, leaving me to start my long walk home alone. But then he reached out and stopped me, and told me that while he didn't recall the young man I'd spoken of, he did remember something else from a great many years before, when he'd first arrived on Serenitas.

He'd stopped one evening by the side of the road, he said, to drink from a well by a house. As he'd lifted the bucket to his lips, he'd seen a woman much like the one I'd described, standing a short distance away in the twilight. He'd lifted a hand to call out, but when he saw that she wasn't alone he held back, not wanting to intrude.

She was standing in her garden facing a little away from him, he said, toward the mountains. In her arms she held a child, and together they were watching the rising moon.

Thomas A. Day was born in Bremen, Germany and raised on diplomatic posts around the world, including Berlin, Chile, and the Middle East. Educated in the sciences, technology and business, he has worked as a senior manager in the aerospace industry, a now-and-again nighttime cargo pilot, and a freelance software developer in the artificial intelligence field. He currently works as a forensic software and intellectual property analyst, serving as an expert witness in high-stakes technology litigation. He lives with his wife and two sons in Portland, Oregon, and is completing a second novel.